Dogs with Bagels

A Novel

Maria Elena Sandovici

Maria Elena Sandovici
elenasandovici@gmail.com
havewatercolorswilltravel.blogspot.com/

To My Mother, Who Loved New York

It is what it is.

—Andre

{ 1 }

Homeless in the Big Apple

Some people adopt chinchillas or sugar gliders. Others ask their most exotic friend to move in. It's dangerous, becoming the exotic pet of a wealthy friend, but it has its perks. You get to wear borrowed designer clothes and go to cool clubs. Then one night you become an embarrassment and get sent home in no uncertain terms.

Except you have no keys to the apartment (not your fault; you asked repeatedly, she just kind of laughed it off), no money in your purse, and you are being ushered into a cab by the guy whose advances you spurned, which resulted in you being sent home in the first place. You smile and pretend all is well. What else is there to do? You entertain the feeble hope that he might give you cab fare. But he doesn't, so now you're sitting in a cab with no cash and no keys.

Breathe. Relax. *Alle gute dinge sind drei.* (That's German. I'll explain later). All good things are three. (See? Not as charming in English.). It might not help much in a no-keys-no-cash-no-home situation, but let's address this crisis as a three-step process:

1. How did I get here?
2. Is this happening for real? (This step is the most painful. In shitty situations there's always this moment of disbelief, when you realize this is your life, not a video game. Here's one instance in which living in the moment is not all it's cracked up to be).

And finally:

3. What do I do now? (Hopefully by the time I get to this step I will have an answer).

But first things first. My *Tati* used to drive a cab. So, pet chinchilla in fancy borrowed heels, have some decency. Don't do your soul searching with the meter running. Swallow your pride, admit you have no money. Give the man your last crumpled dollar bill. And get out of his cab.

Now, I wish I could say the crisp night air is sobering. But Manhattan summers are hot and humid, like a drunk person's breath. I sit down on the dirty curb. And I cry – for like the n-th time today. An eternity later, I dry my swollen eyes, and try to think. Back to the three-step program.

1. How did I get here?

It started off like a perfect day. This morning I woke up feeling light and happy. I woke up late in my Upper East Side bed, in Egyptian cotton sheets that are not even mine. I'm not a luxury prostitute. I'm just mooching off my best friend. She's a trust fund baby, my age, my size, and pretty much as lost as I am, except when you have all that money it's not as big a deal. I am the disappointing daughter of hard-working immigrant parents. She is the cherished baby of a rich dysfunctional family. She has a natural born talent for the kind of sophistication that comes with old money and summers of mild debauchery on the French Riviera. I have a talent for secretly talking to myself in foreign languages.

Anyway, back to my day. This morning I woke up and it was Saturday and I was happy. G and I lounged in our jammies watching bad TV. We started talking about what to wear tonight. I knew it was an important night for Gretchen because she sort of has a crush on this guy Bob, so she wanted to look her best, and me to look almost as good, but not quite. We ordered delivery sushi and Gretchen protested when I tried reaching for my wallet. I was relieved, because as usual I was broke. But then we had barely opened the sushi, I had barely squeezed soy sauce into one of G's tiny porcelain dishes when she said the thing about boundaries, which she learned from her therapist. It went something like:

"You're welcome for the sushi, but you know, L, there have to be boundaries. I've thought about it, and really, I cannot treat you to the hair appointment. Your hair is your responsibility."

I tried to keep a straight face, but my chopsticks got out of whack, and I dropped my *unagi.* I considered just washing my hair. Washing it with Gretchen's caviar shampoo, then styling it myself. I fished my *unagi* out of the soy sauce. It was too salty.

G read my thoughts.

"You can't go without a professional blow dry, L!" She sighed like an exhausted mother, sick of explaining the basic facts of life to a slow learning child.

"Especially with your ethnic hair." She stressed 'ethnic.' I felt that thing again, the angry thing that I recently started feeling. I mean, aren't we all ethnic? I tried to imagine a whole generation of robots, devoid of ethnicity - human-like, but with flawless skin that never grows hair in undesirable places, sweat glands that smell like roses, and porcelain teeth that don't ever need brushing. Their doll-like heads grow smooth silky hair the color of clean cotton balls, a blank slate for whatever hue they wish to dye it. They grow in fields, these people. Fields and fields of generic yet beautiful creatures. Kind of like in the Matrix.

G snapped her fingers.

"Earth to L! I pulled a lot of strings to book this appointment. You need to look your best tonight. You are getting a Brazilian blow dry!"

I almost snickered. 'Brazilian blow dry' sounds dirty to me. In real life it's an anti-septic procedure carried out in an immaculately white room with mirrors, a cross between a hospital and an art gallery, where people sit in ergonomic chairs drinking cucumber water, and make sophisticated small talk with hair ninjas wielding hot metal plates and very sharp objects. I submitted to the ritual. I tried to tell myself that if I drank enough cucumber water, and looked at the whole thing as an elaborate show (which it was), I'd get more bang for my buck. I kept my lips shut. Though to be fair, the assistant ninja allocated to me didn't seem too interested in conversation. He was eavesdropping on the gossip between Gretchen and the master ninja in charge of her hair. Myself, I tried to zone it out. Sophisticated small talk is not my specialty. Internal monologue in foreign languages is.

Je crois que j'aimais mieux mes cheveux ce matin.

I think I liked my hair better this morning. Never understood why it's such a virtue to have your hair straightened, when it naturally comes in waves.

When all was said and done it cost a small fortune. I felt guilty. *Mami*'s best friend works in a salon, though mind you, one that serves stale coffee in Styrofoam cups, not spring water infused with the flavor of organic cucumbers. Still, they do hair there. They would probably have done this whole blow out thing just fine (though maybe not Brazilian), and *Mam*i's friend would have made sure I got it for free. But then it would have all just gotten sweaty and sticky and nasty on the subway, and well, spring water with cucumbers was kind of a nice touch.

"You have beautiful, thick hair!" the cashier said, taking my hard-earned money, leaving me destitute. "Where you from?"

"Er… New York?"

I watched her put my cash into the register. I looked around for the pitcher of cucumber water. At these prices, would it be wrong to ask for a refill?

"But where you from from?" she insisted. People always do.

They say if you live in New York for ten years, you become a New Yorker. That's obviously a lie, because in my case, fifteen years and counting didn't even begin to do the trick. It's like I had it stamped on my forehead or something. Imported. *Importata.* Blah. Of course, most of New York is imported. Some of the most interesting elements of it are, in fact, foreign. Even the Brazilian blow dry is, supposedly, from Brazil.

"Where's your family from?" the cashier insisted.

"She's Romanian!" Gretchen jumped it. "Isn't that exotic?"

"Can I have more cucumber water, please?" the exotic Romanian girl asked. *Pot sa mai am apa cu castraveti, va rog?* In Romanian it sounded kind of dumb, which cheered me up. Until Gretchen said:

"Isn't that, like, so different?" She meant being Romanian, not the cucumber water. I wanted to smack her. I really haven't been a decent pet chinchilla lately.

Anyway, back to my story about today and how I ended up alone, cashless, and with no keys. I'll skip the rest of the going out preparations and go straight to the scene at the club. The club was fancy and full of beautiful people. But I'd spent too much on an apple martini, and I was having a bad time.

G wanted me to flirt with J.J., Bob's friend. I found J.J. annoying. In fact, I found all three of them annoying, and I was not trained well enough to disguise my boredom. I don't think I was outright rude, but I wasn't a good sport. I could sense G was furious. I excused myself to go to the ladies' room. I needed an escape.

The bathroom wasn't a good idea. As soon as I stepped in, I saw the old woman standing there, by the sinks, wearing a black dress and a white apron. My heart sunk. I hate how in these fancy clubs there's women whose job it is to wash people's hands. Of course, I know these women don't wash people's hands (G laughed at me once when I said that). They just hand you towels and lotion. Still, I think it's sad that this is someone's job. So sad, in fact, that tonight, when I saw the old woman, I started crying like an idiot.

I hid inside a stall. I know this is ridiculous and I promise I'm not some kind of freak. But old people are special to me. I was raised by my grandmother, like many Romanian kids of my generation. Well, in fact, I was raised by my grandmother, my great grandmother, and a nanny. But that only lasted until I was eight, when I left the country with my parents and my stupid brother and moved to stupid Queens. After that I never saw my grandmother again. Or my great grandmother, or *Tanti* Grosu, the nanny. *Mami* and I cried rivers over this, and in time, my affection for the three women turned into a general sense of loss and an inclination towards liking older people. My memories sometimes mislead me, too. I'm not sure, for example, who taught me the prayer about the little angel, but I still say it every night, although *Mami* laughs at me, because the prayer is for children, and I am, by some standards, grown. I can't remember who first showed me how cute birds are when they drink water. Their little throats move like little pumps, and they have to tilt their heads back to swallow. But give me a puddle and some doves (*porumbei*), and I'll probably start crying.

So I hid in a stall, trying to blink back tears. I forced myself to count the tiles on the floor. It's a trick I learned from *Mami*, a technique she came up with when she realized we would not be able to function in the new country crying rivers every day. The tiles were all the same cream color, some shiny, others matte. Each of them probably cost more than a plate of *Mami*'s fine china. I counted nine shiny ones, and twelve matte ones, then added the two numbers, then tried multiplying the sum by seven.

I finally felt brave enough to face the lotion woman. I smiled at her as best I could, and washed my hands quickly, avoiding eye contact. Then she held out a towel.

"You like lotion, Miss?"

I did not. What I wanted was to run away before the tears came back. But I didn't want to be rude, and so, the lotion process started. We held hands, the lotion woman and I. Her touch was warm, but her skin felt rough. How did people get skin like that? Was it old age? Housework? I wondered what the lotion lady did in her free time. What had she done in her youth? How did she end up here, in Manhattan, in the bathroom of a bar for spoiled rich kids? I looked at her tip jar. Just a few dollar bills. I wished I could afford a proper tip.

I closed my eyes and tried to concentrate on absolutely nothing. There was a sort of intimacy to the hand massage, a sense of closeness. Something I longed for in this big city, where I felt so alone tonight.

I dug inside my tiny clutch, fished out my last ten dollar bill, and placed it in the tip jar. I was officially out of cab fare.

I left the bathroom as quick as I could.

"What's wrong?" Gretchen asked when I got back. I could tell she was miffed. "You ok?"

I gave her my best pet chinchilla smile.

"Maybe those apple martinis are catching up with you. I'll ask J.J. to hail you a cab."

That was my cue to disappear. Once I was gone, JJ would probably hook up with a friendlier girl, and Gretchen could go home with Bob.

I air kissed G good night.

"Sit tight, gorgeous!" JJ said, and leaned in to give her a kiss on the cheek. Bob laughed. They were all a bit drunk. I wasn't even jealous.

Then J.J. hailed me a cab, and I was too embarrassed to admit I had no money.

Which leads me to #2. Where I am now. I told you I don't like this part, and since I really am under a lot of stress, I'll keep it short. Not that it really matters.

Here I am, alone on a dark street with no cash, no keys, no cell phone, no quarters, and most importantly: no clue. It's ridiculous. I should be home, safely asleep under *Mami*'s duvet which smells like spring and dew and loving care and too much time spent tending to the laundry. But I can't click my designer heels and go home. I cannot make myself disappear from the dark lonely street and insert myself neatly into Mami's bed. *În patul lui Mami.*

So yeah, this sucks, and to tell you the truth, being alone at night in a place I don't know in Manhattan has always terrified me. So, let's skip to Number 3.

3. What to do now? Where to go? All my things are in Gretchen's apartment. Even my toothbrush. The maid should be long gone by now. The doorman might let me into the lobby, but will probably not let me into the actual apartment.

If I at least had a stupid Metrocard, I could ride a train back to Queens, and go to *Mami*'s. But how can I show up like this, in the middle of the night, after three months of being away and bragging about my glamorous life in the city? What would *Mami* think?

Besides, *Mami* wouldn't approve of me riding the subway late at night. Plenty of thieves and rapists there. And creepy guys who stab people. Anyway, I don't have a Metrocard, so it's a moot point.

Calm down. *Calmează-te*. Chill out. Breathe. Think. There's gotta be a simple solution to this. There's gotta be somewhere I can walk. Someone I can call. Collect, of course. I can only call collect. To think I used to laugh at *Mami* for carrying a bunch of quarters in her purse.

I'll walk. That's what I'll do. It's painful in these stupid shoes, but I'll walk. Uptown seems safer. The stupid straps of Gretchen's stupid shoes dig into my flesh. But the further uptown I get, the better I feel. There is more light, the sights are more familiar.

In front of the Plaza, I'm greeted by music and flowers, by horse-drawn carriages, and the sparkle of diamonds underneath pashminas. I love these elegant people, so marvelously civilized.

The doorman greets me as if I belong here. It never fails, the magic of the Plaza. You step through the golden door, and you're transformed. Even tonight, I'm no longer a cashless vagabond with sore feet and no place to sleep. I'm a princess.

How lovely it would be to be a guest here! How grand to stay at the Plaza, even for just one night! I smile my happiest smile as I take it all in. For a few seconds, my problems disappear. There's chandeliers, red carpets, people, commotion, laughter. It never fails to impress me, the lobby of the Plaza. And yes, I've been here many times. Though I have never stayed. In fact, I've never even had as much as a cup of tea here. I've stopped by as a trespasser, a girl with no money, but plenty of time, craving a little luxury. I've spent so many hours wandering the streets of New York, with nothing to do, and no cash in my pockets. Nice hotels are my places of refuge. You can always go in if you need to pee. Nobody asks you your business, and the restrooms are always clean.

In fact, the restrooms are lovely. It beats going to *Starfucks*, buying a cup of coffee you don't need, then having to pee again after drinking it. Seriously. Luxury hotel beats coffee bar any day. But there are caveats. There are, sadly, lotion ladies here too, expecting tips. And you know how I feel about lotion ladies.

Tonight all I want is to use the pay phone. I'll call Momo collect and pray to God she's home. But not immediately. You have to be careful, if you're a penniless vagabond in the lobby of a world-class hotel. You can't make a rookie mistake and blow your cover. You have to act like you belong there. You better have a story.

My story, if anybody asks, is that I'm meeting my friend George at the bar. I've only had to use it once. And then I had to sit cross-legged on a fancy barstool, look at a menu advertising overpriced drinks, glance impatiently at my watch, and pretend I was being stood up.

But if nobody asks, then you walk past the doorman, past the receptionist, and head towards the restrooms. Walk normally. Walk with confidence. Yet be aware that in the midst of everybody else's drama, you are inconsequential, a grey mouse. Nobody is looking at you. They are always busier thinking of themselves. So I walk swiftly through the crowd telling myself I'm nothing but a grey mouse (*un şoricel gri*), dull and inconspicuous. Almost invisible.

I cradle the receiver to my ear and say a little prayer before telling the operator the number. Please let Momo be home. She's not. The phone rings. Empty. Futile. Sad. She's probably at *Tati*'s. It's Saturday night after all. I picture Momo and *Tati* coming home from dinner, having wine on his balcony. I feel a heavy lump in my stomach at the thought of my father. What would he say if he saw me right now?

I walk hesitantly towards the reception desk. It's unlikely that they'll have a free room. And even if they do, I won't be able to afford it. But I do have a credit card, and this is an emergency. I imagine the room, the big white bed, the soft sheets against my skin, the bathtub, and those little soaps they give you in hotels. How much am

I willing to pay for my own little soap from the Plaza? How much to see the inside of one of their rooms?

It would be financial suicide. It would push me over my credit limit. It would take ages to pay back. I'd have to sell my kidneys on the black market. But the least I can do is ask.

The woman behind the desk gives me a stern look.

"The only rooms we have available right now are twin rooms." She types something into the computer. "But I would be able to give you a special rate of six hundred fifty dollars plus tax."

Her smile is so fake that I almost recoil. She can probably tell that I'm an impostor, a gray mouse with not enough money to stay at the Plaza. For just one second I wonder if I have enough credit left for six hundred fifty dollars plus tax. I doubt it. I think of *Mami*, who uses only cash, and thinks sixty-dollar shoes are expensive. What would she think of a six hundred fifty dollar tiny bar of soap?

I thank the receptionist, and walk away defeated. Outside, I take off Gretchen's stupid shoes. My feet are killing me, and I have to walk thirty blocks uptown. The hot pavement feels comforting on my bare feet. Some late-night stores are still open on the Upper West Side, flowers and fruit displayed in stands on the sidewalk, busy people buying things inside. I like seeing people around me, even at this late hour. But the knot in my stomach is still there. And it feels worse the closer I get to his house.

The doorman buzzes upstairs. "Mister Pop, Liliana is here." He drags out my name the way most Americans do: Leahleahahnna. It sounds like an exotic plant. That's what Alex used to say when we were kids.

Tati's building is decent, but pales in comparison to Gretchen's. Back in the day, like when he first moved here, or even later, when I started going to CUNY, I used to be impressed with this lobby. Now I find it completely unremarkable, an average lobby in an average building on the Upper West Side. It looks nice enough, but you wouldn't call it elegant, not if you have the misfortune of being familiar with the type of elegance reserved for the very rich.

In the elevator I try to put my shoes back on, but my blisters are way too painful. I look in the mirror. My makeup is smudged, my eyes puffy, my hair in disarray. So much for the expensive blow dry. Why on earth didn't it last longer? I dip my finger in my mouth. I try to wipe off the black stains under my eyes. I make a face at myself in the mirror. The elevator stops. I feel like I swallowed a rock. I wish I could evaporate or something.

It's Momo who opens the door. Momo in a white dressing gown, her dark hair pinned up. Her makeup is gone. But even so, she's beautiful.

"What on earth is going on, Lili?"

I suddenly feel very tired.

"Nothing. Can I come in?"

But she's still standing in the doorway, a worried look on her face.

"What happened to you? Have you been crying?"

I shift my weight from one foot to the other. I'm angry with Momo. I'm angry that she's even here, angry she wasn't home to rescue me so I wouldn't have to go through this.

"Can I come in, or are we gonna stand in the doorway all night?"

Momo sighs, and crosses her arms.

"Do you know what time it is, Liliana?"

I puff through my nose like Gretchen. Even pronounced correctly, I still hate my full name.

"You go to bed late anyway, so why does it matter? I'm surprised you guys are even here."

"Well we are, and what time we go to bed is nobody's business. You can't just show up in the middle of the night and pretend all is normal. I mean, look at you!"

"Whatever. Can I come in?"

I brush past her, almost pushing her out of the way. I walk straight into the bathroom and stick my dirty feet in the tub, run the water, and slather my toes in Momo's expensive soap.

I grab a white towel, wipe my feet, then throw it on the floor. I take a deep breath, brace myself, open the door, push again past Momo, and head straight to the living room.

In his early fifties, *Tati* is still handsome. Gretchen, who met him once, said he was one of the most handsome men she'd ever seen. I wouldn't go that far, but he's good looking.

"Hi, *Tati*. You mind if I crash here tonight?"

Tati frowns. My heart sinks. He's gonna say yes, obviously. But what else is he gonna say?

"Can I stay here, daddy? Just tonight?"

I hold my breath. His dark eyes look me up and down. I can only imagine what he's thinking.

"Yes, sweetie, you can always stay here. You know that. Mona will fix your bed."

His voice is warm, conciliatory. I'm waiting for the other shoe to drop.

"If she apologizes. And only then," Momo interjects, the hurt in her voice a little too obvious. "She can't just come busting in here like a savage, be rude to me, and demand to be served."

I swear she's driving me crazy tonight! I am so very tired. I know I've been rude, and I do feel sorry, but I really don't have the patience to deal with her right now.

"Is either of you listening to me?" Momo whines.

Tati gives her a look of irritation. I suddenly feel sorry for her.

"I'm sorry Momo," I say. "You know I love you. It's just I'm tired, is all. And my feet are killing me. Will you please fix my bed?"

Still pouting, she goes in search of pillows, sheets, and a comforter.

"*Plapumă.*" I smile, looking at the bulky load Momo is single-handedly struggling with.

She smiles back. She finds it funny, my random use of Romanian words. It's gotten us past many awkward moments.

"Don't just stand there, Lili. Help me!" Momo admonishes while straightening the sheet on the leather couch, and tucking it in. "This ain't your mother's house!"

It sure ain't yours either! But I don't say this out loud. Instead, I pretend to help with the sheets. I've been unpleasant enough for one evening.

"Are you gonna tell me what's going on?" she prods one more time. She's dying to know. She is my confidante of sorts. Momo certainly knows more about me than Gretchen does. I've dramatically inflated the number of men I've slept with, for Gretchen's benefit, suspecting that her admiration might falter if she knew the truth. Momo knows that I've only been with two men: my ex, and a much regretted one-night-stand fueled by alcohol, and by Gretchen's matchmaking skills. The former left me with a broken heart, the latter with a vague feeling of disgust. In both cases, Momo generously supplied condoms, advice, and a shoulder to cry on. She also insisted than neither of the two young men were good lovers, and that the best was yet to come.

So yes, we're close, in a way that *Mami* and I have never been, and probably could never be, as it surely must be unnatural for a mother and daughter to talk about intimate things.

Momo is sitting on the couch, lighting a cigarette. *Tati* has gone to bed. We're alone in the living room, and I know Momo expects me to talk to her.

I wish she wouldn't smoke. I hate smoke. And I hate the fact that all Romanians, other than *Mami*, are smokers. I wish I could tell Momo not to light up in here. After all, it's *Tati*'s apartment, and he himself smokes only on the balcony. He usually airs out the place after Momo leaves. I've even seen him spray Febreeze into the pillows of the couch, but I've never told her. It would be cruel.

"Let's go sit outside, Momo. I feel like watching the cars go by."

Outside, on the balcony, her cigarette bothers me less.

"It's Gretchen," I finally say. "She wanted to go home with this guy and she didn't realize I have no way of getting in."

"So you still don't have a key."

Why does she have to state the obvious?

I lean over the edge of the balcony and look down. I love to see Broadway stretching down below, with all its lights, and still, at this hour, people and cars going about their business.

"And by the looks of your feet you still have no money, not even for a lousy cab. What do you do with your paychecks from *Bella*? After all, you don't pay rent."

I bite my lip. Can Momo even imagine what it's like to work in retail? She probably spends on a dress what I make in a week.

"You know I could help you with managing your money," Momo says. "If only you'd let me."

I swallow. She knows quite a bit about money. She works in finance, after all. She makes money by doing stuff with money. The difference between her and most other members of 'the community' is that Momo has a cool profession, and she actually practices it, here in America. But then again, like me, she came over at a young age, and studied here. Nearly everybody else was a doctor, a lawyer, an engineer, or an architect, like *Tati*, back in Romania. They had careers over there, but once they came here they became taxi drivers, shop assistants, and such. Momo never had to do that. She went to business school, and now she works in a glass building downtown, wears tailored suits and real designer shoes, eats gourmet food, and is never out of carfare. What pisses me off is that I had the same opportunities she had, and look where it got me.

I yawn strategically.

"I'm really tired. Can we talk about it tomorrow, please?"

"You do look exhausted. But you know, you can't keep making excuses just to run away from your problems. Do you have any idea how worried your father is about you?"

Momo's dark eyes search mine. I swallow hard. Sometimes I just want to smack her. "I know he doesn't say much, Lili. Victor is like that, he doesn't express himself, but you should know, he's terribly worried about you."

Bullshit. He expresses himself plenty. In fact, I'm sick of him telling me how worried he is, and how irresponsible I am.

"I really need to go to bed, Momo. Can we please talk tomorrow?"

She looks away. Distractedly, she stubs out her cigarette. She plays with the pack in her hand. I hope she's not going to light another.

"Well, I guess we better call it a night, then," she finally says. "But I have to leave early tomorrow. I won't be here when you wake up."

I yawn again and I give her a big hug.

It's a far cry from the Plaza, but the sheets smell clean, like lavender or something. Sweet and soothing. *Tati* is probably using a better laundry service these days. I like how the couch cradles my body. What a relief to finally feel comfortable.

I didn't draw the blinds. I like seeing the city lights. I can never have enough of that, the red sky of Manhattan. As a child, shortly after arriving here, I felt totally bewildered by the New York City sky. It never seemed to fully get dark. I wondered if I'd ever see the stars again. The sky looked almost red. After all these years I'm still not used to it. But I have come to enjoy it. *M-am invățat să-mi placă.*

{ 2 }

Sunday with *Tati*

When Victor gets up the next morning, Lili is still asleep, curled up in fetal position, her mouth slightly open, a strand of drool leaking onto her pillow. He would find this disgusting in anyone else. But his little girl sleeps like a baby, her balled up fist so close to her mouth, it almost looks like she is sucking on her thumb. Definitely still a child. And a troublesome one at that.

She still has so much growing up to do. At times he's irritated that she's still so immature. She's twenty-three, after all, but in so many ways she's still a little girl. He's worried that she might have chosen to grow up too fast. When she left home, he panicked. It wasn't just that it was irresponsible, crazy, in fact, her arrangement with her friend. Neither here, not there. He was worried about her. He didn't think she was ready. He knew he was being overprotective, and a bit patriarchal, in this one instance very much a Romanian father, but he realized he didn't like her being on her own. He wanted to still know, each night, that his little girl was sleeping safely next to her mother. Instead, Lili chose to haphazardly and irresponsibly throw herself into the world.

He was right to worry. Last night, she seemed so lost, showing up barefoot at 2am, looking like a deer caught in the headlights. Her voice sounded just like a child's. He couldn't even open his mouth to ask what happened. He wasn't afraid of what he'd say, but rather of how she'd take it. He's not an angry man. He's always been capable of controlling himself. But whatever he said recently, whatever arguments he brought, Lili took offense. She's accused him of ridiculous things, of not giving a damn about her, of abandoning her, of not wanting her to be happy. None of those things are true, and he hopes she doesn't really believe them. He especially hopes she doesn't think he abandoned her. He left one day, it's true, taking all his possessions in two black garbage bags. But the truth is more complicated than that. He wonders, sometimes, what Maria chose to tell the children.

He's made mistakes, of course. But he always tried to be a good father. Attentive, involved, understanding even. Compared to most immigrant parents, Victor likes to think of himself as reasonable. He doesn't expect his children to achieve the things he wanted for himself, but had to give up in order to make ends meet in a new country. He doesn't throw in their faces the sacrifices he made. Though these are plenty, he doesn't use them for emotional blackmail. It never even occurred to him to push either of his kids into architecture, the profession he loved but had to give up. He did mention several times, that according to him, architecture, medicine, and the law, are still the soundest careers out there. But he declared repeatedly that whatever path his children take, he'll be supportive, just as long as they make practical choices and prepare themselves for standing on their own two feet. This is exactly where Lili, for all her intelligence and charm, has so far failed, and continues to struggle. His little girl has no idea what it takes to survive in this world.

Not that she's stupid. She did well in college. But she got a B.A. in English literature with a minor in Italian, choices he advised against, yet dutifully paid for. Now she is wasting her education, working in a high-end boutique, a job so strikingly similar to her mother's, that the irony of it all never ceases to amaze him. He came to America hoping for a better life for his family. And here they are, fifteen years later, his bitter wife and his chipper daughter, both intelligent, both educated, both gainfully employed selling leather goods. Maria has no choice. She is a poorly adjusted immigrant, who will forever speak bad English. Lili, on the other hand, has no excuse. She had every opportunity to succeed, she still does, and she obstinately chooses to make nothing of it. He once told her he almost regretted paying for college, and the little brat spat out that after all, CUNY was cheap, and that she saved him a bundle by living at home. He then accused her of being unappreciative of him for putting her through school, and of her mother who cooked, cleaned, and did laundry for her for all these years. Her reply came quick as lightning: "Unappreciative? Of *Mami*? Ain't that your job?"

Victor frowns. He needs his coffee. He badly needs a smoke.

He pours himself one large, steaming mug, and takes it outside, to the balcony. He likes his coffee strong and black. And he enjoys a cigarette with it above all else. Mona left early, quietly, as not to wake him, kindly starting the coffee on her way out. She's probably the most considerate girlfriend a man could ever hope for.

The coffee tastes just right. His tastes have never been simple ones, and living in a city that has everything to offer, he's probably grown too sophisticated for his own good. Once his business started making money, he began exploring the culinary variety of Manhattan. His fridge and pantry started bursting with gourmet items, and slowly but surely he started to flirt with the idea of cooking. He has to admit, he used to think cooking was a woman's job. But living on his own, he missed that homemade flavor that no restaurant can recreate. What upset him most was that he specifically yearned for his wife's cooking. He missed the flavor of her food even more than he missed her touch, her voice, or the scent of her skin. It was his body's ultimate betrayal, craving the nourishment prepared for him by the hands of a woman he so deeply resented.

He learned to cook as an act of revenge. It was an empowering, liberating coup. By now, he's probably good enough to rival Maria.

It's past noon when Lili finally begins stirring. Yawning and stretching, she emerges with messy hair and swollen eyes from her crumpled sheets. He's already had breakfast, coffee, and two cigarettes (he tries to be disciplined about his smoking and only allows himself one on weekdays, two on weekends). He's already gone through the new issue of Architectural Digest, and a catalog of furniture sent to him by a warehouse in New Jersey.

Lili comes out to greet him. She stands in the doorway, smiles and yawns. Always a restless sleeper, she's managed to un-tuck the bed Mona prepared for her, and has slept the last few hours with her cheek directly on the leather couch. He can see a line on her skin from the edge of the sheet.

He offers her orange juice, but to his surprise she wants coffee instead. She comes back with a steaming cup, and comments on how good the French Roast is. It sounds more like a question than a statement, and she pauses, as if awaiting his reply. Setting her mug down on the table, she pulls Mona's bathrobe tighter around her body, and adjusts the belt. With her left hand, she brushes the hair out of her eyes. Then she grabs her coffee mug again. She smiles. She seems reluctant to sit down with him. She probably thinks there's another lecture coming on. It upsets him to realize, she's actually afraid of him.

"It's a nice day out," he says. "What do you say you eat some breakfast, and then we go to the park? We haven't had a proper walk together in months."

Her face relaxes a bit.

He suggests a peace offering:

"We could get pizza, then ice cream."

She smiles and nods, her eyes now bright with sunshine.

It's a beautiful day, a bit hot in the park, but neither of them minds it. They end up having ice cream first. Dripping cups of Mister Softee, which he doesn't really enjoy, but agrees to buy to please her. They sit on the grass, and he studies her appearance, trying to guess from her face just what kind of trouble she's in.

There are no clues in her face. She looks beautiful, still a bit puffy from sleep, with the sun in her hair, and ice cream dripping down her chin. He reaches over and wipes it off with his napkin. She smiles, knowing how he can't suffer a mess, and for a moment, her face takes on that familiar expression, her mother's expression from when she was young, before life and kids, and marriage, and this country made her bitter. After all these years, when memories of Maria sneak up on him, it still shocks him, in a way that is pleasant and painful all at once.

He stands up.

"It's hot here. What do you say we go see a movie?"

There's something French playing at the Paris. They both enjoy it, and walk off feeling happy, playfully speaking French to each other. He's proud of his daughter's French. He had no idea it's gotten so good.

He remembers the effort he put into teaching her, when she was just a little girl, the used copy of *The Little Prince* he bought to read to her at night. It was expensive for their meager budget. His wife got upset, and so the next time he bought his little girl a French book, he hid it from her. Maria found it later, of course, but she just smiled, half amused, half annoyed.

He takes Lili's hand, and asks playfully:

"*Ou avez-vous envie de dîner ce soir, mademoiselle*?"

Where would you like to dine tonight?

They end up at one of her favorite restaurants, close to his apartment, on the West Side, a place that serves a simple yet delightful grilled chicken salad, and quite exquisite desserts. She's enjoying her chocolate mousse when he finally asks why she needed to spend the night.

She tells him her roommate, Gretchen, forgot to give her a key. He knows how a father should react to this type of story. But he decides to keep quiet. He doesn't want to tell her once again what he thinks of Gretchen, or of their living arrangement. He's met this roommate once. L introduced them at her high school graduation, an event both he and his wife dutifully attended.

After dinner, Lili borrows his cell phone so she can call her friend. He's irritated that she still has not replaced the phone she lost a few weeks ago, an expensive phone he had gotten her as a gift. But he doesn't want to ruin the evening by scolding her.

L seems happy after a short conversation he tries hard not to listen to. She just found out that Gretchen has returned home, and now she's in a hurry to get back. Apparently, there's some kind of crisis going on, and her roommate needs her ASAP. And besides, Lili assures him, Gretchen really IS a wonderful friend, friendships just have their ups and downs, and the thing about the key is an innocent oversight, nothing major. Most importantly, she says, it's a wonderful place to live, and he really shouldn't worry, her arrangement with G is rock solid.

He decides against voicing his doubts. Instead, he surprises himself by offering her to stay with him, for as long as she needs. She laughs, declines, thanks him, hugs him, and tells him to stop worrying. She keeps giggling and shaking her head. "Oh, *Tati*! Come on!" Does she know how hard it is for him to make such an offer, how he hates the idea of sharing his space, of giving up his solitude? He doesn't insist. But he feels uneasy for the rest of the night.

He sees her to a cab, and gives her three hundred dollars in cash. He reminds her to buy a new cell phone, tells her as kindly as he can that he hasn't stopped paying her monthly bill, and that it's neither safe nor practical to go without a phone in this day and age.

Walking back home, he decides to allow himself a third cigarette, and when he finishes it, he craves the fourth one, but doesn't give in. He walks into his building, greets the doorman, who has become almost a friend over the years, and strikes up a short conversation. Oddly, he feels the need to talk to someone. He's almost sorry he told Mona not to stop by tonight. He talks to the doorman about sports. By the time the elevator comes, he has pretty much satisfied his need for conversation.

He's happy to get into his big bed, turn on the flat screen TV, and enjoy his single malt scotch. He falls asleep watching sports, and when he wakes up to turn off the lights, he has the feeling it's been a good day. The thought of some of the new furniture orders crosses his mind. He'll take care of those tomorrow, at the store. It also occurs to him that he has not asked his daughter for her phone number at her friend's house or at that silly place she works at. He makes a mental note to call his wife tomorrow and ask for Lili's numbers. Shortly thereafter he drifts into a dreamless sleep

{3}

Friendship

By Sunday night it's clear that Bob was just another one-night-stand. No, he hasn't called. No, he hasn't replied to Gretchen's seven (or was it twenty seven?) text messages. And he ushered her out of his apartment quite rudely this very morning, not even offering coffee. Gretchen is curled up on her beautiful white couch, with a bottle of her favorite wine, some chips, a melting carton of Ben and Jerry's, and a box of tissues. Between sobs, she repeats over and over that he was so rude, he practically told her to leave.

I realize it would be in bad taste to bring up the trifling matter of the key at a time like this. I've never seen G this distraught before. Though I've seen my fair share of G's post-party meltdowns. Hold your judgment, though. It's really not the way it sounds. Yes, Gretchen goes home with the wrong guy every now and then, and yes, she gets upset when they don't call her afterwards, but it was never this bad before. Some ice cream, a pizza maybe, a cocktail or two, a few jokes about men being pigs, and she'd cheer up and be her usual self. But tonight she's really upset and I'm starting to get concerned. None of the usual tricks in my pet chinchilla repertoire seem to cheer her up this time.

"He practically shoved me out the door, L!" she says for like the millionth time. She blows her nose, defiling yet another innocent tissue, then tosses said tissue behind couch. The maid will have a heart attack when she sees this place tomorrow.

"Like, like… like I was garbage, L. Like a prostitute or something."

G sobs. Her face is swollen beyond proportion, and her nose looks like a red bell pepper. *Ca un ardei gras roşu.*

"You're exaggerating, G! He's just a guy, he's stupid, and he has no manners. He's a pig."

"You have no idea what a pig he is!"

Gretchen takes another sip of wine, then refills both our glasses. I shudder. I can already feel a headache coming on. Please God don't let me be hung over at work tomorrow!

"Can you get out another bottle, L? I'm just too weak to move. And I really need to get drunk tonight!"

While opening the wine in G's immaculate kitchen, I glance at the digital clock on her state of the art oven. 11:45. Fat chance of going to bed before one, the way Gretchen is carrying on. I wonder what is best, to stop drinking and just pretend to sip, or maybe to chug like a pig in the hopes of finishing the bottle fast, going to bed, and hopefully falling into an instant coma.

Surrounded by discarded tissues, Gretchen is holding out her empty glass.

"Oh, L, you have no idea! You're such a sweet little girl, you've had such a sheltered life! You have no clue how people are!"

I try to not take offense at that. It's G's pain speaking, that's all. I smile and take a sip of wine.

"I mean, L, maybe if I grew up like you, if I had a mother, instead of three older sisters who just treated me like a fucking mini-adult since I was five, who just took me to parties and gave me clothes and never told me not to smoke, not to do drugs, or drink, or let a guy get to third base… Well, you know what I mean. I just… I didn't even have a childhood. I just experienced it all, and well, you'd think I should know better. You'd think I'd be wise enough by now not to let people use me. But it's the same thing all over again, L. He used me! And I let him. I'm such an idiot. I just let him use me, and then he shoves me out the door and…"

Her voice breaks. I feel sad and guilty. Poor Gretchen really needs a friend. And lately I've been so resentful of her wealth and privilege, that I forgot all the bad things in her life. Yes, she has a trust fund. And her daddy and older sisters spoil her rotten. But that's mostly because her mom died when G was a baby. And no matter how much money and how many presents her family dish out, they'll never make up for the fact that she grew up without a mother. I can't even imagine what that's like, can't imagine my own childhood without *Mami*. I can't even bare to think of what I would have done if my *Mami* had one day disappeared.

And so I drink more wine, and try, as best I can, to comfort Gretchen. Poor G! Motherless, and then to have such bad luck with men all the time! Yes, probably it wasn't the best idea to get drunk and go home with Bob. But he did seem nice, and G had such a crush on him, and they are considerably young. And it's 2004, for God's sake! Going home with a guy shouldn't be such a big deal anymore.

"Oh, G," I say, "stop beating yourself up. You had no way of knowing he'd be such an asshole. You didn't do anything wrong, you just..."

"L!" Gretchen sits up and fixes me in a serious, yet very drunken gaze. "You know nothing!" Her voice slurs. Her puffy face seems darker. "Let me tell you something. But you have to swear, and I mean swear, you won't tell anyone."

I swallow. I wish G were not this patronizing.

"You don't know nothing!" G says, and I cringe at the double negative. Not because it's grammatically incorrect. In fact, to me, it's über cool. *Super tare*. Poetry of the streets. But it's my own linguistic über coolness, my poetry of the streets. It's fake and wrong on Gretchen. She stole it from me, stole the one cool thing that I had.

"You think that I went home with Bob?"

G laughs, and for a second, I don't understand.

"You went home with JJ?" I ask incredulous. Haven't we been talking about Bob all along? And why would G go home with JJ, when it was Bob she was interested in all along?

G holds up two fingers.

"Both, L." She sobs so hard she can barely continue speaking. "I went home with both. I slept with both. I'm so stupid, L, I was drunk, and they told me all these nice things, they flattered me to no end, like I was some sex-goddess and they couldn't help wanting me, oh God, they actually said that, and I was so drunk, and... I fell for it, L! I thought it'd be hot, and that I was so cool for doing it with two guys, and they both seemed so crazy about me, and..."

I try hard not to look horrified. But the bouquet of the wine suddenly makes me want to vomit.

"Don't ever tell this to anyone, L! I mean nobody, nobody can know. It's you and me, and well, Joan knows, but that's it! You understand?"

Wait... What?

"You told this to Joan?" If I ever had a threesome, or anything remotely sexually adventurous, Joan would be the last person I'd confide in. But then again, Joan is Gretchen's sister, not mine. Maybe to G she seems less judgmental.

"Yes," Gretchen says. "I shouldn't have, I know it. But I just felt so awful, L, and I was here all alone, and you don't have a damn cell phone so I couldn't call and tell you to come home. Damn, L, sometimes I really hate that you don't have a cell phone! So I called Joan, and we had takeout brunch, and well, it was horrible. She just... She said I need to learn how to deal with people, that I always let guys use me, and other people too, that I'm too kind, and too naïve, that I try too hard to make people like me, and that I should know better..."

She reaches for the carton of ice cream, and in a clumsy gesture, knocks it over. I watch as a puddle of chocolate spreads over the hardwood floor. I'm tempted to go get a sponge and wipe it, but just then, Gretchen grabs my hand.

"It's true, though, isn't it, L? I do let people use me. I am a pleaser. How pathetic is that? A pleaser! And my life is a mess! I have to start organizing it, don't I? I have to become tougher and stronger! You'll help me, right?"

I wake up the next morning parched and with a monster headache. It's one of those yucky post-drinking mornings, when I feel dirty even after taking a shower. But what can a girl do? Life goes on, duty calls. I struggle into my couture and my heels (or rather G's couture and her heels), cast a regretful look towards the coffee maker I won't have time to use, and almost sprain my ankle running out the door.

In spite of the bile building up inside me at the thought of swallowing anything, coffee is all I dream about all morning. Rich, dark, strong, fragrant, slightly acidic, potent coffee. The killer of all headaches. The surrogate of sleep.

With no bus fare, I have to run to work in heels. At an intersection, waiting for a light to change, I feel a man pushing his body a little too close to mine, and my stomach turns. God, they really are pigs! G's story looms over me, like a dark cloud. It's so awful and so revolting, I wish I never heard it. The whole world seems so ugly right now, I can barely stand it. What the hell was G thinking? Why on earth would she sleep with those guys?

Groggy and ill humored, I stumble to work, dreaming about the cup of coffee I'll finally buy at lunch. The guy at Starbucks will pitch a fit at the sight of one of *Tati*'s crisp hundred dollar bills, but so what? A girl's gotta do what a girl's gotta do.

Bella is a small but exclusive boutique specializing in handcrafted leather goods from Italy, most of which Francesca personally purchases during her trips to Milan. I envy her glamorous lifestyle, just as I envy her slender figure, so comfortably yet elegantly wrapped in cashmere.

It's not Francesca's slender figure that I covet most though. I'm a size 2 myself. Alex calls me bony. It's rather something about Francesca's grace and elegance that I wish I could steal. Something I can't really put my finger on. It isn't beauty, though I can name a few beautiful women, like *Mami*, who have a similar type of grace. Francesca isn't even beautiful. *Mami* certainly is. I, however, inherited neither beauty, nor grace. I'm a klutz, my sense of style would be nothing without G's help, I have bad posture, and the list could go on.

As I contemplate all my faults, my hand slides over the soft leather of a bag I've been coveting for ages. I love the simple style, the tender, malleable texture, and of course the intoxicating scent of leather. This bag represents luxury to me. Luxury, class, and elegance. The kind of beauty I always long for but can never afford. Most of all I want it because it's the same bag that Francesca wears herself.

"*Ti piace, cara*?" My boss asks from the other end of the store. "I'm thinking of putting it on sale, *sai*? You should really buy it, use your discount on top of the sale price?" Francesca's enthusiasm is, as ever, contagious. I can't resist. It seems like the price is worth it, just to honor her friendly invitation.

I use *Tati*'s cash to get the bag. Francesca congratulates me repeatedly, gives me a beautiful cloth sack to store the bag in, and throws in some of the special lotion for free, the one she is adamant all fine leather should be cleaned with. She insists that I transfer my belongings to the new bag immediately.

Strolling to Starbucks on my lunch break, the new bag bouncing softly on my shoulder, I experience an exhilarating mix of dread and delight. I love seeing my reflection in store windows. The large, soft, creamy leather satchel almost makes me look chic. It shows off my delicate figure. And it certainly draws a lot of attention, making the rest of the outfit -a simple black dress, and hurtful six inch heels - seem much less drab. (Seriously, this is the saddest part of my fashion trouble: Even the coolest clothes look drab on me).

I am in love with my new bag. But I regret spending *Tati*'s cash. Sometimes I really have no self-control. And I can't even return the stupid thing. What would Francesca think? So I just squandered $265, which could have been used to pay down my credit card bill, not to mention buying a new phone, and surviving until my paycheck. Oy! I shudder at the thought of my elegant yet frugal mother. *Mami* would die if she knew how much I paid for this bag. I mean, it's just a bag, even if it comes with a cloth sack and its own skin-care regimen.

Well, to be fair, at least I didn't charge the bag itself, so at least, I won't pay interest on it. Plus, I now actually have change, and can buy a much needed cup of coffee. And bus fare! I have bus fare!

After work, holding on to those bars on the bus I feel jittery and anxious. I guess it's because my only meal today was coffee. Then again, it was a giant latte, containing plenty of skim milk. Isn't that protein after all? And it should keep me skinny. They show all this stuff on TV about skim milk melting away fat, right? Plus, skipping lunch after making a major purchase is only sensible from a financial point of view.

By the time I get home, my stomach feels like a painful hole, a burning little crater, menacing to get deeper and deeper and kill me. Can a girl die from no food and too much coffee?

There's never food in Gretchen's fridge. Just Fiji water. So I stop and get some burgers and fries off the Dollar Menu at McDonald's. I order two of everything. One for me, one for G. I try, once again, not to think of *Mami*, who would never in a million years allow Alex and me to eat fast food.

Although she complains about fat and calories, G loves her burger. And she eats most of my fries in addition to her own. But she isn't impressed with my new bag. *Bella* carries quality leather accessories, imported directly from Italy, but G finds it too mainstream. She also thinks a cream colored bag looks hideous with an all black outfit.

Once again, she has stolen my word. Hideous. *Hidos.*

I love that word. Original, and oh so versatile. I mean, now, for example, it describes just how I feel after breathlessly devouring my hideous burger. I promise myself never to eat fast food again. I also promise myself never to show a new purchase to Gretchen.

Later on, I'm in my bathroom removing my makeup with Ponds cold cream and a cotton disk, a trick I learned from *Mami*, when Gretchen knocks on my door. I quickly hide the cold cream. Too low brow for the likes of G.

"Ahm, L..." Gretchen starts, seeming uncomfortable. "I don't know how to say this correctly, but you've been here three months, and..."

I feel my knees soften. I never thought she'd actually throw me out.

"...I was talking to my therapist and, well, she thinks our friendship is another place where I don't have good boundaries, so... I'm not saying you're trying to take advantage, L,

I know you're a true friend, but, you see, the thing with Bob was just such an eye-opener for me. My therapist says I need to learn to learn to take better care of myself. I need to stop trying so hard to please others so... Well, anyway, you know I love to have you live here, but, you know..."

My stomach hurts. I wish she'd leave so I could curl up on my bed and cry. If I still have a bed, that is.

"Look, L, I don't mean to be a hater," G continues. Another word she stole from me. A word I borrowed from the music Alex blares in his room whenever he's home from college. I wish I could snatch it back from Gretchen's mouth and claim copyright or something.

"Anyway, L, you seem to be doing so well with your job, buying new things and, well, all this time you've never offered to contribute. I mean, I know I own this place, but the maintenance comes out of my estate, you know? And maintenance in this building is not cheap. I think if you contributed a thousand a month that is way reasonable for Manhattan, especially for a place like this, right by the park. And well, you know, you've been here three months, and let's say the first one was on me, but after that, really... What I'm trying to say is: You owe me two thousand dollars in back rent for June and July, and then August just started, so that's another thousand... I think it's a fair deal, and I'm only doing this in order to be, you know, fair, and honest, and good to myself."

She takes in a deep breath, as if recovering from a huge effort.

I don't know what to say. I shift my weight from one foot to the other. To think I walked into this trap, eyes wide open. How could I believe I would really live here for free? Like a parasite. *Ca un parazit.*

"*Gute Rechnung, gute Freundshaft*," I finally say.

Gretchen gives me a blank stare.

"It's German, G. It means something like good calculation, good friendship."

Maybe the mention of German will make Gretchen soften up. After all, it was my interest in the language that started our friendship. It was in high school that I decided I didn't fit into American society, and that my entire family would be better off if we moved back to Europe. I used to scan the names of kids in my class, singling out the ones that sounded European. Gretchen's stood out. I walked up to her and asked timidly: "Are you German? Were you named after Gretchen in Faust?" Gretchen had once fallen asleep during Faust, and had absolutely no German origin to claim. But she thought I was very interesting at a time when she herself was very bored. That's how we became friends.

The silence in the room is heavy. I guess I have to produce more in way of a response than a German saying.

"Well," Gretchen says, "It's important to get uncomfortable matters out of the way, in order to be good friends. And really, L, it's such a ridiculous amount, it's just symbolic, you know. Kind of like a symbol of the trust and …er, friendship between us, you know?"

I stifle a sigh. In the circles I grew up in, nobody would talk of two thousand dollars and counting as a symbolic amount.

But it's nothing to Gretchen. I've seen her donate clothes to charity that had price tags higher than that still hanging on them, clothes she had never worn.

It's an understatement to say that she is filthy rich and obnoxiously spoiled. She got a BMW for her high school graduation, and a two-bedroom apartment overlooking the park for barely making it through college, which really just meant surviving four years of intense partying.

I myself worked hard in school. I had a full scholarship in high school. Then I went on to CUNY because it was cheap and in the city, but I graduated *summa cum laudae*. It's true that I lived at home with *Mami*, and unlike American kids, I was never pushed, or even encouraged, to get a job, or even to do my own laundry. *Mami* never even let me wash the dishes. All I had to do was go to class, schlepping used copies of paperback novels, and my dog-eared Italian dictionary back and forth on the subway. At home, *Mami* would cook delicious meals, keep the house clean, and not just wash, but actually iron every little piece of clothing I used. Even my underwear. *Tati* would give me a weekly allowance. He'd come get me on weekends and take me to visit his friends in 'the community', or take me back to Manhattan to go to the park or the museum. A few times a month he made sure he took me to what he called a real cultural event, a play, or a concert, and Momo sometimes joined us.

Yes, my life has been good and sheltered. But what was given to me always had its limits. *Mami* cooked the most delicious meals, but insisted we eat the leftovers. She was meticulous about ironing, but would never ever spring for a new outfit. The house was clean, but there was never enough money to get cable, or the internet. We watched a small ancient TV, hooked up to an antenna. *Tati* gave me an allowance, but it was never more than a hundred bucks or so. I could shop at TJ Max, but never at Bloomingdale's, not to mention Barney's, or any of the designer stores on Fifth or Madison.

My college graduation present was that both parents attended. Even Alex came from upstate, looking presentable and acting less obnoxious than usual. *Mami* baked one of her famous chocolate cakes, all made from scratch, decorated with candied hazelnuts (*alune*) and laced with real rum. She stayed up most of the night to arrange the layers, and still had to work the next day, so she looked frail and tired. *Tati* gave me an envelope containing not one hundred dollars, as usual, but actually two (!), and brought an excellent bottle of red wine that we all loved. My parents, like most Romanians, don't give a damn about underage drinking.

A cake, two hundred dollars, and a bottle of wine! That's all I got. That, and a rather uncomfortable silence around the table when I announced my future plans: working at *Bella* in order to save money for a trip to Italy, and living with Gretchen in Manhattan. After the long silence, *Mami* exclaimed with carefully contrived cheer: "Well, that sounds like lot of fun! You should be enjoying the life when you are young." She raised her glass to toast to Italy.

Tati gave her an angry look:

"Go on, encourage her! Don't you see she's completely irresponsible?"

Then *Mami* and *Tati* started arguing.

Alex and I cleared the chocolate covered plates and placed them in a pile on the kitchen table. It didn't occur to us to actually wash them. We just stood there with a table full of dirty plates between us. I was trying to think of a topic of conversation, just so we wouldn't have to listen. But we both really wanted to listen, in the same way that people feel compelled to slow down and look at a car wreck on the highway.

Tati kept his voice low. His anger tends to be controlled. *Mami* usually makes up for it by being quite dramatic. She's a screamer, a thrower, and on occasion a hitter (She never spanked Alex or me, but I've seen her hit *Tati* a few times). Every now and then, we could hear her crying out in an exasperated, almost pleading voice:

"What she is doing wrong? She just wants to live the life!"

It was *Mami*'s rule early on, that only English would be spoken in our household. Yet of all members of our dysfunctional family, she's the only one still struggling with it. Still, she will not give up. That is *Mami*'s way.

So basically, for graduation, Gretchen got a lovely apartment. I got a cake, some wine, two hundred dollars, and courtside tickets to yet another championship fight between my parents. All of these things, however, I can never say to G. What's the point of telling people how much your own life sucks?

So I smile, shrug, and admit she caught me off guard.

"Gee, Gretchen. I never thought of it that way… I mean, I thought I could just crash, but I don't want you to feel like I'm taking advantage. I'll just, well, you know… I'll just give you the money."

Gretchen is still standing there, expectantly. Does she think I'll write her a check right now? Does she imagine in her crazy little head that I have that much money in my checking account? Or that I have a hidden pile of cash in a shoebox in my closet, prepared for just such an emergency?

It's a long awkward moment before she finally bids me good-night and leaves.

That night I cannot sleep. Good calculation, good friendship. Where am I gonna get that money from? I mostly earn commission at *Bella*.

I was really planning to save for Italy. But there is just too much expensive fun to be had in New York City proper. Having to commute all the way to Queens, I never before enjoyed this much freedom, the excitement of so many things to do, so many places to go to. I've been spending my paycheck before it even gets deposited into my account. I'm always struggling to make minimum payments on my credit card, and the only thing I can be proud of is that so far I've somehow managed to make due. Other than that I have nothing to show for myself. Most of the time I try not to think of this. After all, I've only been on my own for three months. Nobody would expect me to have saved enough for a trip to Italy in such a short time, would they?

But now suddenly the situation is beyond disastrous. Now I've accumulated a monstrous debt towards my best friend, a friend who has been kind enough to give me clothes and shelter. And sheets of a gazillion count Egyptian cotton. I'll have to find a way to pay her back. And then I'll have to find a way to keep paying to live here.

I toss and turn all night. I don't know if it's the coffee, the hideous burger, or Gretchen's unexpected demand for money that's keeping me up. I only fall asleep close to dawn, and then I have the most disturbing dream. My parents are sitting on a park bench together. *Mami* is wearing a lovely red silk dress, a dress she used to wear in Romania, in the 80s. She's holding a cheeseburger, wrapped in yellow wax paper. She holds it as if it were a curious object, and looks at it with disgust. She takes a small bite, and chews slowly, with obvious discomfort, as if she were chewing a mouthful of cotton. "You call this food, Victor?" Her voice is shrill, her eyes angry. She throws the burger at *Tati*. "You call this a life?" I wake up nauseous, wanting to cry. Throughout the day, *Mami*'s voice echoes in my ears. You call this a life?

{ 4 }

It Is What It Is

Maria hates the subway. It's hot, it smells bad, and there's always construction. And she saw rats, on more than one occasion. Unfortunately, she has to ride the subway every day. If she added up all the hours of her life she's wasted on the subway… But no, she's not going to think about it right now. She'll try to forget that she's even here. She'll continue reading, and she'll imagine herself somewhere else. She takes another sip of coffee, trying not to spill the contents of her travel mug on her paperback novel.

She likes to get to the store early, so she can slip into the back room and change out of her sneakers. She hates the look of sneakers, always has. But life is too short to put up with sore feet. She's no longer that young. After all, she just turned forty-four.

She slips into a pair of black patent leather flats. She then rinses her travel mug, washes it, dries it with paper towels, and places it in her tote bag, which she stashes in her locker. Next, she brushes her teeth using her favorite cinnamon flavored toothpaste. She takes a minute to arrange her dark brown hair in the mirror, pretending not to see the strands of white, pretending not to care. She applies a fresh coat of lipstick. Lastly, she removes her black work blazer from its hanger, puts it on, and dabs her wrists with her signature musky fragrance, the name of which she would not even reveal to her best friend.

When the store opens, Maria is, as usual, at her station, smiling, ready to go. She's good at selling scarves and gloves. Not that it's something she ever aspired to, but it's a job. It gets her out of the house, and it pays the bills.

She has a special power over customers, and she likes that. It will end, of course, soon enough, when her looks are gone. But for now, she can still charm people into buying expensive things they don't need. And after all these years, she still gets a thrill from the thought that they envy her, these rich women who buy five hundred dollar scarves with the same ease that she would buy a loaf of bread. It's more than flattering. It's actually ironic. Envy, of course, is nothing new to her. She's always been beautiful, so beautiful, in fact, that even she herself could not ignore it. She's been the object of people's jealousy all her life. She has suffered great pain and loneliness because of it, especially when she was very young. But in the gloves and scarves department, envy works in her favor. Here envy is empowering, enjoyable almost. Sometimes she feels like an exotic princess who is only selling gloves as an act of generosity, giving of herself to women who so desperately need to borrow a bit of her glamour.

If only they knew how little glamour there is to her life! But she's not going to allow herself to feel sorry for herself. Self-pity is forbidden. She banned it from her life a long time ago. She's made of steel these days. Yet still, sometimes, her former self creeps in, the woman she used to be when she was younger. The woman who was unable to contain her disappointment when she saw her dreams ruined, her life stretching dreary before her, like a pile of dirty dishes to be washed in cold water day in and day out.

She's tried for years to let go of her anger and frustration. In fact, she's almost made peace with herself. Still, every now and then she feels pointless and all alone. An aging woman whose looks are rapidly fading, whose husband has traded her in for a newer, fancier model (though she's aware of the gross unfairness of such claim, she still allows herself to think it every now and then), whose children no longer need her, and seem to not like her enough to want to see her, who has very few, and rather distant friends, who works hard at an overall shitty job meant for a girl half her age, who lives alone in a depressing apartment, in a neighborhood she detests.

These are the thoughts that keep her down on bad days. On good days, however, she sees herself as a relatively young woman with grown children who are finally out of the house. She might have done a bad job at it, but the ordeal of motherhood is over, and though she has not excelled at it by any means, she deserves some credit for trying her very best for the past twelve years at least. Her children might even come to realize this, once they truly mature. Maybe once they have children of their own and see for themselves how hard it is. Not that she necessarily wants them to have kids of their own. She'd rather put up with them being ungrateful and unappreciative forever, than watch them sacrifice themselves to parenthood the way she had to.

She has to catch herself whenever she starts thinking like this. She has to make herself stop. There's no use complaining, after all. It is what it is.

That phrase irritates her son to no end. He declared it the ultimate platitude.

"Literary, my ass. You'd think a woman who studied fucking poetry and shit would find a better way to express herself."

She so wishes he didn't hate her. But she is powerless to change it, so it is best to just not think of it at all. After all, this too is what it is.

All she can do now is let go of the past and try to enjoy the prospect of her future. She's waited many years for it, and her time has finally come. At last, she's free. And she has to remind herself that she's still young enough to enjoy it.

The thrill of new-found freedom puts a smile on her face. A genuine one, not a customer-service goddess one. Not that anybody knows her well enough to tell the difference. Victor might have, at some point. Or rather she desperately wanted him to. But now she's old enough to pry apart her own wishful thinking from harsh reality. Victor was never as fine-tuned to her as she assumed him to be. She knows now that Victor never saw anybody as clearly as he sees himself. But then again, can she blame him? Aren't people inherently selfish? Especially men. Women, sadly, were raised to revolve around the men they love, and, of course, around their children, to read their thoughts before these are even formed in their heads. It took her a long time to realize she was trying to do that constantly, while Victor mostly just saw through her.

Maria opens the glass counter. She starts rearranging her favorite gloves, letting herself enjoy the scent of fine leather. She tries to relax, to liberate herself from all her toxic thoughts. She hates it when her mind starts spinning around the same ideas, distilling them into hideous clichés. She smiles. It's L's word. Hideous. *Hidos.* Which one has she just used, in her thought process, the English, or the Romanian? Funny how whenever she tries to figure out what language she thinks in, there is no way of telling. She probably thinks in broken English. Hideously broken English.

She calls L on her lunch break, while eating the roast chicken sandwich she brought from home. She's hoping L is also taking her break. Will she also eat a home-made sandwich she's packed carefully in the morning? She tried so hard to teach her about proper nutrition, something Americans seem really clueless about. She's also explained how much money one could save by not eating out. When L started going to CUNY, Maria packed her a healthy lunch each day. But she soon discovered that L was feeding it to the pigeons, or throwing it in the trash, or best-case scenario, bringing it back untouched. She preferred to spend her allowance buying all sorts of crap she'd eat in unsanitary places. Maria eventually let the issue go. It's one of the frustrating facts of raising children, that they refuse to follow perfectly good advice, and that there is no way of making them.

Then again, it is what it is.

The Italian lady finally summons her daughter to the phone.

"L, my sweetie! How is my beautiful girl?" Maria chirps into the receiver. She realizes how retarded she sounds, but she can't help herself, she's too excited to be talking to her baby girl.

Besides, she's cool in her own way. For example, she is the only member of the family who agrees to call L L instead of Lili, or the much dreaded longer version, Liliana. Maria is very good at indulging her children's harmless little eccentricities. This earns her quite a few points in L's book. On the other hand, it is one more thing that irritates Alex.

"You healthy and beautiful? Why you not come visit *Mami*?"

Maria wipes the corners of her mouth with her napkin, while listening to L's excuses about being busy, having lots of fun, and life overall being just too fabulous for her to drag herself to Queens.

"Why we don't meet then, in the city? I know you having fun after work. But why we don't meet for lunch one day? *Mami* will treat, ok, my sweetie? Tuesday?"

The thought of seeing her daughter makes her happy. She decides to get off the phone before L has a chance to change her mind.

"You needing anything, my sweetie?"

That has been her final question ever since L moved out in early May. And the answer has so far invariably been no. She has to give it to her baby girl. L is so competent in taking care of herself in spite of the naïve and sometimes silly image she projects. Maria is so proud of her! She herself had trouble standing on her own two feet, and she was older than L, and with much more experience. She's happy to see her baby girl living life on her own terms, not crawling back home to Queens defeated, the way she herself was forced to do, the one time she wanted to leave. She once again promises herself that on some momentous occasion, maybe when L gets a real job, or when she comes back from Italy, or when she moves in by herself, maybe when she decides to go to graduate school, whatever the next milestone worthy of a special mother-daughter moment, she will sit her down, open a good bottle of wine, and tell her the story of the horrible thing she did, the one she'll never be able to forgive herself for. The one her husband could never forgive. She knows L is smart enough to understand. And she knows it will inspire her to pursue her own dreams, not somebody else's. She knows that L will avenge her, that she will make her proud.

She sighs. Reluctantly, she dials the next number. It's taken her two days to return his call. And mostly it's because talking to him is so unpleasant. He doesn't just make her angry. He actually still makes her nervous.

Maria and her husband have not shared a bed for ten years now. They have not shared an apartment for eight years, and a bank account for seven. All those have been her choices. She has particularly insisted on the bank account, more than on any of the other separations. The better his business did, the more she insisted on not partaking of his money.

The only thing she could not stop him from was giving allowances to the children. She would pay for their rent, their meals, their clothes, their subway fares. He could provide them with frivolous spending money if he wanted. They didn't need it anyway.

Of course, when it came time for the kids to go to college, it was just understood that he would pay. Just as it was understood that their children would go to college. Still, although she never told this to him, or to her children, Maria felt the need to save for Alex and Lili's education herself. She didn't quite come up with a sufficient amount, but it made her feel good to know that, if Victor forfeited the bill, her savings, combined with student loans could help put her kids through college.

Her stomach tightens as the phone rings at his furniture store. She scolds herself for being nervous. Especially since she knows he won't answer. She's purposefully calling at a time when he's bound to be out. He always goes to lunch with people: clients, suppliers, people from "the community," or maybe members of a club called "My Wife is a Witch." Maybe right now he's having lunch with his hot young girlfriend.

The phone rings five times, and then, just as her stomach relaxes and her breath gets back to normal, there it is: Victor's voice. Of course, it's just a recording. He's changed the greeting for the store. She has to admit she likes it better with his voice on it. The bastard.

Quickly, in an artificially friendly tone, she leaves the numbers for both Gretchen's apartment and *Bella*, the place where L works.

There. Now it's done. She exhales sharply, then looks at her watch. Her lunch break is over, and she hasn't even had time to look at the real estate section in the paper, something she's been looking forward to all day.

She'll have to put it off for later, when she'll take a few minutes to eat a piece of fruit, invariably an apple or an orange. For now she'll have to return to her station.

Every day, Maria walks four extra blocks on her way home. She's been doing this ever since she noticed the little bulge of fat building up on her previously flat stomach, the thick upper arms, and a shocking new need for larger bras. She hates the idea of getting fat, hates the cellulite on her thighs, on her arms, the general loss of firmness she knows is unavoidable in old age. Unless, of course, you can afford lipo. Not that she would do that. She's had enough painful medical interventions for a lifetime, what with having children and all that horror. And she's never been good at handling pain.

So she walks. At least it's moderately useful, sometimes enjoyable, and free. She prefers to walk through the city, sharing her daughter's distaste for Queens, a distaste she has carried with her since her arrival in the new country. She can remember it so vividly, the day they got to this horrible place, she can taste it still, can still feel the muggy July evening on her skin. The humidity felt filthy. So did the large and decrepit car her husband's friend picked them up in. The seats smelled weird. Old plastic in a dirty city. Such an unfriendly scent. She hated it, and as they drove on, she also hated the graffiti on the bridges, the gloomy neighborhoods of exposed brick. She shuddered at the thought that such a place would be her home. She never grew to like it. But after rebelling in every way she could, she finally decided (or was she forced to this decision?) to stifle her dissent and carry on. What else could she do? It is what it is, after all.

So nowadays she walks a few blocks in Manhattan, before finally descending into 'the gutter' as her daughter calls it, the overheated, smelly New York subway, where fat rats roam freely among the tracks, but every now and then she can hear the melancholy sound of an accordion. It's always a nostalgic song, a song that makes her think of home, her real home, the faraway country she fled from, a country that no longer truly is, the country of her youth and of her past, the only time and place where she was happy. She always gives the gypsy playing the accordion a clean, crisp dollar bill. She's done so even in her times of need and misery, in the days .99 cent boxes of macaroni and cheese for her kids were an important budget item. Even then, it was a habit, giving him money. But she never ever talks to the man. She makes sure she has the dollar bill out before she approaches him, and she has mastered the art of dropping it into his tip jar without looking at him, and most importantly, without stopping.

Tonight her detour is longer than usual. Her feet have a will of their own, and she smiles when she realizes where she's going. There she is, looking up at the number indicated in the newspaper ad she carefully circled earlier today. She counts the windows, gazing up to the seventh floor. Seven is a special number. It has mystical powers. She knows that much.

A light is on in the windows. She can make out the color of the wall behind it, warm and pleasing. A pigeon rests briefly on the window frame. She smiles again, considering it yet another sign, a blessing.

She stands there, looking up for nearly an hour, forgetting that she's hot and tired. The delicious smell coming from a store finally reminds her that she's starving. Feeling slightly naughty, she steps inside, buys a slice of crunchy, juicy pizza, and devours it like a hungry child.

By the time she gets to the subway she has a spring in her step. She gives the old accordion player five dollars, and hurries off quickly before he has a chance to talk to her. When she gets home she does something unprecedented. She feeds the leftover roast chicken to a cat lingering on the fire escape. Fuck the chicken. She's finally free!

{ 5 }

Hide and Seek

Things have been awkward at Gretchen's lately. I wish I were invisible. Leaving before G gets up is easy. Staying out late, to avoid awkward hours of hiding my room is a bit trickier.

Early one Moday morning, I found a key on the kitchen counter, accompanied by a little pink card: "I had Juanita make this. Sorry for the delay, roomie." There was a little heart above the 'i,' and a smiley face next to Gretchen's signature. I crumpled up the card and threw it in the toilet. I wanted to do the same with the key. But I needed the key. And I didn't want to clog the toilet.

The toilet clogs anyway. Juanita, the housekeeper, a middle aged Puerto Rican woman with little sense of humor, informs me of this development matter-of-factly.

"I had to call plumber," she says, while putting on her sandals. Juanita wears sneakers to work, but puts on cute shoes when she's getting ready to leave. Today it's pink suede sandals, so delicate and feminine that I have trouble reconciling them with the image of her always scrubbing. I'm embarrassed about the toilet. And I'm afraid they'll add the plumber bill to my tab. God knows what plumbers cost in Manhattan.

I also hate Juanita's pretty shoes. *Mami* does that. She changes into pretty shoes. I hate to think Juanita is like *Mami*, and *Mami* like Juanita. Could it be, that while other people move up the social ladder, my *Mami*, just like Juanita is stuck somewhere between ugly sneakers and cute shoes? I guess my mother is a servant to rich people too. It's not that different, really, being in sales, high end as the department store might be. For the first time, I kind of see *Tati*'s point. If I go on at Bella, I'll be just as stuck too.

But what else could I do? I've never had another job. I was lucky Francesca hired me, in my last semester of college. I was so happy to finally wither *Mami*'s resistance and start working, so happy to be dealing with those beautiful bags, and to be speaking Italian every now and then… *Mami* begged me to wait until college was over (Romanian parents think having a job takes focus away from studying). But I wanted to start working at *Bella* right away. I loved it from day one. Then it got boring, even a bit oppressive. But what choice do I have? Especially now that I need money more than ever so I can pay my stupid rent. Still, looking at Juanita's pretty shoes, I want to quit right now. If I stay on, and let things slide, I can just see myself one day: middle aged and poor, walking to work in ragged sneakers, my feet too sore to accommodate normal shoes. *Pantofi normali.*

"Do not throw tampon in toilet!" Juanita warns me, as a parting thought. "No tampon in toilet!" She gathers her purse, which once matched her dainty sandals, but now shows so much wear that it seems from a different era. *O eră diferită.*

"Que verguenza con esta chica, viviendo aqui come si fuera su casa… Y no paga nada"

I'm not supposed to hear this. I'm not supposed to understand. But Spanish is not that different from Italian. Or Romanian, really.

No paga nada. She pays nothing. Has Gretchen complained to Juanita about me?

I've never felt more like a trespasser. I need to start paying Gretchen. I will start paying Gretchen. I repeat the thought like it's my new mantra. I will it to chase away my fears of impending homelessness. I badly need a distraction. I need to get out. I have neglected everybody since I moved here. I need to call people. I need to go visit others for a change. I make a list in my head. I'll call Rachelle first, then Momo.

Rachelle is not Jewish, although that's what I thought when I saw the name of my assigned lab partner in biology class last year. I wrote down the name, and imagined a Jewish girl in a white lab coat. Curly hair, high cheekbones, designer glasses, killer purse. I imagined myself dissecting frogs with a Jewish American Princess. We would become fast friends, and she'd teach me a few things in Yiddish. But the person who met me in the hallway of the yucky smelling biology building was obviously not Jewish. She was Black.

Rachelle later scolded me, explaining that the two categories were by no means mutually exclusive.

"So why do you think that just because I'm Black I can't be Jewish? What if my mother was Jewish?"

That was just the start of a long rant.

"Why would you look at a person's name and wonder if they are Jewish? Does it matter if they are Jewish?"

I only partially managed to redeem myself by explaining my interest in language, words, culture, and my fascination with Yiddish. Rachelle said it was another stereotype to expect a young Jewish woman to know Yiddish. I felt that expecting a student to be young was a stereotype too, but I kept that to myself, because the thing was, I liked Rachelle, and I really badly wanted to be her friend.

Initially, Rachelle was distant. She acted like she was annoyed, though just a tiny bit flattered, by my eagerness to gain her attention. She told me I was immature, spoiled, and a bit irritating, but that I made up for some of those flaws by being occasionally amusing, a much needed diversion for a single mother working full time and taking night classes at CUNY

I call Rachelle at work, and she seems happy to hear me but doesn't have time to meet up. I wish I'd had the foresight to book a get together two weeks in advance. Rachelle has school and work, plus a baby. This week she says she has no babysitter, and that she can't afford her subway fare, let alone going out. Rachelle is the only friend I have who has no problem admitting she has no money. I find this utterly refreshing.

I offer to come over and bring pizza.

Rachelle declines. I insist. She gives in.

So Tuesday night, cheered up by a rather pleasant pizza lunch with *Mami,* who seemed uncharacteristically happy, I take the tramway to Roosevelt Island. The thought of having pizza twice in a day makes me queasy, but I cannot disappoint Rachelle. Besides, I only had a slice at lunch, as *Mami* practically forced me to eat a side salad and some fresh cut mango.

Rachelle's place is much cleaner than usual, though Jurron is running around with a roll of toilet paper he spreads all over the floor.

"Quit messing with that paper, Jurron!" Rachelle calls after him. "I've just finished cleaning, and I've had a hard day, and I'm tired."

She places the pizza box on her kitchen table, and gets out plates and napkins. Other than *Mami*, she's the only person I know who actually uses real plates for pizza.

"You didn't have to bring over pizza, girl. Thank you, though."

Rachelle opens a bottle of wine and pours it into real glasses.

The leather couch that was there last time I visited is gone, so we sit on the floor. Rachelle still manages to eat with decorum, while I spill both tomato sauce and wine on myself. It occurs to me later, while Rachelle is dabbing the spots with seltzer, that the shirt is Gretchen's, and that it probably cost more than a brand new laptop. I feel the sting of fresh tears, and I have to blink hard, then improvise a quick mathematical exercise involving the number of cans on top of the fridge. I can't cry in front of Rachelle.

She'd go on a rant about me being a spoiled white child. *Un copil alb alintat*. Her own life was not easy. She grew up in the projects. One of her sisters died when she was little. She made a mistake getting involved with Jurron's father when she was only sixteen. She couldn't go to college because she had to work. Then, when she finally signed up for night classes she discovered that she was pregnant. She had to suck it up and deal with it. She had to finally break up with Jurron's father, and move away from her mother's in order to raise her child in a different environment.

"But do I sit around feeling sorry for myself like a silly white child with nothing better to do? No, girl! I go on! Somebody has to pay the bills, somebody has to diaper the baby, and somebody had better go to class if she ever wants to get her degree!"

I'm fascinated by Rachelle's life. I admire her. But at times I find her cold and unsympathetic.

After Rachelle finishes cleaning my shirt, she motions for me to sit back down and finish my wine.

"And don't spill it this time, child. Watch yourself."

Jurron wanders back into the living room, still dragging the toilet paper behind, but with less energy.

"You wanna help me give him a bath, L? Not that you'd know anything about bathing a toddler. Just to keep me company. I've got to put him to bed before it gets too late."

I'm not crazy about kids, but I'm fond of Jurron. I also like the lavender scented bubble bath Rachelle uses. I enjoy standing there, watching her coo over her baby in the little tub. *În căduță.*

Bathtime allows for bits and pieces of conversation, which I am desperate for. As much as I hate the scolding and diatribes, I cannot have enough of Rachelle.

"So what classes are you taking this fall, Rachelle?"

She shrugs.

"I was going to take Medieval History, and also Geometry. But I think I might have to withdraw."

That's weird. At the rate Rachelle is going, she'll never graduate.

"Why withdraw? I thought you liked History."

Rachelle looks at me like I came from another planet.

"Whether I like it or not, I don't have my Pops to pay my tuition for me, girl. Somebody has to pay the rent and feed the baby. And as you might have noticed, Rhonda is gone."

Rhonda is Rachelle's roommate. Rachelle never complains about her, but I can tell there's no love lost between them.

"So you finally had enough of her?"

"It's more like I had enough of her entourage. If I didn't care who my child grew up around, I would have stayed at my mother's house. Plenty of free baby sitters there, and low rent too. But I do care. And Rhonda was bad news. So she had to go. But it's hard making ends meet without her."

"Will you find someone else?"

"I put an ad up at school. But it's hard. I mean, I really have to be careful who I let into my house, and around my child. I was hoping to find someone sooner, so I could stay in school. But it looks like I'll be asking for a refund for that tuition money."

She smiles sadly while rubbing baby oil on Jurron's belly. He giggles, and moves his fat little feet around. He seems perfectly happy.

"How much is your rent?" I ask.

"What do you care, missy?"

Rachelle raises an eyebrow, then turns back to Jurron whom she is now wiping dry with a fluffy white towel.

"Well, maybe I might…"

"Might what?"

"Be your roommate…"

"And why the fuck would you do that?"

Rachelle doesn't curse. She says it's important to speak politely, yet firmly, and also to speak properly. She says society expects Black people to be uneducated, and all ghetto, and she wants to challenge that stereotype.

"Because you need a roommate, and I…"

"You what? Want to help? Now why would a white child like you want to help a sister like me?"

I'm taken aback. I'm used to her setting me straight, but this time it's unwarranted. And why does she have to bring the whole race thing into it?

"It's not just that, it's also… I would like living with you."

"But you already have a place to live. In Manhattan."

"I'm not sure it's working out."

Rachelle claps her hands together and starts laughing.

"Oh, listen to this one! This child's incredible! It's not working out! And she just moved there. Just moved there. I'll tell you what, miss I-wanna-live-in-the-big-city-and-have-a-lot-of-fun: If it's already not working out where you are, then why should I take you in? Do I need more trouble? Do you think I've got time for your drama in my life?"

I leave as soon as Rachelle is done putting the baby to bed. She seems relieved to see me go. I walk slowly along the East River trying to convince myself I hate the place anyway. It's too much like being back in Queens, exposed brick and all. Isn't it actually part of Queens? But every whiff of salty air from the river makes me long to live here. As I stare into the dark water from the tramway and say my goodbye to the Island, I can't shake the feeling that this would be a nice place to live. If only for the thrill of riding the tramway every day.

Back in Manhattan, my mood is so gloomy, I need major cheering up. So I walk to nearby Bloomingdale's, a place I worship, but where I've never shopped. It's nearly closing time, but navigating through the cosmetics counters like an expert, I manage to buy a small bottle of Angel perfume. I stroll home feeling like a sexy, sophisticated woman. *O femeie sofisticată.* A woman in whose life wonderful things will happen. And what better way to celebrate it, than an ego-boosting late dinner with Momo tomorrow night? I'll wear my new sexy scent, a pair of Gretchen's Manolos, and my new leather bag.

I suddenly realize that Rachelle did not compliment me on it, or on anything else about my appearance, which has dramatically improved now that I'm wearing Gretchen's clothes. Hater.

At home, I sneak quietly into my room and hide my new fragrance in the pocket of an ugly sensible coat *Mami* bought me long ago. This thrills me somehow. My new secret fragrance. *Mon parfum secret. Parfumul meu secret.*

The next day I slip out before Juanita gets there. I drag around a headache all day, and I feel like I'm going to fall asleep on my feet. Not even a double espresso from Starbucks helps. Instead it gives me a burning feeling in my stomach. I have to buy a bagel just to calm it down.

Luckily Momo will treat me to dinner tonight. I anticipate quite the culinary delight. Momo has good taste, and she's generous. I freshen up in the bathroom at *Bella*, and spritz on plenty of my new *parfum secret*. I'm wearing a taupe dress, and a pair of gold sandals, both belonging to Gretchen. I leave work feeling well put together and sexy, but seeing my reflection in a shop window, I regret matching the crème purse to the taupe dress.

I have three hours to kill until Momo gets off work. Three hours with no cash and uncomfortable shoes. I sit myself down in the nearest Barnes and Noble, and start studying a travel guide on Italy. Bad choice. The pictures make me want to cry. Maybe I'll never ever go there. Not with life in the city being so expensive, and my debt towards Gretchen. I mean, where am I gonna get a few thousand dollars in cash? I wish Gretchen took credit cards. I can just imagine myself, swiping my Visa through her mouth. That wouldn't even help though. I'm almost up to my credit limit. I'll have to wait for the next paycheck and just give Gretchen what I can, then ask to pay the rest later. I put the Italy book away, and spend most of three hours sulking, staring at people, unwilling to get up from the couch, though several seatless readers shoot me angry glances. I feel lethargic, heavy. And strapped cruelly into Gretchen's Manolos, my feet are killing me. *Ma dor picoarele*. See, I'm already turning into *Mami*.

{ 6 }

Happy Anniversary

August fifteenth is the day Maria hates most. Each year she tries not to think about it, but her mind refuses to obey. Finally, a few years back she decided to give in and allow herself a secret celebration. Nothing big, nothing too conspicuous. Just a little treat to get her through the day. A consolation prize of sorts, to divert pain and anger: a bar of 80% dark chocolate from Fauchon, a piece of black Spanish soap, a small cup of gelato on a park bench. A cappuccino maybe. A really good one. Served in a china cup, not in a paper cylinder with a plastic lid.

But this year her treat is something big, something exciting and crazy, something she's been aching for all these years. She's not sure it's appropriate, and she's not sure it's the right decision. She's not even sure she's going about it the right way. But it might be her last shot at happiness.

She doesn't know if it's nervousness or excitement, but she slept poorly the night before, and she couldn't bring herself to eat any breakfast this morning. She feels jittery, and has trouble hiding the trembling of her hands. Her stomach feels heavy, like a rock. But she keeps telling herself it's the beginning of a bright new future, and that she should be proud of taking such a big step on the saddest day of all.

Dressed in a crème linen suit, which was a bargain, but looks like it cost a fortune, wearing Italian leather sandals that kill her feet but show off her perfectly pedicured toes (her only friend works in a salon, and treats her on occasion), with her shiny dark hair falling neatly on her shoulders, Maria knows she looks presentable. She could pass for one of the well-groomed women who shop at her store. But her knees are shaking, and she can't stop staring at the clock on the wall, willing its arms to move faster.

She arrived at the bank early, taking the whole morning off, and having decided to even treat herself to lunch in a fancy little bistro later. It took her forever to fill out the application, which she peered over with a dictionary, and help from Madalina. Now, holding the form in her hand, she tries to compose herself. She wants to act confident, relaxed, like a woman used to walking into banks and asking to borrow large sums of money. In truth, she never before applied for a loan, and she doesn't use credit.

Her friend Mada, the quintessential consumer, who charges up a storm in every sale known to womankind, laughed when Maria confessed her estrangement from the financial world. She went through great trouble, sharing knowledge about loans and banks. But Maria opted for the only bank she herself was familiar with, the one Victor uses, the one whose name was printed on the checks he wrote out for the kids' college tuition. She even decided to go to the very same branch. It's nerve racking, of course, the thought that he could actually wander in, and see her here, but it is almost worth the risk, because the place where Victor banks must be a sound, reliable institution. She hates to admit it, but he's very competent. He's the kind of person who takes risks, risks that drove her to despair when they were still together, but which paid off in the long run. She still remembers how angry she was when he borrowed money to start his business, how she yelled at him, how she refused to speak to him for days, and how she cried herself to sleep at night, quietly, so her daughter wouldn't hear. And here he is, nine years later, a successful entrepreneur, while she still toils away for an hourly wage in a department store.

She looks at her wedding ring. She decided to wear it today, hoping a little jewelry would make her look more worthy of a loan. It feels unnatural on her finger, like a shackle, weighing her down.

Twenty-four years ago, in her youthful infatuation and total ignorance, she committed her life to Victor, his fascinating persona, his needs, his wishes, his desires, and most importantly, his dreams. It was the happiest day of her life. But in hindsight she knows it was the day she gave up on herself. How ironic that her entire family gathered in the lush greenery of her grandmother's garden, to congratulate her, wish her well, drink champagne, and celebrate that Maria, from that moment on, would cease to grow, and eventually cease to exist, that she would slowly but surely become her husband's shadow.

Of course, at the tender age of twenty, and madly in love, she didn't see it this way. She'd already known Victor for two years then, and had grown downright obsessed with him. As part of an amateur theater group, she met him at an impromptu party after a performance. She only played a small part, if one could even call it that. She played a tree. She didn't even have any lines. All she had to do was stand there, her arms stretched out towards the sky, tulle flowers hanging from her fingers. Ironically, it was the most exciting role she'd ever get. Her incorrigible shyness, which she had hoped to cure by acting, and her lack of talent, prevented her from getting good parts, in spite of her beauty. She got to play bystanders in crowds, and once, years later, in her last performance, she got to deliver a line. But it was as a communist worker, in blue overalls, complete with a ridiculous protective helmet, and her line was: "Everlasting glory to socialism!" She quit shortly afterwards.

In the fall of 1978, however, she was quite happy to be playing a tree. The role even seemed challenging, as holding up her arms for such a long time, yet giving them, as the director had instructed, some natural grace, the roundness, kindness, and miraculous beauty of a tree, was difficult. After the play, her arms were sore, and when a tall, dark and handsome stranger extended a champagne flute her way, she smiled, but declined it.

Yet later she danced with him, and she was happy he asked, in spite of her clumsy refusal of his drink, and in spite of her shyness, which, as all her friends told her, was usually perceived as lack of interest, possibly even as the conceitedness of the most beautiful girl in the room. This was, she knew, one of the reasons young men didn't court her.

He told her he was an architect, and that he had designed their costumes, paying most attention to that of the tree, as he considered it by far to be the most important role. "Really?" she asked, staring at him in disbelief.

"Of course. It is the only character who remains on stage from the beginning to the very end. It holds the whole piece together, don't you think?"

She smiled proudly and told him she had even been instructed to stay there during intermission. He laughed, and though she was serious, she laughed with him.

"Well, you see now, why I thought it was important for the tree to look best. I've repeatedly commended the casting people for picking you."

She was confused. There were no casting people. Apparently there was no costume designer either. He was joking. Though he really was an architect. She was embarrassed for thinking he was serious. Whenever she liked a man, she lost every ounce of wit she possessed. This was another reason nobody courted her. She was shy and clumsy.

But Victor was persistent, almost aggressive. It seemed that once he made up his mind to have her, nothing could stop him. His desire and his persistence attracted her like nothing else before. Whenever he disappeared for a few days, whether he went on a hiking trip to the mountains, or to the Black Sea with his friends, she was tortured not just by his absence, but by a deep and painful fear that he would not return to her, that he would lose interest, that he was maybe at that very moment dancing with another girl, or lying on the golden sand next to the tan voluptuous body of a smarter, more experienced woman, a woman who knew how to please a man. But Victor returned to her after each of his trips, resumed taking her out, and tried once again to extract more than a few passionate kisses. He mocked her prudishness, and her reluctance to participate in the trips he so often went on with his group of friends. He kept assuring her teasingly that her virtue was safe, that he was indeed desperate to have her, but that he wouldn't take advantage of her in some mountain resort. She blushed and made excuses about having to study. She was embarrassed to admit her mother wouldn't let her go.

It wasn't until way into their second year of dating that she agreed to go to the Black Sea with him for May Day. She was impressed that he weathered the mockery of his chauvinistic male friends (whom she had overheard saying quite vulgarly that 'he should have banged her by now') as well as the additional expense, and gotten her her very own room overlooking the sea. She was almost disappointed, as by now she had worked herself into a frenzy and convinced herself that she should sleep with him, because she really loved him, and he wanted her so much. She had gone from wishing to be the kind of proper girl her mother had raised her to be – which required, among other things, holding off until marriage in order to make sure he wouldn't 'fuck her then leave her' (the way her own friends vulgarly put it) - to wanting to give in to him, to please him above all else. She was afraid she was making him suffer too much, and the thought of him suffering, of him being denied even the slightest wish, pained her deeply.

When they got to the resort, she was amazed how beautiful her room was, how lovely the view. The Black Sea is not aqua blue and translucent like the Mediterranean. Its deep waters turn dark, mysterious shades as they transform like a chameleon from navy to a somber green. Occasionally, Maria thought she saw hints of purple. And what amazed her most was the intoxicating smell of salt and fish, which she inhaled greedily, as if it were her last chance for air before drowning in that very sea of darkness and seaweed and sunken ships. But as much as she loved filling her lungs with the delicious salty air, she had no patience to sit on her little balcony and look at the water. Her restlessness almost made her cry. Her thoughts and feelings were more agitated than the waves themselves, and they all revolved around Victor and her momentous decision to finally sleep with him, a plan complicated by her having this lovely room all to herself.

On their first night at the resort, emboldened by an extra glass of wine at dinner, she ended up inviting him over, saying something stupid, pretending she was afraid of the dark. He slept in her bed, and he held her all night. It was tender, and quite romantic, but she wanted to scream in frustration. She wanted to slap her own face for her inability to initiate anything. She simply didn't know how. She was shy and inexperienced, and she knew that any attempt at seduction on her part would be ridiculous. So she just lay there, awake in his arms, until the sun rose across the deep blue sea.

In the pale melancholy of early morning, she finally peeled herself away from Victor, gently, as not to wake him. She carefully opened the balcony door. He slept on soundly, looking happy.

It was chilly on the balcony, damp with the salty sea breeze, and somehow lonely. The whole resort was asleep, and the morning looked bluish gray, depressing. The sharp cries of seagulls, and the sound of waves greeted her indifferently as she shivered in her cotton nightgown. Guilt overcame her at the thought that she wore this in front of Victor, that he could feel her skin through the light fabric. Last night it had seemed like a good idea to let him see her almost naked. Now she was embarrassed. And above all, she was cold. Yet she was reluctant to go back in, afraid opening the door again could wake him. She settled into a wooden framed beach chair, sinking into its sun-faded cloth, which smelled moldy, like the whole resort, took in the sea breeze, hugged her knees to her chest, closed her eyes, and pretended she wasn't freezing.

It was on that same balcony, late in the afternoon, that he proposed to her and she accepted. He then lifted her salty sunburned body, carried her to bed, and made love to her. It wasn't what she expected, though for the longest time she couldn't admit to herself it was rather boring. Afterwards, basking in the afterglow of it, while he was enjoying a cigarette, she worked hard at convincing herself that it had been quite lovely. In truth, it had been awkward and painful, though not as excruciatingly so as some of her friends had told her. She tried to focus on the positives: the feeling of his weight on her, the touch of skin on skin, the actual closeness of the act. It made her tingle all over to think of his lips on her, everywhere, the roughness of his stubble on her tender sunburned skin. She took a long shower, and put on her best dress, a white linen dress her mother had had tailored for her that spring. She felt sad at the thought of her mother, whose trust she'd betrayed by sleeping with Victor. But as they later strolled leisurely down the boardwalk holding hands, she felt beautiful, loved, and happy. At dinner she devoured a large grilled pork loin, drank a bit too much wine, and indulged in her favorite dessert, *papanasi*. She was feeling a little sick when they returned to the room, and suddenly very tired. After making love again, she was sore, and couldn't fall asleep. She sat on the balcony for most of the night, wrapped in a blanket. The sky was dark. The sea seemed to flow into it. The lonely lights of ships shone far away. Stars and seagulls were her only companions. She read one of the books she had brought with her. Sartre. She shivered under the hotel blanket, which smelled like mildew. She hated Sartre. And she was too anxious to concentrate. Her mother would kill her if she knew she'd slept with Victor. At four in the morning, cold, frustrated, and bored, Maria picked up her fiance's cigarettes, and smoked two of them on the balcony. He rose at seven, smiled at her sitting there in his shirt, smoking, proclaimed it very sexy, and carried her off to bed again.

They were married three and a half months later. It was a small family gathering in her grandmother's garden, at the outskirts of Bucharest. That morning they stood ceremoniously at city hall, between a Romanian flag and a red, communist one bearing a hammer and sickle, and signed their marriage certificate. By that point Ceausescu had pretty much outlawed religion, and people were afraid of even stepping inside a church. But Maria wanted a religious wedding, and a priest had agreed to marry them at her grandmother's house, with a few friends and family present.

It was unbearably hot, the way Bucharest gets in August, when people start discussing record heat waves, and temperatures of forty degrees in the shadow (Celsius, of course). After the religious ceremony, which took place in the house with the drapes drawn, the guests sat in the shade of the grape vine, drank home-made wine, and ate the food prepared at great cost by her mother and grandmother. In 1980, with the communist economy suffering shortages, it was already hard to find certain meats and produce. Store shelves screamed of emptiness, and people stood in line for hours to buy daily necessities. Those living in the country had more luck. Her grandmother, who raised chickens, slaughtered the last ones for the wedding. Victor's friends were instrumental in securing rare treats. Though his connections, real butter, good quality Chinese powdered milk, Russian chocolate, Havana Club rum, and even large cartons of eggs materialized in her grandmother's kitchen days before the wedding.

Somebody brought champagne. It was not French, of course. Even people with connections, who were occasionally able to shop at stores destined exclusively to foreign tourists, had difficulty obtaining French champagne. The champagne was Romanian, and it was very good.

"*Champs Elysse*. Produced for export," one of Victor's friends said with a wink. He had brought a whole case.

Another friend brought a few bottles of Johnnie Walker. In between that, the champagne, the Havana Club, and the chilled home made wine, there was plenty to drink.

Maria almost got tipsy, but her mother snatched away her last glass of champagne, whispering, so the guests wouldn't hear, that there was nothing as disgraceful as a drunk woman. For a second, Maria feared she might drag her into the kitchen and smack her.

Of course, nobody objected to Victor having more than his share of Johnnie Walker. As a taxi took them to his apartment late at night, Maria was annoyed that he was drunk. But she smiled, and helped him to bed.

She sat on the balcony, unable to sleep, not willing yet to start unpacking. She had anticipated this for weeks, the day she would finally move in with Victor. He had an apartment in a gorgeous prewar villa, which had survived the 1977 earthquake. The first time she visited, Victor explained to her what a sound construction this building was. He even showed her a book on the architect who designed it. She was appropriately impressed, but mostly she was excited at the prospect of moving away from her mother's, of sharing her home with Victor and being his wife. She was only twenty, young enough to be mesmerized by the idea of having her own home. She couldn't believe that she was now the lady of the house.

The night of her wedding, while her husband slept off his whisky, Maria walked through the apartment admiring the large rooms and the solid wood furniture. She loved the bedroom above all. He had bought it for her. He had promised it one hot and mellow summer afternoon, as they lay exhausted from passion on his old bed, the dark blinds pulled low to keep out the sun, and an ineffective communist fan struggling to blow cold air towards them. The whole world seemed to slumber in a heat-induced lethargy. The fan was buzzing at the same rhythm as an unfortunate fly hitting its head repeatedly against the windowpane. She stretched like a cat, yawned, and offered to go make coffee before heading back to university. Those were her days of sneaking behind her mother's back to sleep with Victor, cutting classes, weaving herself into a web of lies.

He didn't like her leaving. He wanted her all the time, he couldn't have enough of her. He would have married her that very second just so she'd stay in bed with him all afternoon. Over coffee, two tiny cups of strong and fragrant Turkish brew, they engaged in their usual playful banter, where he would tease her, mercilessly, about taking other lovers, ones who didn't have strict mothers and could stay in bed all day.

She laughed, stepping into her summer dress, the fabric cool and fresh against her skin. Although she hated leaving, she was almost looking forward to the summer heat outside. She was happy. The afternoon seemed perfect, glorious. She knew Victor wanted her, and only her. But she played along. She pouted and told him to make sure and change the sheets if he wanted her to ever come back. In fact, she said, adjusting her makeup and her hair, she'd like him to refurnish the whole bedroom, to get a bed just for her, and above all a new vanity with a bigger, better mirror.

To her surprise, shortly after that, he took her furniture shopping. Not in stores, mind you. In people's houses, in grand magnificent villas and humble stooping cottages, in ugly standardized apartment blocks, and dusty attics, smelling sweet and faded, like the paper of old books. She picked a mahogany bedroom set, extravagant, dark, and solemn, fit for a queen. He bought it without hesitation.

And now here she was. She was married! This was her home. The grand mahogany bed, her own bed. She lived here now, in this wonderful apartment, together with the man she loved. Still, the night of her wedding, wandering through her new home alone, surrounded by luxury and beauty, she felt dissatisfied. The champagne buzz had worn off, leaving her with a slight headache.

In the morning she called her best friend and woke her. She needed to gush about the wedding. She mentioned casually that she was slightly annoyed that her husband was drunk, and how stupid it was for her mother to monitor her own champagne intake.

"She just doesn't want you to look ridiculous, especially in front of Victor and his friends. She worked so hard for the party to turn out right. You didn't even have to do anything, other than show up."

This much was true. In general, Maria didn't have to do much. Her only task in life so far had been to pursue her love for Romanian literature at the University. Basically, she just sat around and read plays, poems, and novels, while her mother and grandmother provided for her every need.

Things wouldn't change much now, although she was a married woman, with her own household to run, a situation she considered very dignified and glamorous (she doodled '*doamna Pop*' on all her lecture notes, and was so afraid Victor would find them, that she actually ripped some of them up, then did poorly on the respective exams). Her mother helped her find a suitable cleaning lady, who would cook occasionally, as well as, of course, iron all of Victor's shirts, Maria's clothes, the bed linens, table cloths, and everything else necessary.

On Sundays they had long, elaborate lunches at her mother's house, sometimes at her grandmother's. They left loaded with enough food to last a week. Always Victor's favorites, the delicacies his mother in law liked to spoil him with. Maria didn't mind. Her fridge and pantry were always full, her husband was happy, and she herself never had to move a finger. Sometimes she considered learning how to cook, just so the food he loved so much could come from her own kitchen. Repeatedly, she asked her grandmother to teach her, but the old woman laughed and shooed her away.

The first years of her married life were happy ones. She enjoyed her new home, loved the spacious rooms, the mahogany furniture, the shade of the walnut tree underneath her bedroom window. Oh, how she loved that tree! And how deeply, how painfully she would miss its round leaves in the years to come! A symbol of death, that's what they are, walnut trees. Old stories and poems in Romanian folklore are punctuated with them. They're always a bad omen. One shouldn't be fooled by the promise of cool, deep shade underneath their green leaves. There's nothing but death lurking in its depth. As a literature student she should have known that. Could she have changed things, maybe, if she had paid attention to this somber warning? Could she have averted the end of her marriage? Could she have kept the love of her husband, or at least, that of her children?

But she was blind back in those days. Blind, naïve, totally unaware of how quick her luck could turn. She had no feeling of impending doom. Her life was full happiness and sunshine. And she was foolish enough to think it'd last. She loved her life. She loved everything about it. She loved her home, the new seamstress who made her fancy dresses, with Victor's encouragement, and away from the scrutinizing eye of her mother. She loved her courses at the university, the few girl friends she gossiped with in frequent coffee breaks, the books she read on quiet afternoons in her big mahogany bed, light filtering in through the leaves of the walnut tree. She loved having dinner with her husband when he got home, loved their walks together in the park on Sundays, their frequent escapes to the mountains or the sea... Above all, she loved living with Victor and being his wife.

He seemed constantly pleased with her, his appetite for her insatiable, and she was flattered and overjoyed by the ravenous hunger he devoured her with. She loved that he was proud of her beauty and of her sense of style, that he liked to show her off at social events. She still was not able to say much whenever she was in a group, but now her shyness was disguised as smugness at being the wife of such an attractive and successful man. Most people thought she was aloof. Her mother warned her that it was not good for a young woman to be so conceited. But Maria couldn't help it. Whenever she was in a group, her tongue was tied, and all she could do was stand by her husband's side, surveying the world from underneath her long eyelashes, drifting away from conversation into her own inner world. In truth, she didn't care how she came across. She was happy to be with Victor, to feel his strong arm around her waist, and see that sparkle in his eye whenever he looked at her. Her world revolved around the two of them.

Both her pregnancies came as surprises. Lili, in her first year of marriage, was welcomed, cheered, and applauded. Alex was a happy occasion too, but Maria found herself faking the big smiles that went along with the announcement.

Accidental pregnancies were common, as Ceausescu had outlawed all means of birth control in an effort to increase population. When she got married, one of her more savvy friends advised her to secure some kind of pill, off the black market. But Maria was shy about broaching the subject with Victor. Female issues were not sexy, and she was embarrassed to ask him to use his connections to get such a pill. Innocently, she trusted her body to fate. In a way she almost hoped to get pregnant with Lili. It seemed like the natural thing to do. That was what people did. They fell in love, got married, had kids. Everybody wanted babies. It was a core value of all Romanian families, and women especially cherished it.

Maria knows now, much too late, that she never really wanted a baby. What she wanted was the elated feeling of being pregnant. She wanted the happy look on her husband's face. She wanted her mother's and grandmother's display of joy at receiving the news. She was just twenty and only recently married, but they were as happy as if she had been barren and waited decades hoping to conceive. She even wanted the little belly, and the cute pregnancy clothes her seamstress soon began fitting her for. Having people give up their seat on the bus was an extra perk. They had of course, done so before, for such a beautiful young woman, but they seemed more enthusiastic now.

In some ways, despite the physical discomfort and her growing fear of childbirth, pregnancy was enjoyable. Having the baby, on the other hand, was completely anticlimactic. All attention shifted away from her. But Lili was adorable, and Maria found motherhood easy. Having a full-time nanny helped. She herself never had to change a diaper. She did have to get up in the middle of the night for feedings, but since her course schedule at the university was not demanding, she didn't really mind. Her major concern was the possibility of the baby waking Victor. But he slept soundly, even when Lili cried.

When she didn't have class, Maria would take Lili to the park in a stroller. Sometimes her grandmother came along. They'd sit on a park bench, rock Lili back and forth, and talk about babies. Maria loved it. She finally felt like she'd been admitted into a very exclusive club. Though, to be honest, it seemed like her membership still needed confirmation.

Her mother and grandmother both mocked her lack of competence. She had a baby, yes, but that didn't mean she knew anything about them. In fact, she started off on the wrong foot, by making a big fuss about giving birth. It was as if there was an acceptable level of complaining, and she had unwittingly surpassed it. The nurses in the maternity ward made mean jokes at her expense, and Victor had to pacify them with gifts of cigarette cartons, nylons, and coffee. He assured Maria that they were jealous because she was so young, so beautiful, and had such a perfect little baby.

Indeed, Lili was nothing short of a miracle. Maria would stare at her for hours, not being able to believe that this was her child, hers and Victor's, born of their love. Still, she considered not having another baby. Pregnancy had been easy on her young, healthy body. But childbirth was too traumatic, physically and emotionally—she just couldn't get those awful nurses out of her mind, no matter what her husband said. She never wanted to go through that again. Also, she noticed that after nursing Lili, her breasts shrunk, a development that made her question her attractiveness to Victor.

She finally got up the courage to ask him to get her the pill off the black market. Her friend assured her that it made her breasts fuller, and her skin beautiful. But even with Victor's connections, obtaining birth control was complicated. She waited. In the meantime she used the calendar method. She'll never know if it was her lack of mathematical precision, or the fact that she could never say no to Victor, but she found herself pregnant again. The same joy overcame her friends and relatives. Victor too was happy. Still, he asked her an unexpected question:

"How do you really feel about it?"

She faked a big smile.

"I'm happy, of course."

"Are you sure?"

"Of course I am."

They didn't talk about it again. She knew, of course, that there was an alternative. Abortions were illegal, and highly dangerous. But some doctors still performed them. And au lieu of birth control, she knew that lots of women had them, almost routinely, like pulling out a tooth. Her own mother confessed to this, in private, years ago. But Maria didn't want to even consider it. She was not so dead set against having another child, plus she was getting that euphoric feeling again, the delight of knowing she was carrying Victor's baby.

The pregnancy turned out to be an easy one. She was even spared the delivery experience. She had a C-section. She ended up with a painfully healing scar, which she'd have for the rest of her life, but overall that was nothing compared to the agonizing pain of pushing Lili into this world. And Alex was a baby she simply adored.

Something strange happened to her this time, though. Her breasts shrunk again, but her feet grew larger. She could no longer comfortably fit into her shoes. This was a bigger problem than she initially suspected. For all of Victor's connections, purchasing new shoes that met his young wife's standards for quality was impossible. She tortured her poor feet for years, out of vanity, trying to walk around in her old ones.

And it was in the era of sore feet that Victor started feeling unhappy. His discontent was not with her, thank God! She thought back then that if he stopped loving her she would die. Though she knows now she underestimated her own resilience.

His discontent was with his career, and with some aspects of life under communism. She hated herself for not being able to do anything about it. But try as she might, those were two things she simply couldn't fix. Victor was successful as an architect, but the repressiveness of the communist regime was at its height, and it led his career on paths he never envisioned or desired. More and more he was asked to design industrial complexes that went along with the socialist dream. He hated those projects, but conformed. At night he'd tell her how dull his work was these days, how uninspiring. He wanted to build houses, not socialism.

And then, in 1985 he was assigned the worst project of all, the one he could hardly bring himself to work on. It was a set of apartment blocks in a village on the outskirts of Bucharest.

"Who will live there?" Maria asked. She always listened when he talked about his work. She was happy that he included her, that he took her questions, and even her opinions, seriously.

"The farmers," Victor declared, covering his face with his hands.

It was a tragedy, according to him, that the nationalization of agriculture led small farmers to give up their land and their animals, forcing them to work collectively for state owned cooperatives.

Cooperative agricole de productie. Landwirtschaftliche Produktionsgenossenschaften, German-speaking peasants called them in the small village where his grandparents lived, in Transylvania. The last time they visited that village, for his grandmother's funeral, Maria found that talking to the peasants depressed Victor more than the old woman's death itself. He told her that they were witnessing the destruction of a lifestyle, the destruction of an entire culture.

After returning from his grandmother's funeral, the apartment blocks he had to work on bothered him even more. He knew that the farmers' houses would be torn down, against their will, to be replaced by 'the socialist dream' of living in modern apartments. He told Maria that he had nightmares of farmers killing themselves. People who were used to having their own garden, growing tomatoes, peppers, raising a few chickens, maybe a cow, stuck in apartments, with sad little balconies overlooking the highway. People who for generations had cherished their connection to the soil and its life-giving powers, to the dirt and its fruits, would now be stuck in blocks of concrete.

It was in one of their late night conversations that he first mentioned America. The children and the nanny, *Tanti* Grosu, a robust woman from the country, were sound asleep. Maria and Victor were secretly listening to Radio Free Europe in their bedroom, with the sound turned so low they could barely hear it.

"I could get us there. But would you go?"

At first it was a distant dream, her husband's dream, a dream that had the power to make him happy again. She enjoyed hearing him talk about America, because it made him feel good. She had no idea what a dangerous temptress America would turn out to be.

It was a fantasy, an adventure they liked to imagine together, a secret game they played. Victor would list all the advantages they'd have, in America, even silly things, such as being able to go to a store and buy anything they pleased. There would be a never ending supply of consumer goods, sparkling on store shelves, just waiting for her to pick them up. She could finally get shoes her size, and he promised to buy her the very best. Fine, soft leather, and perfect craftsmanship, made in Italy, or maybe Brazil. She'd have a pair in every color. She'd have a walk-in closet full of pumps, flats, sandals, wedges, and sexy knee-length boots in black patent leather. She could of course get birth control in America too. And anything else she wanted.

When she realized he was being serious, she panicked. She loved her life, her home, her few friends, and her extended family. It would be crazy to trade all that for political freedom, reproductive rights, and a closet full of Brazilian shoes. But she was willing to consider giving it all up for her husband's happiness. And so she never mentioned her misgivings. This was Victor's dream, and Maria was careful not to express anything but support and enthusiasm.

Still, as much as she cheered him on, he sometimes questioned her resolve:

"It would be irreversible, you realize. There would be no way to come back. We'd have to leave everything behind. And everyone. Are you sure you'd be willing to do that?"

He looked at her, and she avoided his eyes. She thought how for him, she'd be willing to do anything, no matter how painful.

"You realize you might never see your mother again, or your grandmother?"

It was true. Leaving the country in those days, especially fleeing to the West, was illegal. There was no turning back. Once you were gone, you stayed gone. Even Maria was aware of this.

Yet she laughed it off, saying that one never knew, things could change. And that she couldn't live for her mother, anyway. She had to live her own life. Deep down she didn't believe this. The conversation struck a painful chord. But she buried her fears deep inside and kept smiling.

It took years to accomplish Victor's plan. Taking along his children and his wife from the very beginning was a non-negotiable, and this made their escape more complicated. She never understood exactly how he managed it.

When she finally learned that they were to indeed leave for America, via Germany, she panicked. She considered telling him that she could not go, that she wanted to follow him to the end of the world, but that she couldn't. She was ashamed of her reluctance, of her cowardice. What would he think of her for changing her mind after he tried so hard to get them out? Would he be angry? Would he be disappointed? Would he stop loving her? Would he go anyway, without her?

The day she finally worked up the courage to tell him, they got some dreadful news: The beautiful villa they were living in would be demolished, together with their entire neighborhood. Blocks of flats would be built instead.

Victor took it with stoicism: "See, Maria, I know you have your reservations about leaving." How did he know? She'd never expressed them. "But we do have to leave. We cannot go on here. What is happening here is simply horrible, and it's only going to get worse." She had to agree with him. That night, after they made love, she stepped out of the house, and sat underneath the walnut tree, smoking a cigarette. It was early March, but it was warm outside, and she was comfortable, wrapped in her spring coat. She thought of how she would miss it, the yard, the tree, the bench. She thought of how she would miss their house. But then she had to remind herself that she would lose it anyway, that it would be torn down. Victor was right. They had to leave. It was the right thing to do. But then why was she so scared? Why did she feel like somebody was about to tear her heart out? Why did she feel that she was making an irreversible mistake?

She was terrified of telling her mother. But when she finally did, her mother was supportive, though sad at the thought of such a separation, a separation that would probably be forever. It broke Maria's heart to see her around the children after that, the way she kissed their little hands and faces, the way she hid from them so they wouldn't see her cry.

Nobody was able to tell her grandmother. Maria never forgave herself, but she just didn't have the heart to do it. She loved her grandmother most of all. She was the one Maria would run to for comfort whenever she was in trouble. She was the one who'd brush her hair, wipe away her tears, and speak to her in a soothing voice. She was the kindest, wisest woman Maria ever knew. But her wisdom was the simple, raw, peasant kind. You laugh, you love, you toil away and eat the fruits of the earth, you play with your children, and you bask in the sun. Then one day you lie down and die, and there is peace, and the sun shines on. Who'd ever heard of moving across the ocean in pursuit of happiness?

The day of their departure her mother kept feeding her little greenish pills, *extraveral*, a mix of valerian extract and other plants. She insisted it was a natural tranquilizer, totally safe. She also insisted Maria should not let her husband or children see her cry. The pills made her feel loopy, but helped her control her tears. She didn't cry as they rode away from the house she would never see again. She didn't cry when she hugged her mother at the airport, when she felt her firm grip on her shoulders and wondered if she'd ever be able to touch her again. She didn't even cry when she waved at her for the very last time.

Later, on the plane, she felt dizzy and nauseous. Her children wouldn't sit still, and she realized Victor expected her to calm them down. She wondered if slipping them a little green pill was ok, it was made from plants after all. One of the stewardesses brought them a children's magazine. Communist cartoons, little pioneers marching around, printed on rough, porous paper. She looked at the familiar images, and realized she'd never see such things again.

Suddenly the knot in her throat gave loose, and an uncontrollable wave of grief erupted, tears like hot lava, burning on her cheeks. It is to this day one of the most embarrassing episodes of her life, sitting on that plane, weeping uncontrollably, in front of all those strangers. No matter how hard she tried, she could not stop herself. She felt that the pain in her heart could never be contained, that she would never be able to stop crying. All of the sadness in the world had gathered up inside her, and she would surely die and feel the same, she knew it.

She can't recall much of the months they spent in Germany. They stayed with friends of friends of friends, who treated them coldly, but were actually generous to put them up. It was Victor who kept reminding her of their generosity, in a reproachful tone, as if she were a spoiled child who was being unreasonable. She was scared that one day his patience would run out, that soon enough he'd sound like those unfriendly nurses in the hospital himself. She knew by now that he was disappointed with her for her constant crying, and for her inability to control the outbursts of energy of their children. Lili and Alex were eight and five by then, and they embraced their new life with so much curiosity and enthusiasm that she could barely stand it. She herself was terrified of just how strange everything and everybody looked. At Frankfurt International Airport she wanted to run and hide at the sight of so many foreign people, people of all creeds and races, people wearing clothes she'd never seen before, sporting turbans and saris, green spiky hair, and nose rings (!). She was scared, and deeply disappointed. If this was what the West looked like, she wanted none of it. But Alex and Lili were full of excitement for everything new and foreign they encountered. And since neither she nor Victor had the heart to tell them they were never going back, they showed no signs of homesickness.

The only person who was homesick was Maria. She missed things she never even registered before. The cracks in the ceiling at her mother's house, the postal worker who delivered their mail, the stray cat who sometimes came to their yard, the way the rain smelled in early spring, the light fixtures in her bathroom. All of the mundane details of her previous existence, once of little significance, were lost to her forever, and as she tried to embrace the memories, to capture the taste and feel and smell of what was lost, she realized that it was gone forever.

For most of their time in Germany she hid in the bathroom, crying. One day her hostess knocked on the door. "Water is very expensive," she explained in German, and then, when Maria didn't understand, in English. Finally, Victor had to translate for her. She spent most of the other days in their room, crying in bed, hiding her face in the pillows.

Finally, in the summer of 1989, jetlagged, feeling filthy and battered after the journey, her patience tried severely by her two overly active children, but with dry eyes and mascara that would finally stay in place, Maria arrived in New York City, and took up residence in the borough of Queens. From that moment on, her marriage to Victor would uncontrollably and unequivocally spiral into an abyss.

Looking into the blank face of the bank employee in front of her, Maria is overcome by despair and hopelessness. The young man hands her a pile of documents. Useless as they may be, Maria thanks him. She knows she's been wasting his time. As she walks out of the building she curses the moment it occurred to her to schedule her meeting for today. Of course, on any given day, her financial situation would be the same. But looking for an outlet for her anger, it's too convenient to blame it on the date. This anniversary is nothing but a commemoration of disappointment and betrayal. How could she ever think such a day would be good for business?

She starts walking in the direction of the store. She briefly contemplates throwing her stupid wedding ring into the East River. But the gesture would give her little satisfaction.

She no longer feels like having a fancy lunch. She buys herself a hot dog from a street vendor. Halfway through eating it, she gets disgusted thinking of the meat processing facilities. She feeds the leftovers to a bunch of pigeons. On her walk back to work she discovers that she smeared ketchup on the sleeve of her favorite suit. What a perfect fucking day!

{ 7 }

Food Fight

I wake up late on a beautiful Sunday morning. Outside the sun is shining, but I feel tired and sore, as if ten hours of sleep were not enough. I've been working overtime recently, hoping my commission would amount to something. But August is the slowest month in New York City retail. Most people with money flee the muggy heat of Manhattan. *Bella* is empty and quiet, and I spend my time waiting uselessly for customers, tallying up the extra hours I've put in, and hoping that Francesca will find some way to reward me. But Francesca is my boss, not the tooth fairy. Come pay day I'll get my stupid commission, nothing more.

I have trouble falling asleep these days, and then more trouble waking up. I'm in a codependent relationship with the snooze button on my alarm clock. Just five minutes, please, five more minutes. Then the five-minute naps pile up, and I'm already late. Mornings are cruel that way. Twice I got to the store after opening. Francesca was not pleased.

Today, at least, there's no alarm, nowhere to go. It's Sunday, and I'm happy to sleep in. Still, I don't feel relaxed or rested, but rather weak and drowsy. I want to go back to sleep. I'm glad I declined Gretchen's invitation to brunch. At least sleep doesn't cost any money. I stretch lazily, like a cat, and enjoy the luxury of letting an indefinite amount of time go by before finally getting up. This is worth saying no to Gretchen. It was the first invitation to hang out together since that awkward conversation about money. I wanted to say yes. But I'm behind on sleep and short on cash. Fifteen bucks for eggs Benedict, and another fifteen or so for each Bellini? Ouch. Before, I might have hoped Gretchen would pay, but the way things stand now, I doubt she'd even offer.

On my way to the kitchen, I make a face at my reflection in the mirror. My features are puffy, and my hair is dull and messy. I'm wearing white pajamas, a gift from *Mami*. She likes getting me pajamas for my birthday, and underwear and socks for Christmas. Yuck. To make matters worse, they're always plain white cotton. So not sexy.

I brew a fresh pot of coffee, and congratulate myself for buying milk, bread, and a jar of Nutella last night, in preparation for eating breakfast at home. *Mami* would have paid half of what I paid, shopping at the grocery store, not the luxury deli downstairs, but at least making breakfast at home is a step towards thriftiness. I have to give myself credit for that.

Oddly enough, my milk carton looks like it's been opened. Gretchen probably wanted some last night. It feels light, like she drank half already. And it's not closed properly. I hate it when people leave milk cartons open. Still, given the pristine emptiness of the fridge, the milk smells fine.

I pour coffee and cut two slices of bread. The jar of Nutella feels sticky. The cap is smeared and *de-geu-lasse*! Disgusting, which even *en francais*, is still pretty darn disgusting after all. G has eaten most of it, straight out of the jar by the look of it. I place it on the counter, wipe my hands on my white jammies, and contemplate whether I'm willing to eat Nutella laced with Gretchen's drool. I'm craving chocolate, damn it!

As I rummage for a knife, I hear a key in the door. I freeze. I feel like I'm being caught red-handed, though it's my own Nutella I was planning to attack.

The hairs on the back of my neck stand up. Gretchen is not alone. Joan comes in, talking in a low voice on her cell-phone. She holds her index finger up towards me, silencing me before I even have the chance to speak. Finally, she snaps her cell phone shut.

"Leahanna. Good morning. Or should I say, good afternoon?"

She looks at my Nutella-smeared white jammies with disgust.

"Liliana," I say. "L for short."

"Elle," Joan frowns. "Gretchen and I had invited you to brunch, to discuss your little situation, but I see you are too busy to join us." She puffs though her nose, and under her scrutinizing gaze, I wish I could evaporate. "So I had to take the time and come all the way here to discuss your situation."

I hate the way she stresses every syllable. Harmless words seem threatening this way. A situation can be good or bad, but a si-tu-a-tion is certainly a problem.

"My sister told me that you still have not paid the back rent you owe, and you have in the meantime accumulated yet another month's debt, so…"

I interrupt.

"I…"

"Don't interrupt. I just wanted to tell you that I have advised Gretchen to start charging you interest. Against my advice she decided not to evict you, but I have insisted on the matter of the interest and…"

"I really…"

"Let me finish."

"I have to go."

Joan and Gretchen both look at me in disbelief.

"Go where?"

"To…eat? Breakfast? Out?" I stammer. My disjointed utterances come out like questions. What am I asking for? Permission?

Gretchen seems peeved.

"You wouldn't have brunch with me, but now you're going out?"

I shrug.

"I have no choice. You ate my Nutella."

Before they can say anything else, I slip past Joan, and grab my Italian leather bag.

Joan stares me down.

"You are going to breakfast? In the middle of our conversation? In your pajamas?"

"Yes, ma'am."

I don't catch my breath until I'm in the street. *În stradă.* My whole body's shaking, and I have to slow down to catch my breath. I keep looking back, expecting Joan to follow. I need to take refuge somewhere, just in case. I duck into the nearest subway station, and ride the train aimlessly for hours. Tears roll down my cheeks. I wipe them with the sleeve of my pajamas. I blow my nose in it too. I don't care what people think. They're welcome to think I'm homeless. Am I not, after all? They can think I'm insane. I don't care. I grab my old battered CD player from my purse. My headphones will protect me from the world. Soon I start finding comfort in watching the people around, people who don't look at me, people who are absorbed in their own lives. Strangers distracted by ipods, cellphones, blackberries, and the occasional book. I'm pretty sure that among them I'm the only one riding the subway for no reason, with no place to go, and that seems sad. And at the same time liberating.

Later that afternoon, feeling lighter, as if I cried off twenty pounds of worry, I find myself strolling towards the park. I sit on a bench in the sun, and soon a dog emerges next to me. It's a mid-sized mutt, with fur of an indistinct yellowish color, parted by asymmetric black lines. It licks my hand, then, encouraged, places its front paws on my shoulders and covers my entire face in slimy, hot, and stinky dog kisses. I laugh, not even trying to shake off the overfriendly mutt.

"Bobby!" A man's voice calls out. "Down! Down, boy! Down!"

The young man belonging to the dog apologizes profusely, and offers to buy me coffee.

An hour later we are sitting in front of a bakery, Bobby snoring happily on the sidewalk. I have breathlessly devoured an enormous pastry, and am covered in confectionary sugar.

"So is this the day you usually hang out in the park in your jammies, and make out with innocent people's dogs?"

I laugh. He's not hot, and that puts me at ease. If he were hot, I'd want to impress him. But he's totally average, and I'm thankful for the opportunity to relax. I never really understood the phrase 'uncomfortably handsome.' It should be 'so handsome he makes you uncomfortable.' I guess that's a mouth full. And luckily, it doesn't apply. I'm so comfortable that I give myself license to lick the confectionary sugar off my fingers.

"It's a long story."

"I bet," he says. "So can I take you out again, so you can tell me all about it?"

Here's the Catch-22. If you like a guy and try to act your best, he'll somehow through some completely unfair law of the universe be repelled. But if you don't like him, well, I mean, if you really don't give a fuck what he thinks about you, you can wear your dirty jammies to the bakery, eat like a pig, lick your fingers, let his dog drool all over you, and he'll still ask you out.

I make a date with Greg, 25, law student at Columbia. I accept mostly because I know he will pay. Also, I enjoy the attention. And if we really do end up together, wouldn't that make a cute story? We met in the park, I was wearing my jammies, and his dog was the one who picked me up? Then again, why on earth would we end up together? I'm not attracted to him. He's cute, maybe. But not that cute. Then again, doesn't Momo keep telling me to stop falling for hot guys who are assholes? Maybe I'll grow to like him eventually. He seems nice. And what is he saying now? That it would be funny if we went to a movie right now, with me still in my jammies? Well, yeah, it would be funny. Besides, I dread going home to Gretchen. And it's been ages since I've seen a movie. Or been on a date for that matter.

At the end of the night I feel happy. It's been an interesting day. We had pastries, went to a movie, ate a late Chinese dinner. He wanted to spend time with me, I wanted to delay going home.

It's almost midnight when Greg hails me a cab, which he generously pays for. I'm hoping Gretchen is asleep, or out, or at least unwilling to come out of her room and confront me. I take the stairs, although it's quite a hike, and although *Mami* always warned me to stay away from stairwells. Women get raped on stairwells. But I am more afraid of Gretchen. The closer I get to our floor, the worse I feel. My greasy Chinese dinner is making me nauseous. All of the wonder of the day has worn off.

The apartment is dark. I tiptoe to my room, close my door, and for the first time ever, I lock it, hoping Gretchen can't hear the little click. I turn on the tap, and throw up. I lie in bed sweaty, exhausted, unable to sleep.

{ 8 }

Phone Call

Maria puts on some music, brews some chamomile tea, and proceeds to remove her makeup. It's an evening like any other. She's tired, and she feels trapped between her own walls, which paradoxically are her source of comfort. She hates this place so much, and yet, it is the only place where she can relax at the end of the day, where she can cast off her torturous shoes, get into her bed with a good book, and pretend that the outside world doesn't exist. She closes her eyes, and gently massages Ponds cold cream into her eyelashes. It's not a spa treatment, but it's soothing.

The phone startles her. Her heart jumps. Who would call her this late at night? What if something happened to Alex or Lili? She looks at the clock. 9pm. Not that late, after all. Still, the sound of the phone makes her panic. She quickly removes the cold cream from her face, and runs into her bedroom. Her eyes sting from whatever traces of lotion she left behind, and just for one second, she regrets not having one of those cordless phones.

She's gone through great lengths to acquire a stationary phone with a rotating device. When she finally found one, L proclaimed her cheap. Alex just rolled his eyes. But she really wanted this phone, because it was the type of phone she had in Bucharest, back in the 80s. L said she understood, but pointed out that they could still get a cordless in addition to it. It was, after all inconvenient, having only one phone, which Maria insisted on keeping in her bedroom. This kept her teenage children off the phone, and with their noses stuck in books instead. Until they both got cell phones from their father, of course.

L also pointed out that the rotary phone was impractical because so many businesses require callers to press keys nowadays. Maria shrugged. “Tough then.” She liked that expression. She learned it from Alex, who used it every time she complained about his refusal to do any of the little favors she asked for, like filling out a form, or translating a phrase she couldn’t understand.

Maria brings the receiver to her ear.

“Hello?”

She likes the familiar feel of the receiver in her hand, the roundness of the plastic pushing against her cheek.

“Hi, Maria.” It’s Victor’s voice. Curt, dry, a tad impatient, the way he usually speaks to her. “I hope I didn’t disturb you.”

Not in a million years would she confess to him that she was getting ready for bed. He needn’t know she leads a lonely life. He probably suspects it, anyway. Sometimes she forgets how badly she wanted to be alone back in the days when her husband and children were all still here, pulling at her, demanding things, bleeding her dry of energy. She forgets that she relishes loneliness, that she would pick a night in bed with tea and a good novel over a hot date any day. Damn, she thinks. I wish I had a hot date.

“No. What you want?” she spits out.

“I need to talk to you about something. Can I take you out for lunch tomorrow?”

He almost sounds cordial. She suddenly dreads lunch, dreads what he wants to tell her in a nice, amicable, only slightly condescending way.

“Tomorrow not good. You invite Lili?”

“No, just you and me. Wednesday then?”

She swallows hard. Just you and me, he said.

She has not been alone with Victor in years. The two of them don’t get together for meals, unless it’s a family event, for the benefit of the children. Sometimes Victor stops by to drop something off. The check for Alex’ tuition. Or L’s purse she inadvertently left behind in

Victor's apartment, then been too busy to retrieve herself. Things like that. Maria asks him to drive to Queens. She meets him downstairs. Goods exchange hands with little conversation. The difficulty of finding parking makes it obsolete for her to explain her choice not to invite him upstairs.

There's only one reason she can think of, why he would want to see her alone.

"Lunch is bad for me. No time."

"How about dinner? My treat. Anywhere you like."

Dinner would be even more pathetic. She feels like shouting an insult and hanging up. But that would be childish. She's known for a while now that this was coming. She realizes that now, with the children out of the house, their little charade is over. Maybe that woman is pushing him to get married. The younger, more attractive woman he's sleeping with. His girlfriend.

It's a perfect time for Victor to ask for a divorce. She would do nothing but humiliate herself by fighting it. He might even think she's jealous, and he would certainly be smug about it. He'd know it's out of spite, the spite of a bitter, frustrated, lonely woman. How unfair that at his age, for Victor, the world is his oyster, yet she'll end up alone. Not that she wants a man. She's had enough of love. She doesn't mind the solitude. What she resents is not having a choice. What she resents is him having a life. A better one. As if she never was. But then again, this too is what it is.

She'll agree to the divorce. But not on his terms. It will be civilized, but she'll never allow it to be friendly. She doesn't want to pretend, doesn't want any of this day-time television reconciliation bullshit. She's not going to break bread with him and smile and wish him well. She's going to sign a piece of paper, and that's it. No smiles, no handshakes. She doesn't see why they should meet in person. Don't people get divorced by mail these days?

"Is this necessary, Victor?"

She can hear him lighting a cigarette.

"For God's sake, Maria, do you have to be so difficult? It's only dinner!"

It's as close as he ever comes to losing his temper.

She sighs.

"We can talk on phone."

"Maria, there is something I would rather discuss with you in person. Can't we have dinner like civilized people?"

Her heart sinks. What's the use?

"Fine," she says. "Next week?"

"How about this week, Maria? Really, what are you doing that is so important?"

"A lot. I have the life too, you know."

"I never said… Never mind."

"Fine." She concedes. "We go Wednesday. But I can't stay late. I don't like to be on subway late at night."

"I'll drive you home."

He sounds amiable, as if he really cared about her getting home safely. As if, now that the kids are grown, if she dropped dead one day, it wouldn't make his life a little easier.

"Where would you like to go? On me."

She rolls her eyes. He does do well for himself, but does he have to rub it in? She makes up her mind to insist they go Dutch.

"Wednesday I come to your store after closing," she says. "Indian buffet around corner is fine."

That place smells like curry from miles away. She happens to love the food. And the meals are so cheap, that even if Victor ends up paying, it can hardly be considered a meaningful treat. Besides, you have to pay up front, so separate checks are pretty much the norm.

"We could go somewhere nice, you know. There is a new Spanish place two blocks from my store. They make some excellent…"

"I don't care what they make! I don't care what you want. Indian is good. And buffet is fastest."

Her harsh tone makes her mispronunciation stand out even more. *I don't care vat you vant.* "See you Wednesday," she says and hangs up.

She goes to bed and tries to immerse herself in her book, but it's impossible. She reads entire pages without paying attention to the plot. As much as she tries, she cannot get the divorce off her mind.

{ 9 }

Coming to America

The decline of their marriage began the day they arrived in the new country. Perhaps it even began the day they left home, or even when they first decided to leave. Or maybe it was written in the stars for them all along, and it all began the very day they met. Maybe their courtship and the good years of their marriage were all just preparation for the hatred and bitterness that followed.

But to Maria the day of their arrival in New York would forever be marked as the beginning of the end. There was just too much irony in their moving here. They came to America in the summer of 1989. They had given up everything to come here, and they had done so for two reasons: to escape communism, and to salvage Victor's career as an architect. Ironically, a few months after their arrival, communism collapsed. As for Victor, he never worked as an architect again.

He replaced his love for architecture with his fascination with the United States, his love for New York, which, feeling stifled in their unattractive neighborhood in Queens, Maria could not understand.

They also felt differently about the collapse of communism. One of their first fights came in January 1990. For weeks they had been watching the news of the Romanian Revolution, perplexed, hypnotized by the images on TV. The coverage started in mid December, and, even as the fighting in the streets simmered down, images of the violence and bloodshed that ensued were still being broadcast. They had limited access to news on their small second-hand TV, hooked up to an antenna. It was funny, she thought. In Romania they had no access to news because of communist censorship. Here they couldn't afford cable.

They would walk across the street to the neighbors', who had a satellite dish. Victor could not get enough of the news, but Maria found it depressing. At some point she even had to cover her daughter's eyes, as images of tortured dead bodies appeared on the screen. The other parents didn't seem to mind their children watching.

The political discussions bothered her even more than the images. While people were waiting for the same news segment to be played over and over by CNN, as if they had not absorbed it completely, they sat around talking, mindlessly eating the dishes Vica, the host's wife, prepared. The other women, with the exception of Maria, would help Vica serve food and beverages. Maria just sat around braiding her daughter's hair. Lili was fascinated by the African braids of some girl at school. Maria was shocked when Vica told her how expensive such a hairdo was. Some of the other women chimed in to explain that there was no way Maria herself could achieve such a hairstyle, and besides, why would she want to? Still, braiding kept Maria's hands and mind occupied.

It was not just the news coverage, but also the political discussions that were making her sick. In spite of all the bloodshed, in spite of the war-like images, in spite of the young people machine-gunned to death, and the chilling discovery of underground torture-chambers, in spite of having cried for days, frazzled, until she finally managed to reach her mother on the telephone, Maria saw the revolution as a positive event. Some images haunted her at night, but others were uplifting, glorious, the victory of a people who had won back its freedom. Her biggest regret was not being there to actually enjoy it. If only they had delayed their departure, if only they had waited a few more months, they could be there right now, continuing their old lives in a free country. She would have loved to be there to take in the scent of freedom. Even from a distance, she thought it was the most exciting thing she'd ever witness.

Vica's guests, however, kept smoking, frowning, and bickering. The room stank of stale smoke and pessimism. Some said civil war would follow. Others mentioned anarchy. Others placed bets on how long it would take for another communist regime to seize power. There were some who mentioned fascism, or military rule. Some expected Soviet tanks to march in.

Maria kept her eyes on Lili's hair, and her thoughts to herself. She was too shy to talk in a room full of people, all louder and more opinionated than herself. Besides, she disliked them so intensely by now, that she didn't find them worth talking to.

Instead, she told Victor that she thought the images were bad for the children, and that maybe she should take the kids to a park or something, instead of keeping them in a smoky room, where people talked about politics, and dead bodies were shown on TV. Victor agreed. She insisted that he continue attending these gatherings. She knew he liked them. He was a central figure in the political debates. And she really wanted Victor to have a good time. She was worried that his new job as a night watchman in a parking garage would depress him, or that their new state of poverty would bring him down.

So Victor attended news-fueled political discussions, while Maria pushed a sulking Alex on a swing in the park, or wandered through the supermarket aisles under the guidance of Lili, who knew enough English to read the labels on the mesmerizing variety of products available in America. They walked through stores the way people walk through museums. They couldn't afford anything. But wasn't it interesting to see that there were so many different kinds of shampoo out there? She tried to find diversions for her children. But mostly she wanted a diversion for herself. She needed something to take her mind off the Romanian Revolution. Nothing worked. She couldn't help thinking of it while she strolled trough the pharmacy aisles, and she couldn't help discussing it with her husband in the few hours they spent together.

"Victor, why do these people all think it will be bad? Why can't they see that something good is happening?"

He smiled at her. She hoped she still looked beautiful to him, in her cheap cotton gown, and torn grey sweatshirt, hand-me-downs from Vica, who had wanted to 'help them settle in.'

"Don't you know how pessimistic our people are? It's in their genes." He laughed. "No matter what happens, good or bad, Romanians will embrace it with hard-core cynicism."

"But you don't think it's bad, do you?" She was stating the obvious. Victor was always arguing that democracy would succeed in their country. Eventually.

"No, I don't. I'm glad the communists are gone. But I'm not going to be naïve and think this will be an easy transition. Still, yes, it does make me happy. I knew it was coming. For years, I knew."

Maria was shocked.

"You knew? How could you know? Nobody knew!"

"Look at what was happening all around us. Things were stirring in other places for a while. *Glasnost* and *perestroika* were just the first steps. Besides, a tyranny that harsh was bound to collapse eventually. The worse things got, the more I thought the end was near."

Maria looked at him in disbelief. She snapped shut the book she was reading, and placed it on the cardboard box she used as nightstand.

"Well, if you knew, then why did we leave? Why did we come all the way here?"

Victor sat on the bed, and tried to take her hand.

"Because, my love," he said in a tender, patient voice, "I didn't know when it would happen, how it would be, and also, I knew things would be tough afterwards. Do you think the transition will be easy? There will be poverty, there might be violence, there will be all kinds of hardships. We have the chance for a better life here. People back home have some hard years ahead."

"And our lives here are easy, Victor?"

She looked around the room. They slept on a futon mattress on the floor, though they had bought decent twin-size beds for the children, who were sharing the other bedroom. She had no idea who Victor had borrowed the money from, or how he would pay it back.

Cardboard boxes were the only other furnishings in their room. She had been pleased to discover that in America, apartments came with closets already built in, though theirs was made of a flimsy material, not much better than cardboard, just like the walls themselves, through which she could hear the neighbors. The nice dresses she brought from Romania were hanging in the closet on wire hangers she got from the dry cleaners upon Vica's advice. Next to them was all the ugly crap people had given her. She soon came to be grateful for those rags, as she realized that in America people did not dress up much, but rather wore what was known as 'casual' clothing. Her two-piece tailored suits and raw silk dresses drew strange looks in the supermarket. She was trying to get used to wearing the jeans and T-shirts that had been shoved down her throat by those busy-bodies in the 'community.' Next to her clothes, Victor's stuff was lined up in neat little piles in a construction he had assembled out of card-board boxes. His night watchman uniform stood out, like an ugly dark spot.

The room was too cold for her. They were keeping the thermostat low, to save money. She slept in a thick sweatshirt, and she wore socks to bed. She secretly considered thermal underwear, but it was too unsexy. Not that socks were exactly attractive either. It's true that being cold was not new to her. In the last years of communism, there had been shortages of heat, electricity, or water, all utilities having been controlled by the government. Their apartment here was not much colder than their house had been last winter in Bucharest. Still, she found it ironic that having moved to America, she still had to suffer being cold.

She raised her eyebrows, waiting for Victor to respond. Did he not see the difference between this makeshift room, this joke of an apartment, and the beautiful villa they used to live in? Did he not feel the lumps in the mattress they slept on? Was he not disgusted by the thought that other people had slept on it before them, people they didn't even know? People who might have been filthy or diseased, who probably had fucked, masturbated, sweated and peed on this bed, who maybe had died on it? Did he not miss their solid wood furniture, the sculpted mahogany bed with hand-embroidered crisp linens, where they, and only they, had made love so many times? Did he not miss the sun shining through the big oval leaves of their walnut tree, as they lay in their bed reading on Sunday mornings, drinking Turkish coffee out of real china, not clunky mugs from the dollar store? Did he not miss the aroma of that coffee, or the scent of lavender on their starched white sheets?

He caressed her hand, and spoke tenderly, as if to a child.

"This will be hard on us, Maria. We will have a few hard years. But things will get better, I promise. Our children will have much better lives here. They will be happy."

She felt a wave of rage. Wasn't her life important too?

Such thoughts made her feel ashamed of herself. All the people she knew put their children first. Romanians seemed to live for their children, to sacrifice everything for them. Why couldn't she? If other mothers felt the same, none of them ever voiced it. And she could never bring herself to ask. She wasn't close to anybody anyway.

"Our children were happy before," she said. "They were already happy. Lots of people were perfectly happy."

Why wasn't he looking at her? Was he even paying attention?

Her voice grew sharp.

"I was happy. Why would my children not be happy in a place where I was happy, where lots of people were happy? Is it written on their foreheads that they can only be happy in America?"

Victor stood up and walked to the window. They had a view of another similar exposed brick building. She hated their view.

"What special children we have, Victor! They can only be happy in America!"

Her own voice surprised her. Where did that sharp edge come from, or the sarcasm?

Victor turned around and faced her, his arms crossed over his chest, his gaze distant. He spoke in a calm controlled voice. She would soon learn that, to her despair, he rarely lost his tempter.

"If you didn't want to go, then why didn't you fucking ever say so?"

She was taken aback. He had never sworn at her.

She felt like hiding under the blanket, but she knew she had to roll with the punches.

"You knew I didn't want to go. You knew it!"

"Don't wake the children."

She bit her lips. She felt bad for yelling.

"It's not my job to read your fucking mind, woman. When you want something, you should say it."

She stood up, to be closer to his height. She was not nearly tall enough.

"Well, I'm saying it now," she yelled. "I hate it! I hate this house, I hate this place, I hate this life! I hate it! Fine? I hate it!"

His face twitched with impatience and irritation.

She waited. It was his turn. He had to say something, anything. But he was quiet, and she could not stand it. She wanted to scratch him. She wanted to scratch him until she drew blood.

"I hate you!" she screamed, throwing a pillow in his direction. Recalling the fight later, she'd be embarrassed by the childish gesture. He picked up the pillow with a sigh, and placed it on the mattress.

"I have to go to work," he said.

After he left, without as much as another glance in her direction, she stayed up all night, shaking with anger, frustration, and shame. In the morning, when he came in, she pretended to be asleep. She did not rise until she heard him snoring beside her. She did not speak to him for two days, until she woke up one morning to the smell of warm cinnamon buns and coffee. He said he wanted them to have breakfast in bed, and told her about the amazing aroma coming from the bakery at dawn, as he was finishing his night shift. Sleep still in her eyes, she smiled. The smell of cinnamon and sugar filled the room as they started kissing. She could not stop giggling, as he teased her: "I think you're a liar. You don't seem to hate me much at all." Yet in the middle of their lovemaking, she got distracted, thinking of how much the cinnamon buns and coffee must have cost.

Later she heated the cold buns in the oven. Of course, the children ate most of them, and she was left with just a bite, just enough so she could crave more. The cold coffee was watery. She could not believe Americans paid money for this shit. She poured it down the drain, and washed the paper cups, placing them carefully next to the sink to dry.

Later she had to go back into the bedroom to retrieve a pile of laundry. She hated laundry day. They didn't even have their own machine! She had to push their dirty clothes in a little cart to a coin-operated laundromat a few blocks away. That day it snowed, and she dreaded stepping through the dirty slush, laundry and kids in tow. As she was contemplating the horror, she saw Victor sleeping, a blissful expression on his face. She stood there for a second watching him, her arms full of dirty clothes. On her way out she slammed the door as loud as she could, then cried out to her kids at the top of her lungs: "Alex! Lili! Coat on! We go laundry!"

Another one of their early fights stands out in her mind. They had been invited to a barbecue at the house of a wealthy Romanian family, on Long Island. Some friends of Victor's offered to give them a ride in their mini-van. Maria didn't like any of these people, especially since Victor often used them as examples of how Romanian immigrants did well in America. She also was sick of hearing about how all these nice compatriots had helped them, how they continued to help. She was tired of charity, tired of being thankful for every worn out item others found it in their hearts to toss her way.

For the party that day she put on a red silk dress, her favorite dress in fact, sewn by her seamstress in Romania. She was too dressed up for a barbecue, but she didn't care. Victor seemed pleased with her appearance. He proudly put his arm around her shoulders, as they huddled with their children on the back seat of the mini-van. Maria and Victor had insisted on letting their hosts and their children take up the more comfortable seats. She was miffed when they accepted without further protest. Normally, at home, people would have politely turned down each other's offer, and gotten gridlocked in a lively argument, each insisting the other ones take the better seats.

Lili was sitting on Maria's dress, wrinkling it, and the sole of her little shoe was rubbing up against Maria's taupe suede pump. It was ironic that after almost a year in America she still wore the same undersized shoes that hurt her feet. But it seemed frivolous to splurge on shoes, when they could barely pay the rent! She'd seen lovely shoes, in the windows of expensive stores in Manhattan, but she had forced herself to look away. Of course, there were cheap ones out there too. In America the selection of merchandise was broad enough to accommodate every taste and budget. But Maria had yet to discover shoes destined for people with exquisite taste but minimal budgets. It would take years for her to learn how to hunt for such bargains. In the meantime she put up with sore feet.

The Long Island neighborhood of clapboard houses was stifling and depressing to her. The houses, all the same, spacious, brand new, and expensive, looked boring. Conformist. Like the uniform she'd worn in high school in Romania. Ugly and made of plastic. If doing well meant living in a neighborhood where all the houses were the same, everybody drove a bloody mini-van, and you could practically see into your neighbor's living room, well then she'd probably want to drown herself in the small oval pool that invariably decorated each tiny back yard. She couldn't believe Victor bought into all this. Where was his taste, his love for art and self-expression? Wasn't this just the kind of soulless conformity he had rebelled against?

She arrived at the party with her dress wrinkled, and her toe-pinching, torturous shoes dirty. She told herself it didn't really matter. For all she cared, she could wear a garbage bag for these people. Their opinion meant nothing to her. And they disliked her anyway.

Her persona as an arrogant stand-offish woman had followed her to New York. Her aloofness, as usual, masked her shyness. But it also masked her unhappiness, and the fact that she did not share these people's conviction that life in America was better. They similarly did not share her nostalgia for the old country. If they had ever been homesick like her, they had gotten over it years ago.

The only person Maria could relate to was an old woman who was equally unhappy to be here, but had come for her daughters, who needed help with their children. Like Maria, Mrs. Stoica spoke no English. Maria tried to pick up a few phrases here and there, which she insisted on using on her children, but Mrs. Stoica felt too old to learn. Maria wished she had a similar excuse. Learning English was torturous for her. She kept the TV on while cooking and cleaning. She wrote down new words every day. But other than to her children, she did not dare speak to anybody. Victor insisted that her lack of practice held her back. She had to push herself, he said. But Maria was sick of pushing herself.

Mr. Grecu, the host of the party, was grilling *mici*, sausage links, and pork cutlets, for his many guests. An upstanding member of the community, he had been in America for twenty years, and had been an invaluable source of help to many new arrivals, including Victor. It was Mr. Grecu, who, through connections, and, from a distance, had facilitated the Pop family's flight from Romania and their political asylum in the United States. It was also he who helped Victor find that dreadful job as a night watchman. Maria hated him with a passion.

He motioned them over, cheerfully waving a sausage link, which he offered to Alex. He engaged Victor in an animated discussion, while Maria sulked a little too obviously. She hated having to endure such boredom for the enjoyment of her family, and for the sake of free grilled meat.

Unfortunately, Mr. Grecu felt the need to address her.

"So, Maria, Victor tells me you still don't have a job."

She blushed. She was ashamed of not working, but there seemed to be no way to find a job without speaking English. Surely no employer would want her nine-year-old daughter tagging along as an interpreter.

"My English, you know..." she said shyly, and felt utterly and profoundly stupid.

"Yes, yes, many of us had that problem at the beginning. It will get better. And you don't always need English to get a job. You know, I talked to my friend Ion, the one who owns that bakery, *Amandina*. He said you could help his wife, decorating cakes. You don't need English for that."

Although she had longed for a similar job, Maria felt insulted. She could not explain why.

"Thank you," she said. "But I'm not interested in that kind of work."

At that point, a lot of people's attention turned to her. She had spoken louder than intended. She blushed. These people considered her arrogant enough, without her giving them extra evidence.

Mr. Grecu laughed. He was a chubby man with rosy cheeks and a potbelly. A *bon vivant,* Victor called him. Had she met him back in Romania, under different circumstances, she would have probably liked him.

"And, what, pray tell, would you like to be doing? What kind of job *are* you looking for?"

She felt people's expectant eyes upon her.

"I'm a librarian," she said.

Mr. Grecu was copiously amused, and so were the others. The host's wife, a cheerful matron, with the same stout build as her husband, came to her rescue.

"Come child," she said, taking Maria's hand. "Let's get you fed. Don't mind him."

As she was being led towards a table full of salads and grilled meats, Maria looked back to see her husband apologize to Mr. Grecu for her behavior.

On the drive back she was fuming. She could not say anything in front of the people driving them. But as soon as they got out and the mini-van sped off, she turned to Victor, and shoved him, hard.

"Why didn't you stand up for me? Why did you apologize?"

Victor gave her one of his standard 'not in front of the children' looks. He turned away and walked towards the building, holding his son and daughter's hands. Maria walked behind them, feeling left out, like a stranger stalking them.

"Why didn't you defend me?" she yelled in the lobby, following them into the elevator.

Instead of answering, Victor calmly pressed their floor number. She banged her fist on the "Open Door" sign.

"Why didn't you stand up for me?"

"Why didn't you take the job?"

This time Maria punched the "Open Door" sign so hard it hurt.

"I'm a grown woman. I'm not a child. I don't need you to apologize for me. Don't you dare apologize for me! I have a right to my opinion. I'm a fuckin' grown-up."

Victor removed her fist from the button. The elevator finally took off.

"Then start fucking acting like one."

She was so ashamed. For days afterwards she felt worthless. A bad wife, a bad mother, a person who refused to work, was a burden on her family, and then complained about it, and even cursed in front of the children.

There was no cinnamon bun reconciliation after this fight. Victor continued to talk to her, but was cold and distant. Ashamed of her behavior, she was polite, but she tried to stay out of his way.

She walked the kids to school each day. Then, to keep out of the house, she went grocery shopping, something she would usually do on afternoons and weekends, with Lili's help, whose English was quite good. Two years before their departure from Romania, Victor had hired a private tutor to give the children English lessons. Maria had considered it ridiculous, but had not shared with Victor her concern that the children were too young to learn. It turned out that she had been wrong. Her children were doing ok in the new country, though school proved difficult at times. There were many differences in the way subjects were taught, even something straightforward such as math. Handicapped by her ignorance of the language, she could not be much help. It was Victor who sat patiently at the table with Lili and Alex, trying to figure out whatever it was they didn't understand.

Pushing her empty cart around, Maria wondered if her family even needed her at all. At least she cooked and cleaned as best she could. Sometimes she thought of herself as a machine that provided food, sex, and clean laundry. She imagined her family being better off with a robot, rather than a flesh and blood woman. A robot would work quietly, and they could switch it off and store it away when its work was done.

Of course, her work was never done. She knew the house was never clean enough for Victor's taste. Back home she would have fired the housekeeper if she'd done as poorly. But she did not like cleaning, and with two children running around, there was always too much to do.

As a cook, at least, she was improving. She had first started experiencing with food under her mother's guidance, in preparation for moving to America. She had wanted to master a few of Victor's favorite recipes. Even in her blind naïveté and her ignorance about what lay ahead, she had suspected that in America they might be unable to afford help, at lest at the beginning. Plus, what if American cooks did not know how to prepare Victor's favorite dishes?

{ 10 }

Dinner Date

The main reason I accepted Greg's invitation is that I'm starving. *Flămândă.*

With only five dollars in my checking account (three of which will be eaten up by my bank's evil minimum balance fee), I subsist on a diet of coffee and bagels.

Bagels are the city's solution to world hunger. I've loved them since I was a little girl. *Mami* would buy them as a special treat, and hand them to us whole, like donuts, expecting us to just bite in. *Mami* has her own word for bagels, a funny Romanian word: *covrig.*

There's a deli close to *Bella* that serves toasted bagels with cream cheese for just a dollar. That tends to be my dinner. For breakfast I buy a 75 cent cup of coffee as well. I ask for plenty of skim milk. It keeps me fuller that way. And it has calcium.

I'm bored of bagels. *Plictisită.* I feel like I'm carrying a rock in my stomach. And I hate to think what all those carbs are doing to my body.

I get ready for the date at work, in the back room. I'm wearing a light blue dress *Mami* bought me on sale at Daffy's. I like it, but it's more appropriate for a picnic than dinner. I threw it on in a rush this morning, before racing to *Bella* and still getting here late. If I could go home after work, like a normal person, I would pick a different outfit. But I live like a refugee these days, totally *clandestina.* I try to be home as little as possible. Sleep and shower, it's all I ever do there any more.

Unable to change my dress, I freshen up my makeup, and splash on my *parfum secret*. It's liberating to go on a date feeling no butterflies in my stomach. I'll actually enjoy my meal. None of that silly pushing food around too nervous to chew, scared that steak juice might dribble on my chin, that taking a big bite might make me look unfeminine, or that the cherry tomato I'm about to stab with my fork will launch itself across the room.

There are advantages to going out with someone I'm not into. Besides, didn't Momo say it's good to date someone who likes me more than I like him? Didn't she say it's best not to be crazy about a man, but instead to learn to appreciate him for being nice and being good company? I usually find such suggestions depressing. What's the point of being with someone you're not crazy about? What's the thrill in that? But quite possibly I'm maturing, because I'm finally willing to give it a try, finally ready to accept there are no fairy tales. Maybe Momo is right, and if you lower your expectations, there are good guys out there, guys who deserve a chance.

Francesca gives me a critical once-over:

"*Stai, bellissima, cara! Sempre bellissima*!"

I'm surprised she likes my simple outfit. She tends to prefer clothes that are expensive and with an edge.

"It's a lovely dress for after work," she says. "But I would appreciate it if you tried to dress more consistently with the look of Bella, yes, *carina*? This week you look a bit, *no se*, like girl next door, *sai?* Like you work in the Gap, not an exclusive Italian boutique. You need to pay more attention. I have seen you in better clothes."

I swallow. I've been hesitant to wear Gretchen's stuff lately, though it's still hanging in my closet. I'm terrified of running into Joan or G, and having them point out that, in addition to being a squatter, I'm a wardrobe parasite, a shameless little free rider. Like a moth. *Motte. Molie*.

Francesca has a point. My own clothes are a bit shabby, and quite limited. I look neither polished nor sophisticated these days. I look like myself: a poor girl from the boroughs, with little flair for faking high-end style on a low-end budget, the way *Mami* does. *Mami*, of course, has more artistic sense, and many years of practice. Plus, when you're beautiful, it's easier to look well put together.

Greg brings me a bouquet of daisies. *Margarete.* How old fashioned and sweet! People don't buy each other flowers anymore, but it's such a nice thing to do! My mood brightens instantly, and I cheer up even more when he agrees to dinner at a steakhouse nearby. It's wrong of me to pick such an expensive place, but temptation is an atrocious animal.

The steakhouse is elegant in a dark and austere way - wood paneling, dim lights, crisp white tablecloths. I find it fitting. Eating steak is a serious business. A hungry girl should know.

"Would you care for some bread?" Greg asks, extending the basket.

"No, thanks."

I've eaten enough dough to last me a lifetime.

"So tell me more about yourself. Will you finally tell me where your family's from?"

I take a sip of wine. I move my glass in a slow circular motion, observing the dark liquid inside.

Greg's gaze lingers on me. I wish I found him attractive.

"Well," I say. "Maybe you can guess?"

I try not to be annoyed. I hate people's fixation with my origin.

"Ok." Greg says, smiling. "I'll take you up on that challenge."

"Ok." I smile back. "It is in Europe, and…"

"I know that much. I think Eastern Europe."

I cringe. People tend to lump all of Eastern Europe together, as if it were one big entity. They mostly think I'm Russian, and many times, as I correct them, I realize that to them it's all the same. Not that there's anything wrong with Russia. But if you know anything at all about Romania, you'd know that you're comparing apples and oranges. It's never ceased to bother me that people find the particularities of a rich and fascinating culture of so little consequence as to not even try to distinguish them from another entirely different one.

"Yes," I say. "But let's see if you get this. It's not a Slavic country. We speak a romance language, you know, a language based on..."

"Latin. So you are Romanian?"

I did not expect this. Nobody ever knows anything about Romania. And when they do, it's about gymnasts, vampires, or communism, topics I find irrelevant - or at best passé - and irritating. It's just as ignorant as saying that the quintessence of American culture is McDonald's. What frustrates me is that nobody knows what a beautiful country Romania is, how lovely the mountains, the sea, the wildlife, the virgin forests, the architecture. Nobody brings up Ionesco's plays, Cioran's philosophy, or Brancusi's sculptures. Why would people rather remember the most brutal communist dictatorship of Eastern Europe, rather than the most notable artist of the twentieth century, or the inventor of absurd theatre? I guess humans thrive on horrors: vampires and violence. No wonder I hate discussing my origin! Even with Greg, who guessed correctly.

Luckily the steaks arrive. I ordered a filet mignon with a side of asparagus. *Sparanghel.*

Greg watches me enjoy the first bites of my steak. I notice him staring and I feel embarrassed. Does he know how hungry I am? Does he have any idea how good this steak tastes after all those bagels?

"I love watching you eat," he says. "You gotta love a girl who orders her steak rare."

"I sure am a big fan of the raw dead cow!" I say jokingly.

The conversation drifts on. At times it feels like an interview, and I have to remind myself to be polite. It's only fair that I sing for my supper, and some of his jokes are not bad. At least he's a distraction. Gretchen, the rent, Francesca, my bank account, and all the bagels in the world seem far away.

Later he walks me home. An uncomfortable thought enters my mind. Will he kiss me? We stop in front of my building. I hold my breath as his face draws closer. He goes for my cheek, and I feel relieved.

Upstairs in the apartment, I venture into the kitchen to get a vase. I arrange the daisies in it, and place them on my nightstand. *Margarete.* For the first time since Gretchen mentioned the money, I'm able to appreciate the beauty that surrounds me. I open the window, letting in the sounds of the city. Lying in bed, next to my bouquet of daisies - *margarete*, I feel that everything will be all right. I will pay Gretchen back, I'll come up with a plan. Funny how those little white flowers restored my faith in life, how they helped me feel comfortable again, in a room where only yesterday I felt hopeless, and threatened.

{ 11 }

A Different Dinner

Wednesday night. Her nerves are tense, dread coursing through her veins like poison. It was hard focusing at work. Her brain is in a fog. She's afraid she might faint, or perhaps evaporate. She wouldn't be entirely surprised if she disappeared into thin air. The thought of seeing him and discussing their divorce makes her want to vomit. Dinner never seemed like a stupider idea.

She changes into a pair of high heel sandals. Walking in them is hell, but her ego is worth suffering for. She has to look her best. She cannot stand the thought of him no longer finding her desirable. She wants him to feel the occasional pang of regret, the way she does when she sees him. It's like a shock, each time, setting eyes on Victor and finding, over and over, that her body is still drawn to his. Just like a stupid animal. Not that she'd ever want him back, but it still hurts like a broken limb that will never fully recover.

Her only consolation is that maybe, just maybe, when he looks at her he feels the same. She knows it isn't true. She's not blind, after all. As much as it hurts her pride, she has to accept what she is: his aging, no longer attractive wife, once beautiful beyond words, now used up, wrinkled and jaded, with circles under her eyes, and lots of cellulite. A bitter, boring woman, impossible, and hopelessly alone, whom he's going to divorce in order to marry his young, fun-loving mistress. Who probably has not an ounce of cellulite on her slim body. Not that Maria's ever seen her, and for that she thanks her lucky stars. She couldn't stand it, to be face to face with the woman sharing Victor's bed.

But it is what it is. She'll sign the papers and move on with her life. She only wishes she could do all this without obsessing about her appearance, without clinging uselessly to whatever shreds of pride and vanity she's still got left. Didn't she already waste enough time choosing her stupid outfit? She dressed more carefully for dinner with Victor than for her interview at the bank! Her final selection was a flattering yet casual top, white, a color she always looked stunning in, with enough cleavage to make her appear voluptuous, without looking like she put any effort into her appearance. It's a plain cotton top, something a woman would throw on for a stroll to the market on a summer day. Under no circumstances is Victor to know she dressed up for him!

To be honest, she knows why she's so worked up about her looks, while she wasted her time dressing and undressing, hating all her clothes, why she tossed and turned in her bed all night causing the dark circles under her eyes to deepen to a dangerous shade of purple. It's not just unpleasant, seeing him, dealing with the papers, being discarded, and traded in for a newer model. No, it's not just humiliating and plain horrible. It's also bloody unfair! After all, it was she who no longer wanted Victor, she who rejected him, who kicked him out of her bed, and then out of her house! He didn't leave her. She left him. She packed her bags and left. She abandoned her marriage, her kids even, and although she came back, wasn't she the one who asked him to leave in no uncertain terms? Wasn't she the one who refused to sleep with him? How sick and wrong for him to turn the tables on her now! How sick and wrong for *him* to want to discard *her*, when all along it was she who wanted out! How dare *he* not want *her* anymore? It was always the other way around. He wanted her, and she said no. He stayed with her, but she asked him to leave. Not that she ever wanted a divorce. As much as she needed her freedom, as much as she wanted to escape the daily pain their marriage had become, she could think no further than him moving out. She never wanted to imagine a next step.

She wishes it were all her idea. She even wishes perversely that today, over lunch, she can sit there and nonchalantly say that she's relieved, because in the end, she's wanted the divorce for years now, but didn't want to bring it up because of the kids. She was never much of an actress, but if she can deliver that line convincingly, well, she'll just have to treat herself to a good bottle of Laurent Perrier to drown her sorrows in.

She arrives at Victor's store in a cab. It's a splurge, but there is no way she could walk all those blocks in heels. And she can certainly not go to dinner with her soon-to-be ex husband carrying beat up sneakers in a tote. It would be like admitting she's a loser. It's already hard enough to see his store, each time more polished, more sophisticated, the furniture on display more modern, and more expensive. Her reflection in the window looks shabby, and as she pushes the glass door open she feels like she's entering a place where she doesn't belong. It's one of those lovely stores where she wishes she could shop but will never afford to.

The young woman sitting behind the desk is new. Maria doesn't know her, yet she is seized by instant hostility. As they greet, she recognizes a Romanian accent. But she continues the conversation in English.

"I'm here to meet Victor," she says.

"He went for a smoke. He'll be right back." The young woman is paging through a furniture catalog. She doesn't seem to pay attention to Maria, who realizes with irritation that, after all, there is no reason why she would be given any deference. She's not a customer. She's just a soon-to-be-ex-wife whom the young woman has never even met. In fact, she's nobody.

She walks around looking at the furniture. She recognizes Victor's style. Clean lines, quality materials, simple colors, no bells and whistles, no excess. She knows him well enough to understand why he selected each and every piece. This hurts. It always hurts to be reminded of good traits in people you lost. It hurts to think that you'll never forget. If twenty years from now she'll walk into a room he decorated, she would recognize his style. And even worse, she would like it. It's a relief to know she'll never enter such a room, that she doesn't socialize with the wealthy people whose apartments he furnishes. That she will never ever visit his apartment. And that in fact, after today, she'll never ever come back here. She looks around almost fondly. She never knew how to say good-bye to places, never knew how to act when she was looking at something for the very last time. Is there a mental snapshot people take? Is there a way to recall colors and textures and scents? She has no clue how to keep memories alive. She only knows how to lose them.

She lets herself sink into a lovely armchair. She might never afford to buy it, but at least for now, she can enjoy its comfort. Her sore feet need a rest.

"You cannot sit on the furniture, ma'am!" The receptionist rushes over, as if trying to avert a real crisis. "These pieces are for display! You cannot sit there!"

Maria crosses her legs and leans further back. It is so bloody comfortable. And it smells like a brand new luxury car.

"I can sit where I want," she says. "I'm Victor's wife!"

She loves to see the shock on the young woman's face, loves to hear her little gasp of surprise. She wonders if the woman knew Victor was married. She probably met Lili and Alex, and must have imagined that these children have a mother. She wonders if she also met the lover. She must have.

Maria smiles. She enjoys this twisted situation, and she might as well milk it while she can. Soon she'll be divorced, and she will no longer have the satisfaction of shocking Victor's acquaintances with the fact that, while he and his girlfriend are such a public item, he does, indeed still have a wife.

She hears the chime of the door and sits up straight. The sight of Victor makes a chill run through her spine.

"Maria," he says, coming towards her, trying to act cordial. "You look lovely, as usual." Even as a formality, she still likes to hear him say it.

"Hi, Victor."

Her greeting is frosty. There will be no pretense on her side. Being polite takes a superhuman effort. Being pleasant is absolutely impossible.

"I see you met Gina. She's from Braşov, you know?"

"I don't care," she snaps. "Let's go."

He holds the door for her, and on their way out, his hand lightly touches her waist. It's one of those useless, outdated gestures, protective and polite, yet, she knows, meaningless. He probably didn't even think of it, it's just a habit. But for a second, the warmth of his hand lingers, and just for a second, she is fool enough to enjoy it. She inhales sharply. Underneath the cigarette smoke, she recognizes his old familiar scent. She straightens her shoulders and hastens her pace. Why on earth need he stand so close to her?

They walk side by side silently. Victor lights another cigarette, and she realizes she'll have to slow down for him to be able to keep up with her.

He shifts around so he can walk on the outside of the sidewalk, shielding her from traffic, something Romanian men were taught to do, part of their code of manners. She has mixed feelings about it. Is it chivalrous, or is it patronizing? But even as she questions it, she's touched. So touched, in fact that it hurts to remember, once more, that her husband is now another woman's man. Whatever tenderness he still feels for her is probably mixed with contempt and pity. What type of shabby consolation prize are such small gestures anyway, in the face of the unavoidable?

She can't believe she's getting so melodramatic. After all, she hates his guts. She wouldn't take him back if he was the only man on earth. His stupid mistress is welcome to him, if she's willing to put up with him being cold and condescending.

"How have you been?" he asks.

"Fine," she says, and raises her eyebrows, indicating that she'd rather skip the pleasantries. But he ignores her cue.

"Anything new and exciting?"

The question annoys her. Is he mocking her dull life?

They get to the restaurant and she grabs the door before he can hold it open for her. She marches to the cashier and orders:

"Two buffet dinner. Pay separately."

She already has her money out.

Still, there is a brief argument before Victor gives in and lets her pay her share.

As they sit at the small table, their plates full of fragrant Indian food, Maria finds herself unable to eat. The presence of her husband, and the conversation ahead, kill her appetite. The scent of spices, cream, tomatoes, and basmati rice, tease her taste buds, but all she can do is sip her water and wait. She forgot to tell the waiter that she wanted no ice. She never got used to drinking cold beverages, the way Americans do.

She feels uncomfortable sitting across from Victor. Is it her imagination, or is there sexual tension between them? She doesn't know which is worse, the thought that her lonely life and empty bed are making her delusional, or the idea that he too feels the charged mix of desire and resistance floating in the air.

How silly, she is! Victor is enjoying his food, unaware of the drama in her head. Through all of life's crises he never lost his appetite, or his ability to sleep. As if he's not a human being. As if his heart is made of stone.

"This place is really good!" he says between bites. She watches him load his fork with saffron rice and juicy pieces of meat. She takes another sip of water. It's so cold it actually makes her shiver.

"I can't believe I haven't been here before. Good call." He's obviously relaxed. As if he's having dinner with a friend, not his estranged wife. He seems totally unaffected by the significance of their bloody meeting. She's so hurt she's fighting back tears. This is beyond humiliating. If he wanted to be cruel he wouldn't do a better job of it.

"There is a reason I wanted to see you." Victor finally says. She feels nauseous. Her legs start shaking under the table. But it's almost over, she tells herself, almost done. She inhales deeply, takes another sip of water and braces herself to hear his words.

"I heard you applied for a loan at the bank," Victor says.

That's not what he was meant to say.

"How you hear that?" she asks.

"From the bank. You went to my branch for a loan, and since we are still married, they forwarded me some of the correspondence."

What is he talking about? Why even bring this up? She takes another sip of water. For the life of her, she can't understand what he's getting at. And she'd better stop drinking the water, because she doesn't trust her shaking legs to carry her to the ladies' room.

"This is what you wanted to talk about?" she asks.

"Yes," he says. What does he mean 'yes'? Is this what she went through all this agony for? She's too irritated to even feel any relief. Here she is, completely humiliated, thinking he's about to divorce her, when in fact he's dragged her out on the town to discuss her finances?

"I was wondering…" Victor continues, but she interrupts.

"Is none of your business, Victor. I don't know why the bank tell you my information. Is my loan. And is nothing to do with you!"

"Well, since we are married, legally we are one financial entity."

She feels blood rushing to her face. She takes a sip of water to calm herself down.

"No, we are not! We have separate accounts! We have our own separate money!"

"We do." His voice is conciliatory. He reaches across the table, but she pulls her hand away. Then she realizes he wasn't going to touch her, he's just pushing the glass of water towards her. "And I respect that," he says. "It's the bank's mistake."

She takes a sip of water and does her best to calm down. "Anyway," he continues. "That's not the issue. What I wanted to talk to you about is the fact that you are obviously trying to buy an apartment."

Maria reaches for the *naan* bread, and twists off a piece. She has no intention of eating it, and instead starts kneading it into a ball. Does he even know how patronizing he sounds? She doesn't want to discuss her plans with him. She's been coping without his help for years, but now he feels entitled to lecture her about real estate just because he's a man?

"I think that's a great decision," he says. Her irritation grows.

She squeezes the *naan* ball flat between her fingers.

"I don't care what you think, Victor. I don't need your approval!"

"I know you don't." There's almost a trace of affection in his voice. "What I mean, is, I'm happy for you. Is it a nice apartment?"

"You ask me to dinner to ask if the apartment is nice?"

"Don't get so defensive. It's just a question. Is it nice?"

She rolls her eyes. In all their fights, she always came out looking like the bad guy. He is just too infuriatingly polite.

"It doesn't matter, Victor. I'm not buying."

"Why not?"

She exhales sharply.

"None of you business. Really!"

He waits, staring her down. She fumbles with the napkin on her lap.

"I don't have enough money, ok? Down payment is too large. You happy now?"

She immediately regrets telling him. It makes her feel like such a pauper. She looks down at the glass plate covering the table. There is a little smudge in one corner, where somebody, probably herself, has dropped a bit of curry. She scratches at it with her fingernail.

"How much do you need?"

She feels the sting of tears in her eyes, and she tries blinking them away. She stalls, taking another sip of water. The pressure in her bladder is unbearable by now, but her throat feels dry, like somebody is strangling the life out of her. His eyes on her are persistent. She has to do her best to look away, has to do her best not to cry.

"Twenty thousand," she finally says, hating herself for having agreed to this humiliating dinner.

"You know I could give it to you, don't you?"

There's an infuriating amount of kindness in his voice. He's trying to be charitable, and she just can't stand it.

"I'm not asking," she says.

"I know. But I'm offering."

She shakes her head, and forces herself to look at him.

"Why? Why would you give me twenty thousand dollars?"

It's not that she doesn't want the money. But if she took his charity, how would her pride recover? And seriously, why would he give her money? Why would the man who is no longer truly her husband, the man who shares his bed with another woman, give her twenty thousand dollars, just like that?

"Well, I thought that if I helped, maybe you'd soften up." He winks. "You know, give me some sugar."

"Some sugar?"

Is he suggesting what she thinks he is? She takes a sip of water. Her heart is racing. Is this for real? He's propositioning her in exchange for money? Perversely, she's turned on.

"Sugar," she repeats caustically. "You are asking me to…" She cannot bring herself to say it.

Their eyes meet. She feels her face burning. She has to look away.

"Yes, honey. I'm asking you to sleep with me."

Well, at least that settles the question of whether he still wants her. Some crazy part of her enjoys this. Yet it's disgusting and demeaning. How dare he?

"Excuse me?" She raises her hand to cover her cleavage. Her face still burning, she reaches for her iced water. She knows Victor has little respect left for her, but she never thought he would be such a pig. "How you dare even suggest that?"

He laughs. It angers her beyond words that he's having fun at her expense.

"Well, princess, it's not that outrageous, if you think about it."

"For me to sleep with you?" she asks, shaking her head in disbelief. "And you to give me money?"

"You are my wife," he points out. "Neither me giving you money, nor you sleeping with me would be all that shocking."

She should get up and leave, that's what she should do. If only her knees would stop shaking.

"Seriously," he continues. "What's the big deal? We've had sex countless of times. Thousands, perhaps. Seriously, do the math, for ten years or so, we did it almost every day, sometimes several times a day, so..."

She stands up, and places her napkin on the table. She's let this go too far.

"Sit down, sunshine. Your virtue is safe." Victor grabs her hand, and gently pulls her back towards her seat. "I'm only joking, of course. God, you are such a fucking prude!"

Now on the brink of tears, she collapses into her chair and takes another sip of water. Her bladder is about to burst. She has no clue where the restroom is, and no force left to drag herself up again.

She looks at him in disbelief and anger. For all his faults, Victor has never been this cruel before.

"I'm serious about the money, though," he says, trying to meet her eyes. She looks down at the food she hasn't touched. She's not just angry. She's hurt. She has to summon all her willpower not to cry. She tries to count the holes in the white paper doily under the glass plate of the table. There are ten holes in a pattern. And ten little flowers to go with them.

"I'll write you a check," he says. "No strings attached."

He takes out his checkbook and an expensive looking pen.

"I will not take it," she says, trying to conceal the hurt in her voice. "Not in a million years. I will save and buy something later. I don't want your money. I told you so years ago. I want to have nothing to do with your money."

Victor signs the check and slides it across the table. She doesn't touch it, but she can't help looking. He made it out for thirty thousand dollars. Bloody generous. Or rather, bloody arrogant motherfucking showoff!

"I won't take it, Victor."

"Please take it, Maria. I want you to have it."

"No."

She slides the check back across the table. It physically hurts to push it away, all that money, all her dreams. But her pride will not let her take it. Especially after that distasteful joke.

He sighs.

"Well, if you wanted our financial affairs to be so separate, you should have divorced me years ago, princess."

She takes another sip of water. The sting in her bladder cuts like a knife.

"Don't be so stubborn. Take the money. Get yourself the apartment. I know you want it."

She looks at him defiantly.

"I already say I not want it," she says. "You think you are so good? You come in here, shove your money in my face? What you are trying to show Victor? That you are a good man, that you do the right thing? What you are trying to buy with your money? A clear conscience? You want to go home and know you did the right thing?"

She hopes he can see the hate in her eyes.

"Mark my words, Victor. You will never do right by me. Never."

He sighs, and reaches into his pocket, taking out his wallet again. He'll put the check back in, she knows it. It hurts to think of all that money, and how she could have used it. It will take her years to save up that much. She'll be an old lady before she moves to Manhattan. She can't watch him put that check back in his wallet. She has to look away.

"I'm not trying to," he finally says. "And for the record, sugar ray, you will never do right by me either."

He stands up to go, and reaches for his cigarettes.

He's holding a fifty-dollar bill.

"Stop being such a self-righteous cunt. Take the money." He places the fifty on top of the check and slides it across the table to her. "And get yourself a fucking cab back to Queens!"

He pushes his chair back and walks off. She sees him light a cigarette outside. A few steps, and his tall dark silhouette is gone. She's left with a feeling of emptiness and shame, just like the old days. That, and a check for thirty thousand dollars she knows she should rip up.

But not right now.

First, she'll wait for her knees to stop trembling, then she'll get up and use the ladies' room. She needs to pee like there is no tomorrow.

"More water, miss?" the waiter asks, holding out the carafe.

{12}

New Beginnings

September announces itself as a happy month. Or at least, I try to see it that way. There are a few things to look forward to: Rachelle called out of the blue wanting to have lunch, Greg's taking me out tonight, and, most importantly, I'm getting paid today! I'm hoping my check will be enough to cover the minimum payment on my credit card, and allow me to give Gretchen a few hundred dollars.

At *Bella*, Francesca is waiting for me with a cappuccino, and congratulates me for selling a record number of bags and accessories last month. "You outdid yourself, *carina*! The slowest month of the year, and here you go, selling, selling, selling!"

I wonder what my commission will be. I want to ask, but I'm afraid to. Then I burn my tongue on my coffee, and take that as a sign that it's better to shut up.

My tongue is still sore when I head out to lunch. I'm almost late, and Rachelle hates lateness. Still, I stop by an ATM, just to withdraw a twenty. I look at the receipt. I don't want to believe this. But there it is, black on white: Minus the twenty dollars I've just withdrawn, my account contains one thousand thirty two dollars, and seventy eight cents. *O mie treizeci şi doi de dolari şi şaptezeci si opt de cenţi.* The stupid cappuccino was a consolation prize.

I'm terrifyingly poor, and I'm late for lunch with Rachelle. We're meeting at an *Au Bon Pain* across the street from her work. Rachelle hates waiting for people, and her lunch breaks are short. But as I come galloping along, I see her smiling, pleased to see me.

I hug her with enthusiasm, and shriek with joy, a childish habit I cannot outgrow. Rachelle shushes me, embarrassed. We stand in line to order. I love the sandwiches here, especially one with roasted red peppers and crusty bread with rosemary in it. *Rozmarin.* I also love the chocolate croissants and the delicious French roast coffee. My stomach hurts. I'm dying for a sandwich. I covetously eye what others are buying. How I wish I could bite into a crunchy baguette! But there's nothing I can afford today. Although this is an inexpensive place, which is why Rachelle and I keep coming here, today everything seems out of my price range. Even the bagels are two dollars, something I cannot bring myself to pay. I'm tired of bagels anyway. When my turn comes to order, I stammer:

"I think I'll just have a glass of tap water, with ice in it. I burned my tongue on this coffee this morning, and, well, I can't eat."

Rachelle gives me a strange look, and proceeds to order a chicken sandwich and a cup of soup for herself.

As we sit down, I try not to look at her sandwich, try to ignore the steam rising from the broccoli and cheddar soup. I have a killer craving for a piece of juicy chicken breast on a baguette with just a tad of garlic mayo. I pretend to enjoy my water, and pray that my empty stomach will not make any growling noises.

Rachelle takes a few bites of her sandwich, a few spoons of her soup, then pushes her tray torturously close to my side of the table, straightens her back, and gets right down to business.

"Look, L," she says. "I have to go back to the office soon, so I'll just have to come out and tell you, with no embellishments, why I'm here. I have not had much time, with my work schedule, and though I've interviewed a few people, I have not found anybody I trust. So if you'll still consider it, I'll take you on as a roommate."

I open my mouth, but she holds up her hand. She's not done yet.

"Now, don't flatter yourself, child. This is not out of friendship, and I sure have limited trust in you, but you seem to be the best out of a bunch of screw-ups who want that room. I'm not sure you'll work out, since, honestly you don't seem to have your life together, but I do want to take my courses, I do want to feed my child, and I do want to not live in squalor." She pauses to take a sip of her diet soda, and something about her demeanor tells me that it's not wise to interject anything just yet.

"I want you to know, you'd be on probation," Rachelle says, giving me a look that intimidates me more than I care to admit. "You mess up on paying the rent, the bills, or you engage in any funny business in my house, and I'll kick your white ass as far as New Jersey. I want us to be clear on that before you even consider it."

I nod.

"And there would be a lease. I've drafted it and had a lawyer friend look it over. I want you to know this would be legally binding."

"How much is the rent?" I ask.

"Five hundred dollars."

"That's it?"

"It's for the one bedroom only. I have the master bedroom, and Jurron has a room for himself, although he mostly sleeps with me. You'd just have the one small room, the one Rhonda stayed in. You have use of the kitchen, and of the bathroom. But you sure would not be welcome to lounge around my living room and watch my TV unless you a) pay half the cable bill or b) get invited by me. Anyway, five hundred is a third of the rent. That's to make clear, you'd only be renting the one room."

In spite of all the restrictions, this sounds like my one chance for freedom.

"That is awesome, Rachelle, I…"

Rachelle holds up her hand again.

"Girl child you sure have lots to learn about life! Look at you getting all excited. Now you need to sleep on it, so don't answer me right away. I made a copy of the lease for you to look at. It explains the utilities and all. And there's also a list of all the rules for the apartment. Like cleaning, and all that."

Rachelle takes a folder out of her tote bag, and hands it to me.

"Would I get a key?" I ask.

Rachelle gives me a puzzled look. "Of course you'd get a key! How would I ever rent you a place without giving you a key to it? Now I gotta run back to work, but you think this over and call me. But don't take longer than two days, please. If you're not interested, then I've gotta drop out of my classes and I better do so while I can get a refund. I would of course prorate September's rent until you can move in. But if you want in, you better chop chop. I can't afford to wait too long."

I watch Rachelle disappear into the sliding glass door of the building across the street. I wait a few moments to make sure she's truly gone, then reach over and devour the leftover sandwich and cold broccoli soup. *Supă rece.*

I call Rachelle later that night. The next day we meet at a deli. Over toasted bagels with lots of cream cheese, I hand her the signed lease, and a check. A little thrown by my plan to move in that very night, Rachelle gives me the key, saying: "You better guard this with your life, white child! I hope you read what the lease says about replacing those locks!"

I swallow a chunk of bagel that goes down my throat like a brick. They're about as satisfying as eating concrete. I really wish Rachelle would lose the commanding tone. Even my offer to pay for lunch was met with a snort: "Really child, what are you gonna go and do that for? Just pay for your own food!"

I sneak out of Gretchen's apartment at night, like a thief. All I'm taking is an oversize garbage bag (*un sac de gunoi*) full of my own crummy clothes and less than glamorous shoes. I say goodbye to a closet full of Gretchen's couture. I paid dear money to have everything dry cleaned. I've left the dresses in the plastic bags from the cleaners, and I've arranged all of her shoes in a neat row at the bottom. On my way out of the apartment I leave my key on the kitchen counter.

I take the subway to Roosevelt Island, dragging my garbage bag full of clothes up and down several filthy flights of stairs, getting lost, then running to catch the train. Once in the empty cart, I hug my possessions to my chest. I forgot to worry about thieves and rapists, and now here I am, alone, at night, on the New York City subway. When I finally get to my new apartment I'm sweaty and completely exhausted.

I unlock the front door as quietly as possible, knowing that Rachelle and the baby are asleep. I walk to my room slowly through the darkness, hoping the garbage bag will not make too much noise. I fumble with the light switch. I'm greeted by nothing but darkness. I place my bag down and sink to the floor next to it.

As my eyes adjust to the darkness, I realize that my room is empty. I raise the blinds, and see the East River, glowing red from the city lights, like a big stream of dirty blood. Somewhere out in the night, there are sounds of ambulances, cars, helicopters, people... *Salvări, maşini, elicoptere, oameni...*

{13}

Labor Day

(*Ziua Muncii?*)

I'm standing outside my new building, waiting for *Tati* and Momo to pick me up. Luckily they are running late, so I don't run the risk of them wanting to go upstairs and visit my new apartment. I don't want them to see my empty room. The first night I slept on the floor, my head on a rolled-up sweater wrapped in a T-shirt. I used another T-shirt as a towel the next morning. When I got out of the shower, Rachelle was in the kitchen, making breakfast for Jurron.

She looked at me and shook her head.

"Now please tell me, honey child, that you do have some furniture somewhere that you're planning on bringing into that room! Do you?"

I said yes, but it sounded unconvincing.

"I did not mean to look in there. That room is your own business. But you did leave the door wide open!"

Rachelle motioned for me to help myself to toast and coffee.

"Got any milk?" I asked happily.

"No child, I got creamer. And I know you don't like it, Miss Priss. But guess what? If you want milk in this house, you gotta buy it yourself. And today is an exception, because I see you've got nothing, and no clue about anything either, but if you want coffee, you gotta brew it yourself. And you gotta brew it using your own darn coffee and something called a 'filter'. And that, white child, you also have to buy. And if you want toast you buy bread… and butter, and jelly, or whatever the h-e-l-l you want on it! That's just how things work in this house!"

Rachelle handed Jurron a plate of cereal he started eating with his hands.

"And if you want to not sleep on the floor, princess, well then you need to buy yourself a bed. And if you want to not sleep on a bare mattress, well then you buy yourself sheets. And those, child, you wash, and dry, at the laundry on the third floor, using laundry detergent, and quarters. Because, guess what, honey child, your mama's not around to wash them for you! Oh, Lord, what have I done? What have I done asking this white child to move in! I bet her mama fed and diapered her until she was old enough to vote, don't you think so, Jurron?"

I realized I'd never hear the end of the furniture and sheet rant. I could have kicked myself for not asking ahead of time, for not knowing that somehow, these things would not be provided. But later Rachelle asked me into her bedroom, where she dumped some flannel sheets, a blanket, a towel, and a pillow into my arms.

"I want to make it clear that this is the first and last time you use my stuff. And I want to make it clear I don't have to lend it to you. I'm doing you any favors. As soon as you get your own stuff, and that better be soon, baby girl, you will return these to me. And they will be washed, folded, and smelling of fabric softener and dryer sheets, if you know what's good for you!"

The sheets feel nicer than the bare carpet, but after almost a week of sleeping on the floor, my body is sore in all sorts of places. I tried to make the pain go away by running this morning, on the island, and stretching afterwards. It was to little effect, and when Momo jumps out of the car to hug me, I have to fight the urge to flinch from a sharp pain in the neck.

Momo smells light and flowery, and seems to be in a good mood. She volunteers to let me ride shotgun, and moves to the back holding the bottles of wine and the bouquet of flowers we're bringing to the party.

It's a nice day outside, still warm but not too hot. The barbecue is a small event, just two other couples, a little older than *Tati*. The hostess, Mrs. Ionescu, shows Momo and me her garden. Mr. Ionescu is grilling the traditional *mici*, some sausage links, and pork chops. His wife made roasted red pepper salad, and *salata de boeuf*. The other couple brought tomato salad. Big chunky tomato slices mixed with onions, and good olive oil, sprinkled with coarse salt and fresh ground pepper. It's a simple pleasure, one of my favorite summer treats. Tomato salad. *Salată de roşii.*

"These organic tomatoes," one of the women says, "they taste just as good as tomatoes back home."

Funny how conversation always turns to food. Romanians can spend hours comparing a piece of cheese to other cheeses. A lively discussion starts, whose main purpose is to assess the tomatoes in terms of size, color, texture, aroma, and sweetness, and ultimately decide if they measure up to the golden standard of tomatoes in Romania.

I happily spoon a large heap of *salata de boeuf* onto my plate. I like the way Mrs. Ionescu makes it. Though it is not as good as *Mami*'s. *Mami* firmly believes that a good *salata de boeuf* starts with a small amount of homemade mayo mixed with tangy mustard. She's also partial to using chicken, rather than beef, and roast chicken rather than boiled one. She uses baked potatoes, and she never ever adds peas, which to her are a filler. Of course, the other essential thing, are the pickles. *Castraveţii.* They have to be salty and crunchy, squeezed well, and cut just the right size.

Mami's *salata be boeuf* is so good it deserves international awards. But that doesn't prevent me from enjoying Mrs. Ionescu's, in spite of the store bought mayo and the filler peas. At least, Mrs. Ionescu is extra generous with the pickles.

I have to agree with *Mami*, though, that some people's *salata de boeuf* can be gross. Still, I always try at least a small scoop at each party. I've probably sampled a dozen varieties, produced by a dozen different Romanian women. I could establish my own Zagat rating for *salata de boeuf*, and just about all the dishes omnipresent at Romanian gatherings. The thought would probably make *Mami* have a heart attack, *Mami* who always tells me to be careful in my food choices at parties, because some people are bad cooks, and one can get sick. I wonder if the way she feels about the cooks shapes her opinion on their food. But since she's never present at parties in 'the community,' I take license to enjoy whatever I want.

This feast is a welcome change from my daily bagels.

The conversation is now carried out exclusively in Romanian, an indication that the elderly couples are really getting into it.

"My mother, may God rest her," Mrs. Ionescu sighs, "she always bought her produce from the same woman at the market. She used to get these tomatoes, they were fleshy and juicy all at the same time. They were so good, you could eat them like apples. And in the summer, that's what we ate for dinner when it was very hot, just tomatoes plain and simple, with cheese."

Maybe others would find this gathering boring, but to me it's heaven to sit here, indulging in pure gluttony, and listening to old people reminisce about the produce of their youth in a faraway country I myself have such fond memories of. So what if they're crazy to talk about tomatoes for so long? So what if I've heard them say the exact same things so many times before? It's soothing, like an old familiar song. And they are all sweet and kind people. Especially the hosts!

They keep filling my plate, smiling affectionately. "My sweet little girl," Mrs. Ionescu coos, offering me another pork loin. "So skinny! You need to put some meat on those bones!"

They tend to treat me like a child. I don't mind. Though I'm not sure how I'll manage to eat yet another pork loin after stuffing myself with *salata de boeuf*, eggplant spread, roasted peppers, and the much discussed tomatoes.

Hours later, I'm full to the point of bursting, and I'm starting to get bored. Romanian parties last forever. Mrs. Ionescu asks if we want coffee. And by the way, coffee is not an indication of the end, just a break in the feast, which could go on for hours. I'd love a cup, especially since Mrs. Ionescu offers Turkish coffee, *cafea turcească*, one of my favorite things in the whole wide world.

"And if you want, I tell your fortune," the other old lady says, with a wink.

The women go inside to help prepare the coffee and bring out the cake. I offer to help too, but Mrs. Ionescu protests: "No, no, you stay with daddy."

The two older men are still busy grilling.

Tati and I sit quietly for a moment. I'm playing with my napkin, wondering if maybe, after coffee and cake I can squeeze in another *mic*.

"Have you spoken to your mother recently?" *Tati* asks out of the blue.

"Yes, last week." I realize I should call *Mami* and tell her I moved.

"And?" *Tati* asks.

I shrug.

"She's fine."

"Nothing new?"

What new thing does he expect? *Mami* is always the same. And as far as I can tell, she's fine, I mean, as fine as *Mami* can be.

"You sure?"

I give him a puzzled look. Is something going on with *Mami*, that I don't know about?

"Do me a favor, Lili. I know you're busy, but please take the time this week, and call your mother. Ask her how she's doing. And then call me and let me know."

He takes a few drags from his cigarette. He's quiet now. I wonder what is going on.

"But please, don't tell her I asked."

The women come back with little cups of foaming, fragrant Turkish coffee. They also serve a chocolate and vanilla coffee cake, something people simply call *chec.* It's good, but *Mami*'s is much better. *Mami*'s is fragrant with vanilla, and the upper crust has a moist crunchiness to it that only *Mami* can create. I suddenly miss her, and I feel sad and guilty. I forgot to call her. I haven't visited since I left, and here I am, having a good time with *Tati,* his girlfriend, and a bunch of people who probably hate *Mami,* who have probably been mean to her at some point. Though, honestly, I can't imagine Mrs. Ionescu ever being mean to anyone. I feel tears coming to my eyes. It's probably time to stop drinking.

Luckily, the caffeine gives my morale a little boost. And the fortune reading is delightful. The old woman examines my cup, then smiles, and declares with enthusiasm that she sees a ring. *Un inel.* Mrs. Ionescu grabs the cup, to look at it herself.

"Yes, yes. I see it too. There's clearly ring in here! Watch out Victor, there's ring in her cup! Your little girl is getting married!"

Everybody laughs, and *Tati* pretends to be upset. He finally looks into the cup himself.

"It's just a bubble," he says.

The women laugh, and ask if I have a boyfriend. To old Romanian women there's nothing more important in life than marriage. Except, possibly babies. I feel sorry for Momo. After all, for her, both marriage and children are out of the question. But Momo smiles, just like the others.

"Oh, come on! Tell us!" Mrs. Ionescu urges.

"You must have boyfriend, Liliana!" the other old woman says. "How can pretty girl like you not have boyfriend?"

"Leave her alone!" Mr. Ionescu protests, but it's all in vain. The women keep asking and prodding, their eyes full of expectation. They look so well-intentioned, and so eager. I hate to let them down.

"What about this nice young man you've been going out with, L?" Momo asks. "He seems promising, doesn't he?"

I'm relieved that *Tati* has followed Mr. Ionescu into the house for an after dinner brandy. I don't want to discuss my love life in front of him. Mrs. Ionescu seems to read my thoughts:

"Come on, your daddy can't hear you! Tell us all about him! Who is this guy? Where you meet?"

I can feel myself blushing. How could I have forgotten Greg? He's not someone I like, but at least he's worth mentioning, isn't he? After all, he did bring me flowers.

The ladies' eyes light up with hope and joy, as I start telling the story of Greg, with a few embellishments. Mostly, I exaggerate how much I like him. I do it to please the old ladies. What's the harm in that?

{14}

Social Call

After Labor Day, I feel compelled to call *Mami*. Or rather, I am shamed into calling her. Especially after *Tati* asks me to lunch so he can give me a present of sorts: a new cellphone. He is gracious enough not to mention the money he gave me to buy a new one, the money I spent on a purse. I swallow my guilt, and give in to a blissful feeling of relief. The phone situation has been unbearable lately, what with Rachelle not having a house phone, and Francesca frowning each time I make a call from *Bella*.

Tati programmed his own numbers, as well as *Mami*'s, into the phone. "You really should call your mother," he says.

He seems concerned, and I begin to worry. Is there something wrong with *Mami,* that I am not aware of? I cannot bare the thought of her being sick, or of something bad happening to her.

But when I finally make the call, waiting with trembling hands and a lump in my stomach to hear some dreadful news, *Mami* sounds just as usual: over the top excited to hear me. She doesn't have any news to share, and wants mostly to know about me. It takes considerable effort to get her to talk about herself, and when she does, it's nothing out of the ordinary. Work is tiring, but overall ok. She's reading a new book she really likes, and which she highly recommends. That's about it.

I stall, making her talk about the book. When it becomes unavoidable, I give her my news. I'm afraid she'll be worried, or that she'll even disapprove. But my announcement is greeted with enthusiasm.

"I really want to see new place, my sweetie. I want to meet new roommate!" There's no way to talk her out of it. I should have seen this coming! After all, *Mami* also insisted on visiting Gretchen's before I moved in. Of course, back then I posed no resistance because I knew she'd love it, and *Mami* did. Actually, if anything, *Mami* liked it too much, and was too exuberant in showing her excitement, like a child in a candy store, clapping her hands and marveling over all the wonderful features of Gretchen's apartment. It was embarrassing and sad.

But her seeing Rachelle's place, and my unfurnished room, is unthinkable. She'll probably faint if she sees I sleep on the floor. I've no choice but to buy a cheap futon mattress and have it delivered. This drives me to the full exhaustion of my credit line, a tragedy with ramifications I try not to think of. I regret every useless purchase I ever made, every single penny I have lost access to. I even regret buying *mon parfum secret*.

Some of my last cash goes towards sheets in a pleasant shade of lavender, a cheap lamp, towel, pillow, and some hangers. I arrange my clothes and shoes inside the closet, and make my makeshift bed as neatly as I can. I air out the room, and drag around Rachelle's oversized vacuum cleaner (*aspirator*). I wish I had enough money to buy flowers. But I can hardly afford to eat, let alone beautify my space.

Rachelle laughs when I ask if it's ok to have a guest.

"Did you actually read those rules I wrote out for you, child? Of course you can have guests, as long as they stay in your room and are quiet. And as long as you don't smoke anything, and that includes cigarettes."

Then her curiosity takes over:

"So who is this guest, anyway? Is it that guy Greg you've been seeing?"

I frown. The thought of Greg visiting is not an attractive prospect. And what's up with all these otherwise sensible women getting so dreamy eyed when asking about him?

"It's my mother," I say, embarrassed.

Rachelle cracks up.

"The white child's mama! Now that's a woman I'd like to meet! I better make sure I'm home when she's coming!"

Much to my dread, she makes good on her promise. She is indeed home the day of *Mami*'s visit. It's Sunday, my least favorite day of the week. Though I miss *Mami*, I'm dreading her arrival. On top of everything else, I have to worry about how she and Rachelle will react to each other. Rachelle will probably think Mami is weird. And I've no clue what Mami will think when she enters the living room to find a woman holding a baby. *Un bebeluş*.

Still, I'm more worried about Rachelle's impression of *Mami*. Rachelle can be difficult and harsh. And *Mami*, in spite of her beauty, has never won a popularity contest. I should be used to it by now, but it still hurts. As lovely as my mother is, as beautiful and sweet, people tend to be hostile towards her. For as long as I can remember, I've wanted to protect her, but never knew how.

I worry all morning. Then *Mami* finally arrives, and her smile fills the room. She looks older and tired, but she's still beautiful, and extremely happy to see me. I'm embarrassed that Rachelle gets to witness her display of affection. I'm also embarrassed that *Mami* came laden with packages. Why on earth did she have to drag the whole house with her? Why do Romanians always have to carry around so much stuff? My irritation melts slightly when I notice the baby blue fluffiness of one of her favorite towels peeking from one of the bags. She brought me good towels! How did she know? I cannot help myself, I jump for joy and hug her.

But my excitement wanes at the sight of *Mami*'s worn sneakers peaking out of her tote. What's the point of her dressing nice and wearing one of her best pairs of shoes, if she comes in here looking like a bag lady with all those packages, and if she carries her stupid sneakers in plain sight for Rachelle to see? Then it occurs to me that my roommate too, carries her shoes in a bag on her daily commute. So hopefully she'll understand!

I hold my breath as *Mami* looks around the room, taking in the clean but modest furnishings. Her eyes rest on the living room window, and light up when they see the East River.

"Nice view."

"So you are roommate?" *Mami* smiles, extending her hand to Rachelle a little too enthusiastically.

"Yes. I'm Rachelle."

"I'm Maria," *Mami* says in her heavily accented English. "I brought you cake." She hands Rachelle the flowers and a little brown bag. Graciously, Rachelle offers to relieve her of her packages (*pachete*). She opens the brown bag, and much to my delight, takes out a tiny rectangular cake, carefully wrapped in plastic.

"I made myself." *Mami* says still smiling a little too widely. That smile works miracles in retail, but in the real world it seems a bit forced. *Forţat.*

I take the cake and flowers, and go off in search of a vase. The cake smells of vanilla and cocoa. It's exactly the type of cake I've been craving since the Labor Day party. As if *Mami* somehow read my mind.

"And who you are?" I hear *Mami* ask. I hear the baby laugh. I start to relax. Maybe I worried too much. This doesn't seem to be going that bad. I take pleasure arranging the flowers in an empty pasta jar (*borcan*). Little yellow mums. *Zambile?*

"I once had Black friend too," I hear *Mami* say. Oh shit! Only *Mami* can say something so inappropriate! As if she came from a different planet! *Altă planetă.*

"Yes," *Mami* carries on, oblivious to the fact that she just set herself up for one of Rachelle's tirades about race. I wonder what she's gonna add now, to make matters worse. "She was my first friend in United States. I watch her kids for her."

"You watched her kids?" Rachelle retorts. The hostility in her voice is obvious. I wish I could think of a good way to extract *Mami* from this conversation.

"Oh, yes," *Mami* continues, unaware that she's treading on thin ice. "I watch her kids. It was my first job in United States. I was like baby-sitter, during the day, when she was working."

I run the water on high so that the noise will prevent me from listening further. I remember *Mami*'s friend, Josephine, and her two children. Alex and I used to go to her place after school. I remember sitting on a nice couch, watching TV, lots of TV.

When I finally dare abandon the kitchen, I'm bracing myself for an uncomfortable situation. To my surprise, *Mami* and Rachelle are sitting next to each other, seeming to have a pleasant conversation. How on earth did this happen?

As I place the flowers on the coffee table, Rachelle turns to me and says:

"L, honey child, why don't you cut up that nice cake and put on some tea? Your mother is going to think we don't know how to treat a guest."

As I serve tea and cake, I realize my mother is having a good time. She and Rachelle are talking about food, *Mami*'s favorite topic besides books. She is instructing Rachelle on how to make the perfect apple pie. *Plăcintă cu mere.*

"I make very easy crust with butter and sour cream. Equal measures. Is easy to make, and I usually make twice that I need. It freeze nicely, wrapped in paper from butter."

She seems utterly satisfied with herself, and Rachelle follows her every word as if she were saying something truly important. Of course, knowing *Mami* she will not stray too much off the safe topic of food, although to tell the truth, her reminiscing to Rachelle about Josephine was surprisingly forthcoming.

It takes me a while to figure out what made them bond so fast.

"You have to learn to cook tasty and nutritious meals cheaply when you are mother like us," *Mami* says. "In this city are children who starve."

Rachelle nods her head emphatically.

"And other children who get way too fat." *Mami* sighs. "Mothers like you and me are in very special category, very difficult to manage, because our children are in danger of both. You'd think is spoiled rich kids who get fat. But really, I look around and I been thinking of it for years. Is poor children, who eat crap who are most in danger. Most of cheap foods have little nutrition and lot of crap. Fatty meats, processed carbs, corn syrup, nitrate, MGS, and all junk. Is hard to come up with balanced meal, all the vegetables, all the vitamins, on a budget."

Rachelle nods. It suddenly occurs to me that she is just as obsessed with Jurron's proper nourishment as *Mami* was with ours. No wonder they get along! Listening to them, I feel ashamed and guilty, thinking of my own eating habits, the gallons of fatty cream cheese, and the dozens of bagels I've been subsisting on.

To my horror, Rachelle seems to be thinking of exactly the same thing.

"So how come you never thought L how to cook?" I find this an inappropriate question, asked in a rude tone of voice. But *Mami* laughs.

"L never show much interest. And I figure, let her study. After all, college degree is hard to get. Cooking is easy. And L likes food. So I thought, well, if she'll be hungry, she'll figure it out. And if she can't, she can always come back and ask me to teach her."

Mami takes another sip of tea from her little cup. *Ceșcuță*. I guess I should have asked her to teach me. Not just to cook, but to magically transform a few measly dollars into proper meals.

"Much more important get college degree, don't you think?"

I only wish college had taught me how to avoid subsisting on bagels.

After cake and tea, I show *Mami* my room. Her face stays bright and hopeful as she surveys the emptiness. If she's horrified, or at least disappointed, she doesn't let it show.

"So clean, my sweetie. Very nice."

She touches the sheets, rubbing the fabric between her fingers.

"This cotton?" she asks.

I nod, and *Mami* declares herself satisfied. "Nice color. You know, I brought you more sheet and towel. I show you." Then *Mami* starts unpacking all the wonders she brought from home. They smell like her closet: a mix of soap, loving care, and lavender satchels. *Lavandă.* I suddenly miss home.

Dogs with Bagels

{15}

Long Lost Friends

Maria changes into sneakers in the elevator. She's going to walk back to Queens across the pedestrian bridge, then get on the subway once she's had enough exercise. Walking through the projects doesn't faze her. It's a nice, sunny day, and she's in a decent mood, although the visit to her daughter made her nostalgic.

She feels silly having mentioned Josephine, her Haitian friend, to Rachelle. After all, other than skin color, the girl has nothing in common with her former friend.

Maria met Josephine in her aimless days of wandering through supermarket aisles, trying to avoid being home with Victor, and trying in vain to prove to herself that shopping and cooking were as useful to her family as taking on that stupid job at the bakery would have been. Her self-esteem was so low, she would not speak a word to anybody. Most cashiers knew her by now, and scanned her food without asking questions.

But every now and then there'd be a new person behind the register, one unfamiliar with Maria and her ignorance of the English language. How she hated the attention such situations brought her! If the cashiers asked her a question, they usually spoke way too fast. She'd try to convey this in her broken English, or she'd try in vain to communicate through gestures. The salesperson would generally repeat the same question, louder and louder, as if Maria were deaf, not foreign. By now, other customers would stare, and she'd be so embarrassed she'd just want to disappear. One time she actually ran out in tears, leaving her groceries on the counter, the labor of hours spent scanning labels, and comparing prices.

To survive these moments of humiliation, Maria created a persona. Whenever people kept addressing her louder and louder, whenever they displayed impatience with her lack of understanding, she would answer in French. This threw them off, and it made her feel better. It restored a little bit of her pride to remember, and let the world know, that, while in the English-speaking world she was a total idiot, she was fluent in French, a language these people did not have the vaguest notion of. Or so she thought.

One day, as the cashier kept asking louder and louder about her choice of paper versus plastic, and Maria replied, once more in French, a voice from behind her offered graciously:

"*Peut-etre je peux vous renseigner, Madame*?" Maybe I can help you?

She turned around, and, to her surprise, she saw a tall Black woman, in her early thirties, looking sharp in a well-tailored coat. This was Maria's first meeting with Josephine. It was also the first time she actually talked to a Black person. She felt curiosity mixed with awe. There were no Black people in her home country, and she had never met one before. She'd seen them, along with people of all ethnicities on the streets of New York, but she never had the chance to interact with them. The only people she had actually had any dialogue with in New York, were members of the Romanian community, a world she found more and more confining.

Stunned by the novelty of the situation, she accepted Josephine's invitation to coffee. It was the beginning of a friendship Maria would come to cherish.

Josephine was Haitian, and spoke fluent French in addition to English and Creole. She had two children, and was raising them alone, with occasional help from her sister. She took to Maria immediately. She was excited to meet someone with older children. The fact that they were neighbors facilitated the friendship.

Josephine worked all day, selling gloves, scarves, and wallets in a chic department store in Manhattan. But she was always happy if Maria came by, in the evening, for coffee or tea, and a chat, while Victor did the homework with Alex and Lili.

Maria's first trip by herself on the subway would be to visit her new friend at work. It was a terrifying trip, one she hesitated taking, but she was too embarrassed to admit to Josephine that in spite of her carefully written directions she was still afraid. She managed to not get lost, and finding the store was one of her early little victories over life in the new country. She felt excited and energized, having had a small adventure all by herself. She brought Josephine homemade chicken sandwiches, which they enjoyed on a bench in Central Park. It was the first time Maria saw actual beauty in New York, beauty she could relate to. Until then, the city had seemed hostile, dirty, and cruel. She never understood why the world celebrated it. But sitting in the park with Josephine, the buildings and trees looked beautiful, and for the first time in longer than she could remember, she was in awe of her surroundings.

Before Josephine she had been hopelessly lonely. Now she finally had someone who would listen to her complain about her new life, about her husband and her children, and about how useless she felt. Josephine tried to convince her, that even without a job, she was useful to her family.

"You watch the children. You shop. You cook. You keep the place clean. You do laundry. Why do you think these things are useless just because you don't actually get paid for them? Do you know how much one would have to pay to have somebody else do all that? How much would you have to pay for a cook? Or a cleaner? Or a baby sitter? Or to drop off the laundry somewhere?"

Maria did not confess that in Romania she had people who did just such things for her. She started feeling a little less useless. She began feeling unappreciated instead.

Josephine did not just try to boost her self-esteem. She actually helped her, by giving her her first job. It was a mutually advantageous situation. Josephine stopped taking her children to daycare, which was expensive, and Maria began spending her days at her neighbor's house, watching the children, whom she could thankfully communicate with in French. Josephine did not pay her much. In fact, she made less than minimum wage, something she did not question until much later. She made next to nothing, but it was still an amount she could shove proudly into Victor's face.

More important, still, she finally had a refuge. She'd spend hours on Josephine's comfortable couch, watching TV, while the children were coloring, or napping. Josephine had all the premium channels. Some days, Maria was too depressed to do anything other than lose herself in shows she did not really understand.

Josephine was a good friend in many ways. But like any friendship, theirs had its shortcomings. During their three years of knowing each other, Josephine would let Maria down on more than one occasion.

Josephine was the only person she told about her failed attempt at leaving Victor and the children. She didn't tell her before the fact, though she did let her know she had a problem and wouldn't be able to babysit anymore. When she returned, she did not explain, and Josephine did not ask. Things went back to normal. They were friends, and Maria continued to look after the kids. But after what she'd done, normalcy did not suit her. She needed to confess to someone. She hoped that if only she could bring herself to tell Josephine, and if Josephine would be even a little sympathetic, she'd begin to forgive herself.

It took her months to bring herself to tell her what really happened when she disappeared, to confess that she had actually run away, trying to leave her husband. As soon as she said it, Josephine grew animated.

"I knew it! I knew it!" she screamed. "I knew that creepy bastard hit you! I just knew it! Oh, Maria, I wish you'd told me sooner. You always acted so withdrawn..."

Maria tried to protest, tried to argue, to explain that Victor had never in his life hit her, that he would never do such a thing. Actually, if there was a perpetrator of violence in her household, it was her. But she could not bring herself to tell this to Josephine.

The more she protested, the more Josephine grew convinced that Victor beat her, and that Maria was too scared to tell anyone, too embarrassed to tell even her closest friend.

"I know women don't tell anyone. I know it. The girl across the hallway, that tiny little thing, her husband choked her and threw her down the stairs. Me and my sister heard her screaming, and he was cursing at her and threatening. But after the cops came, she said he didn't do it. She had blood running down her chin, and bruises on her face, and she still said he didn't do it. She said she fell!"

Maria did not want to continue the conversation. She couldn't stand the shame. That battered woman had stood by her husband, and she, Maria, whom Victor had never dared lay a finger on, had tried to abandon her husband and her children. She realized she could never tell Josephine the truth. She felt sorry that she had even tried, because now, she felt even more ashamed than before.

A few days later, Josephine gave her a pamphlet on a women's shelter. Maria didn't protest, thanked her, and put it in her pocket.

Later that night, locked in the bathroom, she read it. She tore it to pieces and threw it in the toilet. She wished she had never seen it. What those women had suffered disturbed her on so many levels. She wondered if she herself would have been able to survive.

She also felt a new wave of appreciation for her husband. After all, the issues she had with Victor were minor compared to what these other husbands had done to their wives. She felt heartsick at the thought that she had a good man, yet that she was not able to appreciate him. Years later she would marvel at her own stupidity in thinking those thoughts. If not beating her was her criterion for judging a good man, than she sure as hell had low standards.

In any case, her appreciation for Victor came at a time when their relationship was no longer salvageable. She'd felt it for a long time. But on a cloudy Sunday afternoon, she finally learned for sure. He was no longer hers.

They were at a party in the 'community.' On her way to the bathroom, she overheard two women gossiping.

"They sleep in separate beds, in separate rooms. He sleeps in the boy's room in a twin bed, and Lili sleeps with her in the bedroom. Lili told this to Dana. And don't you see how she acts? I'm telling you, they are done."

At the same party, she noticed a woman flirting openly with Victor. It wasn't unusual. Women always liked him. Maria never minded before. Before, it was harmless, a game, a joke, nothing for her to be concerned about. But that day it was different. She could feel it. The little hairs on her arms stood up at the sight of that woman sitting next to Victor. They were talking about something, and the woman was laughing and looking at him affectionately. She even reached over to straighten his hair, and picked up a little piece of meat from her plate, picked it up with her fingers, and fed it to him, directly into his mouth. In that small gesture, Maria knew. There wasn't just flirtation there. There was intimacy. Her husband, and that woman, they had slept together, or if not, they soon would. She felt like she'd been punched in the stomach. She had to summon all her self-control not to lunge over and grab the other woman by her hair.

That night, she told Victor:

"I will never go see those people again. None of them. You can go with your children if you wish. But I will never go there again."

She became more and more isolated. Her only friend was Josephine.

Which was why, when Josephine announced her departure, Maria was unable to conceal her disappointment. She didn't even manage to fake excitement when her friend described the better life she would have in Chicago.

"Please write!" Maria asked, in tears. Even as she said it, she knew letters would be little consolation. What she really wanted was for her friend, her only friend, not to leave her.

"Maria," Josephine insisted. "Get real. You know I'm not going to be your pen pal. This is life. People move, things change. I'll always think of you fondly, but I'll be in Chicago. I'm not going to pretend I'll send cards and make phone calls. I'll be busy with my new life, and you should be busy with yours. You should be making new friends, girl. You finally got yourself a real job!"

As part of her moving preparations, Josephine had pushed Maria to interview for her old job at the department store, arguing that by now her English was good enough. And it was. She got the job immediately, and was quite happy, proud, and thankful. But she did not want Josephine to go, and she could not conceal it.

Josephine got angry with her.

"You need to learn to let go, girl. There's too much nostalgia you're dragging around! If you want to make it in this world, you need to learn to let go of people and things of the past. Like that friend of yours who died, the old lady. How long are you going to cry over that one? She was old, she was sick, and now she's dead. That's life. You're a young woman, and really, if you had dropped dead one day, that old woman would not have cried half the tears you did. You need a thicker skin, girl. This life's not meant for the sentimental kind!"

Mrs. Stoica's passing had shaken Maria deeply. Her own grandmother's death the year before, had not affected her as much. Unable to be there, and not being confronted with the unequivocal presence of a dead body to bury, Maria had not been able to mourn. When Mrs. Stoica passed, however, it was as if the grief for the two deaths, combined, erupted inside her. She felt as deeply bereft as after leaving Romania. Once again, she thought she would never stop crying.

Mrs. Stoica was the only person in the community Maria felt close to. And although Mrs. Stoica herself chose to be isolated from her compatriots, she deeply disapproved of Maria's choice to do the same. The two women shared a dislike for having to adapt to a new country and a new environment. They shared nostalgia for the lives they left behind. But Maria had been wrong to assume that they also shared the same hostility towards the community. Mrs. Stoica didn't want to associate with people, mainly because a lot of them talked too much about new things she didn't understand, and this made her tired. She was old and had already learned enough about life. She was now due some rest. However, she thought Maria ought to make an effort to be friendly, and to fit in. She owed it to her children to get along with people. This is what Mrs. Stoica thought, and she never hesitated to say it.

Still, in spite of having to listen to such criticism, Maria liked visiting Mrs. Stoica. She took the children with her on weekends when Victor worked. He no longer was a night watchman, but drove a yellow cab. It was a better paying, but demanding job. Still, he seemed to like it. It gave him an opportunity to talk to all kinds of people. He'd always been a people's person, and Maria assumed, with envy, that his pleasant nature earned him extra tips.

She complained to Mrs. Stoica about Victor incessantly. Under Josephine's influence she had now taken to noticing how unappreciative he was, how he took everything for granted. She once told Mrs. Stoica that she hated him for always taking everything she gave, until she felt completely drained. She said she felt cheated because she put all of her efforts into pleasing him, yet he hardly ever did anything to please her. She was all consumed with taking care of him and the children. He too, was all consumed with taking care of exactly the same people. Nobody was there to mind her, and her needs.

Mrs. Stoica shook her head, and smiled:

"You know what my mother always said, may God rest her? The person eating seven breads is not stupid. The person giving it to them is."

Mrs. Stoica had an old saying to suit any situation. Maria remembered an afternoon when she was there with her children, and they got into an argument about Josephine. That was quite a bone of contention between them, as Mrs. Stoica never really understood her choice of socializing with, and working for, a person so utterly foreign.

"You turned down a job in a bakery, to go take care of that Black woman's children?"

Mrs. Stoica said "Black" with a mixture of fascination and fear. Maria understood that this was a woman who, until her mid seventies had never set eyes on a Black person. She remembered how she herself, had been shocked to see people of various races and ethnicities at the international airport in Frankfurt, and then later on the streets of New York. In communist Romania, everybody looked pretty much the same, and they all dressed in a similar fashion, the fashion she was accustomed to, and liked. In America she was confused to see people running around in low-rise jeans, in saris, and turbans, do-rags, dread-locks, mullets, yarmulkes. It made her feel even more foreign, like she was on a different planet, not just a different continent. So, yes, Maria could understand how a woman who had not experienced diversity until her mid seventies, would be fearful. But by now she herself knew enough about the world to identify her friend's attitude as racist.

"Black, white, what does it matter? She's my friend. She has done more for me than anybody else since I came here."

"That's because you won't let anybody help you, Maria. You are too proud to take your own people's help."

"I don't need their help."

"Of course you do. We all need each other's help. We are all in a new country, adjusting to new ways, making ends meet. It's not good to be so proud. You need to learn to accept help."

Maria sighed.

"I do accept help. I've already told you that Josephine has been helping me."

"So you'd rather accept that Black woman's help than your own people's?"

Maria sighed.

"My people's? What makes them my people? How are they really my people, more than any other person? If you speak about how we all came here, poor and clueless, and how we need to help each other, don't you realize, Mrs. Stoica, that we're all in the same boat? Black, white, Asian, Hispanic, mixed, Romanian, Puerto Rican, Chinese, Haitian? Who cares? People come here from all over the world. Why should it matter who helps whom? At the end of the day, aren't we all really the same in coming here and trying to make new lives for ourselves?"

Mrs. Stoica shook her head.

"People do come here from all over the world. So many people come here from so many places. They think in America, dogs run around with bagels on their tails. *În America umblă câinii cu covrigi in coadă.*"

Maria smiles. *Covrigi.* She remembers Alex, sitting by the window in Mrs. Stoica's kitchen, paging absentmindedly through a schoolbook.

He looked up.

"*Covrigi,*" he said. "*Mami, mami, vreau covrigi!*" I want bagels!

How old was he back then, ten maybe? It seems like ages ago. And it seems odd to think of him sounding so excited about something so trivial. When was the last time he said anything remotely nice to her? He grew up and stopped calling her *Mami.* He got into saying 'mom' instead, always irritated, always condescending.

She sighs. She's fed herself memories all the way home. How silly, and how utterly useless. It doesn't help to remember, and it doesn't help to dwell on the past. You're still here, still now, and it still is what it is.

She turns the key in the lock, walks in, and heads for the phone. She tried hooking up an ugly black contraption to it, an answering machine. She's hoping, still, to hear from her realtor. But the answering machine refuses to work with her old rotary phone. Besides, would the realtor even call on a Sunday? She heard that these people work day and night, that they are desperate to sell. But they probably only break their backs for people with real money.

She sits down on the bed, and looks at the useless machine. She did, finally, after sleepless nights, cash Victor's check. Her hand trembled when she signed her name across the back. She wonders if he had an endorsed copy returned to him.

Of course, by the time she brought herself to cash the check, the apartment she liked was gone.

"It's been sold two weeks ago," the realtor said. "Welcome to New York real estate, lady. You gotta move fast if you want something. A place like that isn't gonna stay on the market long, not at that price. Now, let's see… I could show you a bunch of other places, but don't expect them to be like the one you wanted."

The very next day, she took Maria to see five different apartments. They were all more expensive than the one she'd liked. And all were hopeless, hideous.

"I'm sorry, lady," the realtor said. "They don't sell mansions in your price range. I'll call you if anything better comes up."

Maria knows she shouldn't hold her breath. With a determined gesture, she unplugs the answering machine, folds its cord neatly, and puts it back into the ugly box it came in. She'll return it tomorrow.

{16}

Uneasy

I've been seeing Greg for about a month. I like his company at times. But I'm not sure I should continue. He obviously wants me, but for me, the attraction is just not there. I guess it's time to end things, but I don't want to hurt his feelings?

I share my misgivings with Rachelle. She raises her eyebrows.

"I can't tell you what to do, L, but it's about time you make up your mind. Either you take it to the next level, or you dump the poor guy. Otherwise you're just leading him on, and that's not fair."

I know. But how would I justify my decision? Telling him the truth would be beyond cruel: Sorry, Greg, you've been nothing but nice to me. But I am not attracted to you, and I can't sleep with you. Let's just be friends, ok?

As I keep turning things over in my head, I realize that Francesca is fixing me with a less than friendly gaze. For a few days now she's been rather cold. And she keeps criticizing my outfits.

"You used to dress nicer, *carina*. What is going on?"

I miss G's wardrobe. But oddly, I don't miss living in her lovely Upper East Side apartment. I'm more relaxed now. Life seems easier, less claustrophobic. I still get that panicky feeling every now and then, though, if something or another reminds me of Gretchen, and of my unpaid debt, or if Francesca frowns while looking at my shoes. In fact, Francesca is looking at my shoes just now, and I wish I could just sink into the ground.

In need of an escape, I grab my bag, and announce that I'm taking lunch early. Francesca frowns, and mutters something. But the hour is appropriate. Just to make sure, I look at the digital clock on the counter. That's when I realize it's September 11th. No wonder, I'm having such a crappy day.

While chewing a bagel I leaf through the newspaper somebody left on the table. It's full of 911 stories. It was three years ago, and I remember it like it was yesterday.

That morning I was in the apartment in Queens with *Mami*. She didn't have to be at work until later, and I only had an afternoon class. Alex left early in the morning, on the subway. He was still in high school back then.

Mami was in the bathroom, fixing her makeup. I was drinking a glass of orange juice and eating a bowl of cereal. That was before I started liking coffee. For some reason, I felt compelled to turn on the TV. At first I thought the news coverage was a segment from a science fiction movie. Once I realized the images were real, I ran to get *Mami*.

We watched together, hypnotized, as the second tower collapsed. *Mami*, on the verge of tears, and pressing a hand to her chest as if trying to keep her heart from jumping out, was the first to speak:

"Go call your brother's cell phone. Tell him come home right away. Then call your *Tati.* See if he's ok."

I went into the bedroom. With trembling fingers I dialed the two numbers, one by one, over and over, until I finally got through.

Mami stood in the doorway, holding my unfinished juice as if it were a holy relic, capable of protecting her from the horrors of the day. She stood there while I talked to Alex and *Tati*. When I finally put the receiver down, she was still standing there, with the juice.

"This old," she said. "I make fresh one."

Mami thinks juice loses its vitamins if you don't drink it right away. I couldn't believe she was thinking of that at a time like this.

Tati materialized at our apartment a few hours later, and to *Mami*'s relief, Alex was with him. They had met in Manhattan and walked across the bridge together. The subway was not running.

Mami made us all fresh juice, as if vitamins could keep us safe from terrorism.

I sat on the couch with *Tati* and Alex, watching our crappy prehistoric TV, regretting we didn't have cable, talking about what had happened, what was going to happen. *Tati* and Alex kept talking about how this would affect people's perception of immigrants, especially Muslims.

They watched the news and talked, while *Mami* busied herself in the kitchen. I don't know whether she wanted to avoid *Tati*, the news, or the facts of life. But *Mami* cooked all day. She made a vegetable stew. *Ghiveci*. More vitamins, I guess.

As Alex and *Tati* were deep into their political discussion, and *Mami* was busy chopping vegetables, I slipped into the bedroom and called the person everybody seemed to have forgotten about. Momo cried when she heard my voice.

Three years later, eating my cold bagel, I have a revelation. Nobody is better equipped than Momo to give me advice on my conundrum with Greg. I'll have to call her today, and if I'm lucky, she might even buy me dinner.

Walking back the few blocks to *Bella*, I'm in a better mood. But then I freeze dead in my tracks. The well-dressed young woman opening the door to the store is unmistakably Gretchen. My heart pounding, I duck into a telephone booth, where I wait the excruciatingly torturous minutes until she leaves the store.

By the time I venture back to work, I'm late. Francesca points at the clock on the wall, shaking her head and pursing her lips. She tells me in a displeased tone that my friend Gretchen just stopped by, and that Gretchen really needs me to call her.

"And frankly, I am sick of taking messages for you, *carina*. I don't know what kind of issue you have with this Gretchen person, but I really would appreciate it if you kept your personal life away from my store. This is a high end boutique, not a messaging service!"

I feel my world collapsing. I cannot take my life anymore, this dead-end job, Francesca's disapproval, the frightening thought that out there, in this city, Gretchen is looking for me, and that I owe her money. Feeling tears coming on, I excuse myself to go to the ladies' room, and call Momo on my cell phone.

Momo is having a hellish day. She says she'll probably have to stay at the office until nine. She has been working late all week, and is exhausted.

"Please, Momo,"I beg. "I know you're busy and tired, but I really really need to see you. I'm having such a horrible day."

Momo gives in. She's good like that. She always tries to be there when I need her. She's too tired to go out, though, so she asks me to stop by instead.

She's still wearing her business suit when I arrive. And she does look like she's had a stressful day. But she welcomes me with a big smile and a warm hug. She cuts up bread and cheese, then sets out a dish of garlic stuffed olives, some giant capers the likes of which I've never seen before, and two glasses of wine. Good Momo! She must have sensed I'd be hungry, and stopped by the store on her way home.

I devour the offerings like the hungry little animal I am. Momo puts on music, and retreats to the bathroom to remove her makeup. When she comes out, dressed in a white terrycloth robe, similar to the one she keeps at *Tati*'s, she reaches in the fridge for a paper bag containing cold cuts.

"I'm so tired, Lili, I don't even know where my head is!" she says, while extracting a large Versace platter from her cupboard, dusting it with the sleeve of her robe, and arranging slices of prosciutto on it. "I almost forgot what all I bought for us! But here' hon'. Here you go. This is pretty good stuff. Even Victor likes it!"

I grab a few slices of meat, while Momo lets herself sink onto her leather couch, and lights a cigarette.

"So what is going on, love?" she asks. "You didn't sound good on the phone earlier."

I try to finish chewing a mouthful of food.

"All kinds of crap, you know," I say, while fishing for another slice of cheese and a sun-dried tomato. They are delicious. Who needs to cook when they know a good deli, and can afford to shop there?

"Work and stuff."

"I thought you liked working at that store."

"I did, but… Well, it seems like I'm not doing that well and Francesca keeps bugging me. It's about stupid things, really, like I was late coming back from lunch today, and sometimes my outfits aren't cool enough, and well, maybe I've been making too many calls, I mean, it's nothing really serious, but if you put it all together…" I sigh. I don't want to tell it like it is, but lately I've been afraid of losing my job. "I don't know, it's just that... I feel like I'm in trouble at the store."

"How much trouble can you be in?" Momo asks, taking a puff of her cigarette. "I mean, it's a job selling bags. If you get fired, you get fired. It's not that big a deal."

Her comment annoys me, and I think it shows on my face, because she quickly corrects herself:

"Oh, sweetie. I'm just trying to help you gain some perspective. You're not planning on selling bags for the rest of your life, are you?"

"I guess not."

The topic of my future is something I consider best unaddressed.

"So it's just a temporary job. Something you do now, for a while, to pay your bills while figuring things out. If you get fired it's not a tragedy. You'll get another job."

"I guess," I sulk. This conversation is not helping. I need some serious comforting, not someone to feed me cold cuts and tell me it's ok if I lose my job.

Momo smiles.

"Oh, honey, come on! Don't be so down on life! You probably won't even lose your job! You're just having a bad workweek. That stupid cow who owns the store is probably having her period or something. Here, have another glass of wine, you'll feel better, I promise!"

"I hope you're right," I say, as I let her refill my glass. "Maybe it's just a bad workweek. But actually this is not what I need to talk to you about. I need to talk to you about this guy I'm seeing…"

"Greg." Momo smiles. After singing his praises at the Labor Day party, I don't know how to tell her the truth.

"Yes."

"Is he still being nice to you?"

"Yes, but…"

"But?"

I stare at the slices of meat and cheese on my plate.

"I don't know how to say this. I don't think I can sleep with him."

"Is he pressuring you?"

"No."

"Good." Momo lights another cigarette. She smokes too much, and I hate it.

"Do you want to sleep with him?"

I shrug.

"Do you like him?"

"Yes."

"But?"

"I don't know. I like him, but…"

"He doesn't really turn you on?"

"I guess not."

"Do you like the way he looks?"

"I guess."

"Do you have a picture of him?"

After two more glasses of wine, and a shared slice of cheesecake (*prăjitură cu brânză*), we google Greg on Momo's laptop.

"Oh, he's adorable," she pronounces. "So here is what I think. You're probably afraid because you haven't had much experience with men. Maybe you are just shy, or maybe a little repressed. He's a nice guy. He looks healthy. I think you should just go for it. But use protection, of course."

I roll into a ball on the couch. I'm a bit drunk.

"L, honey," Momo insists, "all you really need is more experience. Sometimes you can't even know if you like a guy before sleeping with him. And it certainly takes a while for a woman to be able to learn what she truly likes in bed. Look, you are young, you should live your life. It's always better to regret what you did, than what you didn't do."

I nod, though I'm not sure I agree.

It's interesting that the two women I admire most, *Mami* and Momo, are both very keen on me living my life. In very different ways, of course. I can't imagine *Mami* encouraging me to experience sex with various men. Still, as odd as it seems, Momo and *Mami* have something in common, a pushy enthusiasm for all sorts of new and exciting adventures they want me to embark on. I wonder what it is that makes them so eager to see me live life to the fullest.

Of course, *Mami* missed out on a lot of fun. But what exactly did Momo miss out on? Momo went to a good university, then got a good job as an accountant. She partied through the eighties and nineties, and had several lovers before meeting *Tati*. And now she's in a stable relationship with a man she adores.

"Sweetie, why are you afraid?" Momo asks.

I wonder if I really am afraid, or just uncomfortable.

"I'm not in love with him."

"Is he in love with you?"

"I'm not sure."

Momo lights another cigarette.

"Love is not all it's cracked up to be, you know. Love can actually mess up everything. It makes you lose your head, and do stupid things. Trust me, it makes the strongest women weak and needy. Do you remember how miserable you were when you broke up with your first boyfriend?"

I nod. I'll never forget that.

"It's better sometimes to just find someone you like being with. We all need companionship. And, even though you have not learned this yet, we all need sex. You'll understand someday. If you can find a good companion, that's usually the best you can hope for."

Momo takes a drag of her cigarette. She blows the smoke out pensively.

"This guy seems like a good guy. A nice person. He adopted a dog from the pound, what a sweetheart! And he's studious, and all around sweet. Maybe that's why you're not that hot for him. We usually fall for the bad guys, the hot bad guys, right?"

I laugh. Now, that is true.

"But the hot bad guys always break our hearts, love. Trust me on that. Maybe the key to happiness is to just find a nice, stable, guy, maybe not the hottest one out there, and just stick with him. And seriously, L, as jaded and crazy as New York is, a guy like that is almost impossible to find. You saw how men act out there, right? They all want to hook up with no strings attached. You told me that yourself!"

Unfortunately that is true. No hot guy in Manhattan wants a girlfriend. The atmosphere is too sexually charged and there are as many beautiful girls as there are trendy clubs and overpriced cocktails. Nobody wants to limit their options. They want to try everything the city has to offer, and the city never stops offering up new things. Fuck buddies and hot one-night-stands lurk around every corner. A nice boyfriend is harder to find than a cab during rush hour on a rainy day. So what am I doing throwing away a good man?

{17}

French Connection

At the end of the month, I get fired. Francesca says my wardrobe has gone from shabby to grungy, complains about my lack of punctuality, and about Gretchen calling the store incessantly.

"*Bella* is a high-end boutique, not an answering service!"

My financial situation is beyond bleak. After paying the rent and the minimum payment on my credit card, I'm looking at another month of eating bagels.

Depressed about my money troubles, I agree to a date with Greg, hoping he'll cheer me up. I end up getting drunk. Once the second bottle of wine is uncorked, I tell him about getting fired from *Bella*. I meant to keep it a secret from everyone, until I found a different job, but the wine loosens my inhibitions, and I end up confessing. Under the influence of alcohol, I cannot even remember why my financial troubles are normally so embarrassing to discuss. I even tell Greg I've been living on bagels. The only thing I keep to myself is my debt to Gretchen.

Greg listens, and seems not to judge. He says most young people struggle with money at some point, and he encourages me to apply for a better job than the one at *Bella*. According to him, it was a job with very lousy pay, and I'm better off without it. He thinks I should forget all about retail, and instead try for a secretarial position that requires language skills.

"You might not make a lot of money, definitely not as much as in some of the better-paid retail jobs, but you'll have something to put on your resume if later you want to shoot for a better job, or maybe apply to grad school. Nobody cares that you spoke Italian selling bags, but if you work in an office, you're likely to get more skills, and that type of experience looks good."

He sounds a bit like Momo, but for some reason I'm not irritated. In fact I feel lucky to have him advise me.

I decide to attack the job market with patience and determination. Greg says it might take longer to find a decent job as an administrative assistant, but I'm willing to put in the time and the effort. Greg helps edit my resume. He moves the languages section to the very front because it's my most marketable skill. Seeing my resume dressed up restores some of my hope. For two weeks, all I do is apply, wait, then apply again.

I'm nervous. I never understood much about the economy, but I know the Clinton years are gone. Now there's this awful war in Iraq going on, and overall, everybody is talking about things going poorly. I never paid attention before. I considered going to an anti-war protest once, but that had nothing to do with the economy. I just hated the idea of people dying, and of us taking over other countries, just because we can. The economy was the last thing on my mind. I thought I was immune to it. After all, I had no money, no stocks… Funny, I never realized just how vulnerable I was.

To survive without an income, I'm stricter than usual with my diet of bagels and coffee. Following Rachelle's advice, I start buying frozen bagels from the supermarket, and tubs of store brand cream cheese. I now eat all my meals at home. It reassures me that I can feed myself so inexpensively. But it's a minor consolation. Deep down inside, desperation is building up. What if I don't find a job? How long will I be able to buy bagels? How long will I be able to pay rent? At night, unable to sleep, I add up numbers in my head. My life is cheap these days, but no one lives for free. Especially in New York City.

Aside from bagels, my only expense is the paper I buy each morning. I read the ads carefully, circling the ones that even moderately match my skills. Each day, I arm myself with courage to make the calls. I'm probably over my minutes on my stupid cellphone. I don't want to imagine *Tati*'s face when he gets the bill.

In the afternoons I feel tired, discouraged. I sit on the couch like a bum, watching my new favorite show, Judge Judy. I've started to imagine myself on the show, a defendant in Judge Judy's courtroom, and Rachelle standing there accusatory, reciting a laundry list of reasons to evict me. Number one being, of course, inability to pay the rent. Because really, even while starving on two bagels a day, if I don't find a job, I won't be able to pay next month's rent. I'm probably looking at a future of homelessness. And Judge Judy.

But being sued by Rachelle is not even my worst nightmare. When I succumb to the darkest levels of depression, an even more terrifying fantasy plays out in my head. I'm once again the accused in Judge Judy's courtroom, but this time the person suing me is not Rachelle. It's Gretchen. Over and over again I imagine Judge Judy ordering me to pay Gretchen back, scolding me for leaving in the middle of the night, betraying a friendship, and not repaying kindness.

Things take a turn for the better once I start getting interviews. At least now I have a reason to get dressed in the morning, to comb my hair, apply makeup (not too much of it, and definitely no perfume – that's Rachelle's advice), then spend the day in limbo between various offices, dull and institutional as they are, where other young people in cheap suits wait clutching briefcases and manila envelopes, hoping to be selected for some crappy underpaid position. It's no walk in the park, but it sure beats spending the day on Rachelle's couch in my jammies.

Sometimes I make it home in time to catch the end of Judge Judy. It's lost part of its power to terrify me. In fact, one day, I even catch myself thinking, that it will be sad to have to miss it once I get a job.

Once I start believing in it, it happens. One day, my cellphone rings, and I'm told I got a position as a receptionist at a small finance firm whose main clients are French. *Français!* It's not the best paying job, but I did find it moderately interesting, and was able to show some genuine enthusiasm during the interview.

After hanging up and jumping up and down a few times (*Mais oui!*), I go out and buy a miniature bottle of French champagne, and a slice of pizza. I rent a French film to watch by myself on Rachelle's TV. It's a small private celebration. Of course I should celebrate again with Greg. I can't wait to tell him about the job! *Le boulot!* I'll buy him dinner this time. I owe him for all the times he's treated me, and I need to thank him for his advice.

Rachelle comes home while I'm still watching the movie. She sits on the couch next to me and gazes dreamily at the screen.

"You're so lucky to speak French, L. I wish I spoke another language."

In a good mood, and slightly tipsy from the bubbly, I offer to teach her.

"Are you serious?" Rachelle asks with her usual skepticism.

"Sure, Rachelle. It's the least I can do. You've been so good to me."

Rachelle sighs.

"Child, you really are clueless, aren't you? How exactly have I been that good to you?"

"Well, letting me live here and all."

"That's not me being good to you, child. You pay rent here, remember?"

On the screen, Paris in the rain (*la pluie*) looks mellow and romantic as ever.

"Now how much are you gonna charge for teaching me French, child?"

"I wouldn't charge you, Rachelle."

Rachelle sighs again, *exasperée.*

"I'm trying to teach you something, white child, and you won't listen. You don't go around offering people stuff like that for free. Because if you do, they will take it. And when they take it and they don't give you anything in return, well then you only have yourself to blame. I'll give you ten dollars an hour to teach me. We can do two hours every week to start, and if it goes well, we might go up to three."

I nod. I don't want to argue with Rachelle.

"Now, normally it would not be any of my business what you do with your money," she continues. "But since you were stupid enough to not even ask for it in the first place, I'll make it my business. You better save my money, honey child, and do something sensible with it. Don't let me catch on that you bought one more of those overpriced purses with it."

"What if I bought *you* a purse?" I volunteer. "For your birthday, you know?"

Rachelle has never acknowledged my Italian leather bag. I thought it went unnoticed until one night, when she couldn't find room for something in the freezer, and took it out on me:

"Do you think you could have any more cheap frozen bagels, child? Well, I sure am glad you're running all around town with a three hundred dollar bag! That sure is worth eating nothing but frozen bagels!"

I was shocked to see that Rachelle had not only noticed the bag, but that she knew exactly how expensive it was. I thought she was jealous, and wanted one herself. That's why I offered.

But Rachelle rolls her eyes:

"Well, if you buy me a bag, you're a fool, L. Because when your birthday comes around, you're still not getting more than a twenty dollar present out of me."

Luckily Rachelle's negativity can't bring me down. I know my life is about to drastically improve. A few days later, I invite Greg to lunch at a cheap little French place. My days of eating bagels are over. I order grilled chicken salad, and contemplate having chocolate mousse for dessert. I feel at peace and happy. It's a nice autumn day, and we got a good table by the window. But suddenly I almost choke. The woman walking by outside is Joan. And they say you never run into people in New York. I want to hide under the table. But you can't do that, just like that, while having lunch with your sort of boyfriend, can you? Luckily Joan is too immersed in a conversation on her cell-phone to see me. But the encounter reminds me that, even if things are looking up, my troubles are not over. I promise myself to start saving and pay Gretchen back. Suddenly, chocolate mousse for dessert is not such a good idea. Still don't I deserve a little treat for getting a new job?

More days pass, days of eating chicken sandwiches, clam chowder, and chocolate croissants (*pain au chocolat!*). I settle into a pleasant routine. Each morning I walk to the tramway enjoying a steaming cup of coffee, ride above the dark waters of the East River, prying into people's floor to ceiling windows as the tram comes to a halt, take a brisk walk to work, to spend pleasantly dull hours typing French words on the computer (*l' ordinateur*), with nothing but the occasional phone call to interrupt the sound of my keyboard (*tastature*). I hardly notice the imminent arrival of New York winter. Each day it gets dark earlier, and each day it gets colder. I'm comforted by my new routine. It has an aesthetic quality to it, just like the French words on the screen. Black and white. *Balnc et noir*. Symmetric. What more can a girl wish for, than editing French business letters? I feel like I'm working on a piece of abstract art.

I buy a new fall coat to match the French-ness of my job. I take to pairing it with cute scarves that I tie just so. Greg says I look pretty. He likes to meet me after work. Sometimes he brings his dog, and they walk me to the tram.

When he doesn't have to study we go out for dinner. Wey try out different restaurants, we talk and laugh, and sometimes I get a little buzzed. It's a pleasant life, safe and predictable. But invariably the night ends with an awkward good-bye on the tramway platform. I offer Greg my cheek. But his kisses linger, moving towards my lips. They are soft, gentle kisses, warm and tender, romantic, maybe, but not my cup of tea. They are not passionate kisses, not the kind that make my knees weak, not the kind that leave me dizzy, aching for more.

Riding the tramway home I stare into the dark water of the East River, feeling sad and guilty. What is wrong with me? Greg is a nice, sweet, gentle boyfriend. Why am I not happy to have him? Why am I not in love with him by now? Am I romantically challenged? Do I have issues with intimacy? Has growing up in a twisted household with parents who hated each other, who separated but never divorced, ruined my capacity for affection?

I share my frustration with Momo. Of course, I leave out the part about growing up witnessing my parents' fights. I'm closer to Momo than I am to *Mami*, but I would never betray my own mother.

"So you don't like the way he kisses." Momo's says. "That doesn't really matter, L. That says nothing about how he is in bed, or how suitable you are as a couple. Besides, you can train a guy to kiss the way you like. I would not worry too much about the kissing. Just take things to the next level, and see how *that* goes."

"Maybe I'm not in love with him," I whine.

"Love," Momo sighs. "L, honey, you don't even know anything abut love. You are addicted to what you think of as love, which really is just lust with a few bells and whistles. Infatuation. Nothing more. Infatuation goes away, L. Love is deeper. Trust me. You are still young enough where you can avoid this trap. Don't pick the passionate kind of love. Pick someone good and steady with whom you can build a real relationship. Someone who will really stand by you, who wants to marry and have children, and be there for you in the long run, not someone with whom you experience fireworks, but who can't offer you anything else."

"I'm only twenty-three, Momo. I'll probably meet other guys."

Though frankly I have my doubts. I've never really had much success with men.

"Oh honey, they are not that easy to find. Don't let this man go, L. You will regret it later. You're young, but it's not too early to start thinking of the future. Trust me, hon', if you want to get married and have children, the reliable guys are the ones to pick, not the exciting ones."

Odd advice, coming from Momo. I wonder if she has regrets. I know *Mami* does. I guess as the next generation, it is my job to do things differently. But differently how?

{18}

Thanksgiving

Despite leading separate lives and not liking each other's company, Victor and Maria spend all major holidays together, for the sake of their children. This includes Thanksgiving, although it's not a Romanian tradition, and not a holiday Maria particularly likes. She doesn't see why she has to roast a giant bird in order to celebrate the rape and murder of the Native Americans. But she cannot deny her children the holiday. So each year, she dutifully cooks turkey and sides, and joins Victor, Alex, and Lili in giving thanks for being healthy and together. Though really, they are not truly together, and their situation is nowhere near healthy.

Her recent efforts to spice up the holiday were met with disapproval. Last year she suggested to L that she'd make a turkey curry instead of the boring roasted bird. Her daughter looked at her as if she were insane, and Maria decided to take a more traditional route, by preparing a delicious fried chicken instead, with collard greens, candied yams, and corn bread. Victor loved it, and complimented her on the excellent meal. Alex pushed the food around on his plate.

"How exactly does this have anything to do with Thanksgiving, mom?"

She smiled encouragingly and pointed at the candied yams.

"There is sweet potato."

Alex rolled his eyes. But he had no problem helping himself to seconds and thirds.

This year, thank God, she will be spared the unpleasantness. Alex decided not to come home from school. He needs to study, or so he says. She suspects that he's actually partying, but she accepts his excuse without comment. Criticizing him would only make things worse.

Lili also has plans. She'll be spending Thanksgiving with her boyfriend's family. Maria was not even aware that her daughter had a boyfriend. She feels hurt that L doesn't share much about her life. And she hopes that this mysterious boyfriend is just a silly infatuation, nothing serious.

Of course, there's also Victor to take into account, but with the children unable to attend, the idea of him coming to Queens for Thanksgiving is absurd. Maria cannot imagine being more relieved. She has not talked to him since the day he gave her the check for her down payment. She really doesn't want to talk to him. Their last meeting was too unpleasant. Plus, she's embarrassed to have cashed the check she so firmly rejected. He'll probably gloat, discreetly, in his own way, and then he's bound to ask too, if she has found a place yet.

Unwilling to call him, she asks L to communicate to him that, since both children have other plans this year, there will be no Thanksgiving dinner at her house.

"What will you do, *Mami*?" L asks.

"Don't worry about me, my sweetie. I'll be fine."

"Will you go anywhere? Maybe you can go to a dinner somewhere else?"

Everybody seems to think that Maria should go somewhere. Her colleagues at work invite her over, and even insist, when she declines politely. Mada, her only friend, offers a selection of parties they could go to. Or should they take a small trip, a cheap little cruise or something? Maria laughs. To her knowledge, there are no cheap cruises, in fact there are no trips she can afford to go on, and she knows Mada has just as little money. For a second, she entertains the idea of blowing some of Victor's cash on an exotic trip. After all, it's been years since she's been anywhere remotely nice. She envisions her and Mada drinking mango margaritas on the beach and enjoying hot stone massages in a fancy spa. But no, she needs the money for her down payment, in case she ever finds a place.

Besides, she has no desire to go anywhere, margaritas and hot stone massages be damned. She doesn't want to be standing in long lines at the airport, with luggage, and irritated people. Just the thought of the crowds makes her cringe. Traveling must be hell these days, with the terrorist threats and people's hysteria. She'd rather just stay home. And she doesn't want to go to somebody else's party either, to eat their overcooked turkey and canned cranberry sauce, and force herself to be sociable. She'd rather spend a quiet evening with a book. She even signed up to work the Saturday after Thanksgiving.

But Mada won't take no for an answer. She gives up on the unfortunate idea of the cruise, but she can't accept that Maria will spend Thanksgiving alone, when there are so many nice dinners one could go to.

"No, Mari, an evening alone with your books does not sound like fun. It sounds depressing. And besides, you are being selfish! Maybe you want to be alone, though for the life of me I don't understand why. But what about me, Mari? You know I don't like to go to parties alone. Would it really be that hard for you to show a little solidarity and come with me?"

Against her better judgment, Maria concedes. At least Mada associates with a different group of Romanians than Mr. Grecu and his lot. And she seems convinced that among her circle of acquaintances, she can find a Thanksgiving party Maria will like.

"Tolerate," Maria corrects. "I'm only going for you, so you don't have to go alone, remember?"

But Mada insists that, in spite of her social phobia, her friend will enjoy the party she ultimately selects.

"Mari, these people are nice. She's a professor at NYU, and he's a software engineer. They are young and cool. And their friends are nice. I promise! There will be people there you've never ever met.

And it's not even a dinner, it's a real party. There will be drinks, maybe even dancing, but really, people will just mingle and talk to each other."

Maria sighs. Mingling and talking? Not her forte. But still, on Thanksgiving night she does her hair and makeup, puts on a black wrap dress that accents her waist and cleavage, dabs on some perfume, steps into yet another pair of torturous shoes, picks up a bottle of red, and takes a cab to Manhattan to accompany Mada to the house of complete strangers.

The party is not bad. Mada is in a good mood, and really happy to see Maria. The hors d'oeuvres are excellent, and there is plenty of good wine. The people seem nice, and quite a different crowd than the one Maria so intensely disliked. Still, being her usual shy self, she keeps quiet and sticks to Mada's side. At some point, however, her friend drifts off, deep in conversation with a man who seems to like her. Left to her own devices, Maria tries to work up the courage to mingle. New people keep arriving. The room is getting fuller and fuller. For Maria's taste, it's too loud, and too smoky. She decides to escape to the balcony for just a few minutes.

She's trying to make her way through the crowd, when someone taps her shoulder. It's a soft, feminine touch, and as she turns around, she's faced with a beautiful dark-haired woman. She searches her face, trying to recognize her, but her mind draws a blank.

"Are you Maria Pop?" the woman asks. Her face is one big smile. Maria wonders where they could have met.

"Yes."

The woman extends her hand, and Maria shakes it.

"Monica Simion," the woman introduces herself. Maria feels a cold chill going down her spine. "I've been wanting to meet you for such a long time. I've heard so much about you. From your children, from Victor."

Maria wonders if she should just turn around and leave.

"I'm Victor's girlfriend," the woman finally offers.

Maria cannot breathe. She wipes her palm on the fabric of her dress, as if trying to wipe off the other woman's touch. She takes a step back, inhales sharply, then says:

"And you had the bad taste to think that I would want to meet you? Get away from me!"

Just then, she notices Victor, standing on the other side of the room, looking straight at her. The bastard! It has never occurred to her that he and his girlfriend could be here tonight, otherwise she would not have accepted to come. She hoped never to meet this Monica Simion.

She turns around and heads for the bedroom, where the guests' coats are piled up on the bed. She cannot wait to leave this party. As she blinks away tears, she's hoping that awful woman will not follow her to see her cry.

But it's even worse. The person following her into the bedroom is Victor. She looks away, and keeps digging through the coats, not even acknowledging his presence.

"Maria, I'm sorry. I didn't know you would be here tonight."

She drops the coats and looks at him. She knows her eyes are glazed with tears, but she can't help it.

"Please don't look at me that way," he says. "I really am sorry. I had no way of knowing you'd be here."

She tries to blink away her tears, but it's too late.

"Maria, please don't cry. I really am sorry."

She can think of nothing but leaving this awful place.

"I want to go home, Victor. Can you please take me home?"

She knows how absurd her request is, how unlikely for him to leave his girlfriend at this party in order to drive her home. But there seems to be genuine concern, genuine warmth, in his voice when he asks:

"You want me to take you home?"

Her eyes meet his. There is a fleeting moment of kindness between them. A cease-fire of sorts.

"Please," she says. "Take me out of here."

He reaches for her coat, and holds it so she can slip it on. He places his hand on the small of her back and leads her out of the room.

They walk in silence to his car. She can't think of one single thing to say. Why did she ask Victor of all people to take her home? She hates being alone with him.

Victor holds open the car door. She sits down, fastens the seat belt with a shaking hand. The interior of his car smells like expensive leather. It reminds her of the gloves she sells. She tries to take comfort in it, but she can't. His car feels foreign to her, like enemy territory, like the frozen plains of Russia. From the dashboard, machine eyes cast their lifeless glances at her. What is she doing in his car? She should have left alone. She should have taken a cab.

The silence is oppressive. Victor lights a cigarette. He's blowing the smoke out the window. He seems miles away.

Her mind is spinning uselessly. She keeps trying to think of something to say, something neutral, something to ease the tension. But she has no clue, and she has no courage. It was too bold of her to ask him to take her home, too bold and too presumptuous to think he wanted to rescue her. And why on earth did she think she'd be comfortable being alone with him? Why did she think she'd be able to tolerate his frosty politeness, his unspoken judgment, all the way home?

He doesn't get on the Queensboro Bridge. She wonders where he's driving. She can't find her voice to ask him, can't think of how to phrase the question. They drive in silence, her staring at the cars ahead, him smoking. He steers the car uptown. He's taking her to his apartment. Her muscles tense up. She knows she should protest, but the words won't come out.

He parks the car, and comes around to open her door. Now is the time for her to walk away, and get a cab. Instead she follows him into the building.

They stand side by side in the small elevator. With a mix of dread and excitement it slowly sinks in. He still wants her, yet he must hate her at the same time. Her nervousness is bordering on fear. Yet she's not sure exactly what she's afraid of. Adrenaline courses through her veins, as if anticipating danger. But she doesn't try to stop the elevator. She doesn't try to leave. Whatever lies ahead, she's drawn to it, like a moth to a flame. It's surreal, being here, in his building, in this elevator, going upstairs. With Victor.

He opens the door. She steps inside. He helps her out of her coat. She's cold. She's never been here before, to the place where he lives. She's thought of asking L to describe it so many times, but was embarrassed to show curiosity. And now here she is, surrounded by the objects that furnish Victor's life without her. Will she be strong enough to weather the frozen fields of Russia?

He turns on a dim light, and pours two tumblers of scotch. Straight up.

"Drink this. You seem to need it."

Her hand is shaking visibly. She takes a small sip, and the golden liquid spreads a wave of heat throughout her body.

He comes closer. She can feel the warmth of his breath, can smell the hint of tobacco and whisky on it, the scent of his skin, so manly she can barely stand it.

"Drink faster," he says, and she downs her whisky like a shot. He takes her empty glass and places it on a table. The thought briefly crosses her mind, that he should use a coaster, that there will be a wet ring on his expensive table, and she clings to that thought, as if that ring of water were the lifebuoy that can rescue her from Victor, from her own feelings, and her fear. She should leave. Now. Trembling visibly, she inches away from him, towards the wall, but he comes closer. For one long moment, she's weak with anticipation. Then he finally touches her, and she shivers at the boldness of his hand on her thigh, on her breast, the forgotten feel of a man's fingers on her flesh. He lifts her off the ground, and he is rough, yet at the same time careful, his hand cradling her head, as he presses her against the wall. It always turned her on, the way he could pick her up, as if she were weightless. Her heart is pounding, vibrating like an Asian gong. She feels it in every fiber of her body. Her evil, treacherous heart, threatening to explode, to melt into hot lava, to wash over her in waves of heat and kill her.

{19}

The Walk of Shame

Maria is sitting on the New York City subway, with her coat wrapped around her, taking little sips from a cup of Starbucks coffee. Her head hurts from lack of sleep, her bloodshot eyes are burning, and the soreness between her legs intensifies with every shake of the subway car. She blushes.

She feels as if the people on the subway know what she's been up to, as if they can see her wrinkled party dress underneath her coat, as if they can tell that she's carrying her bra in her purse, that she's not been able to find her underwear, that she hasn't had a shower, or even washed her face. Can they smell it on her, the scent of Victor, combined with the sinful smell of sex? She herself cannot understand why she feels so embarrassed and guilty at the thought of sleeping with her own husband. Is it because they're separated? Is it because it's been over ten years since she's been with a man? Or is it because this was a different kind of sex than anything she's ever experienced before? It was mostly good before, when they were still together. But it was never this wild, this intense.

She lowers her eyes, afraid people might be able to read into them, to see the images coursing through her head, the images she's trying to erase, but can't.

Maybe the reason she feels so embarrassed in the light of day, is that she's allowed herself to lose control, as if her body didn't belong to her, but to a completely uninhibited woman, a woman who was wild, free, crazy, and loud. She never behaved like this before.

She felt so uncomfortable waking up in Victor's bed, next to his naked body, the sight of which immediately made her blush, though she had seen it many times before. But that was in a previous life, and his body too back then was different, though it hasn't changed over the years as much as hers. She shakes away the image of her own naked body, the breasts that are larger, but not as firm, the little ring of fat around her waist, the cellulite on her hips, the scar from the C-section when she had Alex, which now forms a little valley through the small cushion of her belly. The thought that he saw all this makes her want to die. But she remembers not caring about any of it in the heat of passion, and she also remembers, much to her horror, him taking the time to look at her.

She wishes she had something to read, anything to distract her, anything to make her stop thinking about the night before. But of course, all she has is the small purse she took to the party, now stuffed beyond capacity with her bra. She wishes she had a toothbrush. She would of course not have brushed her teeth at Victor's. She was extremely careful not to wake him as she tiptoed around collecting her things from wherever they were scattered. She would not have taken the chance of waking him by running the water. She even waited until she was at Starbucks to use the restroom. In her hurry, she even gave up on finding her underwear. She heard the bedsprings creak as Victor was turning, and felt such a strong surge of panic at the thought of having to face him, that she decided to just grab her coat and purse, and leave, holding her shoes, stockings, and bra in her hand. She stepped into her shoes and stockings in the elevator. Even call girls must be classier than that.

But call girls do not really have to feel uncomfortable afterwards. For them the deal is clear. A simple business arrangement. Whereas she knows, she's swimming in muddy waters. What, if anything, will happen next? What will Victor do? Part of her is furious with herself for being a coward. She should have had the courage to stay and find out.

What would he be like in the morning? Would he be tender, would he at least be friendly, or would he, again, be cold and distant?

Would he want to talk about it? Or would he act like nothing happened? Would he want her to stay for breakfast? Would he want to go to bed with her again? Would he want her to just leave? Would he drive her home? Would he promise to call? Would he make her coffee? Would he bring her breakfast in bed? Or would he expect her to make breakfast for him, to serve him, the way she used to while they were still together?

She'd love to know, and part of her wishes she'd stayed. But she was afraid that he'd wake up and resent her, that he'd be cold, maybe even unkind. She couldn't bare that, can't bare to even think of it, in fact.

She decides to forgive herself the cowardly escape. After all, she should give herself license to be uncomfortable. Yes, she's a bit of a prude. But she's a woman who has not been touched by a man in more than ten years. She's never ever been with anyone other than her husband. And the man she went home with last night seemed like someone else, a cross between the Victor she knew, the one she'd loved and hated, and a stranger. It felt oddly familiar, and yet completely foreign. It was strange.

There wasn't much of the tenderness that dominated their lovemaking, even in their final years of living together, when she started feeling used, like a passive observer, somebody, maybe even something Victor had sex with. Last night she certainly was an active participant, but the tenderness that used to be there between them was gone. She could pick up little traces of it here and there, small vestiges of the past, but what happened between them seemed completely different. It was pure lust, wild, with a rough quality to it. And she liked it. A lot.

Still, now, in the light of day, it shakes her to think that maybe that was all he wanted. Just sex. Just her body. She's flattered that her aging body can still awake such desire, but, in the light of day, it all seems empty to her. Is that all she is to him? Maybe it was not even the actual attractiveness of her body that ignited such passion. Maybe it wasn't even lust on his side. Maybe it was just an ambition. Maybe he wanted to prove to himself, and to her, that he could wear down her resistance, that the woman who had pushed him away, still wanted him. She suddenly hates herself for having allowed herself to go home with him, for having let him touch her, for enjoying it, for letting him see just how much she enjoyed it.

She gets off the subway at the stop closest to her house. She's in no mood for walking, and her body feels sore. After all, she got plenty of exercise last night. As she climbs up the stairs from the subway, her cellphone's ringing startles her. She opens her purse and the bra falls out. She picks it up, embarrassed, just as somebody's about to step on it. Then she retrieves her ringing cell phone, and without even looking at the screen, she turns it off.

When she gets through her front door, she feels better. Her apartment is warm, familiar, comforting. She hates this place, it's true, but now she embraces its time-honored safety. How good it is to be home, in her own apartment, after weathering the cold plains of Russia! How soothing to sink back into the mundane setting of her daily life. She kicks off her torturous shoes, drops her coat and bag on the floor, and walks into her bedroom where she unplugs the phone with such determination she almost rips it out of the wall. She's tired, and weary, a war survivor, in fact. Her body's sore, and her eyes are burning. The whole wide world can just fuck off and leave her alone.

She runs herself a hot bath. All she wants to do is soak. She pours some lavender oil into the water. She unwraps her dress, and looks at her naked body in the mirror, hoping to find it more beautiful than she remembers. But here it is, the same old body. Less firm, more puffy than she'd like it to be, and very pale. She wonders what Victor thought of it, as he undressed her.

She notices two big bruises on her thighs. She tries hard not to recall exactly how they happened. She remembers knocking over something, a shattered sound, and neither her nor Victor stopping to look at the damage. There was broken glass on the floor, and she carefully stepped around it earlier this morning. She blushes again at the thought that they behaved like animals. Exhausted, she sinks into the bath. She wishes she could just wash the previous night away.

{20}

A Different Point of View

Halfway between sleep and waking, Victor can feel the intoxicating scent of Maria's skin. He longs for the warmth of her body. He reaches for her, though even half asleep, he's afraid of her pushing him away. He opens his eyes looking for her, and finds that the bed is empty. The crumpled sheets smell like her, but she's gone.

He hopes she's on the balcony, or in the kitchen, making coffee. He reaches for a sheet to wrap himself in, and goes in search of her. He feels a sudden pain, and realizes he's stepped on something sharp. It's a piece of glass, part of the lamp they knocked over the night before.

There's nobody in the living room, nor in the kitchen, on the balcony, or in the bathroom. She left. She snuck out like a thief in the middle of the night. The front door is unlocked. All her stuff is gone. There is no coffee.

His foot is bleeding onto the hardwood floor. He rummages through the bathroom, trying to find something to bandage it with, and realizing that he simply doesn't care, he wraps it in a towel. He puts the coffee on and lights a cigarette, which, contrary to his habit, he smokes in the living room.

Why the fuck did she leave?

He felt relieved, the night before, to realize she wanted him too. When he decided to take her to his place, he assumed she would protest, ask him to pull over, get out slamming the door. He would not have insisted. He would have driven her to her apartment. But she didn't say anything. She followed him, like a little lamb. Did she maybe not want him after all? She was extremely nervous. He wanted to make some kind of comforting gesture, but he was afraid to show he still cared for her. All he could bring himself to do was offer her a drink. And then he was not even able to wait for her to finish drinking it. He did not even ask her to sit down, did not extend any of the small courtesies one would towards a guest. He did nothing to make her feel at ease.

But then again, did she not pull him close herself? Did she not kiss him back? Did she not give more than enough signs that she was thoroughly enjoying it? These sound like the excuses invoked by date rapists. Did he, in fact, rape his wife?

Why is he even thinking such a thing? He's not a violent man. He would never do such a thing. Still, what if she thought of it that way? What if, in the light of day, she woke up to find herself a victim? If anybody can undergo such a transformation, it's Maria. She's capable of blaming him for things he didn't do, for thoughts he didn't think. She's capable of blaming him even for the thoughts coursing through her own head.

Did she, in the light of day, reconsider, and take offense? But what exactly is there to be offended by? She's a grown woman. She went home with him of her own free will. They had sex. She enjoyed it.

It's true that he did not make love to her the way he used to when they were still together. He fucked her. And she liked it. A lot. Would she be hypocritical enough to be offended by the fucking, after enjoying it so much?

He pours himself a cup of coffee, lights another cigarette. He decides to call her, and ask her why she left. As he's waiting for her phone to ring, he realizes he's nervous. Her answering machine picks up on the fifth ring. "Is Maria, leave a message." Her voice on the recording is abrupt, impatient. The way he heard it many times before. He hangs up.

When he calls again, a few hours later, the phone goes straight to voicemail. She must have turned it off. He calls her house phone, that antiquated contraption she keeps in her bedroom. There's no answering machine attached to that thing, so he cannot tell if she's unplugged it, or if she's sitting there, refusing to answer.

A new wave of hatred towards Maria rises in him. As he walks aimlessly around the apartment, his foot still hurting from that damn piece of glass, he hates her once more for all the mean and hateful things she's done over the years. He's already taken a long, hot shower, trying to scrub her scent off his skin. But it lingers in the apartment in spite of the open windows. Her scent mixed with the cold of the late November day, with the sounds and filth of the city.

He doesn't know what he hates her for most. Is it her small acts of bitterness, her early frustration, her hysterics, or is it the big stuff she did? Is it the day when she announced coldly that he should sleep in Alex' room from now on? Is it the day she asked him to leave the apartment?

He remembers that morning so well. He was coming home after spending the night with another woman. It was a meaningless fling. He cannot even remember her name or her face. He should not have spent the night with her. But it was in his days of driving a cab, and he sometimes drove night shifts. He knew that's what Maria would tell the children if he didn't show up, and it eased his conscience. He shared a bottle of wine with that other woman, smoked a few cigarettes, joked around. She was easy to be with. He let her talk him into spending the night. It was the promise of a lazy, relaxed evening that made him stay.

At that point, being home was completely unpleasant. His wife barely spoke to him, and when she did, her comments were meant to hurt. He felt like he was performing a balancing act, trying to avoid her sharp daggers, and at the same time trying to avoid his children seeing him get ripped to pieces. He was tired. Driving a New York City cab was the hardest thing he had ever done in his life. He needed to come home and relax. Instead he came home to a place where you could cut the tension with a knife.

The night he spent with that other woman was fun. He even managed to sleep through most of it. In the morning she made coffee, and offered to cook breakfast, but he had to leave. He wanted to get out in his cab early enough to make a full day's worth of tips.

Around lunchtime he happened to drop off a customer in his own neighborhood, so he decided to stop by the house for a quick bite. Even in her days of intense unpleasantness, Maria would leave meals out for him, meticulously arranged on the table, ready for him to eat.

He didn't expect her to be home. She was supposed to be at work. But there she was, sitting at the kitchen table, in her cheap nightgown and frayed pink bathrobe, holding a half empty cup of coffee, staring into space. She looked like she'd been up all night, and she looked like she'd been crying.

She shot him a poisonous look. He thought that she would hit him. He was preparing to counter her blows, something he did poorly, because he was always afraid of hurting her. She could hit hard for a small woman. She had sharp little knuckles that could do a lot of damage.

But she did not hit him. Instead, she looked straight into his eyes and spat out:

"I want you out of this house! I want you to take your things and leave!"

He was shocked.

"I want you gone!" she yelled.

He had never seriously considered leaving her. As horrible as their life together had become, he felt responsible for her, and didn't want to abandon her in the foreign country where he had taken her, where she was unhappy and didn't fit in. He had especially not wanted to leave the children. Although, whenever he thought about it, he realized it was probably better for them not to see their parents fight all the time.

"Fine," he said. "I'll leave. Do you really think I like living with you?"

She looked down. Just for a second he thought she was sorry. But as he was walking out the door, without his lunch, she shouted after him:

"Locksmith is coming today! To change locks! I stay home to wait for him!"

Victor brews another pot of coffee, lights another cigarette. He's smoking in the house, something he never does. In a way he's performing an exorcism. He'd rather have his home smell of cigarettes than of his wife.

Of all the evil things she's done, there is one that he can hardly bring himself to think of. It's something he's never discussed with anyone, one of the secrets of their marriage. This one makes all her other hateful acts pale in comparison. However, it's not something he can easily think of, because it doesn't just fill him with hate, it actually makes him feel guilty.

It's the memory of the day she left him.

It started off like any other day. He came home tired, after having driven the cab all night. He intended to take a long nap. The children would be at school, and Maria would be at Josephine's. She left breakfast out for him when he worked nights. It was usually a skillet with an omelet in it, covered with a plate, something she knew he enjoyed even cold. Other days there were hard-boiled eggs, peeled carefully, next to a few slices of cheese and cold cuts, maybe a few olives, all covered with a napkin. She left his food out on the table so it would be room temperature, not cold. There was always a pot of coffee on, toast on a plate, and sometimes even a glass of fresh squeezed juice. Thinking of the breakfasts she left for him, he usually feels guilty, sometimes even nostalgic.

That day there was no breakfast. It struck him as odd, because she made his breakfast even when she was mad, even when she refused to talk to him. He paced around the kitchen, confused. He opened the fridge, looked at a carton of eggs, and thought it was too much trouble to cook them.

Coffee was on, but the pot was half empty. He poured himself a cup, and bit into a piece of bread, which, not toasted, tasted pretty bland. He thought of Maria's complaints about American bread not having the crunchy crust she liked, and he rolled his eyes. Tasty or not, it was a piece of bread, and it was fine by him.

When he walked into the bedroom he saw the clothes thrown on their bed. By that time he had actually managed to buy a bed and a few other pieces of furniture for the apartment. He had hoped his wife would be pleased, but she had insisted that she disliked it, and that it was too expensive. She had thrown a horrible fit when he had explained to her that he had bought all of it on credit.

At first he couldn't figure out why things were on the bed.

Whenever something dreadful happens, there's always that elusive moment, when things have already happened, but one has yet to find out. That is the moment people wish they could go back to. The moment before disaster sinks in and begins to truly exist, the moment before their world is wrecked. For Victor, it was seeing the clothes on the bed, yet not realizing why they were there. It seemed a bit strange, yet to his knowledge, nothing was wrong yet. He didn't know yet that his wife was gone. Then he saw the closet doors askew, the dresser drawers hanging open, and most of her things missing. One of the suitcases they had brought with them from Romania had disappeared from its place under the bed. He quickly checked the shoebox where they held their savings. Half of the money was gone. It was only a few hundred dollars. He wondered how far she'd get with it. The thought that she had left like this, taking their money, not telling him anything, not warning him, made him sick to his stomach.

He went and knocked on Josephine's door. He could hear the children inside. An unknown woman opened. She said she didn't know where Maria was.

His wife was gone. Without a trace. Just like that. He couldn't believe it.

He felt a surge of terror at the thought that she might have taken Alex and Lili with her. But all of their things were in their room. And where would she go, with two children?

Still, the thought of her leaving them was more shocking than the thought of her taking them with her. How could she leave her children? In spite of what other people said about her, he knew she loved them. How could she abandon them? Had she been that desperate to leave? Had she been that miserable? How could she not have warned him? Or had she? He thought of all her little acts of desperation, her scenes, her crying, her outbursts of anger. Had all those been signs he had chosen to ignore? Would he have been able to stop her, had he paid more attention, had he tried to understand her?

He briefly considered the idea that she had gone away with a man. But he quickly dismissed it. She hardly knew anyone. Where would she have met this man? At the store, at the laundry, at Josephine's house? Besides, Maria was not the cheating kind. But how well did he know her, after all? He never thought she was the leaving kind either.

He was relieved when Lili and Alex came home from school. Although he'd been almost certain she hadn't taken them, he'd still been worried. Their arrival was the best thing that happened all day.

Lili immediately wanted to go to Josephine's to see her mother. Alex wanted to watch TV. He asked them both to sit down, and explained, in a voice he tried to render as natural as possible, that their mother had gone on a short vacation. He told them that she had not wanted them to be sad, so she'd kept it a secret, but that overall *Mami* had been working very hard, and was very tired, and that he'd sent her somewhere nice to get some rest and a breath of fresh air. Upstate. A little cabin in the woods. He had to stop himself. When people lie, they tend to provide too much detail. He could almost picture her at a little cabin in the woods. He only wished it were true, he wished it had occurred to him to send her somewhere to rest, instead of ignoring how miserable she was.

"How come we don't get to go with her?" was Lili's question.

"How come you never get tired?" was Alex'.

As it got time for dinner, he became discouraged. He made an omelet for the children. Lili and Alex took a few bites, then pushed their plates away, asking him to order pizza.

He couldn't sleep while she was gone. Lying in bed alone, for the first time in his life prey to insomnia, he wondered and he worried. Where had she gone? Would she come back? Would they ever hear from her again? Had she disappeared forever from their lives? What would he tell the children if she really never came back? How much longer could he still fool them with the vacation story? To his disbelief they had bought it, and though Lili said she missed her *Mami*, they seemed to be doing ok, and not asking too many questions. But he could not go on lying to them forever.

There were practical concerns too. How long could he go on driving the cab only while the children were at school? He was making less money, and he was more exhausted than before. How long could he afford to order pizza every night? He was already getting sick of it, and the children would too, eventually.

Mostly, however, the questions that haunted him revolved around his wife: Where was she? What was she doing at this exact same moment? Was she able to sleep, or was she lying awake like him, thinking about them? Was she worried about what their lives would be like without her? Did she miss them? Did she at least miss her children?

If he dozed off, even for a few moments, he woke in terror. What if something bad had happened to her, something really bad? What if she was dead?

Then finally, on her fourth evening of being gone, just as he was getting ready to order pizza, the phone rang. It was her.

"Victor?" Her voice was hesitant. He could tell she was crying.

"Where are you?" The curtness in his own voice surprised him. For days, he had been planning what to say, and how to say it, if she called. He had decided to be kind and understanding. But now that she was actually on the phone, he couldn't.

"I'm at… the train station."

She spoke is a small voice, sobbing so hard her words were hard to understand.

"Which train station?"

"The big one, in Manhattan."

"Penn Station or Grand Central?"

"Penn Station."

Pause.

"I… Can I come back?"

"Stay where you are. I will come get you."

They agreed for him to pick her up across the street from the station. He insisted that she not leave, that she wait for him there. He told her it would take a long time for him to get through traffic. And it did.

The whole way there, he worried that she'd change her mind, that she'd disappear again before he could get to her. But when he pulled up in the cab, she was sitting there, on her small, battered suitcase. The laces of her cheap sneakers were untied, her hair was a mess, her eyes red and swollen. She wore faded jeans and a hooded grey sweatshirt. She did not look like his beautiful wife. She looked like a juvenile delinquent.

He stopped the cab, but he didn't get out to open the door for her, or to help with her suitcase. He just popped the trunk and waited for her to get in. He was still breathless from the drive over, from the fear that he'd be too late, that she'd be gone again. But here she was, in the flesh, and quite a sorry sight.

She sat in the back of the cab, like a customer, placing the little suitcase on the seat next to her. He realized she was embarrassed to face him. But her choice to sit in the back irritated him.

"I opened the trunk. You need to close it."

She got out, closed the trunk, came back in. She just sat there, looking down at her hands. For blocks and blocks of slow city traffic, that was all she did. He lit a cigarette. He did not talk to her. He turned the radio on, listened to NPR. They were halfway across the Queensboro Bridge when he realized that in the back of the cab, she was crying softly, trying to stifle her sobs, wiping her eyes and her nose with the sleeve of her sweatshirt.

"You better stop that before we get home," he said. "The kids think you were on vacation."

Her sobs intensified. Her whole body was shaking, and she was gasping for air, barely breathing between bursts of crying. He had to stop the car, and wait for her to calm down. It took forever. He was worried about the children being home alone. He didn't know anybody who would watch them. That woman, Josephine, had been borderline rude to him the other day, when he had once again gone over to ask if she knew anything about Maria. He could tell that she thought he was some kind of monster.

Driving Maria home that night, he felt both guilt and anger. He wondered why she had come back. Had she realized that she was making a mistake, or was it that she had not been able to cope on her own? He didn't ever ask her. But it keeps haunting him to this day.

He felt like a prison warden bringing a fugitive back to the prison. Was that how she felt? Was she simply there because she had no recourse, because she had no other place to go, and no way out? He could not bare the thought of her being miserable, yet being forced to stay with him for lack of other options. He could hardly bring himself to touch her after that. Two years later, when she asked him to move out of their bedroom, he was angry, yet relieved.

Victor pours out the rest of his coffee. He's had enough. He stubs out his cigarette into the dirty cup. It still hurts to think of her attempt to leave him. And the way she snuck out this morning, as if trying, once again, to escape, reminds him of it.

Damn woman! He furiously rips the sheets off the bed. He calls a cleaning service. In a city like New York, you can get anything any time, even the day after Thanksgiving. Once he gets off the phone he feels better. He'll go out for lunch, then maybe go to a bar while they are cleaning.

His cellphone rings while he's enjoying a juicy burger and a paper. For a second, despite himself, he hopes it's Maria. But it's Monica. He forgot all about her. There is no excuse for his rudeness, his lack of any consideration in abandoning her at a party without even telling her he was going.

"What happened to you last night, Victor?"

“I’m sorry, honey. I had to talk to that woman. She is the mother of my children, and I have to get along with her, for the sake of Alex and Lili.”

On the other end of the line, Monica is quiet. He wonders if she’s finally had enough.

“How about I call you later, and we make dinner plans?” he asks.

After a long pause, she says:

“That would be nice.” He’s relieved. She’s letting him off the hook easy, and he doesn’t deserve it. But he’s glad.

{21}

Flowers and Babies

The Saturday after Thanksgiving, Maria goes to work, as planned. Eating her lunch in the break room, she feels it's finally time to turn on her cellphone. Victor must have left several messages by now. With a trembling finger, she presses the 'on' button. The butterflies in her stomach bat their colorful wings. The phone greets her with its customary little tune. She holds her breath, tries to ignore the pounding of her heart. There are no new messages. Irritated, she shakes the phone. Is something wrong with it, maybe? She turns it off, then on again. She waits, dread building up inside her. She calls voicemail again. No new messages. He hasn't called. He simply hasn't. She resists the urge to throw her stupid phone against the wall. She wishes she had not turned it on yet. She wishes she could still bask in the sweet hopefulness that there would be a message.

Her appetite for her sandwich is gone. Why has he not called? Did it really not mean anything to him? Or is he maybe nervous, just like her, unsure of what to do or what to say? Is he regretting their night together? Or maybe he did call but didn't leave a message. It was probably him calling the other morning, when she turned her phone off. She hates herself now for not picking up. But she hates him even more for not leaving a fucking message. It would be so much easier for her then. She'd know. She'd be able to tell from the tone of his voice, and she could prepare herself before talking to him. Angry, she stuffs her sandwich into the nearest garbage can.

She washes her hands, and inadvertently sees her face in the mirror. Although she didn't sleep well, she looks good. Her beauty saddens her. What is the point of being beautiful if all she has is emptiness in her life? What is the point, if he really doesn't care, if even a night of unbridled passion doesn't move him, if he can touch her, hold her, have her, then go on with his life, indifferent?

She chases these thoughts away. If she were not at work, she'd splash cold water on her face. She's angry for giving Victor so much power, for even for a second trying to assess her own worth through his eyes. She's a strong independent woman. Why on earth would she want to be beautiful just for his sake?

She decides to go back to work before her break is over.

The difference between the break room and the first floor of the department store never ceases to amaze her. It's like she's been in another world, a dark, and slightly dirty one, lacking shine and luster, and now she's stepping back into the light. She loves the commotion of the store, the customers wandering in an out, the saleswomen in their black coats, trying to lure people into buying things that look and smell enticing, the counters containing overpriced goods, the natural flower arrangements, the music. It's Christmas music right now, not exactly her favorite. It annoys her that they turned it on immediately after Thanksgiving, and it annoys her that overnight silver reindeer and shiny white fir trees replaced the cornhusks and pumpkins and turkeys. What a big circus one has to put up with, just to make a living!

But in a way it's cheerful, and at least there's always something new. As she's walking towards her counter, taking in the glitter and commotion of the store, she wills herself to enjoy the empty retail glamour. Then, suddenly, she stops dead in her tracks. She cannot believe her eyes! There, by her workstation, is the biggest bouquet of yellow roses she has ever seen. Her hand instinctively goes to her mouth, but is not able to cover her oversized smile. He sent her flowers! She cannot believe it! He actually does care! And he does want her back!

She summons all her willpower to make herself walk slowly, and demurely, towards her beautiful yellow roses. She doesn't want people at work knowing her business. But she cannot stop herself from giggling like a schoolgirl. The butterflies in her stomach are now dancing an elaborate dance, their colorful wings drawing magical circles, whole rainbows of excitement. He actually sent her flowers! It's so romantic that it almost makes her cry. That's why he didn't call. It wasn't good enough, just calling. He wanted to make a real gesture. He does in fact appreciate her. He clearly still has feelings for her.

She slowly approaches the flowers. They are beautiful, like anything Victor would pick. What could be lovelier than yellow roses? She's close enough to smell them, close enough to touch their velvet petals. Excitement courses through every inch of her body. She feels like singing. He actually sent her flowers!

Her co-worker, Tanya, comes over to gush over the roses as well.

"Aren't they beautiful, Maria? Aren't they amazing?"

Maria smiles, but she doesn't like Tanya getting so close to her roses. She has to fight the urge to remove the young woman's hand from one of the flowers. This girl should have better things to do than to mess with other people's things.

But then her eyes fall on the card lying on the counter. Her smile freezes.

"Ray got them for me, girl!" Tanya brags, glowing. "You know, I think I'm gonna marry this boy! I just feel it!"

"Well, good luck to you!" Maria says, and turns away. She unlocks the drawer where she keeps the most expensive gloves. She's going to rearrange them. Finest leather, lined with 100% cashmere. People pay hundreds of dollars for theses. She, of course, could never afford them, but she can touch them anytime, for free. She slides her hand over the soft leather. She closes her eyes, willing herself to enjoy this small treat. Leather smells better than roses anyway.

Ten days later, Maria still hasn't heard from Victor. By now it's clear that she will not. She's determined not to feel sad, abandoned, or sorry for herself. It's hard, because everything reminds her of him. Her own body, which she cannot escape, which she carries with her everywhere she goes, which she tries uselessly to evade in her sleep, reminds her of him. She cannot stand, sit, walk, or lie down, without being aware of it, her own body, aging, yet still beautiful, the body he touched, the body that wanted him, the body that is missing his.

She tries to distract herself by reading. But her favorite pastime has now become a chore. She sits in her empty bed, turning the pages absently, realizing she has completely lost track of what she's reading. Her eyes are on the page, but her mind wanders. For all their comfort and loyalty in the past, books are refusing to offer an escape. They bore her to tears, and in her boredom she feels lonely and dejected.

Frustrated, she sits up in her empty bed, and finds herself staring at the phone with a longing that hurts and humiliates her. How awfully pathetic she is! She knows that there's no way she can make that stupid phone ring. She knows that staring at it will only make her more aware of its silence. He's not going to call her. He really doesn't care.

One night, after staring at the stupid phone for fifteen minutes, she considers calling him. But to say what? And how ridiculous she would seem! He has a life. He's probably busy, with the store, with his friends, with that beautiful younger woman, Monica. She thinks of the two of them in bed together, and it's too painful to bear. It makes her sick with envy. It physically hurts. She tries, instead, to imagine them fighting, to imagine Monica angry after he left her at that party. But it's no good. Invariably, she thinks of them making up, and then again, she pictures Victor in bed with his lover. His estranged wife is probably the last thing on his mind.

The thought that Victor has a life, while she doesn't, bothers her more than usual. She's taken note of it before, with some bitterness, and the occasional pang of regret. But overall she was aware that solitude was her own choice, a luxury, something she was lucky to have. These days, however, she wonders if she has sentenced herself to loneliness forever. To boredom, frustration, and despair.

Maybe it's her punishment for the bad things she's done. Doesn't she deserve, after all, to end up alone and bitter? What did she expect when she left her husband? What did she think would happen when she kicked him out of this very bed, and even worse, out of this very house?

She stands up, walks to the bathroom, and splashes cold water on her face. She cannot allow herself to think this way. She will not allow herself to feel lonely and deserted. She will not wallow in guilt. She needs to stop thinking she deserves this. She needs to find a path to forgiveness. She'll try to find a path back to herself.

But then she walks back to her bed, the bed she used to share with Victor years ago, and her eyes fill with tears. To think that he was here, in this very room. And that she slept besides him. Every night. And that invariably their bodies drifted towards each other, reached for each other in the dark. They made love so often, even when they were mad. She took comfort in it, for years. Things might be bad, but we still want each other, we're part of each other, it's a miracle, and a mystery. Later, she saw it for what it was, a habit, nothing more. Like breathing. He reached for her at night, just like he reached for his cigarettes over coffee in the morning. His tenderness meant nothing. It was like rings of smoke.

But she still had a chance back then. She could at least still try to win him back. She could at least still hope. Every night was a new opportunity to get back his love, his forgiveness. And fool that she was, she gave up, threw it away! Wasn't it so much easier back then, when years apart had not petrified him towards her? Wasn't it easier when he was still hers, at least physically, than now, when she sits alone, in her empty bed, waiting for the phone to ring, knowing full well that he's with another woman?

It's hardest at night, when there is no one to distract her from her thoughts. When she's lying in bed and cannot help but remember his touch, the feel of his body on top of her, inside her. There are specific gestures she remembers, stray acts of tenderness thrown into the rawness of pure lust. His hand, his lips, shockingly gentle at times, as if he really still loved her, just a little. Those are the memories that torture her the most. Sometimes, when she's halfway between sleep and waking she almost believes that those caresses meant something. She lies to herself. She drifts to sleep aching with hope. She dreams that he that he misses her too, that he will call. She has imaginary conversations with him, in her sleep. But then she wakes up, heavy with disappointment, trapped in the same body, carrying those same memories. As sleep drifts from her eyelashes, her dreams give way to cruel daylight. She has to give up hope.

At work it's easier to distract herself. She arranges and rearranges the scarves, wallets, and gloves. She delights in the secret pleasure of touching and smelling the expensive leather. She dresses nicely, smiles brightly, and tries to lure over customers. She tries to have long conversations with them, pushing herself to be more outgoing. She tells herself that she's beautiful, independent, and after all a resourceful woman. She has skills, even in dealing with people. Who would have thought?

On December fifteenth Maria decides to go see a doctor. She asks Mădă for a recommendation, and brushes off her unwelcome questions by pretending to have an important call on the other line.

Sitting on the examining table, in her paper gown, she feels naked and vulnerable. Like a child, she clings to a faint and rather absurd hope. Victor has not called. It's as if she never spent that night with him. But telling the nurse about it makes it real again.

That in itself is reason enough to put herself through a humiliating medical exam, instead of just buying one of those stupid tests they sell in drugstores. Funny, how a woman who used to crave seclusion and discretion, is now so desperate to talk to a stranger about her private life.

She feels frail and delicate, as if she were really sick. The nurse in front of her seems kind. And she is indeed giving her attention, offering care. Maria swallows back tears. When was the last time someone took care of her?

She decides to allow herself whatever she's feeling. Like a sick child, she lets herself cry in front of the nurse. Isn't she a patient after all? Of course, what she has is not a disease, or at least it's not considered a disease by most of mankind (and even womankind). But she feels that it should be rightfully labeled as such. I'm ill, she thinks. I'm suffering from pregnancy. A dreadful illness. A cruel epidemic.

The nurse pats her shoulder in a maternal gesture, and Maria realizes just how much she's been missing a mother's touch. She hasn't seen her mother since 1989. They don't even talk on the phone much. It's fair to say they've never been that close. Is she herself headed in that same direction with L?

"Now, now, honey," the nurse says, patting her back, trying to comfort her. Maria continues sobbing, relishing the other woman's touch. She congratulates herself for having listened to Mădă's advice, and asked for a nurse practitioner instead of a doctor.

"I'm sorry," she whispers, and sobs a few more times. "This is hard for me. I didn't think I would be in this situation at my age. And… my husband and I are actually separated." She cannot believe she's emptying her soul in front of a complete stranger. But it feels good. It's actually the most hopeful she's felt in weeks. Maybe that's why people pay so much money for therapy.

"Now, you do know, you might actually not be pregnant," the nurse says. "You know this could be menopause. Or your period could just be late, for various reasons."

Maria nods, sobbing again. She thought of those possibilities herself. At first she was really scared, waking up in a cold sweat one night, realizing that her period was late, remembering that they used no protection, absolutely nothing. Even teenagers know better. One day the smell of leather started making her sick. She got scared, terrified in fact, and then angry. But in a weird irrational way she felt hopeful, excited.

It's crazy, since she didn't want to have either of her children. In fact, with her earlier pregnancies, she was terrified of the little creature growing inside her, and of the horror of having to give birth to it. Why would she want to be pregnant now, at her age? Why would she want to be saddled again, now when she's finally free?

She recalls each of the times she was pregnant. Her ignorant and superficial joy at being pregnant with Lili, fueled idiotically by everybody's enthusiasm. Her absolute terror at the thought of giving birth again, when she was pregnant with Alex. And then of course, that third, nameless baby, the baby that brought nothing but sadness and trouble.

It was one of the bitter ironies of her family's last-minute flight from communism, that in America, where birth control was legal, she managed to get pregnant again.

She remembers going to see a doctor shortly after her arrival. Vica, Mrs. Grecu's sister, offered to take her. She didn't like Vica, but she agreed to go with her. The doctor prescribed her the pill, something she had been dreaming of since giving birth to Lili. It was a humiliating visit, with Vica serving as translator. Maria was a private person and received an old-fashioned education. She was mortified at the thought of anybody coming with her, but, given the way she was raised, it seemed more acceptable to bring a woman, even one she didn't like, than to involve her husband in such 'female business.' The doctor's visit was expensive. This was shocking to Maria, who was used to free health care. Vica mocked her, saying she really had a lot to learn about life in America. Maria still remembers how the comment, coming at a time when she felt so down anyway, hurt her more than it should have. It was one of those little acts of meanness she was never able to forget. She went out of her way to avoid Vica after that, and Vica, of course, labeled her an ungrateful bitch.

The cost of the pill too came as a shock. Maria silently counted her money and paid, refusing to give Vica a chance to mock her again. She took comfort in the fact that the pills came in a pretty round box, that they looked almost like a case of makeup. She wasn't able to buy herself anything in those days. It was nice to own at least one new object that looked girly and pretty, even if it was birth control, and not cosmetics.

But in the long run, attractively packed as they were, the pills proved disappointing. There was a piece of paper inside the box, explaining side effects, and such, but it was all in English. She had hoped for a French translation, but there wasn't one. She was too proud to ask Vica to translate it, too embarrassed to ask Victor, and surely it would have been wrong to ask her eight-year-old daughter. So Maria had no clue what side effects, if any, to expect. She felt more tired than usual, and, much to her horror, she would go to bed at night, lie next to her husband, and feel no desire for him. This terrified her, and it made her angry. What was the purpose of a stupid contraceptive, if it made her not want to make love in the first place?

She wanted to go back to see that doctor. But she couldn't afford another visit. Besides, she had no idea how to get there on the subway. And she didn't speak enough English to communicate with him. She was too embarrassed to ask Victor to accompany her, embarrassed to discuss in too much detail what was going on with her. She couldn't tell him she thought the pill made her not want him. She would have never in a million years told him she didn't want to make love to him.

There was no way in hell she'd ask Vica or any other woman she didn't like to accompany her to yet another humiliating doctor's visit. Her only choice was to stop taking the pills, and hope for the best. Expensive as they had been, she stashed them away, and waited to see what happened. She did feel better without them. And luckily, her desire for Victor returned.

However, a few months later, she found herself pregnant again. Just like the times before, the prospect of giving birth, or having her body cut open and then stitched back together, filled her with terror. But the nightmare had just begun.

When she told Victor, he was angry. He asked her why she stopped taking the pill. She told him it was making her tired and nauseous. He asked why she didn't ask him to take her back to the doctor to have another pill prescribed, or some other form of birth control. She said she was embarrassed, and he accused her of being a prude and an irrational woman, stuck in the dark ages. She felt stupid herself. Here, where all forms of contraceptives were legal and readily available (though for a price, of course), she had been ignorant enough to get pregnant again.

"But these things are so expensive anyway," she told him, trying to defend herself for not having gone back to that doctor.

"And you think abortions are free?"

She started crying, and locked herself in the bathroom. She had not even thought of that. She'd assumed that she would just have another baby. As terrifying as childbirth was, abortion struck her as unnatural and sad. She knew by then that she was not a good mother, that she was probably not cut out to be a mother in the first place. But could she really allow somebody to suck a baby out of her womb? And how could Victor be so cold? Didn't it matter to him that she was carrying his child?

Later that night, he apologized. She knew he was tired, having just started to drive a cab. So she forgave him, and even felt guilty for making a scene. But then he went on to explain, that they could not afford to have another child, that there was nothing to do, but get rid of it. He spoke of it as if it were as simple as extracting a tooth. She flew into a rage and physically attacked him, pounding on him with her fists, until he grabbed her wrists to stop her.

Later she admitted that he was right, and that they had no other choice. But she stayed mad, and did not allow him to go with her to the clinic. He called to make the appointment, and she went with Mrs. Stoica. Two foreign women, whose English vocabulary combined consisted of less than twenty words. She's still amazed that they found the place, and that she managed to communicate with the doctor. She had considered writing useful phrases on a piece of paper, and just showing it to people. What would that have been like, stopping strangers on the street, pointing them to Victor's neat handwriting: "I need to take the R train for three stops. I need to have an abortion." Years later she told this story to Josephine. By then she was able to laugh about the vision of herself holding up a sign reading "I need an abortion." Josephine laughed too, but then she said that, as liberal as New York was, she might have still run into some pro-life fanatic to kill her.

Humor was the only thing she had to get her through that miserable experience. She felt so rotten, so alone, and so angry with Victor.

She wasn't sure about it yet, or rather, she refused to accept it, but that was when it first occurred to her that he didn't love her any more. To make matters worse, he once again was right. The abortion was not just uncomfortable. It also was expensive, more so than the stupid pills, in fact. Afterwards, she sat in an armchair at the clinic, and cried while Mrs. Stoica caressed her arm, telling her that these things happen, that she'd feel better soon.

Sitting in the doctor's office now, she realizes that for the first time, she'll be genuinely happy to be pregnant. But her odd hopefulness has nothing to do with a real life baby. Just as young women dream of the wedding, but not of the actual marriage ahead, she holds some odd vision of what it would be like to be carrying Victor's child, without really thinking of actually having and raising a new baby.

Her pregnancy fantasy involves first and foremost, telling Victor about it. She will go to his store, maybe with an appointment, maybe unexpectedly. She'll once again do something or other to shock that receptionist she doesn't like. She'll then insist Victor take her to lunch, and this time she'll let him take her somewhere nice. She'll wait until after the salad to tell him.

She knows Victor. He's cold and selfish. But he's a good person inside, and he will try to do the right thing. She knows that now, their circumstances being different (or rather, his circumstances being different) he will not dare suggest she get rid of the baby. She enjoys thinking that he'll offer his support, that he'll assure her he respects her choice. Will this make her feel better? Will it erase the hurt of that other baby, the one he didn't want? Will it erase the hurt of him ignoring her after their night of passion? Will it make her feel special to know she's carrying Victor's child, and that he's being supportive, that he's actually being nice? Whenever she imagines it, she feels happy and peaceful. As if with this baby on its way, her world will finally regain its balance.

Has she completely lost her mind? Does she want to be pregnant just so Victor will be nice to her? Does she really want him to be nice to her just because she's pregnant?

Is she hoping to get back together with her estranged husband by having a baby at forty-four, when their other children are grown? Whenever she thinks about it, she realizes that getting back together is not realistic. It's not even part of her pregnancy fantasy. Once she has this baby, she'll want Victor to be part of their lives, but she won't be able to take him back. Ever. Even if he and Monica break up, which they will, once word starts getting out about the baby. She smiles. She loves the thought of everybody knowing she slept with Victor, and that she's carrying his child. Especially Monica.

But there are even more pleasant things to imagine. Things she and Victor will do together as the prospective parents of this unborn child. She'll keep him at some distance, but she'll allow for certain moments of closeness. They can, for example, come here, to this doctor's office, where this nice nurse works. They'll come together for the ultrasound. Then they might go for lunch. Sort of like old friends. And afterwards maybe shop for the baby. She'll let him get things for the nursery. Maybe Victor will get her a crib from his furniture store. Do they even have cribs at his store? L once explained that one can order a vast array of furniture from a catalog and that it all gets assembled somewhere in New Jersey. Would a crib qualify? If not, for sure, Victor will know where to get a good crib. And they can pick one of those contraptions with animals that spin around to hang above it for the baby to look at.

The nurse's voice startles her.

"I've good news, hon."

Maria smiles like a radiant mother-to-be.

"I just got your results from the lab. You're most definitely not pregnant."

The smile frozen on her lips, Maria starts sobbing again, this time louder, with a force she cannot control. How will she be able to go back to life as it was before? No lunches, no babies, no flowers, no crib, no little pastel animals spinning around. Just her, alone, having to suffer Victor's silence, while he continues being with the other woman, as if Thanksgiving never happened.

"I know, honey, I know," the nurse says, patting her back. "Such a relief! It's ok, hon', it's ok. It was just a scare. You poor dear!"

{22}

Karma and the Jilted Wife

Maria rearranges her favorite gloves. It's nearly closing time, and she's looking forward to going home. She'll draw herself a warm bath, she'll close the curtains and lie in her bed, trying to let oblivion wash over her. She's been treating herself with care and gentleness lately, the way one would treat a sick bird. She will continue her self-indulgent ritual tonight, and every other night, until her pain heals, or until she goes numb enough to ignore it. She knows from experience that she will. Eventually.

She looks up from the gloves, and notices a customer approaching, a tall, beautiful woman, wrapped in a cashmere throw, her shiny black hair bouncing in a ponytail. She looks exquisite and expensive, the kind of customer Maria usually longs for. One with money, and class, who will surely buy something. But today she's not in the mood. She wishes the workday were over, that she were home, in bed, with the comforter pulled over her head. As the woman approaches, Maria tries to summon some energy. She shouldn't let this sale go by. She needs her commission if she's ever going to buy an apartment. Or at least those high-count Egyptian cotton sheets she's been longing for lately. How spoiled she would feel sinking into those, feeling their softness brush against her skin. And why not indulge herself, in the end? If she's going to sleep alone for the rest of her life, and if she's going to spend most of her free time in bed, why wouldn't she at least have fabulous sheets?

She smiles at the cashmere-wrapped woman, trying to lure her over. It amuses her how much of a temptress one has to be, to survive in the world of retail. It's a bit like being a prostitute, except she's selling gloves instead of her body. As the woman comes closer, Maria realizes she's seen her before. It's probably a return customer. She's annoyed with herself for not remembering her. Customers like salespeople who know their names, their tastes and preferences. This woman looks familiar. But Maria's mind draws a blank.

She smiles. Then she remembers where she's seen those perfect features. Her stomach turns. It's not a customer. It's Victor's girlfriend. And something about the determination in her step announces that this is not an unfortunate coincidence, like the night at the party. She didn't come into the store by chance, looking for Christmas presents, she's here to see Maria.

What on earth does she want? Maria should be annoyed, she knows it, but she prickles with morbid satisfaction. As if something in her own sick imagination has summoned up this woman, as if Monica materialized here today because Maria cannot stop thinking about her, cannot stop imagining her in bed with her husband. In some sick way, she knows she wished for this encounter. It's curiosity, or a need for validation, but she's been longing for another face to face.

"You here to buy glove?"

"I'm here to talk to you."

The other woman's voice is dignified yet conciliatory. Maria would prefer hostility.

"I'm happy to talk to you about scarf and glove. This here is some of our finest."

She places her favorite elbow-length gloves in front of Monica. They cost $800. And by the looks of her, the well-dressed bitch can probably afford them!

The other woman's hand cradles the fine leather.

"I need to talk to you about Victor."

Her tone is even, business-like. Isn't she an accountant or something? Maria wishes she had quizzed L shamelessly on the topic. She frowns. Where's the repentance of the mistress seeking reconciliation? Or better yet, the anger of the lover betrayed?

But fine, if the other woman wants to talk business, she herself will be businesslike. With perverse pleasure, she raises her eyebrows, and flicks her hair. Even with a few strands of grey in it, her dark mane can rival Monica's ponytail.

"I get paid to talk to you about scarf and glove. So I will do that. With a smile. But there is nothing you or anybody else can do to make me talk to you about anything else."

"Maria…"

"I'm Mrs. Pop to you. I'm Victor's wife, remember?"

She watches Monica's face twitch as she hears this, watches her eyes darken. So it's not all business, after all. The bitch has feelings!

Maria despises herself for what she just said. She hates being called 'Mrs.' There's nothing more stupid than such a title, nothing more idiotic than defining a woman by whether or not she is formally attached to a man. Yet face to face with her husband's lover, she cannot help herself.

"I need to talk to you," the other woman says.

She has a beautiful face, harmonious, profoundly feminine. But on close inspection, she's not as young as Maria originally thought. She has to be slightly over forty. Why has she always assumed the other woman must be younger?

"I am at work," she says. "You can stay here and buy glove. Or you can go away. I have no interest in talking to you."

But she's bluffing. She's dying to know what Monica has to say. She counts to ten, slowly.

"I'm off work in half an hour. You can wait, and then we go have one drink."

The other woman nods, but she rolls her eyes as if Maria's work is an extravagance designed specifically to annoy her.

Maria plucks the gloves out her hand. "I take you not interested in these."

As she arranges cashmere scarves by color, she tries to think of the things she needs to say to the other woman. This, after all, is not an everyday encounter. She cannot let this opportunity go by. As she arranges the scarves, she's thinking how to phrase things best. Which words will give her the most validation? Which words will she enjoy replaying over and over in her head on all her lonely nights?

Half an hour later, she and Monica are walking to a nearby bar. It's cold outside. In her ballet flats, Maria's ankles are freezing. She feels like she's stepping directly onto the cold hard pavement. But there is no way she would wear sneakers in front of Monica. It's bad enough that in her high-heeled boots (a fine leather creation Maria prices at about $500, just by eyeballing them), the other woman is more than a head taller than her. It's bad enough that she has a beautiful face, and amazingly long legs, legs which Maria cannot help picturing wrapped around Victor's body.

Monica reaches into her alligator purse for a pack of Marlboro lights and a silver lighter. Cartier, no less. Bitch. Everything on her is polished and expensive. As if it's not bad enough that she has Victor. She stops to light a cigarette, and takes a long drag. Unwilling to wait, Maria walks faster, but the smoke catches up with her. Inhaling it, she misses Victor more than ever.

"I want cigarette," she commands, and Monica obliges.

The taste of nicotine reminds her of Victor's lips, pressed against hers, hard and rough, yet unbelievably seductive. She sucks in the smoke, inhales deeply, and for a hallucinating moment she can almost feel the strength of his body against hers. Does he kiss the other woman with the same desperation? Does he make love to her as wildly? Does she feel her whole body tingle when his lips meet her skin? Does she melt in his arms and forget herself the way Maria does?

She straightens her back and walks with more dignity. Monica holds open the door to the bar, and Maria walks in, selects a table and sits down.

"You drink red wine?"

The other woman nods.

The bar is attractive, with simple décor, and subdued music. Just like Monica's outfit, it looks expensive, and very up to date. Maria never goes to places like this. She can't afford it. But she knows how to behave as if she'd been frequenting this type of establishment all her life.

She orders a moderately priced but excellent bottle of *Cotes du Rhone*. If the other woman thinks she has no taste or class, she is wrong. She might be toiling away in the glove department, and taking the train back to her modest apartment in Queens, wearing sneakers, which are not even new, but she knows her food, she knows her wine, and she speaks fluent French.

She waits until the wine is brought and ceremoniously opened.

"So, what can I do for you?" she finally asks.

The other woman looks her in the eye.

"I need to tell you this: The night of the Thanksgiving party…"

Maria's heart starts beating faster.

"That was really uncool of you."

Maria can feel the heat rise to her cheeks. Slowly, deliberately, she takes a sip wine. She allows herself a moment to savor it, to give in to the slight intoxication. She allows herself to play with the dark liquid inside the glass. And in a discreet, studied gesture, she smiles. Just for a second.

Then she looks the other woman in the face and asks:

"How is any of your business?"

"Excuse me?" Monica says. "I went to that party with Victor..."

Maria raises her eyebrows. There are a lot of things she's dying to say to this woman. Things she has rehearsed during her sleepless lonely nights.

"*Vorbesti româneste*?" she asks. Do you speak Romanian?

The other woman nods.

"*Da, doamnă*." Yes ma'am. Maria doesn't enjoy the sarcastic tone, nor the feeling of familiarity implicit in speaking their native language. Any closeness between them would only be sick, and Maria wants none of it. She just wants to say what she needs to say, and she wants to have her words come out articulate, and strong, the way they never would in broken English. She wants to express who she is, and where she stands, then get the hell out of here.

"So you are telling me how to act with my husband." Monica recoils at the word 'husband.' "And I am telling you, it is none of your business."

Monica sighs and rolls her eyes. Her beautiful lips are twisted in a grimace Maria doesn't know how to interpret.

"I am Victor's wife," she says, watching Monica cringe once more. Funny, how she cannot stand to hear 'wife,' or 'husband,' or 'marriage.' She's probably chosen to ignore this aspect of Victor's life. She probably likes to think of him as already divorced. "I have been his wife for almost twenty five years now. I am not just the mother of his children. I am his wife. Whatever you do with my husband is my business, if I choose to make it. But what I do with him is none of yours."

Monica looks away.

"So you were with him that night. I knew it!"

"I think you are not listening," Maria says. "I will not ever give an account of what happens in my marriage, to anyone. Especially not to my husband's mistress."

The other woman inhales sharply.

"If you think you're the wife and I'm the mistress, then you are in denial, lady!"

Maria resists the urge to slap her.

"Maybe you're in denial, Miss. You did know he was married, didn't you?"

"Separated."

Maria feels blood rushing to her face. The nerve!

"Separated. But still married. You should have stayed away from him!"

The other woman's eyes are defiant.

"Maybe it's you who should stay away from him! Your marriage is over. Your children are grown! Maybe it's time you left us alone, Mrs. Pop. This is what I came here to tell you. I want you to leave my boyfriend alone. I don't know what happened in your marriage. He never wanted to discuss it with me, but..."

"Good!" Maria cuts in. "Because it's none of your business."

"Oh, but it is my business, Mrs. Pop." Again, that stress on her name. She speaks it as if it's the most ridiculous thing she has ever heard, and it shakes Maria a little. Because, isn't it, after all? "It is my business, because I love him. He might be your husband on paper, but I am the woman who loves him. And we're together. You're gonna have to learn to respect that!"

Maria puffs, almost spitting her wine.

"You can't just go to a party and leave with my boyfriend," Monica says. "You just can't. And if you're blind, and think the fact that you're still married entitles you to anything, then I am here to open your eyes. Your marriage is over. And I want you to step out of the picture. You made him unhappy. I don't even need to know what you did to figure that out. It's obvious as daylight. You made him very unhappy. Mrs. Pop."

Maria looks into the depth and darkness of her wine. She looks at the face of her rival.

She watches without saying anything at first. Then slowly, she lets her lips contort into a bitter smile. She wants the other woman to feel in her bones, that Maria despises her.

"And with you, he's just floating on happiness, is that right?" She laughs. "That's why you're here. Because the two of you are just so fucking happy. What a perfect relationship you have, Miss ... whatever the hell your name was. Well, congratulations!"

She raises her glass in a mock toast to the other woman.

"Apparently the key to happiness is finding a man with problems in his marriage, sleeping with him, then sitting around blaming all your problems on his wife! Funny, isn't it, how whenever a man is an asshole, there always seems to be a woman in his past whose fault it really is. It's never him who is to blame. Some bitch must have done something bad to him at some point! Some bitch must have made him 'very unhappy,' as you say. The evil wife! Well, maybe you should write a book about it! I bet it'll sell like hot cakes! Besides, that should give you something to do on all the holidays my husband is spending with his wife and children, and you are all alone. How about Christmas? Maybe you can start then? Miss, whatever the fuck your name is. How about I cook a big turkey for my family, and eat it with my husband, whom you love, and I hurt, and you sit home all by yourself, thinking what a bitch I am, and how I made him so very unhappy. Maybe I'll even send you a little doggie bag, to give you some force, you know, so you can comfort him with your love, after I made him so terribly unhappy."

She's bluffing. She has no idea what Victor will choose to do at Christmas.

"You know," Maria continues, "I very strongly believe this, and throughout my life I have found it to be true. Whenever you take something that is not meant to be yours, it will come back to haunt you, and you will pay for it. Call it karma, if you wish. If I didn't know this to be true, I would shoplift from the glove department."

"I am not a bad person," Monica says.

"Maybe you are not. But for the past six years you have been fucking my husband. That is a bad thing to do."

"You are separated!"

"Separated," Maria repeats. "You keep saying that. But when you met Victor, we were not divorced. Actually, from two different ends of the city, we were raising our children together. Surely, you were aware of that. Were you?"

She pauses, waiting for Monica to nod. The other woman just sighs.

"Who did you think you were to decide that we were done with each other when you met him?" Maria asks, her voice rising. "How could you know I didn't want him back? Maybe I did, and maybe you were in the way."

Monica's eyes are fixing her.

"So you do want him back?"

"I will not answer that. As I said before, it is none of your business!"

The other woman puffs like an angry horse.

"Why did you come here to talk to me?" Maria asks. "Why don't you take all of this up with your lover?"

She specifically stresses the last word. Lover. *Amant*. In Romanian it implies something illicit about a relationship, something adulterous even.

Monica looks away. She sighs.

"Of course, you didn't want to upset Victor, did you? Maybe you should be less concerned about him, and think instead about what is good for you."

"You're telling me to leave him?"

Maria shrugs.

"It doesn't matter what I think. You're a grown woman. Figure it out for yourself."

She gestures for the bill, pouring her own wine into the other woman's glass. After sharing a man, she shouldn't mind drinking after her. Maria waves away Monica's gesture towards her purse, and places two fifties on top of the bill.

"Maybe this will help you," she says on her way out. "You and my daughter, Lili, you are close, right? I know she talks to you. She probably talks to you about intimate things. Why not? You are cool, you are stylish, you are older, you are not her mother. I believe you actually care about her, right? If my daughter came to you, and she was in your situation, what advice you would give?"

Leaving the bar, she feels powerful and triumphant. Later, on the subway, the euphoria subsides. Once all is said and done, it's just another Tuesday evening, she's going home to her empty apartment, her ballet flats are wet and dirty from the slush on the street, her feet are freezing, she has a headache from drinking on an empty stomach, and she is a hundred bucks poorer than before. There go her sheets of Egyptian cotton. She's tired, hungry, and cold. And though her pride just got a little boost, at the end of the day, is pride ever really worth it? Once she gets off the subway, she stops at McDonald's and orders a Big Mac with fries. She's ravenous after that wine. And who cares, anyway? She's not pregnant, her children are grown, her husband no longer wants her, and she has already wiped the floor with his beautiful mistress, so isn't it about time she coats her arteries in lard, and lets herself grow into a big fat cow?

{23}

Christmas

Maria takes another sip of coffee. She enjoys the warmth spreading through her body, waking her up. She lets her senses relish in the glorious scent of her apartment. Coffee, fir, vanilla, and the zesty spice of lemon peel. Nothing in the world could smell better.

She remembers her first Christmas in America, when they were not able to afford a tree at all. She cried quietly in the bathroom, missing the lovely scent of Christmases back home, the scent of fir, and of her grandmother's baking. Then, on Christmas eve, Victor appeared with a small tree, and she was so excited! He realized how much she wanted a tree! Although she never told him, knowing they couldn't afford one, he had read her mind, and he went out of his way to please her! He tried to make this easier on her, her first Christmas in the new country!

"I just couldn't stand the thought of our children not having a tree," he said. Her heart sank. She managed to smile, but there was no way to repress her disappointment. She knew it didn't matter, and that she got to enjoy the tree all the same, but it hurt her to know he bought it for the children, not for her. She felt selfish and immature, being jealous of her own children. She told herself that they were kids, and that their joy was more important than hers, especially at Christmas. To make up for her selfishness, she insisted they decorate the tree. She sat up all night making little ornaments out of scrap paper and the glass buttons of a hideous sweater somebody had given her. She unraveled the sweater to hang the ornaments on the yarn. They were ugly, her hand-made ornaments, but the children loved them.

The tree she got this year is bigger than the one they had on that first Christmas in America. It's greener, lusher, with a fuller crown. She didn't even bargain for it. With Victor's money sitting unused in her savings account, she relished in the small luxury of selecting the tree she liked best, and having it delivered, with no further complications. It arrived two days ago. She asked Alex to mount it in its stand, a task she always dreaded. He's home on break, mostly hibernating in his room, in between partying with friends. She caught him in one of his few waking moments, and asked him nicely to set up the tree at his own convenience. As usual, he flat out refused, and she didn't insist. She poured herself a glass of merlot, and decided to do it herself. She told herself that by now there was nothing she couldn't do if she put her mind to it, no task too complicated. She got the tree mounted, and after several tries, it even stood up straight, not crooked. Her hands were sore from the rough wood, but she was pleased with herself.

This morning, while drinking her coffee, she feels almost happy. Her tree is beautiful, and her house smells like Christmas. Three perfect pound cakes sit on the stove, tempting her with their golden crust.

Her body is sore from the effort. Pound cakes are not something she would normally make. But this is no regular Christmas. L is bringing home her boyfriend, an American boy. Alex actually refers to him as a *gringo*, and each time she hears it, Maria has to laugh. She's not pleased that L has acquired what appears to be a serious boyfriend. But as a mother, she considers it her duty to impress the young man. It will have to be a Christmas dinner like he never experienced before. And although Maria is not a big fan of tradition, she immediately decided to prepare the most traditional Romanian dishes she knew: Stuffed cabbage with polenta, then pound cakes for dessert. These are the two most labor-intensive foods she knows how to make, but they are also the most delicious, and the most likely to impress. Besides, she promised Mada a pound cake, for giving her free manicures all year.

Of course, there is another reason why she went through all this trouble. This is the first time she'll see Victor since Thanksgiving. She has not spoken to him since that night. Not even once. But she has, of course, asked L to invite him to Christmas dinner, as usual, and as usual, he has confirmed that he would come. It's not surprising, really. Victor would never miss spending Christmas with his children!

It seems surreal that in a few hours he'll be walking through her door, sitting at her table, eating her food. The last time she saw him, he was lying in bed next to her, naked. The thought of that night makes her jittery. Will she even be able to survive Christmas dinner in the presence of Victor? Will her gestures betray her? Will her children read her secret in her eyes, in her burning cheeks, and her trembling hands?

Whatever happens, she knows that she'll fare best if the meal is impeccable. There is no better distraction for a hostess than serving complicated food, food she'll have to fuss over all evening, food that will hopefully be the center of attention. Presented with delicious *sarmale*, intoxicated by the scent of fresh baked *cozonaci*, her children shouldn't even notice *Mami* being flustered. And she herself will be too busy to pay attention to the butterflies in her stomach, and the weakness in her knees.

As she stretches her aching back, a souvenir of staying up last night, kneading dough like a maniac, she knows that vanity has got the best of her. There is no use denying it. She's gone to incredible expense, and tremendous effort, and the true reason has nothing to do with L's young man. The person she's really been cooking for is Victor. More than ever, tonight, she wants him to enjoy her food. She wants to lay out a feast that will amaze and delight him, a meal that will make him miss her with the same painful intensity that she's been missing him.

She still feels the pangs of rejection from his silence, his refusal to make even a small gesture to acknowledge what happened between them. She still cries over it every now and then. But there is nothing she can do about it. Except serve the most delicious Christmas meal he's ever tasted.

She knows how much he likes stuffed cabbage. Not just any stuffed cabbage. Hers. After all, it's not a regular dish, one that turns out the same each time somebody follows a recipe. It tastes differently depending on who makes it, has a different consistency even. The cook's personality is served along with the meal. She's had *sarmale* that were glorious, but she also had some she could hardly bring herself to swallow. Some people make them too greasy. Others lace them with smoked bacon, a taste her southern European taste buds never grew to like. Others add too much sauce, too much rice, too much salt.

Hers are perfection. She chooses the best cuts of meat, a combination of lean beef and pork, then has the butcher grind them in front of her very eyes. She adds the perfect combination of spices, and just enough rice. She takes her time wrapping each roll, in the best pickled cabbage she can find, making sure each palm sized ball looks the same, and that it is wrapped tightly. She adds tomato sauce, then slow cooks them on the stovetop. Finally, she bakes them in the oven until the juices evaporate, and the top layer is brown and crispy.

The cakes, of course, have a saga of their own. Madalina was an angel to help out. Maria would not have managed the dough on her own. It needs to be kneaded for over an hour, in vigorous continuous motion, until it no longer sticks to one's fingers, and its fragrant yellow mass turns into bursting little bubbles. Only then will the pound cakes come out soft and fluffy, layers and layers of feathery dough, slowly unraveling in one's hand.

Red in the face, and with sweat running down her back from the effort, Madalina laughed at the elaborate process. The yellow mass was stubborn, sticking to their fingers, and refusing to let them manipulate it. They had to tear at it, then slap it hard, and it seemed to rebel. It felt like operating some grueling machine at the gym, and Mada kept saying that she could not believe Maria was actually doing all this.

Mada isn't much for domestic chores, and that's one thing Maria loves about her. She's not traditional. But last night, her lack of skill and patience started grinding on Maria's nerves.

"I can't believe you're going through all this trouble, Mari!" Madalina exclaimed, and Maria rolled her eyes. They had been kneading for 45 minutes. Yes, it was a long time, but they had at least half an hour to go. There was no use complaining.

"So what is next after this? Are we maybe weaving a rug? Or grinding flour?" Mada asked laughing, oblivious to Maria's irritation.

"Move your hands faster, girl. Watch me. You grab it, pull, then smack!" Maria instructed. "Afterwards we'll drink some more wine and you can tell me more about this new boyfriend. And then, I was thinking, while the dough is rising, you can help me wrap the *sarmale*."

Madalina laughed harder.

"S*armale*? And you want us to wrap them? By hand?"

"It is the only way, silly. Besides, the only reason you've never done this is because you don't have children. Lucky bitch."

"I don't recall you going to so much trouble for your children last year… or the year before last…"

"Yes, well, I told you L is bringing home a young man."

"I thought you weren't happy about the boyfriend. Didn't you say you were afraid L might be getting too serious with him?"

"I still feel that way. She's too young."

"So then, what are you trying to impress him for?"

Maria shrugged.

"I don't know. I might not be happy about it, but L likes him. Maybe she's even in love. I don't want her to be embarrassed when she brings him home. Although I have considered opening a can of spam and telling him it's traditional Romanian Christmas fare, and that we like to eat it with our hands."

Mada laughed.

They kneaded silently for another few minutes, then Mada started giggling, still not able to contain her amusement at having to perform such bizarre and outdated chores.

"I can't believe I'm wearing a fuckin' apron, and kneading dough for a whole hour!"

"Two hours, love," Maria corrected. "You know, I think one can measure the level of oppression towards women within a culture by how labor intensive the dishes are!"

Mada laughed, nodding.

"You are unbelievable, you know, Mari? You're such a living contradiction! Only you would insist we do all these insanely old-fashioned housewife things, after complaining for years that mother-hood is awful and oppressive!"

Maria's free hand smacked her, before she even stopped laugh-ing.

"Shut up! I don't want my son to hear you!"

"He doesn't speak Romanian, Mari," Madalina reminded her, rubbing her shoulder with her free hand. "You really hit me hard, you crazy bitch!"

"I'm sorry, love. It's just... Did I really hit you that hard?"

Mada shrugged. They both returned to kneading, but Maria's thoughts kept wandering.

"I used to hit Victor, you know... When we were still together, when we would fight. I would get so angry, and I would hit him. Not like I hit you, not like a joke, but really hit him, with a fist, and hard. I always felt bad about it afterwards."

"I was never much of a hitter. But I used to yell at Doru. And one time I threw a vase at the wall."

"I threw stuff too," Maria admitted. "Lots of things, and some-times I'd actually aim at Victor. He never did anything like that, you know? Always calm, always, you know... civilized. I used to feel like such a savage in comparison."

Mada gave her an affectionate look. She always did that when Maria talked about the past, about her married life with Victor. And in a way, it made it harder for Maria to discuss these things with her.

"You were young, Mari. And you had a lot of shit to deal with... I mean coming here, and being poor, and two kids..." Madalina was the only other Romanian Maria knew, who seemed to understand that raising kids was not all it's cracked up to be. "I cannot even imagine… I would have lost it too, and smacked the shit out of my husband *and* the children."

"Oh, no," Maria shook her head. "Not the children. They drove me crazy at times. Especially Alex. You know he never did anything I asked him to. Never. Even when he was little. Sometimes I just wanted to pick him up and shake him. But I never did. I never touched him. Sometimes it took all the strength I had not to hit him."

"Maybe you should have." Mada was perpetually outraged at Alex' insolence towards his mother.

"I don't know. Mrs. Stoica, my friend, the old one who died, she'd tell me I should beat him. She'd say I should do it after I calm down, never angry, but always point out that it was punishment for whatever he had done. She'd say that then he'd learn to respect me and fear me. But really, I never wanted my kids to fear me. And I promised myself before I even had them that I would never beat them. I don't believe in beating children. I just don't."

"You must be the only Romanian mother who feels that way."

Maria laughed.

"I guess. But you know, it's just so… savage and cruel."

"Yet most of us grew up that way. I mean, didn't you get smacked when you were a child?"

"On and off," Maria admitted. "My mother was not strict, and my father, well, you know, he left, so it was just her and me, and grandma. They spoiled me. Funny thing is, my mother beat me more after I grew up than she did all my childhood."

"Really? How old were you?"

"Well, I was twenty when I got engaged to Victor. He took me to the Black Sea. For May Day. We had separate rooms, of course. But that's where he proposed to me, and…" Maria felt herself blush. Madalina nudged her with her elbow, prompting her to continue.

"Well, never mind," Maria said, concentrating on her kneading. What was she thinking, starting such a conversation?

"Oh come on, Mari!" Mada raised her hands, threatening to abandon the dough in protest. "You never share anything! What happened?"

Maria hesitated.

"Well..."

"You slept with him?"

"Only after he proposed!"

Mada laughed.

"Of course! And?"

Maria sighed.

"...well, we were at the Black Sea for the weekend. And when he drove me home, I still remember that night. It was already dark when he pulled up in front of my mother's house, and I got out. I remember the crisp air and the smell of lilacs, and the salt still tingling on my skin. It was a lovely night and I was in love and happy and floating on thin air, and when I got in the house I started telling my mother that Victor had asked me to marry him, but she stopped me. I guess she could tell by the look on my face what had happened, and she just lost it. She accused me of sleeping with him, and she started hitting me and pulling my hair, and yelling that I was an idiot, that all he wanted from me was sex and that now he would dump me. She would not stop and listen, she just yelled and hit me, until I managed to run into my room. I could not believe it. I mean, she had never done anything like that before. And then she locked me in my room. I escaped through the window, and ran to my grandma's house, all the way to the outskirts of town. The next day I had a date with Victor, and he was supposed to pick me up at my mother's. I couldn't call him, because we had no phone where my grandmother lived. So I just showered and put on one of her dresses, which was big for me, I was so skinny then, a blue silk dress, I still remember it like it was yesterday, and I went back to town on the streetcar to meet him in front of my mother's house. But the stupid streetcar was late, and when I got there Victor's car was already parked in front of the house, and Victor was nowhere to be found. I waited, I worried, I paced back and forth. Then finally I rang the doorbell. And there was my mother, happy and cheerful as can be, acting as if she'd expected me back any minute, acting as if she'd sent me to my grandmother's herself! She was having coffee with Victor! Her new adored son in law, who according to her could do no wrong! Funny how one day she almost killed me for sleeping with him, the next day she was bending over backwards to be the most charming hostess, and from then on she never stopped trying to please him. I mean, after I married him, most of my conflicts with her were over Victor. Whenever she thought I wasn't doing enough, wasn't as sweet, agreeable, and lovely a wife as she thought he deserved, she'd throw a fit. And one time she actually slapped me for eating some meatballs she'd fried for him. I could not believe it, my own mother, slapping me, for eating two meatballs, because she was afraid there would not be enough for my husband!"

Madalina shook her head.

"Romanian mothers!" she said with a sigh. "They always hate their daughter-in-laws, but they treat their son-in-laws better than their own flesh and blood! That's so crazy, Mari!"

Maria gave her friend an affectionate look. She had listened patiently, and had kept on kneading the dough. She was good like that.

"So if she loved him so much, how did she react when you two broke up?"

"Oh, it was a disaster! Even before he left… Once I stopped getting along with him, she just… Well, I'd call her and complain about him. We were already here, and I'd feel so alone, and I didn't talk to her much because it was expensive, but whenever I did, I sometimes told her Victor doesn't understand me, or Victor expects me to do this and that… And she'd always side with him. All the way from across the ocean, my mother would chastise me, for not being a good wife! And when I asked him to leave, she told me I would regret it and that I should have tried to keep him, and… Well, it just got too aggravating to talk to her, and I sort of gave up. So now we talk maybe twice a year, if even that. And of course, she still asks about Victor. Have I seen him? Does he ever come over? Do I ask the children to tell him they miss him? All sorts of bullshit you would not even imagine!"

Maria pushed the dough more furiously.

"What is going on with you and Victor, Mari?"

The question came out of thin air. Only Madalina would have been able to guess that behind the whole tirade about her mother, she was actually hiding her need to talk about Victor. Mada knew her well. She had weathered her silences though so many manicures, had been there to hold her hand when she was depressed. Never asking, never prying. Until now. Yes, Mada was a good friend. For that, she deserved honesty.

"I went home with him at Thanksgiving and I slept with him."

It felt good actually saying it out loud. Though as soon as she said it, she felt the sting of tears in her eyes. She tried to concentrate on the dough, its color, its scent, its texture, to distract herself. And to avoid Mada's eyes, fixing her with a mix of concern and anticipation.

"And? What happened afterwards?"

Maria shrugged.

"Nothing. I went home."

"Just like that?"

"Yes. Just like that."

"Did you talk?"

"No. We just... you know. And then I left while he was sleeping."

"While he was sleeping?"

Coming from Madalina's lips, Maria's early morning escape sounded dreadful. A wave of shame and hopelessness washed over her. She had no desire to discuss this any further. What use was it? Except to tear at her own wounds, and to embarrass herself further?

She spanked the dough a few more times, noticing with satisfaction that the kneading was done. The yellow mass no longer stuck to her fingers. She sighed a sigh of relief.

But just as she was about to announce they were done, and suggest they now wash their hands and place the giant pot somewhere warm so that the dough could rise, Mada asked the most dreadful question of all:

"How was the sex?"

Maria exhaled sharply.

"Excuse me?"

Madalina rolled her eyes, and smacked the dough twice, harder than Maria had thought her capable of.

"Fucking hell, Mari!" This was her favorite curse. "What the fuck is wrong with you? I'm your friend, your best friend, probably your only friend. And you stiffen up like a stick if I ask you one lousy intimate question! You're in love with that fucking husband of yours, but you leave in the morning before he wakes up! Why the fuck can't you fucking open up to anyone ever?"

Madalina struck the dough once more. Maria's head jerked back. She removed her own hand from the batter and started wiping the yellow dough off her fingers. She felt too weak to fight back the tears that were building up inside her, too weak to even stand up straight. So she sat down in the chair Madalina had brought over before they'd started kneading, in the feeble hope that maybe she'd get to use it. Maria had mocked her, saying that kneading dough required standing, that it was a full body workout, and that cooking in general was not something one should do sitting down. It was one of the things she had learned from her mother.

Now Maria herself was sitting down, her elbows resting on the table, her face hidden in her dough-smeared palms, unable to stop herself from crying.

"Mada, you really are a true friend. But I cannot talk about this," she said between sobs, once again feeling acutely her general loneliness in this world, the intense feeling of missing Victor, the giant hole left in her life by his departure, by his indifference toward her.

Madalina inched closer and placed a hand on Maria's back. Maria straightened her stance abruptly, as if wanting to shake off Mada's kindness.

"This is done," she declared, pointing to the dough. "I need to cover it, then you can help me put it up on the cupboard."

Mada sighed.

"Back to the pound cakes, I guess."

It takes all of Maria's strength to lift the pot of *sarmale* and stick it in the oven. There are over a hundred tiny rolls of pickled cabbage in there. There will be more than ten *sarmale* for each person. Of course, nobody can eat ten *sarmale*, but excess is tradition. If there isn't too much, there isn't enough.

Of course, for a Christmas dinner, just *sarmale* and *mamaliga* are not enough. In Romania, Maria's mother would first serve various pork specialties, as well as *salata de boeuf* and other appetizers. Then she would follow that with *ciorba*, a delicious sour soup, a roast, then finally *sarmale*. It's much more food than anyone can eat, but Romanians like to feast.

Maria made Lili's favorite, *salata de boeuf.* She also marinated and roasted a pork loin, knowing it ranks pretty high among Victor's favorites. She'll serve it cold, cut into thin slices. For the rest, she had to rely on store bought appetizers. She chose various salads: smoked fish, grated carrots, green beans, and beets with black walnuts. Her purchases have nothing in common with traditional Romanian fare, but she tasted each item at the deli, and decided they were good. Of course, she also bought several kinds of cheese. She cannot imagine a Romanian gathering without cheese.

She's still thinking of the appetizers and how best to display them, when she finally jumps in the shower. Running hot water over her face, she tries to relax, and to briefly forget about the food, and even about Victor. How typical of her, to spend hours and hours fixing a meal, and leave so little time for pampering herself. She needs to beautify and rejuvenate before her encounter with Victor, or at least to remove the smell of pickled cabbage from her fingers.

By the time she gets out of the shower, slathers lotion all over her body, places Velcro curlers in her hair, and touches up her manicure, it's gotten dangerously late. L and her boyfriend will be here any minute. They're coming early to decorate the tree.

She quickly goes through her clothes looking for her favorite dress, a black wrap that flatters her figure. But then she realizes that it's the same dress she wore on Thanksgiving. She had it dry cleaned, and it now hangs neatly inside a plastic wrap, as if it were new. But it still makes her shiver to think that the last time her husband saw her in it, he untied it and peeled it off her body. There's no way in hell she can wear this tonight!

With no time to spare, and no inspiration, she picks the next best thing. A white silk blouse with a black pencil skirt. Too professional. But still, the blouse is elegant, the white silk flatters her complexion, and the skirt makes her look slender. And after all, it's a timeless classic. The doorbell rings. She quickly steps into her shoes, pulls the rollers out of her hair, and runs to greet her guests.

L is standing there, wearing a cute winter pea coat, and a new red scarf. She looks pretty, but shockingly young. As if since Maria last saw her, she's not been maturing, but turning back into a child. Next to her stands a young man, slightly taller, with a pleasant face, and kind eyes. He's holding a bouquet of flowers and a bottle of wine.

"Hello," Maria says. As usual, when meeting someone new, she feels shy. What is the appropriate thing to do here? Hold out her hand? For him to do what? Shake it, or kiss it? She's not sure what young American men do when meeting their girlfriends' mothers. And he's holding all that stuff, anyway.

"*Mami*, this is Greg. Greg, this is my mother." L takes over in a voice that sounds unnaturally cheerful. She seems overly excited, almost fake. Giggling like a schoolgirl, she retrieves the wine from her boyfriend, so he and Maria can shake hands. So that's the protocol, apparently. Maria thinks the gesture too familiar, too chummy. His touch is too light, and his palm is sweaty, something she always detested. He must be nervous. Good. He should be nervous. He's meeting his girlfriend's overprotective Romanian mother, after all.

"I'm Mrs. Pop. Nice meet you." She flashes him a customer service smile and thanks for the flowers, little white mums, wrapped in too much plastic.

They step inside. L's face lights up with delight at the explosion of scents.

"*Mami*, what did you make?" She heads to the kitchen, the boy trailing behind, like a puppy.

"Greg, you've gotta see this! These are the best cakes ever. *Cozonaci.* And look at this," she says, opening the oven door, where the stuffed cabbage is roasting at low heat. "*Sarmale*! Mami, you are amazing!"

Maria smiles. She feels deceitful. L assumes her *Mami* cooked for her and her young man. When in fact, *Mami* is selfish, vain, and has a completely different agenda.

"Why you don't put on music, my sweetie, open the wine, and you two decorate tree? I go put on makeup, and then I set table and arrange appetizers, ok?"

"Is there *salata de boeuf*?" L asks, clapping her hands like a child.

"Of course, my sweetie."

"Oh, Greg, I told you! There will be a lot of amazing food!"

In her bedroom, while applying her makeup, and looking for some jewelry to go with her outfit, Maria can hear the music L selected. Christmas carols sung by an Austrian choir. She smiles, hearing her daughter sing along. She's really something, her little girl! She actually knows the German lyrics.

There's not much to choose from in terms of jewelry. She settles for a simple gold chain that accents her collarbone, and simple gold loop earrings. It's jewelry Victor bought for her, more than twenty years ago, when they were still in love and living happily together in Romania. She would like to wear something that's not from him, but these are the only decent pieces she has. These, and her wedding ring, which she, of course, will not be wearing. Reaching into her jewelry box, she tries to avoid touching it, as if it might burn her.

By the time Alex comes home, she's already setting the table, using her best linens, a present from Mrs. Stoica. They are hand embroidered, heavy white linens. Unfolding them, Maria still feels the scent of her old friend's cupboards, and it brings tears to her eyes. The old woman brought them with her from Romania, as one of her most treasured possessions, but refused to give them to her daughters. "Their tastes are too modern; they won't appreciate them."

Maria doesn't use them often. They are too precious to her. But she's happy to use them for this special meal, proud that she has real linens, and real cloth napkins, for just such an occasion. She sets candles on the table, and places Greg's flowers in the center, in her favorite vase. She just hopes he won't spill anything on her good linens, or she'll stab him with a fork. There's only so much a woman can take from her daughter's boyfriend!

She's arranging the appetizers in matching china bowls when the doorbell rings again. Her heart stops, and she feels like her throat is closing in. It's Victor.

She lets L get the door, and stays in the kitchen, under the guise of decorating the marinated pork loin with fresh sprigs of parsley. She tries to concentrate on this simple task, but her hands are shaking. She can think of nothing else. He's there, in the next room. She can hear his voice, and it sends chills up her spine. She's not sure she can stand this, not sure she'll be able to face him, spend a whole evening sitting next to him. In vain, she tries to concentrate on the pattern of parsley on the platter. It's useless. She's making a mess. The whole arrangement looks ridiculous, but she doesn't care. She's just hoping and praying she won't drop the roast while carrying it to the table.

She hears Victor's footsteps through the doorway, coming into her kitchen. Her stomach tightens. She has her back to him, but she can feel his presence.

"Hello, Maria," he says. Cold but polite. His usual style. If he feels nervous, he doesn't betray it.

"Hello, Victor," she says, without turning around. She concentrates on grinding fresh black pepper on the meat. She doesn't even like pepper.

"Lili tells me you've been cooking up quite the feast," he says. "I can't believe you actually made *sarmale*!"

He sounds artificially friendly. She hates it when he does that! He's talking to her like she's an acquaintance he doesn't know well, but wants to be nice to. It negates everything that ever happened between them, their whole story.

"Is just food," she says coldly. She finally turns around, and shoves the platter of pork into his hands. "Take this to table, please. And open more wine."

Sitting down with her family she feels flustered and nervous. She can barely eat the little heaps of carrots, green beans, and beets on her plate, though they taste even better now than they did at the deli. Everybody is complimenting her pork loin and especially her *salata de boeuf.*

She smiles at her guests, but she can hardly hear them. It's too much, having to sit here, next to Victor. As usual, he looks so handsome it hurts. And he seems completely unconcerned with her. He's having an animated conversation with Greg, pouring wine generously into everybody's glasses, and appears to be thoroughly enjoying the food.

Looking for an excuse to leave the table, Maria announces that she has to get started on the polenta.

"*Mamaliga*!" L exclaims, and Maria smiles. She loves how her daughter knows the words for everything. She's truly amazing, her little girl.

Stirring the hot mixture of cornmeal and water with a wooden spoon, a task that requires full concentration, she's finally able to get a moment's peace. She likes to watch the bubbles dance around the heavy pot. There's a peculiar combination of simplicity and danger to this task. She throws in a stick of butter, stirs once more, and in one swift motion empties the mixture into a large china bowl. She's proud of her ability to do this with grace, and more importantly, without burning herself.

Her *sarmale* enjoy the success she's been hoping for. While she herself is still too nervous to eat, everybody else devours several, and with each additional helping, the compliments keep pouring. Even Alex, her harshest critic, states repeatedly that she has outdone herself. She smiles at her son, happy to see him content for once. But even this is little consolation.

In the end, what she mostly cares about is Victor's praise. She's trying not to stare, but she is watching his every bite. As he's helping himself to his third portion, he looks at her, and says:

"I think this is the best meal you've ever made!"

It's the superlative of compliments. Still, she can't answer kindly.

"And how you would know?"

It comes out too acidic. She sounds so mean and petty she's ashamed of herself.

"God, mom!" Alex sighs. "Can't you be nice for once?"

But Victor laughs.

"What I meant is that it's the best Christmas meal I've ever had."

He tries to make eye contact, but she deliberately looks away.

"Thank you," she says. It's not the superlative of compliments. It's beyond that. It almost makes her cry. She has to stand up, and go into the kitchen. When she comes back, she's carrying a breadbasket, her lame excuse for having left the room. It's utterly stupid, because nobody eats *sarmale* and *mamaliga* with bread, but luckily they're too engaged in conversation to notice.

She folds her dinner napkin on her lap, and tries to listen to the conversation. They're talking about Romanian wines. Of course, the young man, Greg, is showing a lot of interest in everything Victor has to say. Smart man. Trying to get on the good side of L's daddy. If she were him, Maria would do exactly the same. But seeing him do it, she resents him.

Victor brought a whole case of Romanian wine. It's from a select winery, something only a few stores in the city carry, because it's imported in moderation. Maria has to admit it's one of the best wines she's ever had. Still, the conversation bores her, and after a while, she stops paying attention. While they're all talking about wines, she's carefully studying L's young man. He's reasonably attractive, though not extremely so, and he seems to know it. He displays none of the arrogance typical of handsome men. He actually seems nice enough, and it's obvious that he's head over heels in love with her daughter. Their small gestures as a couple betray it. She wonders if they're sleeping together. After all, young women are freer nowadays, and that's not a bad thing. She searches her daughter's face. Is she happy? Is she in love? She seems to be enjoying Greg's attention. But whether there is love on her side of the equation, Maria cannot tell.

After everybody has had more than their fill of *sarmale*, she stands up and starts collecting the dishes. Greg offers to help, but she demands he sit back down. Kids don't do chores in her household. Of course, her own children know that, and laugh at Greg's initiative. Spoiled brats!

She brings out one of the fragrant cakes, and distributes desert plates around the table. Victor opens another bottle of wine.

Lili offers Greg a brief explanation of the cake. Maybe Victor has been too enthusiastic in pouring out the wine, because the young man seems buzzed. He raises his glass to make a toast:

"To L's wonderful parents, Maria and Victor. An amazing couple!"

Uncomfortable silence fills the room. Did L not explain their situation?

"I mean, amazing people!" Greg corrects himself, blushing. "I just want to say I think it is awesome that the two of you get together like this, like a family, even though you are not…"

L stares at him and frowns. Her irritation is obvious, and Maria wonders once again, if she's in love with him. Greg's voice falters, but he boldly goes on.

"What I mean is, it is wonderful that you are friendly with each other, and able to get together like this, and keep up with tradition."

Yes, Maria thinks. We sure have lovely traditions, Victor and I. We actually just came up with a new one: Every ten years or so, we get together, fuck each other's brains out, and then completely ignore each other afterwards.

She feels sorry for Greg. He's young, tipsy, in love with L, and nervous to meet her weird foreign parents. And then, on top of that, he has committed a blunder. Poor fellow!

"Thank you, Greg," she says. "I really appreciate that. And I'm glad you here with us tonight."

"Yes, thank you, Greg," Victor adds. "It is lovely to see one's daughter in the company of such a nice young man."

L smiles. Victor's approval means a lot to her.

"Actually," Greg says, blushing, "I have something to ask you, Mr. Pop."

Formal, out of a sudden. Maria has a dark premonition.

“I want to ask for your daughter’s hand in marriage.”

Once more, the room goes quiet. L looks down at the piece of cake on her plate. Victor’s face is impenetrable. Greg is watching him like a dog hoping for a treat.

Maria is the first to speak:

“L is grown woman, Greg. If you want marry her, you need ask her, not her father.”

Alex rolls his eyes in exasperation.

“God, mom! Give the guy a break!”

“Actually, I could not agree more,” Victor says. “My opinion in this matter is the last thing that should concern you, Greg.”

He looks at Maria, but she avoids his eyes.

The young man kneels in front of L’s chair. He is holding out a small velvet box with a ring in it. Maria thinks she’s going to be sick.

“L, will you marry me? Will you be my wife?”

L blushes. Then, to Maria’s horror, she nods. The next thing she knows, that ring is on her daughter’s finger, and L, in tears by now, holds it out for her to see. Maria casts an absent glance. She cannot care less about a stupid diamond. What she really wants is to read L’s eyes. Her daughter looks like someone who has just impulsively purchased something extravagant and expensive, and is overcome by the delight of such momentous occasion. But what will she be feeling later, after the thrill and novelty subsides?

Victor expresses more enthusiasm about the ring than the mother of the bride. Even Alex is complimentary.

“Who want coffee?” Maria asks while they are still gushing over that stupid stone. She sets out for the kitchen to look for her Turkish coffee pot. To her surprise, Victor follows her.

“Do you have any hard liquor?” he asks.

“There’s whisky, rum, and vodka.”

“Vodka, please.”

“In freezer,” she says, looking at the water in her pot, waiting for it to boil.

Victor pours himself a big glass of vodka. He starts opening the door to the fire escape.

"Is freezing out," she says. "Just smoke here." It's something she would not allow under normal circumstances. But these are hardly normal circumstances, are they? "And give me one too."

He hands her a cigarette and offers to light it, but she ignores his gesture and lights it from the stove instead.

"Do you approve of this, Victor?" Her voice is sharp, yet she is keeping it low enough so they can't hear her in the other room.

"Whether I approve or not, they will still do whatever they want."

"She's ruining her life. I think we should tell her."

Victor sighs.

"If there's one thing I know, it's that telling young people whom not to marry only makes them stubborn."

Maria looks away. She spoons ground coffee into the boiling water, and turns off the flame. She takes a long drag of her cigarette. It makes her dizzy. It feels good.

Victor's mother never approved of her. Too young, too poor, the result of a broken marriage, a literature student, probably a Gypsy. Not what her mother-in-law had been hoping for. But Victor married her anyway. And he did not marry her out of spite. Back then, he loved her. It hurts to think of it now, but he loved her.

"Is not about who to marry. Is about marrying at all. She's too young, Victor."

"I know," he says. "But she might still change her mind."

"God help us!" Maria crosses herself, something she rarely does. She hates public displays of religion.

She pours the coffee into little cups. She brings it to the table on a tray. On her way out she realizes that Victor has already emptied his glass of vodka.

She keeps searching her daughter's face. L seems a little too hyper. Coffee is probably the last thing she needs, but when Maria offers her a cup, she eagerly accepts.

"You know, *Tati*," she says to Victor, "remember the Labor Day party when that woman read my fortune in the coffee grounds? Remember she saw a ring?"

She beams happily, holding out her sparkly little diamond.

"Ring does not always mean marriage," Maria says. "It really mean fulfillment. Things coming full circle. Completion. Harmony."

Greg laughs nervously.

"Isn't that what marriage is all about?" he asks.

"You be surprised," Maria replies, taking a sip of her coffee.

"On that happy note," Alex announces, "I need to bounce. Thanks for a great dinner, Mom. Bye, Dad! Nice meeting you, Greg, my man! Congratulations to you!"

Alex distributes a set of high fives and handshakes around the room, then off he goes.

Lili and Greg follow shortly after, leaving Maria in the nerve-racking predicament of being alone with Victor. She starts collecting the dishes. When she gets to the kitchen, she sees that he's poured himself yet another glass of vodka. He's smoking again. She regrets having allowed him to do so in her house. Whatever fleeting solidarity with Victor she experienced at the thought of their daughter's marriage, it is gone now. Now the smoke bothers her, his presence makes her nervous, and she wishes that he'd go home.

She places the dishes in the sink, and runs the water. If she starts cleaning up, he might leave. But he just continues to sit there, smoking and drinking, staring into space. When he's finally done with his cigarette, he stubs it out on the small plate he's been using as an ashtray.

He stands up, and comes towards her. Her heart racing, she continues washing the dishes, keeping her back towards him. But it's no use. He comes up from behind, putting his hand around her waist, pulling her close. She can smell the smoke on him, stronger and more bothersome than usual, almost nauseating. His hand is riding up her thigh, lifting her pencil skirt.

"No," she says, loud and clear. "No, Victor, let go of me!"

"Why not?" he asks, his hand already between her legs.

"Mona and I broke up, you know."

He's slurring his speech. He's drunk.

She tries to push his hand away, but it stays in place, pressing harder, until she can feel it with every fiber of her body.

He laughs.

"Stop pretending to be such a prude!"

She hates the vulgarity of it all, hates that she's not strong enough to push him away, hates that he feels entitled to just reach under her skirt and touch her, with no permission, and no preliminaries.

"Victor, I said no!"

He lets go, and she steps away, straightening her clothes. When she turns to face him, he looks confused, hurt even.

"So you seriously don't want this?"

"No."

The look on his face is one of sheer bewilderment.

"Did you hear what I said? Mona and I are over."

She failed to process it the first time. Now that she thinks of it, she's not surprised. And she's not satisfied either. She's just angry.

"So? What do you expect from me? To immediately fill her place? This is not musical chairs, Victor. You can't just swap one for the other."

"You are my wife," he points out.

"What else is new? I was your wife when you were with Mona, too. And before that. That does not mean I have to sleep with you."

"Nobody's holding a gun to your head, woman. But from what I could tell, you really liked it last time. You'd be a hypocrite to deny it. That was fucking awesome, and you loved it."

She blushes and looks away, but decides to be honest.

"Yes. I did. It was really good."

It feels liberating to say it out loud.

A smug smile spreads on Victor's face, and she feels just a little bit like punching him.

"So you liked it. It was good. And now I'm free. And you're my wife."

She has to fight the urge to slap his drunken face.

"I am your estranged wife. And until a few days ago you were fucking another woman. Actually, that's not even fair. You were in a full-blown relationship with another woman. A six-year relationship, if I am not mistaken. And now you just expect me take you back? Just like that? You don't think it actually requires some work to win me back, Victor?"

He laughs. It's more a snort than a laugh, really.

"What the fuck do you expect? Flowers and a serenade? Don't hold your fucking breath! I'm not going to court my own wife!"

"Your estranged wife. And whether you like it or not, you and I both have done some horrible things to hurt each other. It would take a lot of work to patch things up. It's like..."

She's surprised by her calm and patience. She's not sure how long she'll be able to go on without losing her temper, without hitting him. But it's important to tell him where she stands.

"Like an omelet," she says. "You make a bad omelet, you can't fix it. You have to make a new one."

She feels absurd having just said that. It's silly, and even in his drunken state, Victor seems amused by her lack of eloquence.

"Suit yourself, princess. I'm going home."

He starts walking away. She follows him.

"You drank too much, Victor. You can't drive. Stay here tonight."

He looks at her with disgust.

"I don't need your fuckin' sympathy," he says. "And I no longer want to sleep with you."

"I mean in Alex' room."

Although she knows it's an unnecessary precaution, Maria locks her bedroom door. The thought of Victor in the other room unnerves her. When she finally goes to bed, in spite of being absolutely exhausted, her mind refuses to switch off. Maybe she's had too much coffee, or maybe she's had too much wine, but she can't fall asleep. She keeps thinking of that damn boy proposing to her daughter, and of her conversation with Victor. She keeps replaying it in her head, over and over. She keeps thinking of what she said, and how she could have better phrased it. Was it even worth it, explaining herself to him? Can it ever be worth explaining anything to a drunk man who feels like he owns you?

She tosses and turns all night. She keeps thinking of L and her young man. Will they really go through with it? Is there any way for her to stop it? Why does she even want to stop it? Is she maybe wrong, can there be any chance that this is actually a good thing for her daughter, and that she, her mother, is only doubting it because she's a bitter old woman who has messed up her own life?

She keeps thinking of Victor in the other room. She feels like she's been unkind. Though, really, she's proud of having said no. She's also proud of resisting her impulse to comfort him when he looked so vulnerable. After all, kindness to Victor has always been her downfall. But she can't help feeling some sort of tenderness, some sort of concern. She wonders if he's ok after drinking so much. But no, she's not going to check on him, as if he were a sick child. It's crazy and self-destructive to even think of it. But maybe in the morning she will make him breakfast. Maybe then she can talk to him again, sober. Maybe he'll act differently then. Maybe they both will.

She anticipates waking up before him, making coffee, cutting up some of the pound cake and toasting it, squeezing fresh orange juice, frying eggs and bacon, adding hot sauce, to fight off his hangover. When he'll emerge from Alex' room, with a monster headache, she'll be waiting for him with aspirin and a warm breakfast. The thought makes her feel better, and finally she's able to relax. She sleeps a full nine hours. When she wakes up, it's almost noon. As she steps out of her bedroom, rubbing the sleep from her eyes, Alex' door is wide open. Her son's bed is a mess. The other bed is neatly made. Victor already left.

She paces around her apartment, feeling oddly bereaved. Once again, emptiness weighs her down. She's so lonely it physically hurts. And for a woman who so badly longed to be alone, it sure is an unexpected revelation.

{24}

A New Life

It's a white door, covered with a shiny coat of paint. If you look carefully, the way she has, you'll see the individual brushstrokes. She loves these little imperfections.

The door squeaks loudly, and she's greeted by the smell of dust and aged wood, slightly wilted, slightly sweet. To her, this smell is heaven. And if you can't understand why, you've obviously never loved an old house.

She stops to take it all in, the hardwood floors, the beige walls, the large French window, and that lovely scent of days gone by. She's finally home!

It's just one room, and a small one at that. She once stayed in a hotel room that was larger. There are some disadvantages, a fourth floor walk up, a tiny bathroom with a shower and no tub, no separation between the kitchen and the rest of the living space. Still, it's a small studio apartment in lower Manhattan, it's full of light, and worn and lovely, and it's hers.

There is only one window, but it's large, and faces south. She loves the tree whose branches almost touch her one window. It's an ordinary tree. She doesn't know what kind. At least it's not a walnut tree. If it were, she would not have bought the apartment.

She loves the beige walls; they look old fashioned and mellow. She loves the fact that all doors and window frames are painted white.

She knows details like these are unimportant, that she could easily change them. But she is happy that she likes it just the way it is.

She loves the built-in shelves, ideal for her books. And she loves that this tiny place, with its puny bathroom, actually has a walk-in closet, a luxury she's never had before.

Of course, having her kitchen in her bedroom is not something she's crazy about. There won't be enough counter space for all her pots and pans and spices. But then again, with her children grown, her son openly hating her, and her daughter obviously avoiding her, who is she going to cook for anyway?

Buying the apartment has been an ordeal. She never could have imagined all the complications, the paperwork, the inspections, all the people she had to deal with, the calls to and from the bank, the sleepless nights. But finally, she did it! And she's proud that in spite of her bad English, she was able to handle it all on her own. When she recalls her first years in this country, the frustration of stumbling around clueless, her victory in buying this apartment seems even more momentous.

Of course, under normal circumstances she would not have been stubborn enough to try doing this without help. She would have at least asked L to help her translate some of the documents, and accompany her to some of the meetings. But airtime with L is hard to come by these days. Her daughter, noting her disapproval, has decided to avoid her. They had one conversation, over lunch, in January, where Maria asked her directly if she loved Greg. L insisted she did with a vehemence that looked suspicious. Maria didn't even pretend to believe her. L got defensive. She started listing all of Greg's qualities, like a lawyer trying to win a case. Maria eventually gave up and said, "I'm sure he's wonderful," which didn't sound sincere. L left early, without finishing her food. After that, their conversations, on the phone, were short and superficial. The last time they talked, L gushed about the wedding, and Maria felt as bereft as if they were talking about a funeral. At least, L has not set a date yet. But she did express excitement over Victor agreeing to pay for her wedding. "Except your shoes," Maria insisted. "*Mami* will buy your shoes." She hoped this modest offering would appease her daughter. L thanked her, but didn't sound pleased. Later, Maria realized that Victor could afford much nicer shoes. Maybe L already had her eye on something expensive. And now her poor cheapskate of a mother offered to buy her something else instead. When it comes to her children, why can't she ever get it right?

But this is not a day to think about unpleasant things. Today she will celebrate her apartment. Her very own tiny piece of the big apple. She turns the thermostat to 75. She can't suffer the cold. She's happy that she remembered to contact NYSEG and have the power switched on, and that now, on her first day of being here alone, without the realtor, without the inspector, without any of the annoying people she's had to deal with, she actually has heat.

She places her heavy plastic bags on the counter in the so-called kitchen. She takes out a bottle of Laurent Perrier, her favorite French champagne, four sponges, a pair of gloves, a toilet brush, a box of baking soda, vinegar, bleach, dishwashing liquid, and some paper towels.

For the next three hours she scrubs every nook and cranny of her new apartment. She cleans the shower and toilet, washes the inside of the fridge, cleans the window, the floors, the cupboards, and the stove. While doing this, she carries the champagne bottle with her, and periodically treats herself to a swig of bubbly. When she's satisfied with the cleaning, she turns off the heat and opens the window to air the place out. She puts her coat on, and sits in the middle of the floor, holding the bottle. She feels decidedly tipsy. Her movements are slow and clumsy, and she cannot stop giggling. Enjoying her lightheadedness she takes one more small sip, then laughs at the weight of her own arm placing the bottle back on the floor. And in her giddy happiness she feels generous and grateful. All in all, the world has been kind to her. And she feels the need to spread some of that goodness.

She takes off her rubber gloves and washes her hands with dish soap, laughing at the bubbles. She takes another sip of champagne, and reaches for her tote bag. There are a few things she always carries with her. She always likes to have cards and stamps. She buys blank cards with flowers or trees on them. She stocks up whenever they're on sale.

She has taken to writing cards years ago because she noticed it's something nice that Americans do. She remembers receiving her first card, shortly after arriving in the new country. She sent little Alex to a child's birthday party, in Queens. It was an American kid from school, whose parents she and Victor didn't know. She was excited that Alex was going to this party. She thought it was important for her children to meet people outside the community, to make friends with all kinds of other children. She insisted on buying that little American boy a present, a cheap ball. She cut five dollars out of the grocery budget to buy it, and Alex, true to form, hated it. When he returned from the party he pouted and told her that all other kids brought 'real presents,' that real presents were wrapped in nice wrapping paper, or packed in cool bags, and that they came with birthday cards attached. Still, a few days after that party, she received a thank you card in the mail. It was a tiny card, with the picture of a teddy bear on it. "Dear Mrs. Pop," it said, in a hand writing that to her seemed as foreign as the English words. "Thank you very much for the present. Sincerely, Tina, John, and Bobby." Alex refused to translate it, but L read it for her. Maria kept it for years, and is still sorry she lost it. To her it symbolized a new height of grace and friendliness. As soon as she was able to write in English, she started buying cards. She would write them on the subway, on her way to or from work, and drop them in a post box along the way. She wrote cards to other parents, but also to neighbors and work colleagues. As reserved as she was in person, cards allowed her make her own kind of forthcoming gestures.

Taking another sip of champagne, Maria chooses the card she likes best. It's a stylized drawing of a red poppy on a white background. She writes in her beautiful cursive, with carefully drawn rounded letters:

"Drinking champagne in my new apartment. Thank you!"

It comes out a bit slanted, probably because she's a little drunk. But she laughs, licks the envelope, looks for a stamp in her wallet, and copies the address from her leather notebook.

On her way out, bound for the subway that will take her back to Queens, she drops the little envelope into a postal box.

Later that evening, sobering up, and treating her post-champagne headache with aspirin, she regrets having sent that stupid card. What the fuck was she thinking? How on earth could she get drunk and start writing cards? Still, there is nothing she can do about it, short of riding the subway back to Manhattan, standing by that stupid box, waiting for the postal worker to pick up the mail, then assaulting a Federal employee in order to snatch back that uninspired card. All she can do is pray it gets lost in the mail.

{25}

Closure?

Maria is wandering around her old apartment, contemplating packing. She wouldn't mind walking out of this place empty handed, pulling the door shut on her old life, and starting over new. But she's too poor to afford that.

So she pours herself a glass of wine, puts on some music, and starts making a mental inventory of her possessions. She's just starting to get into it, when the rotary phone in her bedroom starts ringing.

Victor's voice takes her by surprise.

"So you haven't moved yet?"

"No."

There is silence on the line for a while. She doesn't know what to say to him.

He states the obvious: "I got your card."

She still doesn't know what to say. She's embarrassed for getting drunk and sending it in the first place.

"Were you drunk?" he asks.

"Quite drunk."

"Nice."

Silence again.

"So, can I take you out to dinner to celebrate?"

"Sure." It slips out before she has time to think about it.

"How about tomorrow? What time do you get off work?"

The next day, dressed in black slacks and a turtleneck, an outfit she hopes looks flattering but relatively casual, wearing her black coat, and her most expensive boots, gloves, and purse, Maria rides a cab uptown to the restaurant Victor suggested. She's nervous at the thought of meeting him, also a little angry with herself for having accepted. But then again, she's still too happy about her new apartment to want to dwell on hard feelings from the past. It's the happiest she's been in a long time. Why ruin it? She's about to start a new life. There's no need to bring old resentments into it. Besides, she's looking forward to having a nice dinner in a nice restaurant. She cannot even remember the last time she enjoyed a meal out. It's a luxury she could never afford after moving to the new country. Of course, she and Victor used to go to lovely places in Romania. Even in the darkest era of communism, when there were shortages of all sorts, menus were limited, and waiters were rude, Victor took her to places that served impeccable meals, where one could enjoy the fragrant shade of tree-filled gardens and be seduced by Gypsy violins. Once they arrived in America, eating out seemed too frivolous for their budget, and more trouble than it was worth, with two children in tow. Still, on their tenth wedding anniversary, Victor insisted on taking her out. And he insisted that it be somewhere special. She knew they couldn't afford it, but she wanted to humor him. She put on her best dress, which by then looked washed out and dated, slipped into pumps that pinched her toes, and entrusted her children to Mrs. Stoica for the evening. They went to an Italian restaurant. The place was beautiful, the service flawless, and the food on other diners' plates looked exquisite. Seeing it, Maria experienced gluttony so acute, that even her pregnancy cravings paled in comparison. But the prices on the menu scared her. The filet Victor ordered for her cost more than several days' worth of groceries. She showed superhuman discipline in eating only half. She planned on using the rest in a stew the next day. Even so, she could not justify the expense. She pushed her delicious steak aside, drank her outlandishly priced cabernet, and smiled at her handsome husband, who obviously wanted her to have a good time. Victor prompted her to eat the rest of her meat. She very badly wanted to. It was a great steak and she was still hungry. But she didn't want to make Victor feel bad by admitting she thought they were too poor to eat in such a nice place. She smiled and said that she was full. "Do you mind if I have it?" he asked. He had eaten his entire chicken entree, but obviously he was still hungry too. She watched him finish her filet, and forced herself to keep smiling, even as she declined having a dessert she really craved. That night she locked herself in the bathroom, and cried for a full hour with the water running, so her family wouldn't hear. By the time she finally came to bed, Victor was asleep, and she felt relieved.

That was the last moderately pleasant dinner out Maria can remember the two of them sharing. After all these years, she should at least try to enjoy the fact that he can now afford to buy her a nice meal. And if he really wants to, why should she make it so difficult for him? After all, she did accept his money. And in her drunken happiness she even brought herself to send that stupid card and thank him for it. So wouldn't it be just ridiculous if she refused to let him buy her dinner to celebrate?

Victor is already sitting at their table when she gets there. She feels awkward. What do people do in these situations? Kiss on the cheek, the European way? Shake hands like business partners? Hug? He stands up to greet her, and his hand brushes hers in a gesture that is neither too familiar nor too business-like. He helps her out of her coat, and she sits down.

She quickly gives him a once-over. He looks good, as usual, the bastard! She wonders if by now there is another woman in his life, or if maybe Monica is back. She wonders if he ever thinks of her, his estranged wife. They haven't seen each other since Christmas, when he made that drunken pass at her. But she can't think of that, not if she's really going to try to be pleasant.

Their first attempts at conversation, about her carbide over, are awkward. They're both trying too hard to be polite. Everything she says rings fake. Her enthusiasm reminds her of something recent, but she cannot remember what. Something she read, maybe, but she's not sure. Not that it matters, anyway. At a loss for words, she smiles, knowing that she looks silly. She's afraid this entire dinner will be an uncomfortable farce, the two of them acting the role of the cordial separated couple.

Luckily the waiter interrupts, asking what she would like to drink. Victor is already nursing a scotch. She likes the thought that even he occasionally needs something to steady his nerves. In fact, she's surprised that he wasn't waiting for her outside, smoking.

"I'll have one of those," she says, pointing to a woman at the bar drinking a light colored beverage out of a tall glass. She feels silly pointing, and ordering the first thing she sees, without even knowing what it is. But she needs alcohol fast, if she's going to relax and act natural.

"Ah, the mojitos are excellent!" the waiter says. Maria smiles. She hopes to God they're strong!

"And we'd love to look at a wine list for later, please," Victor adds. He seems as anxious for alcohol as she is. He's nervous too. She can feel it. She smiles. Victor, nervous! At seeing her, no less!

Her drink arrives. Victor raises his glass.

"To your new apartment."

She smiles. The drink is good, pleasantly tart, with a hint of freshness. She hopes there's an abundance of liquor in there, though she can't really taste it.

"Thank you for agreeing to have dinner with me," he says. "I wanted to see you, so I could apologize in person for my behavior at Christmas."

He sounds too formal, but sincere. She's shocked. He was so angry with her at Christmas, and she assumed that he would stay that way.

"I..." she mutters, unsure of how to respond but willing to acknowledge his effort. After all, it must be difficult for him to apologize. To her limited knowledge, men generally try to avoid that, at all costs.

Just then, the waiter interrupts.

"Here is the wine list, sir. And here are some menus for the two of you to look over. I will be right back to tell you about our specials."

She scans the menu looking for fish courses. She doesn't eat meat during Lent.

"The fish here is excellent!" Victor says, as if reading her mind. "Do you still observe Lent?" Still formal, still overly polite. How long will this dinner farce have to go on?

"Yes, I do."

She smiles at him, like the Stepford wife she isn't.

"I think they have a grouper special today, and it's supposed to be fantastic."

"Lovely!" she says cheerfully, putting down her menu, which she has no patience to read anyway. "I love grouper!"

What a bullshit conversation! And suddenly, she remembers exactly who she sounds like.

"You talk to Lili recently?" she asks Victor.

"Yes. Just the other day."

So he talks to L frequently. Does that mean their daughter is only avoiding her? She feels jealous. But more than that, she's dying to know what's going on with L. She wonders if there's a way of getting him to tell her more, without admitting she feels slighted.

"I heard you offer to pay for the wedding. That's nice of you!" Still fake.

"Of course I will. But first she has to decide on a date."

So still no date. This at least is good news.

She takes another sip of her drink, trying to think of what else she can say that is safe, polite, and will get him to talk more about L.

"You still don't approve, do you?" he asks.

"No," she says. "You think it's a good idea for her to marry that boy? She's so young…"

She starts playing with the corner of her menu. She's not sure she can conceal the gloomy feeling she experiences when she thinks of L's engagement.

"You were younger, when we married." Victor points out. She thinks there's a hint of tenderness in his eyes, but she's not sure.

"And look how great that turned out!" She immediately regrets saying it. It's hard to bring herself to look at him, but when she does, she sees that he too has averted his eyes, that her comment upset him, or at least made him uncomfortable.

"She doesn't love him," she adds, hoping to create a distraction.

"You think she doesn't?" He seems surprised. "Why would she marry him then?"

Maria shrugs.

"He's nice, intelligent, relatively handsome. She likes his company. She's flattered he asked. She's excited about the wedding, the romance... But I don't think she loves him."

"But then…"

She has the feeling he's going to say something important, that he's finally going to agree with her, maybe offer to try talking to L.

But the waiter is back.

"Our specials tonight are grilled filet of grouper, with a cilantro lemon sauce, julienne plantains, and grilled tomatoes. We also have a pork chop cooked in a red wine reduction with…"

"I'll have the grouper," Maria interrupts. She doesn't care about the food. She cares about L. And she wants to continue their conversation.

"I'll have the grouper too," Victor says, handing away his menu.

The waiter is still standing there.

"Excellent! Have you thought of a wine to go with your meal? I can recommend a white…"

"You want red, don't you?" Victor asks, looking at Maria.

She smiles.

"Always red."

Not what most people would drink with fish. But she loves red wine with everything. It's nice of Victor to remember. It's nice of him to compromise, and order a smooth Chilean Merlot, just because she likes it.

"So you think she doesn't love him?" Victor asks, as soon as the waiter steps away. "Has she told you that?"

Maria shrugs.

"No, not really. But I can tell. She…"

Taking another sip of her Mojito, she can finally feel a buzz.

"L doesn't really talk to me anymore, Victor. She's avoiding me."

It's precisely what she meant to keep to herself, but it feels good getting it off her chest.

"My son hates me, and my daughter is avoiding me." She sighs. Maybe she should slow down in drinking that Mojito. She's saying way too much.

"Alex doesn't hate you. He's just immature."

"Ok. My son is immature, and my very mature daughter got engaged to the wrong guy for the wrong reasons. Maybe this is how God is punishing me for being a bad mother." She realizes it sounds a tad overdramatic, but it's how she's been feeling lately.

"Do you really believe that?" he asks.

"Which part?" She cannot help smiling. "That there is a God? That there is retributive justice? That I am a bad mother?"

"You are not a bad mother."

The way he says it, as if it's an undisputable fact, makes her eyes nearly tear up.

"I am a mother who left her children."

She looks down. She should not have said that.

"Ah, that."

He stares at the ice cubes in his glass. The silence between them is heavy. They never talked about this before. It was taboo, yet always there, between them.

When he finally speaks, his voice is gentle, compassionate.

"So everything you've done, all the work you've put into raising our children, all your efforts for all these years, all this is erased by the fact that one day you took a ride on a stupid train?"

She still cannot look up.

"Besides, you came back before they even realized what was going on. From their perspective, it's as if you didn't leave."

She forces herself to be a grownup and face him. It's her past, her guilt. She has to own up to it. In a slow, deliberate voice she admits to the worst part of it all:

"But I did leave. And I did not mean to ever come back. I just... I was not able to manage on my own."

He takes another sip of whiskey.

"You know, I've always wondered about that..." he says.

"Well, now you know, " she snaps, then regrets being so curt.

"I would have felt guilty eventually, of course," she adds in a softer voice. "I love my children, I always have. But I was young and selfish and I wanted to enjoy my life. I was so sick of having to sacrifice everything for them..."

Victor nods, as if he understands. How can he understand something that she herself cannot? She's shocked to see the sadness in his eyes.

"It's not selfish to want to live your life, Maria. It's natural. A mother should not have to sacrifice her whole life for her children, the way you had to." He pauses to take a sip of his drink. She can tell that it's hard for him to talk about this. "For what it's worth, I think you are a great mother. You did a wonderful job raising two kids, on your own, in a foreign country. You should give yourself more credit for that. You're too harsh on yourself, for just the one stupid mistake. So you felt miserable, and you were resentful about having to give up your life. Wouldn't most normal people feel this way?"

She cannot speak at first. Although she's never been able to share the full story of her flight with anyone, she always hoped to hear something like this one day, to have somebody understand. Never in a million years did she think that person would be Victor.

"Wow," she says. "Thank you."

She allows herself a small bitter laugh.

"You know, all my life I've been hoping to hear something like that from another mother. But it turns out that, even if they feel this way, none of these bitches ever admit it."

They laugh. The tension seems to have eased.

"Romanian women certainly wouldn't," Victor says. "Children are supposed to be the point of life."

"No wonder I never fit in…"

For once, she's happy that he's chosen to be kind and generous. But there's another issue, deeper, and more personal to Victor, which she doesn't dare approach. She didn't just abandon her children. She left him. This she can't bring herself to mention. Instead, she tries to say something nice in her turn, something to show her appreciation.

"I did not raise our children alone, Victor. We raised them together, even after…" She doesn't like alluding to asking him to leave. "…we separated. I know I always acted like I didn't want your help, but I was just being proud and stupid. Our children needed you and…"

Before she can finish her thought, the waiter cuts in.

"So, are you guys having a good time?" he asks. To her, this is the stupidest question restaurant staff are trained to ask. "I'm sorry the grouper is taking a while. Our chef likes to let them marinate a little while longer."

Maria sighs. She doesn't give a rat's ass about the fish, the marinating process, or the chef's preferences, though normally such things would hold her interest. Tonight, all she cares about, is talking to Victor. There are meals that are about food, those that are about conversation, and those that are about both. She wishes they taught waiters to make those distinctions.

Finally, the marinated fish arrives. It's really good, but she's already drunk, and wishing she hadn't dulled her senses with so much alcohol. Hopefully food will sober her up.

They eat in silence for a while. The alcohol made her hungry. She cleans everything on her plate. When she's done wiping the last drop of sauce with a small piece of bread, and stuffing it into her mouth, she realizes Victor is watching her, amused. She knows he's pleased that she enjoyed her meal. He's kind and generous like that. He does have his flaws, but at his core, he's a good man. She sighs.

"I never thanked you," she says. "For not telling anyone I left."

"I guess it will just have to stay our secret."

"Well, actually…" She suddenly feels shy. She knows her idea is odd, but after trying to dismiss it many times, she's now determined to go through with it. Under the influence of alcohol, she's hoping Victor might understand.

"If you don't mind, I've been thinking of telling L about it."

"Really? You don't have to do that, Maria." He seems rather bewildered. He must think of it as her way of trying to alleviate her guilt. Her confession. But really, that's only part of it.

"I want to." She takes another sip of wine, bracing herself to explain. She cannot believe that she's talking to him about this. "I just… I want her to know how hard it can be, marriage, having children, all that. I want her to know how things can go wrong, how horrible it can all turn out. Even when you love person you're with."

His eyes grow darker. She realizes she's hurt him.

And before she can add anything to soften the blow, the waiter reappears.

"How was everything? May I take these out of your way? Would you care for any dessert tonight?"

She doesn't want their meal to end. They're not done talking. She didn't mean to hurt him with what she said about marriage. She never realized that talking about the past would be so painful to Victor. And to think that for once she didn't mean to hurt him. It's ironic actually, that after years of trying deliberately to get under his skin, she managed to do so unintentionally, when she was trying to be nice for once.

"Two coffees. And that molten chocolate desert," Victor tells the waiter. She smiles. Apparently he wants to prolong their dinner too.

"The chocolate *Corazon*," the waiter says. "Excellent choice."

The chocolate *corazon* turns out to be a gigantic chocolate soufflé, dark, delicious, molten inside, and perfect with the wine.

"So are you ever going to tell me where you went?" Victor's voice sounds playful. Maybe the hurtful moment is gone, and she should just leave it at that. They are having a nice time after all.

Taking a break between two bites of chocolate, she says with a shrug and a smile:

"Scranton."

They burst out laughing. It does seem funny, in hindsight. Of all the possible places, she ended up in Scranton, Pennsylvania.

When she regains her breath she adds:

"I stayed in a hotel close to the train station and had room service bring me toasted bagels." It sounds absurd, and she's relieved that they're able to laugh about it together.

His hand moves towards her across the table. He places it on top of hers. She feels as if she's been electrocuted, but she fights the impulse to withdraw. His eyes look sad.

She wonders if she should ask him now, if she should finally, after all these years say the unthinkable, apologize for leaving him, and ask the most dreaded question of all. Can he forgive her? She opens her lips, but feels short of courage. She hopes for a second that he might say it himself, that he might volunteer his forgiveness. Instead he apologizes.

"I'm sorry, Maria. I'm sorry I took you for granted. I'm sorry I was cold towards you. I'm sorry you were miserable being with me."

She swallows hard, fighting back tears.

"It was my fault too, Victor. I wish I never…" She isn't quite sure how to say it. His eyes look sadder still. It shocks her, his undisguised hurt. He, who so rarely lets his feelings show. She realizes he misunderstood what she was trying to say, that he took it to mean it was her own fault for marrying him, or for falling in love with him, or something to that extent. In spite of being drunk, she has to concentrate on explaining. She can't mess up this time.

"What I mean, is…"

She takes another sip of wine, and realizes too late, that in moving her hand, she forced him to remove his.

"There are a lot of things I did wrong, and I'm sorry too, Victor. There are lot of things I feel sorry for," she finally says. She's angry with herself for only bringing herself to say something so vague, for not being able to specifically apologize for leaving him, among other things. "There are lots of things I regret. But I don't regret loving you. What I regret is building my life around you, making you the center of my universe. And then later turning into a resentful bitch."

Her cheeks burning, she looks down at the chocolate *corazon.* She's not sure how well she expressed herself, but at least she said some of the things she needed to say. Her apology was not as complete or as deep as she longed for, but at least she tried.

She hopes he'll say something, maybe reach for her hand again, that there will be some kind of affectionate moment, some kind of opportunity for closure.

Just then, the damn waiter reappears.

"Can I take this out of your way?" He gestures towards the half eaten chocolate *corazon.*

"No," Maria snaps. "You can not. It is mine, and I will eat it. And you should learn not to bother people when they want talk to each other. Go away!"

Victor laughs.

"Well, I guess I really am bitch," she says, taking another bite of chocolate.

"Or just assertive." Victor suggests. "I like that."

She smiles. She feels bad for snapping at their waiter, but she's too drunk to contemplate her so far fruitless quest for finding a middle ground between being a raging bitch and a doormat.

"You have to leave the poor guy big tip," she says, laughing. The elusive affectionate moment slipped away, but laughing together feels good. Maybe now that they are civilized to one another, they will have another opportunity for closure down the road.

Later, still giddy from the wine, she decides to show Victor her new apartment. It's nearly midnight, but they are drunk and euphoric, and it seems like a good idea. Never in a million years would she have thought that he'd be her first visitor. As she turns the key in the door she feels like a young girl about to wear her favorite new dress for the very first time.

But as the door swings open, her enthusiasm falters. What if he doesn't like it? After all, he's an architect. He understands space and texture and light in ways that other people don't. His preferences are refined in ways that others miss completely. He'll notice every imperfection. And God knows, there are plenty! Just as there probably are fatal flaws in the structure of the place, which she herself has not been trained to see.

She feels foolish, but her heart beats faster as she watches him take it all in. He walks around the small room, looking at the walls, the ceiling, the light fixtures, the big window.

"Nice," he says.

"You really mean it?"

"Yes. Absolutely. It's beautiful."

They end up sitting on the floor, taking about her new apartment. When she finally takes a cab to Queens, she feels that they have undergone a strange transition. Are they actually friends now?

{26}

Packing Party

After her dinner with Victor, Maria spends most of Saturday in bed. She closes the drapes, and lies down between her clean white sheets. They're not Egyptian cotton, but they feel fabulous. Daylight filters through the drapes painting the room violet, too soothe her hangover. There's a vase of freesias on her nightstand. She bought them to celebrate the closing. Books pile up around her bed, her best friends, her loyal companions. But today she doesn't feel like reading. Her bedroom looks beautiful in the violet light. Will she be sad to leave? Will she miss it?

She stretches, enjoying the familiar comfort of the pillow on her cheek. She smiles. He said she was a good mother. And he liked her new place, he really did. He offered her a moving van, a curtain, and a kitchen island, all for free. She would not have accepted his gifts before, but after last night she will. She closes her eyes and snuggles with her blanket. He said she was a good mother. She wants to remember just how he said it, the exact sound of his voice. She should have recorded it, should have recorded the whole dinner, the whole night, to watch today, over and over, on her beat up TV. If he ever invites her to dinner again, she'll bring photographers, lighting experts, a whole camera crew.

At some point, she's not sure when, she dozes off. By Sunday morning she's feeling fully rested, with renewed courage. She knows just what she needs to do today. She takes her time getting ready, forces herself to spend an hour showering, dressing, and drinking her coffee. She needs to think about exactly how to do this. She feels brave enough today. Ready to do what she knows must be done.

At 10:30 am, she's already ringing their doorbell. It's Rachelle who answers. Maria feels a little inappropriate, coming by unexpected and disturbing her on a Sunday morning. But Rachelle looks like she's been up for a while. It would have been awful if she were standing there is her jammies, with a long face, and eyes full of sleep. But no, she's wide awake, and smiling. Her hair is stretched out on curlers, and she's wearing a navy blue dress.

She motions for Maria to come in. Maria tries not to stare at the pink curlers. She's never managed to penetrate the mysteries of Black hair.

"I think L is still sleeping," Rachelle says, and Maria feels a wave of relief wash over her. L is home. It would all be in vain otherwise.

They walk into the living room. Morning light shines generously through the large window, and a hint of vanilla is floating in the air. Must be one of those air fresheners people plug in. Maria smiles. In spite of the modest furnishings, she likes this place. She finds herself wondering if Victor would like it too. He probably would. The light, the view of the river. He's not a snob, after all. He likes to say simplicity is luxury. She only wishes he had seen her new apartment in the daylight.

Her reverie is interrupted by Rachelle's voice: "L! Get your lazy self out of bed, child! Your mama is here!"

She gestures for Maria to sit down on the futon, and offers her a cup of coffee. It's strong and fragrant, served in a white porcelain mug, complete with matching saucer. Maria thinks it's lovely china, white, simple, and perfectly round. Victor would like this too. She smiles, leans back into a cushion, and lets herself enjoy the rich aroma of the hot dark liquid.

It takes her a while to notice Rachelle still standing there, looking at her expectantly. Is she hoping to make conversation? What's taking L so long?

"You know, L has been teaching me French," Rachelle says out of the blue, and Maria is glad there is something for them to talk about.

"That's wonderful! So, what you can say?"

Rachelle lets out an awkward little laugh.

"Je suis une jeune fille, » she recites, tentatively.

Maria smiles.

« *Non,*» she says. « *Vous etes une jeune femme.* »

« *Oui.* » Rachelle replies, then she pauses, as if looking for words. Maria wonders if she even understood. "I know. But the line from the book was '*je suis une jeune fille*. You know, the book you gave L."

Maria tries to recall what book that is. She's given L several books, over the years, but she never had any indication that her daughter actually read them.

"You know, the one about India," Rachelle explains. "L is really creative as a teacher. She bought me an English copy of it for my birthday. I told her I didn't want an expensive gift, so there she goes, buying me this lovely novel, and then she lent me the French copy you gave her, and suggested I read them in parallel. And she rented the movie for us to watch together."

"With Hugh Grant!" Maria smiles. She rented it for L herself, before giving her the French translation of one of her favorite Romanian novels, the forbidden love story between Mircea Eliade and the daughter of his Indian employer in Calcutta in the 1930s. She thought L felt lukewarm about the movie. The fact that she liked it enough to share, is a pleasant revelation. She takes it as a good omen for her mission today

"What was called that movie?" she asks. She used to know it, but it slipped her mind.

"The Bengali Night."

"You like?"

"Oh, yes, ma'am, a lot."

"Me too. You know, I usually like men with dark hair, dark eyes, like L's daddy. But Hugh Grant, he very sexy."

They both laugh. Maria realizes she wouldn't have made that comment in front of her daughter. No wonder L is closer to Monica than to her!

"I liked that movie very much," Rachelle continues. "But then I like the book much better. I read it several times."

Maria smiles. It's a good book.

"L told me you studied Romanian literature, in college. That must have been fascinating."

Maria nods, shyly. It was so long ago, that she by now almost forgot she finished university, that literature used to be more than a hobby.

She's happy L remembers this about her, that she found it worth mentioning to her friend. Again, a good omen. Maybe there is still hope for them.

Her daughter finally emerges from her bedroom, wearing a pink sweatshirt and grey yoga pants. Her hair is messy, and her eyes are swollen. She almost looks upset, and Maria hopes it's just the sleep settled in her features, not actual displeasure at waking up to find her mother here.

"*Mami*?" she asks in a small voice. She reminds Maria of a baby bird, one who just hatched out of an egg, and is examining the world with confusion and a hefty dose of fear. "What are you doing here?"

"I came see you, of course," Maria answers. "And to talk to Rachelle."

L stares at her mother with a curiosity bordering on panic.

"I came to tell you I bought studio apartment in Manhattan," Maria says. She pauses just long enough to see the surprise on her daughter's face. "I am moving and need you come help me pack."

"You bought a place, *Mami*? That's wonderful! But…"

Maybe it was wrong to spring the news on her without any preliminaries. But despite appearances, L is not a baby anymore. She's a grown woman who needs to learn to face reality. Even in the mornings. Or perhaps, especially then.

"So when you come help me pack, my sweetie?"

"I… I don't know, *Mami*. I am very busy these days…"

As expected, L is trying to brush her off. Normally she would just accept this, and walk away, concealing her hurt. But today she's made up her mind to confront her daughter, using whatever authority a mother is supposed to have.

She's grateful that Rachelle has retreated into the baby's room. She turns towards L, and says firmly:

"Liliana, I am your mother. I gave birth to you, and for last twenty-three years I made sure you have everything you need. I cook, clean, and wash laundry for you, I stay up all night when you sick, and I even came to this bloody country so you have better life. I want you to help me pack and I will not take no for an answer. You pick one night this week, and you come to my house after work, pack, eat dinner with me, and spend the night at my house. You understand?"

L nods. She's looking at her feet, as if her bright pink toenails can offer her an escape from her mother's unexpected tirade. Maria can tell she's embarrassed, maybe even close to crying. Just like her mother, L cries easily. And she's not used to *Mami* scolding her.

"What night you come?"

L's toes dance around uncomfortably. Maria hates that shade of pink. She hates the fact that her daughter feels and looks foreign to her. An unknown young woman. Have they grown that far apart already?

"I…I guess tomorrow."

"Good. What time you be there?"

"Seven?"

"O.K. I get pizza."

*

I've no choice but to show up the next night, as promised. Most of *Mami*'s stuff is already packed. There are still a few piles of things on the floor, and *Mami* is walking around picking up stray items here and there, placing them into boxes. She works methodically, in her typical fashion. Brazilian music is playing in the background, filling the apartment with mellow chords and deep voices. Candles are spreading the warm scent of vanilla (*vanilie*). A bottle of red wine sits on the coffee table. *Mami* is walking around barefoot, humming to the music, leisurely sipping from a large goblet. She seems to be enjoying herself. She even looks younger. She's wearing black yoga pants and a T-shirt. She's probably been up packing late last night. There are circles under her eyes, and most of the work has already been done. I wonder why she needed my help when she seem to be managing fine all by herself. Why did she insist I show up? Maybe she wanted to celebrate the moment. Like a moving party of sorts, with me as only guest. I guess I should feel honored.

Mami is genuinely excited about me being here, but then again, when isn't she excited to see me? She hugs and kisses me, gushing over the smell of my *parfum secret*, complimenting my clothes, the length of my hair, the fact that it's so shiny.

"You have glass of wine. Pizza is coming. I know how my sweetie love pizza!"

She seems more energetic than usual. But restlessness becomes her.

I don't think I've ever seen her this happy before. I feel relieved, yet at the same time sad. It's strange to see our old apartment all packed up. This is where I spent most of my childhood, and my college years. I hated it, but now, on the eve of its being emptied and abandoned, I feel attached to it. I will miss this apartment. I will mourn its loss. In spite of my parents' fighting and my own distaste for the boroughs, this has been the safe haven of my childhood, a place where even now, after moving out, I always thought I could return if need be. Just as I always knew *Mami* and *Tati* would be there for me if I needed them, I always assumed this would always remain my home.

I almost forgot it was rented. The rent is expensive, yet not outrageous, not anything compared to rents in Manhattan. I remember *Mami* writing the checks grudgingly, as if paying for a necessary evil, something that brought no joy, but needed to be paid, like the debt to a bookie. I've known for years she was longing to live somewhere else.

Still, the reality of *Mami* moving is disconcerting. It makes no sense, but having lived in an apartment for fifteen years, shouldn't people be entitled to keep it? It seems surreal that some day I might walk by, look up at our windows and realize that other people live here. The thought of strangers in these rooms seems invasive.

Over wine and pizza, *Mami* tells me about her new apartment. Her face glows with excitement. She looks younger. The new place sounds nice. Though I'm a little taken aback that *Mami* decided to give all our furniture to charity. Apparently she'll have nothing but a big bed and a modern kitchen island in her new place. It's strange to imagine her living in a studio apartment. Manhattan is expensive, and lots of people live in the equivalent of mouse holes, but *Mami* living in one room seems odd. It means I'll definitely never be able to go back to living with her. We used to sleep in the same bed for years, but sharing a bed here, in our old apartment, seemed normal. Sharing a bed in the new studio strikes me as weird and stifling.

After pizza, packing proceeds with *Mami* doing all the work, while still sipping her wine, and me sitting on the floor looking through piles of stuff, trying to find some memories of our former lives that I want for myself. Most of all, I'm hoping to get some of *Mami*'s old clothes.

I still remember the glamorous mother of my early childhood in Romania. I used to think my *Mami* was the most beautiful woman in the world, a cross between a fairy princess and a gypsy. I was fascinated with gypsy women back then. I was in awe of their dark braids adorned with gold, their colorful skirts, and their brazen smiles. My mother, with her chestnut curls flowing freely, and thin gold bangles dangling on her wrists, seemed to have something in common with them. She dressed in bright colors back then, and she smiled a lot, brazenly just like the gypsy women in the street.

Mami's look became more austere in New York. Her beautiful dresses, her lovely high heels, and all her purses were carefully stored away. The gold bangles disappeared too. When I went to prom, *Mami* offered to let me borrow a gold chain and hoop earrings. I asked if she still had the bangles. She said she sold them. It broke my heart.

When I started sleeping in *Mami*'s room, I got to share her closet. I would occasionally reach to the very back, where she kept her old dresses. I'd bury my face in the silk, and inhale the scent of my childhood.

Right now, looking through the piles of things *Mami* set out for me, I'm hoping to find those old dresses. But all I come across are my art projects from school, which I can't believe *Mami* kept, Alex' collection of Lego, a pile of books, and some of my own old clothes and music tapes.

"Where are your dresses and shoes, *Mami*?"

She looks up in surprise.

"Which dress and shoe you want?"

"Your old stuff, *Mami*. From Romania."

She frowns.

"That old junk? Why you want that? That stuff falling apart, my sweetie. But you can look, of course."

She points to one of the boxes that are already packed. It's marked 'Woman,' in *Mami*'s beautiful cursive. I don't even stop to wonder at the reason for this label, I'm anxious to find the dresses.

"Is in bottom of box," *Mami* says. The corners of her mouth contort, as if in disapproval.

There's a wool coat on top, neatly folded and with dry cleaning tags still on. There's a pair of relatively new boots, a few sweaters, smelling of fabric softener, and then finally, underneath, there's my most coveted red silk dress. I almost shriek with joy at the mere sight of it.

I hold it up to my face, taking in that beloved scent, faint, muddled, but still so familiar. It looks slightly different than I remember, very 80s, with unexpected pleats and shoulder pads. But still, it is *the* red silk dress. *Rochia roşie de mătase*. I remember *Mami* glowing in this.

"Can I try it on, *Mami*?"

"Of course you can try, sweetie. But I cannot believe you want that." *Mami* wrinkles her nose. "Is so old. And such hideous fashion. You see shoulder pad? I can not believe I wear such thing."

Before setting out to try on the dress, I dig deeper into the box, hoping to find the taupe suede pumps *Mami* used to wear with it. They are more worn than I hoped, but they still look glamorous to me. I quickly remove my sock.

"Those not fit you, L," *Mami* warns.

"We're the same size, *Mami*! They should fit!"

I slip my foot into my mother's old shoe. It's tight. When I stand up, it hurts.

"See, they don't fit you," *Mami* says. "They too small."

I take off the shoe and start putting on a pair of white strappy sandals. *Sandale cu barete*.

"They all too small, sweetie!" *Mami* says. "They not fit. Trust me. Just put them back. I donate them to women's shelter. Maybe somebody there have small feet."

I still try on a third pair. Too small. I wonder if I can wear them anyway. Maybe they'd stretch in time? *Mami* seems to read my mind.

"No, L, you cannot have them. They too small for you. I give them to women's shelter. Poor women need shoes. And you need not to ruin your feet. Bad shoes are bad for you!"

I wrap them up again, the way *Mami* had, in cloth bags, and stash them back in the box.

"I give all these boxes to women's shelter," *Mami* points to five boxes lined up along the wall, all marked 'woman.' "Is very sad. The women in there, they been abused. They had to escape their homes, and they had no place to go. Some have children. Some brought children with them. You know, L, some women are immigrant women. They don't even speak English. Can you imagine? Being here, not able to speak, like I was, not able to go out there, get job, or do anything really, and then on top of that, be completely dependent on man. Is truly horrible. But as if is not bad enough, imagine the man beats you. Or beats your children, or both. I cannot imagine being trapped in house like that, with that kind of man. You imagine how hard is to escape if you are in foreign country and you don't speak the language? I admire these women who escape. Who go to shelter. But you know, for every one who is there, there are tens, hundreds, thousands in the city, trapped in bad homes, unable to leave because they don't speak English and they don't know anything about this country."

I didn't expect a tirade about battered women. All I wanted was to try on some shoes.

"You know, L, some time I go there, to shelter. I visit with the women. I cannot talk to many of them, they not speak English. Is so sad."

It is. But seriously, where is this all coming from? What's gotten into *Mami*?

"A woman should never depend entirely on man. She should be able to take care of herself, to leave. You never know, L, things can always go wrong, even if they start out right. You should always have way out, an escape. You should always be able to stand on your own two feet."

I hope *Mami* will go back to packing and forget about the battered women. I'm anxious to try on the red dress. But *Mami* is not done.

"I worry for you, L. Marrying that boy at so young age. I know you grown woman and you know to take care of yourself, and I'm so proud of you, but… I guess I agree with your *Tati* that maybe you should go back to school, or…"

I look down at the dress on her lap. *Mami* has never brought this up before. This is *Tati*'s line of nagging. *Mami* tends to stick to advice on nutrition and frugality, and most of the time, even that is too much to take.

"All I'm saying, L, is, if you marry this boy, I just want you to be confident you can leave him, that you be fine without him, and that if, one day you realize you made a big mistake, you be able to walk out and not… I see all these wealthy women, L, some of my clients at the store. They married with such awful men, and they unhappy, but they don't want to let go because their lives would never be same… even with alimony. I just don't want you to fall in this trap, to be attracted by lifestyle that you can not have on your own, and then be stuck with someone because of it…"

I steal a glance at my engagement ring. I know *Mami* doesn't want me to marry Greg. I don't want to know why she feels that way. I was afraid to come here tonight, knowing she'll feel compelled to tell me.

"I'm not marrying Greg for money. He's a poor student!"

Of course, this poor student has wined and dined me at a time when I was living on bagels. But *Mami* doesn't need to know everything about our relationship.

Mami raises her eyebrows.

"Law student. Not going to be poor forever," she points out. "Now I been relatively clueless about life when I was your age, but I was not born yesterday, L. That young man of yours will have money one day. Much more than you yourself can get. Is ok, as long as is not what you see in him."

"No, it is not," I protest. I can feel myself getting red in the face. "I…I…"

"No, L. You don't love him."

Mami pronounces this in a categorical fashion which infuriates me beyond words. Still, I cannot dispute it.

"He's good to me, *Mami*. He's the best man I ever met."

"He might be. But you still very young. And you only been with him a few months. You don't really know him. And what's even worse, you don't even know yourself yet."

"He's sweet, *Mami*. He's so kind. He's the best thing that's ever happened to me."

I can't help it, I feel tears coming to my eyes. *Mami* comes closer, sits down next to me on the floor. She prompts me to blow my nose into the red dress. That would be blasphemy! I use my sleeve instead.

"I've made such a mess of everything else, *Mami*. This is the only good thing I've got going. I just fucked up. I know you're proud of me, and I never wanted to tell you, but I… I can't deal with things on my own. I'm a big failure."

Mami makes a hesitant gesture in my direction. For a second, I hope for a hug. But my mother is not the hugging kind. Instead she gets me a box of tissues. *Şervețele*. When I have at least moderately composed myself, she grabs my shoulders and forces me to face her.

"So, you fuck up," she says. "How you fuck up? You pregnant? Answer me!"

I shakes my head, sobbing.

"No."

"You have HIV?"

"No."

"Syphilis?"

"No."

"Herpes, at least?"

"No."

"You shoot cocaine?"

"No."

"You shoot heroin? Or what you call it, acid?"

"No."

"Crack?"

"No."

"Other drug?"

I wonder if the one time I tried pot counts.

"No."

"You kill someone?"

"No."

"You alcoholic?"

"No."

"You shoplift?"

"No. …But I buy things I cannot afford."

Mami shrugs.

"So does everyone else this country, apparently. You think you fuck up! You twenty-three. You supposed to be running around town and getting in trouble, fucking up, like you say. You should fuck up in all sorts of ways before you figure things out. Just don't fuck up in any big way."

I'm shocked she said the f word.

"Now why you buy these things you can't afford? What you need that you not have, my sweetie?"

I shrug. How can I explain it?

"Beauty, I guess?"

It's probably the lamest thing I've ever said, and if mascara wasn't running down my cheeks, I'd bury my face in the red dress in embarrassment.

Mami looks shocked.

"But you're so beautiful, my sweetie. Trust me, you are unbelievably beautiful."

I've my doubts. But it's not what I meant, anyway.

"No, *Mami*, I'm not talking about me. I'm talking about... Well, about life, you know. About everyday life, and making it a little nicer."

I'm not sure that makes any sense. But *Mami* nods as if she understands. And she laughs.

"You buy things to make your life more beautiful? Oh, L, my sweetie..."

"It's stupid," I say between tears. "I can't even explain it. It sounds even more stupid when I talk about it. But I mean, what do you do on just a regular dull day, when you need a little something special in your life?"

"You just create it, silly. You can learn to do that, L, in little ways, with time. It gets easier as you get older. You know yourself better, and you know tricks."

She shrugs.

"You'll see, my sweetie. You'll learn. Is skill like any other. You just need to learn more about yourself and things you like, learn to appreciate the simple things, and to enjoy them. In the meantime, if you spend too much money, I guess is ok. Is your own money, and you just young, just learning things. Is like investment in learning about yourself. How much you owe, my sweetie?"

I swallow hard. Of all people, I cannot tell this to *Mami*.

"How much, L? I'm not offering to pay for you, you do yourself, and you feel better in the end. I just am curious. You tell me, and I tell you secret too."

"Three thousand dollars on my credit card?" It sounds so horrible. I cannot even bring myself to mention my debt to Gretchen.

"Is not so bad, L. You pay off, you feel better. Is really no tragedy. Not worth crying, my sweetie." She pushes the box of tissues towards me. I dutifully wipe my eyes. "There's trouble, and then there's trouble, L. And most trouble you get in is ok. Pay interest on credit card is stupid, but in the end, is not the biggest deal. But marrying this boy, that is serious trouble. That is really fucking up. And not the kind of fucking up that help you grow."

"But I have to marry him, *Mami*. I promised to marry him, and he's the nicest person, and I just can't stand to hurt him."

"You hurt him a lot more if you go through with it."

I try to compose myself, but my sobs seem to originate from somewhere deep inside, a place of fear and sorrow. A place I can't control.

"You don't love him!" *Mami* screams.

"Momo says that maybe that's a good thing. That love just…ruins everything."

"Is this one of your friends? Momo?"

It's too late to correct my *faux pas*. By the way *Mami*'s frowning, she must know who I'm talking about.

"Monica… *Tati*'s…"

"Aha." *Mami* waves her hand dismissively. "Well, your 'Momo' is a stupid cow!"

I cannot recall the last time I felt this uncomfortable. I pretend to examine the dress on my lap. If only I knew how to switch topics… If only I could evaporate into thin air! (Come to think of it, I've wished for this so many times already, it would definitely be my superpower of choice).

"I'm not saying that because she is sleeping with my husband, and because I resent that. And trust me, I do," *Mami* says. I feel guilty. How could I be so shallow? How could I pretend that my friendship with Momo is not a betrayal? "In all kindness, and fairness…" *Mami* continues, "she may be nice person, whatever. She nice to you. I know. But she stupid, L. She really stupid. And I know. Because I talk to her."

I look up. Is she for real?

"You talked to her?"

"Yes." *Mami* raises her eyebrows as if to show her superiority. "I talk to 'Momo.'" She pronounces the other woman's nickname as if it's the most ridiculous thing she's ever heard. I blush, ashamed to have created such a silly pseudonym. "I had drink with her. And I talk enough to see, she not very bright. She sleeping with a married man, L. Bad choice. And she is stupid enough to fall in love with him. She is completely miserable. And for good reason. Forgive me, for talking bad about your friend, but only stupid woman can stay with man who treat her like that. So you be careful when she give you advice. Is like blind leading other blind."

We fall silent. *Mami* stands up and goes back to her packing. I keep sobbing.

"Why don't I love him, *Mami?* What is wrong with me? It would all be so perfect if only I loved him."

"Oh, sweetie," *Mami* gives me a sympathetic look. "You cannot tell your heart what to feel. It just is what it is."

"But can't I learn to love him, *Mami*? If I try really hard, won't I be able to love him eventually?"

She shrugs.

"There's no saying, my sweetie… You may end up loving him or hating him. Is like Russian roulette. Who can tell? You don't feel what you want to feel. You feel what you feel."

I look at the dress on my lap, smooth out its folds as if caressing a loved being. What was my mother feeling when she wore this dress? Was she in love back then, or was she falling out of it?

"*Mami*, when you stopped loving *Tati,* did you feel sad? Did you wish you still loved him?"

Silence. *Mami* is cutting up a roll of bubble wrap. She seems engrossed in this task, as if it's so consuming that it requires her full and undivided attention.

"This is the way I look at it, L. Is very simple. Even if you love him, is a mistake to marry him. You are too young, too unprepared. You be making the same mistake I made. And that, my sweetie, was one hell of mistake. But you don't even love him. And chance is you never will. So you are making even bigger mistake. Because I don't think you can make yourself love him. But is just what I think. Maybe you know better. I cannot think for you. I just know, me, myself, I can never make myself love someone if I don't."

I'm still wondering if she was sad when she stopped loving *Tati*. If she wished she could love him still. I remember her crying at night, quietly, in bed, next to me. Was she crying because she still loved him? Or was she crying because she couldn't love him anymore? I can't ask that.

I wonder if it'd be rude to go try on the red dress.

Mami's voice startles me:

"How is the sex?"

I didn't expect that. We don't talk about sex.

"I assuming you are not virgin, L. I actually really hope you are not."

I feel my cheeks burning up.

Mami is bubble wrapping a crystal candlestick. The question hangs in the air, demanding to be answered.

"It… it is nice…" I say, blushing up to my earlobes.

"Nice?" *Mami* pronounces the word with contempt, like it's the most ridiculous thing she has ever uttered, more ridiculous even, than calling someone 'Momo.' "The sex is 'nice?' L, honey, I would not in a million years settle for 'nice.'"

I look away. Who is this woman exactly?

"I do hope he not the only one you been with," she says.

I shake my head.

"Well, good. You know, L, I never been with anyone but your daddy."

She says this softly, with a sort of tenderness and a hint of nostalgia that are touching.

"But at least it was hell of a lot better than 'nice.' You ever have better than just 'nice,' L?"

I'm uncomfortable with the topic, but I cannot help giggling and nodding.

"Well, good, then," *Mami* says, laughing herself. "With other man, I assume?"

I nod before I can help myself. Then I see the look of victory on *Mami*'s face. Her raised eyebrows say she's already made her point.

"Of course, sex is not most important thing, and not enough for good relationship. But if even that is not there…" She sighs. She works quietly for a while, bubble-wrapping a vase.

"Ok, my sweetie," she says, taping the box shut, and marking it clearly 'Me'. "Why you not go try on red dress, and show me what it look like on you? Then I make you tea, and I tell you a story."

{27}

Running Away from Home

Despite the shoulder pads, the dress looks good. I love the way the silk caresses my skin. It's a dress meant to make a woman feel sexy. Unless, of course, her face is swollen from crying, her nose looks like a red bell pepper, her mother just scolded her, and she's about to marry someone because she doesn't know how to say no.

When I come out of the bedroom, *Mami* smiles, asks me to turn around, and helps adjust the zipper. Her fingertips, resting briefly on my back are soft and warm, her touch pleasant, but brief.

"If you want dress, I can take out shoulder pad for you," she offers, grabbing at the offending objects. She frowns, but she seems quite taken with me in the dress, in spite of the bell pepper nose and the swollen face, in spite even of the misguided engagement. It dawns on me, surprisingly but clear as day, that my mother will love me no matter what, that she'll stand by me no matter how disastrous my mistakes. Wrong men, wrong jobs, wrong friends, and toxic debt. *Mami* will zip up my dresses and tell me to straighten my back. She'll shrug my troubles away and make me feel lovely despite it all.

As promised, *Mami* makes tea. Chamomile, from loose flowers. *Mușețel.* It's the same tea she brewed when Alex and I were sick, the same she'd offer when I was upset about some teenage drama, or when I was nervous about an exam.

Curled up on *Mami*'s couch, which will be going to the women's shelter, I wait for my tea to cool down. My face still feels puffy, and my bell pepper nose is sore, but a comfortable warmth is spreading through my chest. It's the same blissful feeling as when, on nights when I cry myself to sleep (which has been often lately), I finally start sinking into oblivion. *Mami* sits at the other end of the couch, her body pulling away, as if wishing to retreat into an imaginary shell. Still, she reaches over and takes my hand in hers.

She's quiet for a long time. She sips her wine, and sighs.

"I… need to talk to you, L. And, is complicated." *Mami*'s voice trembles. "You… you think you can listen to long story if I tell in Romanian?"

She seems shy about this request. We don't speak Romanian in the house. Even in the days when *Mami* barely spoke English, she chose to communicate sparingly using the few words she knew.

"I know you understand a lot, L. But this really important. Is important for me that you understand. But is also important for me that I explain well, in detail. Is important for me to be, you know… articulate. Not sounding like uneducated person."

"I understand everything people say, *Mami*."

"Good. You so smart, my sweetie. You have such talent for language! So if you don't understand, you interrupt, ok?"

I nod, but *Mami* still seems hesitant.

"I can do French if is easier for you…"

"No, *Mami*. Romanian is fine. I do understand everything. I promise."

Still, she doesn't start for a long time. And when she finally does, her voice sounds far removed. She seems uncomfortable, as if telling me a story in Romanian is a strange and dangerous experiment. Or maybe it is simply telling a story about herself in the first place, that she's uncomfortable with.

"*Trebuie sa iti spun o poveste despre mine, Liliana*. I need to tell you a story about myself. It is something you've never known, and will definitely not like, but I promised myself that I would tell you. It's something difficult for me to talk about, because it's something really bad I did. And when you think about this later, and even when you listen to me… Well, I want you to understand that I myself know just how bad it is. You can judge me, but I want you to never forget that this is something I regretted for the rest of my life."

Mami pauses, takes another sip of her wine, and gives out a long sigh. If I wasn't dying to know, I'd tell her it's ok, that we don't really need to talk about this.

"So do you understand the language, L? Do you think you can follow me if I speak Romanian?"

"*Da, Mami. Inteleg. Inteleg tot.*" Yes, Mami. I understand. I understand everything.

I cringe at my pronunciation.

Mami sighs and closes her beautiful eyes. Her long lashes tremble. Then she looks down, at her own hands, the long thin fingers, the blue veins protruding from her olive skin, and gives another sigh.

"It is a story about being married young. Or maybe it is just a story about marriage. And it is about being a mother, or maybe just about me as a mother. Maybe I was just unfit, but…"

I open my mouth to contradict her, but *Mami* motions for me to be quiet.

"I know, I know, you'll say I was a good mother and all that, and I know I was in some ways. But I will tell it to you like it is, sweetie, being married and having kids, especially, is not what it's cracked up to be. Even if you marry for love, like I did. Even if you love a good, strong man, like your father. And your father is a good man. Even if he loves you back. Even if you have the most lovely children, and even if you love your children very much.

Life still throws you down, and you might still fuck up. I mean in major ways, in ways that you will regret for the rest of your life, and will never be able to fix. Especially if you are young. Especially if you are ill equipped to handle what may come your way. If you don't take care of yourself, and if you don't know how to, well, then you'll really be screwed when you try to take care of others…"

Her eyes stare into space. She sighs again. Whatever it is, it must be difficult to talk about. Did she have an affair? But no, it can't be that! It's something to do with her children. What on earth can it be?

"I'm sorry, I guess I'm just rambling, and I have not even started to tell you my story. Are you sure you understand the language, L?"

"*Da, mami. Înţeleg.*" Yes, *Mami,* I understand. My accent is so heavy, that I'm afraid she won't believe me. But *Mami* smiles.

"*Bine.*" Good. Finally, she starts talking.

"Do you remember, L, when you were a child, and we were all still in Romania, do you remember your daddy and me actually being happy?"

I nod. In my memories, they were. But then again, I always wonder if that was deceiving.

"Were you, really?"

"Yes. We were happy. Incredibly happy, in fact." She sighs. "I always wondered if you and Alex realized we were not always like this, fighting, and being hateful to each other. Of course, Alex was too little, maybe, but you were older. We have not always been like this, L. Your daddy and I used to love each other, and we were happy together. But I was young and stupid and I loved your daddy too much. I loved him so much I forgot about myself. What I wanted, what I needed, who I was. I put him first, and his wishes. And then we ended up coming here, and I was miserable. But by then it was already too late. And when I finally started saying what I wanted, what I needed, well, as I said, it was too late."

I wonder where she's going with this. It's what I always assumed, that *Mami* gave up on a lot for *Tati,* and that he took her for granted. But why discuss it now? What has it got to do with me? After all, I'm in no danger of loving Greg enough to lose myself.

"I was miserable when we came here," *Mami* says. "I was homesick. I missed my friends. I missed my mother, my grandmother. You missed your grandma too, remember? Remember we used to cry together and I'd ask you not to tell *Tati*? I missed my job, at the library. I missed that beautiful house we used to live in. Do you remember that, L? I hated this horrible apartment, but we just couldn't afford any better. I missed having a housekeeper. I missed having everything provided for me, and not having to worry about anything."

"I was like a princess in our old house. Remember Mrs. Grosu who came and cleaned and ironed, and sometimes cooked for us? I used to not even have to do anything to take care of you and your brother. I'd play with you. I'd do the fun stuff. But it was your nanny, Miss Ani, remember her, who really took care of you. You know I never even changed a diaper until I started watching Josephine's children? Here I was, thirty years old, with two kids of my own, and having never changed a diaper. I couldn't bring myself to even tell her. I just figured it out by myself."

It's weird to think of it this way. *Mami*, is so overwhelmingly competent in everything she does, that it's hard to think of her being young and without skills.

"Anyway, I had a good life before, L, and then it was all taken away from me, and I hated it. I felt like a prisoner here, not speaking English, not being able to do anything for myself. I hated it all, I hated the new people we met, the ones in the 'community', who were all so fucking excited to be here. Who thought I was ungrateful for not liking it. But worst of all, I started resenting your daddy, because it had been his idea."

Mami sighs. Her beautiful eyes glaze over.

"Things just got worse and worse between us. I was so angry with him, for everything that happened, everything I didn't like. I was completely miserable and I took it all out on him. We fought all the time, but mostly really, I felt like it was me doing all the fighting. He stayed so calm, it made me crazy. Anyway, the point is, I felt miserable, and I felt alone. I knew I was losing your father, and sometimes I even felt like I deserved to lose him, like I was nothing but a burden anyway. A wife who didn't work, when we were so poor and he was killing himself to make a living, an immature woman who complained and yelled and screamed all the time. Some days I was disgusted with myself."

I want to say something, but she laughs.

"Yes, L, I bet you didn't know that. I was disgusted, truly, utterly disgusted with myself. It happens, you know? I was young, in a foreign country… And I knew nobody. Mrs. Stoica was my only friend, and she was old, and sometimes kind of weird, and she did not quite understand me. And then, of course, there was Josephine, but I didn't feel like she understood me either."

Mami frowns, gives off a deep sigh. I cringe at the thought of her being so alone. I should have guessed that about her, but somehow I never gave it too much thought.

"I hated my life. There seemed to be nothing to look forward to, nothing that I would enjoy. I knew it was a sin to think this way. I was young, healthy, I had two healthy children, but instead of being thankful, I was depressed. Each morning, when the alarm clock went off, I faced the new day with dread. They were always the same, my days, all drudgery, all unpleasantness. There was a chore for every waking minute, and nothing I enjoyed to make up for it. I'd wake up and already have to rush. I'd fix the breakfast for you kids, and the lunch bags, and then I'd fix your father's breakfast. The kitchen was so fucking cold in the winter. I'd wake up and it'd be dark, and I already would have a headache, but I'd drink my coffee, and fix food for everybody, and make sure you and your brother were out the door in time for school. I'd take a quick shower, and go to Josephine's. I had to be there before she left, and I was always running late, even though it was just a few doors down, and I just looked like hell. A shower was all I could manage, so at least I'd be clean, but I'd be dressed in the most horrible clothes, my hair would be a mess, and I would not even have a chance to get a smear of lotion on my face. But then again, I felt so old and unattractive, it really didn't matter anymore. I'd crash on the couch, as soon as Josephine left. I'd literally fall asleep sometimes, that's just how exhausted I was, and usually the baby's crying would wake me up. When you and Alex came from school, you'd sit with me, remember? We'd watch TV until Josephine came back. I'd try to pretend everything was ok. I'd ask you guys to do your homework while we were waiting for Josephine, but Alex would never listen to me, he'd just sit there and watch Josephine's cable. He'd hog the remote, and eat food from Josephine's pantry, which I'd ask him not to take, which I then had to replace out of my ridiculous pay, and he'd totally ignore me. I finally gave up. I never knew how to make Alex listen to me. I just didn't, and I still don't. I guess if I was really a good mother, I would know, I would have found some way to trick him."

I feel a pang of resentment towards Alex. Why did he always have to be so cruel to *Mami*?

"Of course, as a good mother, I should have really cared that he was not doing his homework and instead watching TV. But really, what annoyed me was that he picked these awful programs that I found really boring. I can't believe I was so immature, L, but I was hoping he'd switch channels more than I was hoping he'd do his homework."

Mami laugh. Her laughter is devoid of joy and it scares me.

"You, of course, were a good child, and you listened to me. You'd sit at Josephine's dining table and try to work. But then you'd run into something difficult and you'd ask me for help, and I had no idea how to help you. It just made me feel stupid, and I'd be so angry with myself for not being able to learn English sooner. Your *Tati* always helped you with your homework. Even when he was tired, even when he worked all night, he'd sit there with you, and help you figure it out. I envied him for being so smart and patient. I myself felt like a useless idiot. After a while, I gave up on insisting you start your homework at Josephine's. I knew you'd do it later with your daddy, so I'd just let you sit on the couch, and we'd watch whatever stupid programs Alex selected for us. On good days I'd braid your hair. On bad days I'd just sit there and stare into space. I'd pretend to watch TV but I wouldn't. I'd just sit there wondering if my life was worth living. And I'd think of how things could be different, how I was still young, and life should be more fun. How I could maybe enjoy living again, if only there were some kind of adventure, some kind of excitement in my life, something, anything to look forward to."

She sighs, as if even now, she can still imagine different lives for herself.

"When Josephine finally came back, we'd rush home, so I could make dinner. If she ran late I'd worry, thinking you guys and your daddy would eat too late, not have a warm meal soon enough, maybe get an ulcer, and it would all be my fault. I usually cooked the night before, so all I'd have to do was warm it up. But I always wanted to make a salad too, to have my kids eat something fresh and green. And Alex liked cucumbers. Well, there is nothing I hate more than peeling freaking cucumbers!"

She laughs.

"But I would do it every night while the meal was warming up, keeping an eye on whatever I had on the stove. Your daddy would be home by then, and he usually started on the homework with you guys before dinner. I always felt like it was my fault you were eating so late. And then, of course, I'd be terrified that the store would close and there'd be no food for the next day. So sometimes I'd just serve you guys dinner, and I'd run to the store. I mostly shopped on weekends, but with the fresh stuff you need every day for a family of four, you always run out of something you need the next day.

I'd come back, and then I'd take a bite of whatever was left, while washing the dishes. Your daddy would be doing homework with you guys, and I'd try to be quiet with the dishes. And then I'd start to cook for the next day, knowing that the following morning it would all start again and that the next night there should be something waiting to be warmed up. After the cooking there'd be more dishes, more cleaning up. It just never ended."

Mami sighs. Her face looks older, more tired.

"The house was never clean enough. I did most of it on weekends, in between laundry, grocery shopping, and cooking. I always hated cleaning. And it would never end. It felt like I'd clean one area of this horrible apartment, and as soon as I'd turn around, there would be a new mess. I always felt bad about my house not being clean enough. After all, I'd ask myself, what am I doing? I'm a housewife. Why would my place not be sparkling clean?"

I want to protest. I never remember our house being a mess. But before I can say anything, *Mami* goes on.

"I felt so guilty for not having a real job. Josephine's was something, but it paid almost nothing. I could get a few odds and ends, and it was better than not making any money at all, but I was not even making enough to prepare a decent meal for my family. It was humiliating.

So I was depressed. I was tired. All I wanted to do was sleep. I sometimes wished I could just lie down in a big bed and have everyone leave me alone. I even wished I could drop dead, and there'd be nothing left but peace and quiet."

I shiver. In my darkest days, I never wished to be dead.

"But, anyway, what I meant to tell you, L, was what I did. And for that, I need you to know how I felt. Because it wasn't something I did on an impulse. I thought about it for a long time. Which makes it worse, I know, but... Well, I told you how sometimes I thought about being dead. I couldn't help it, I thought it would be soothing, to lie down and have all the blood drain out of my body. To simply stop existing."

I hold my breath. The look on my face must be one of pure horror, because *Mami* stops, and shakes her head.

"No, no, honey! I never tried to kill myself. I didn't even want to. I was just depressed, and sometimes I imagined dying as relief. But I didn't really want to die. I just wanted to escape. What I wanted, really, was to leave. Once it occurred to me, I couldn't think of anything else. Sitting on the couch at Josephine's, watching Alex' TV selections, I'd plot my escape. I know it's horrible, but I felt used and tired, and at the same time useless. So I managed to convince myself that everybody would be better off without me. Your father would have one less mouth to feed. And there'd be nobody there to yell and cry and pick fights with him. I thought you'd miss me, but overall, I was a useless mother to you, and I knew that eventually you'd catch on. To Alex, of course, I was just a royal pain in the ass. I just wanted to forget everything about my life, I wanted to rest, to sleep it all off, to just be by myself for a while, and then to start all over again."

She looks at me, as if searching for signs of understanding. I don't know how to react to all this.

"I decided I needed to go somewhere where nobody would track me down. And where nobody knew me," *Mami* says. I hold my breath. Wait... Did she actually do this? How? When? "I started saving my money from Josephine's. Your father did not even notice. I asked Josephine questions about trains. It never occurred to me to take a bus, though it would have been cheaper. If I were to skip town today, I'd do it on a Greyhound. But back then, well, I just didn't know. And it was hard enough to get information from Josephine, especially since I couldn't tell her that I was leaving. I tried to work my questions into conversation. I didn't want to let her in on my plan. I just asked her for a subway map of the city and expressed a lot of curiosity in all things related to Manhattan. I had gone to visit her at work once, and it was such an exciting adventure, that she wasn't surprised I'd want to know more."

Mami sighs. She looks like she hesitates to go on.

"And so one day I told her I'd have to miss the next day, so she had her sister watch her kids. I woke up early. Your daddy was on his night shift, in the cab. I started packing. I didn't think much about what to take with me. I just stuffed jeans, shirts, socks, and underwear in this little suitcase we had. And I took half the money your daddy had saved up for us. It wasn't much, but I knew how hard he worked for it, and I felt horrible for taking it. Still, I told myself that with me gone, he'd save more in the long run."

Ok, I think. So she wanted to leave, she even packed. But at the last moment she must have changed her mind. It's sad, and weird, and I feel a little betrayed, but it's not exactly earth shattering, is it?

"I made you and Alex your breakfast and your lunch bags. I tried not to think about what I was doing. I tried not to think about whether I'd ever see you again, and whether you would ever forgive me. I just kept telling myself that I was a bad mother anyway, and that you both would be better off without me. I knew your *Tati* would take care of you. He was always so strong, so competent, and so adaptable. I knew he'd make it in the new country eventually, and that he'd take good care of you.

I was going to shower after you guys left. I was also going to fix Victor some breakfast. I took down a bowl to beat his omelet, but then I just started crying, and I realized I had to leave quickly, before I changed my mind. Or before he came home.

I dressed in a hurry, tears running down my face, my heart racing, my ears listening for any sounds that could signal his return. Part of me wanted to get caught. Part of me wanted him to find me, and talk me into staying."

That's probably what happened, I think. Or she just changed her mind.

"I nearly raced to the elevator, and I kept praying all the way down that he wouldn't be standing in the lobby when I got there. And on the street, dragging my little suitcase, I kept looking behind me, almost expecting to see him. My heart stopped every time I saw a yellow cab. I made it to the subway station safely. I purchased my token. I even managed to get on the right train. This nice old man helped me. He was not even thrown by my bad English. He helped me look on the map and find the train that took me to Penn Station. And to think people say New Yorkers are unfriendly!"

My heart races. Wait, so she really left? I was so sure that *Mami* couldn't have gone through with it. How could she?

"Of course, once I got there, I was even more confused and more terrified. There were so many people. People rushing, pushing past me. There was a big board showing the trains, arrivals and departures. I didn't know where to go. I just knew I wanted it to be far enough not to be found, yet close enough for the fare to be cheap."

Mami's face is a cloud of unhappiness and sorrow. Her eyes are glazing over, but I'm not sure I can sympathize any more.

"I stood in line in front of one of the windows. I asked the woman next to me: "Where you going?" "Scranton," she said. "Is far?" I asked. "Not really." She seemed kind. I guess I was willing to latch on to any shred of kindness."

She sighs, her eyes lost in space. Does she know I can no longer relate to her?

"I watched her at the window, buying her ticket. I saw her pull out a bunch of twenties. I couldn't make out how many, but I thought, it can't be too expensive if she's paying cash. So when my turn came I said: "Scranton. One way." I had practiced saying "one way" for two weeks.

After I bought my ticket, I looked around for the kind lady also going to Scranton. She had disappeared. I never saw her again. It's weird, but being separated from this total stranger made me sad. I was standing there, in the middle of the station, looking at the big board like a total idiot, trying to figure out which train went to Scranton, and where exactly I could board it. My new friend was gone, and I felt like crying. I hadn't understood what the woman at the counter said to me, so I didn't even know when my train was leaving. In a panic, tears running down my cheeks, I started showing my ticket to strangers, asking: "Where?" Most people brushed me aside. Finally someone pointed me towards my track. I was so grateful, I hugged and kissed him, then ran towards the track. I had to carry my little suitcase down the stairs. It felt heavy by now, it hurt my hand, but I didn't care. My train was there, a big sliver train that would take me away. I got on, and just for a second, I felt excited about my big adventure."

I swallow hard. I'm not sure how I feel. But my hands, holding the tea mug are shaking.

"It wasn't nice at all, on the train. It was ugly, actually rather grimy. It even smelled bad. Like rust, or something. Something metallic, unfriendly, kind of dirty. I got to sit by the window. I cried all the way to Scranton, and then I fell asleep and nearly missed my stop. The conductor was screaming "Scranton" at the top of his lungs. I should have picked a place with a nicer name, come to think of it.

The plan was to check into a cheap but clean hotel, rest the first day, take a bubble bath, watch TV. Then the next day, bright and early I would look in the paper and try to find a job as a French speaking nanny."

She gives off an uncomfortable little laugh, and shakes her head.

"I was so naïve, L. I knew so little. And then, what I learned, well, it was just one unpleasant discovery after another. Really cheap hotels, in this country, are not clean. As my cabdriver told me "If you want clean, and safe, you have to pay, lady." So I had to stay someplace expensive, I mean, expensive for my budget. It was almost nice, actually. But ironically after spending all that money on the cab to take me around, I ended up staying right by the train station. My second discovery was that the only thing I could really afford from room service was a bagel. It cost seven dollars, L, for somebody to bring a stupid toasted bagel with cream cheese to my room. And when it arrived, it was cold."

I smile. How ironic. A bagel, my own subsistence food. I can see myself in a hotel room in Scranton, being able to afford nothing but a bagel, and hating every single bite.

"And then I found that once I showered and ate my stupid bagel, I could sleep for almost forty-eight hours. Once I lay down in those soft white sheets, there was no getting up. I'd wake up for short spells, but would not be able to bring myself to actually rise. I'd just lie there, letting myself drift off to sleep again. I finally emerged, two days later, with a horrible headache and swollen eyes. You know, I read somewhere that too much sleep is toxic. Sincerely, I'm surprised I didn't die from it. Just lying in that big bed, soaking in my own poison.

I took another shower, then made coffee, hideous hotel coffee, if I may borrow your word, weak and tinny. I couldn't even drink it, and I needed it so badly. I ordered another bagel and a paper. All kinds of things were needed in Scranton, but a French-speaking nanny was not amongst them. No need to say that nobody needed a librarian specializing in *fin de siècle* Romanian literature either. I wondered if I was willing to clean houses for a living. Would that be worse or better than the life I'd left behind in New York?

I fell asleep again, with my face on the paper. I woke up to the phone ringing. They asked if I wanted to stay on, or vacate the room. I looked inside my pocketbook, and I started crying. I had newsprint on my face, a bright future as Scranton's worst cleaning lady, and seventy dollars and change in my purse. It couldn't cover an additional night. I had really hoped that by then I'd have secured some kind of employment, preferably as a live-in nanny."

Again, she laughs at her own misadventures, but it's a sad, bitter laugh, as if she's still not able to let go of her disappointment.

"It's funny now, how naïve I was, how I had no idea how this world works at all. But back then I was crestfallen. I realized the only thing I could really afford was to go back to New York, back to Victor, if he'd take me. The thought of facing him at this point scared me so much it made me sick. But with that knot in my stomach, I packed my things, then looked one last time out the window of my hotel room, the lovely room that had been mine for three nights, but which I hadn't really taken the time to enjoy. I pressed my face against the cold windowpane, and wondered when I'd have the opportunity to be alone again."

Her face is filled with nostalgia, as if that moment, suspended in time, is a sacred, yet painful memory. The last moment when she was by herself, in Scranton, in her hotel room. It hurts to think that that's what *Mami* longed for, all these years. Being alone. Rather than with her family.

"I checked out of the hotel and walked to the train station. I managed to purchase a ticket back, but once I got into the city and off my train, I got lost. How ironic that I'd made it all the way to Scranton and back, but then I couldn't figure out the New York City subway and go back to Queens. I called your father from a payphone at the station. I was terrified. I just kept praying, as the phone rang, praying that he'd be home, that he'd pick up, that he'd agree to take me back, praying that he'd come get me in Manhattan.

He did come. He came in the cab. I felt so horrible, I couldn't bring myself to look at his face. He was so angry with me, L. But he was quiet, as usual, cold. I sat in the back of the cab. I was afraid to sit next to him, not physically afraid, of course. Your father never raised a hand at me, and I want you to know that. But I was afraid of his quiet, controlled anger, because I knew that I deserved it. I was so ashamed of myself. I cried all the way home.

We stopped at a stupid diner. He picked up food for us. Meatloaf and mashed potatoes, the worst meal I ever had. I could not touch meatloaf for years after that. I even would not touch anything that had ground beef in it. Meatballs. Remember how Alex always liked my marinated meatballs? I'd nearly throw up after making them, just the sight of them made me sick. But I got over that, of course. It's funny how people manage to get over things. There were so many times in my life when I thought I'd be in pain forever, that I'd never recover, but time heals everything."

She says this, but she sighs, and her face is not that of a woman who's come to terms with her past.

"The only thing I never truly got over was leaving my children. I could never forgive myself for that. I couldn't talk about it to anyone. The only person I told was Josephine, and you know what she said? She said she knew my husband beat me. She really thought that, L. She thought your father was abusive, and that that's why I left. But you know as well as I do, that's not true. I couldn't even imagine it. I still can't. But there are so many women out there who have to deal with that. And if I felt like my house was a prison, can you imagine what kind of hell they must be going through?"

Silence takes over the room. I have long since finished my tea, but am still holding the cup, cold by now. I'm inspecting the rim, studying the pattern of blue flowers bordering it. It's ugly, and I've always thought so, but I'd rather look at it, than look at *Mami*'s face.

"It's funny, L, but that stupid trip to Scranton, that is the only time, in my whole life, that I've gone somewhere by myself. I mean, gone out of town, you know. I've never been anywhere. We used to go on vacation, in Romania, remember? We'd go to the mountains, or to the Black Sea. It was always so beautiful. But I've never gone anywhere alone. Ever. And I've never gone anywhere since. Not even for a weekend. I've never in my life been anywhere by myself. Except to Scranton.

My only independent excursion. And that only to find out that I could not cope in the world, by myself. Do you know how proud I am of you, L? For braving life on your own, at such a young age? You say you fucked up, but sweetie, you've been gone for months, and you haven't come back. And if you ever do, if you ever need to, you'll always know that you can take care of yourself, that you can go out there on your own, and do more than just spend three days in a hotel in Scranton. L, I was thirty-four before I lived independently from your father, before I figured out how to support myself and my children. Thirty-four. And here you are, ten years younger, doing your own thing, putting a roof above your head, surviving. You might think you fucked up because of some stupid credit card bill, but I think you are doing great, and I'm so proud of you.

I guess that's part of why I wanted to tell you this story. So you can know that, if you think you fucked up, I did it so much worse before. So you can be proud of yourself, of standing on your own two feet. And so you can appreciate your freedom. If you want to go to Scranton, or even somewhere real, somewhere actually exciting. If you want to go to Italy, L, and just stay there, you are free. You are not trapped in a bad marriage. And you don't have children who need you. If you go to Italy and buy some ridiculously expensive clothes, well, you might be slightly irresponsible, and you might get deeper into debt and have to pay lots of interest, but it doesn't make you a bad person, because you haven't left your children and your husband to do it."

{28}

Lox and Bagels

Maria is bored. This time of year, suitably outfitted with scarves and gloves, all of New York seems determined to ignore her. They'll be back soon enough, seeking the silk pastels of spring. Until then, she has nothing to do but rearrange her favorite items, soon to go on sale. And worry about L. The way she was sleeping the other night, so peacefully, so innocently, like a child. Yet her daughter is no longer a child, but a grown woman. A woman about to make a stupid mistake that could ruin her life. Next to her sleeping daughter, Maria stayed up all night, praying. It's been two days already. L has not been in touch, and Maria has a heavy feeling in the pit of her stomach each time she thinks of her. Has she, in the light of day, decided to shun her mother, this time for good, this mother who admitted to abandoning her?

Maria sighs and takes comfort in rearranging her favorite gloves. She's so distracted, that she doesn't even notice the customer walking up to the counter, and when she finally becomes aware of his presence she has the feeling that he's been waiting for a while. She looks up from the gloves. Her eyes meet Victor's. Blood rushes to her cheeks. How silly of her to get so flustered! Will this ever stop? Will she ever be able to act normal around him?

"You here to buy glove?" she asks, smiling. From under the glass countertop, she produces her favorite pair, the elbow length ones in the softest leather she's ever encountered. They are a delight to touch, and as she hands them over to Victor she realizes that she's proud of them, as if she made them herself. They are divine and perfect, and it's impossible not to enjoy such craftsmanship.

"Maybe for girlfriend?" she asks playfully. She's dying to know if he and Monica are back together, or if there's someone new in his life. "Surely a handsome man like you has girlfriend, no?"

Victor laughs.

"Actually, I have an estranged wife. I was hoping maybe to take her to lunch?"

Maria smiles.

He's looking at the gloves. His manly hands are caressing the fine leather. She has to avert her eyes. She's always loved his hands, his fingers, big, strong, yet at the same time elegant. She used to think they were a sign of good character, of nobility and endurance. But little good did it do her, that he is such a noble man. Little good did it do her that he is strong, or that he's great with those big manly hands of his.

"This feels fucking amazing!" he says. Maria sighs.

"I know. They're my favorites."

Victor takes a quick glance at the price tag.

"Eight hundred dollars? For gloves?"

She shrugs.

"You want quality, you pay."

"Well, they are amazing," he admits. "Here, let me see."

Before she knows it, his hand reaches for hers, and in slow, deliberate gestures, he's slipping the glove onto her fingers. It feels divine. It feels unbearable. Wrapped in the finest leather known to man, her hand is shaking visibly, betraying her. There's no way to conceal it now, is there? He can see her trembling, so he knows that his touch still sends shivers down her spine, that she cannot, will not, ever in her silly wretched life be indifferent to him. She tries to hide behind her eyelashes, but it's no use.

"It's beautiful," he says. "I'll buy it for you, if you like."

"It's eight hundred dollars!" She laughs. Her voice comes out too shrill. "That's crazy! Beside, I have gloves. I have very nice gloves."

She peels the leather off her hand, and places the object of beauty back in its glass compartment.

"So how about lunch?" he asks.

"Wait here a minute. I'll ask."

She goes off in search of Grace, her supervisor. It's one of the drawbacks of her faulty English. Despite her charm, she's never been promoted. A woman in her twenties, who's only worked here a few months, is her supervisor. Normally, she doesn't give a damn. But today she's embarrassed that she has to ask Grace if she can take her lunch early, that Victor will hear this exchange.

"Grace, I go lunch now," she announces, hoping that her supervisor will not consider this an impertinence. "I go punch out. I be back in an hour."

Grace smiles, and Maria knows it's all right. After all, there aren't any customers.

"O.K.," her supervisor says, then pulls her aside to ask, in a whisper. "Who's the guy? Did you meet someone?"

Maria blushes.

"Is my husband."

She feels good saying it, and she enjoys the look of admiration on the other woman's face. No need to tell her they are separated, and really just friends, that their friendship is new and fragile.

She slips into the back room to punch out, and grab her coat. She can't help but look in the mirror, can't help but swipe a brush through her hair a few times, dab a drop of fragrance on her wrists, and put on a fresh coat of lipstick. She wishes she could erase the circles around her eyes, the wrinkles around her mouth, the time and bitterness they testify to. It's silly, of course to care so much about her appearance. After all, it's just lunch with a friend.

When she returns to the floor, she can't see Victor anywhere. Did she spend too long primping? Did he leave? But then her eyes find him. He's wandered off from the glove department, and is now chatting with a saleswoman from the fragrance section. It's a woman Maria doesn't know well, but who has quite a reputation as a flirt. She's from somewhere in South America, has the most beautiful complexion, wild black hair, and a voluptuous body. She wears low-cut shirts, has a deep sexy voice, and pouty lips. On top of that, her job is to tempt customers with fragrance. What on earth could be more seductive?

Seeing her now, in conversation with Victor, Maria can't suppress her jealousy. There they are, obviously flirting. The way he's looking at her, the way her feline body arches towards him, the smiles, the eye contact. There's obviously a seduction ritual going on, and Maria is not sure who will be seducing whom.

Her first impulse is a childish one. She wants to turn around, go back to the break room, hide there, eat the tuna sandwich she's brought from home, and forget all about lunch with Victor. She wonders if he'd even notice.

Her second impulse is to march over and interrupt their flirting by throwing a tantrum. But that is stupid, and she knows it. She's not going to pull at Victor's sleeve, and she's not going to stomp her feet demanding his attention. After all, she has no claim to him whatsoever. That they are not divorced is only a formality, an oversight on both of their parts.

She walks towards them, and stops about five feet away, unsure of how to act. She notices Victor looking around in search of her, in the middle of whatever tantalizing conversation he's having with the other woman. His eyes find her, before she has a chance to wipe the jealousy off her face. He must have seen it, because he smiles a smug little smile.

Blushing, she smiles back, and walks towards them.

"Here, you should try this," Victor says, and his hand rests on the small of her back. She can feel his touch, even through her winter coat, or maybe she just imagines feeling it. Victor's hand rests on her body as if it's normal for him to touch her this way, as if she belongs to him, just a little bit. Does it mean anything? Or is it just a random gesture from a man used to being around women? Maybe to him, it has no deeper meaning than a sneeze.

She straightens her back. He removes his hand.

The fragrance woman hands her a piece of paper to smell.

"No. Actually try it on," Victor says, and the woman offers Maria the atomizer bottle. It's made of blue glass, and shaped like a star. Aware of Victor's eyes on her, she sprays perfume into her décolleté, then rolls up her sleeve and sprays some on her arm. It still looks young, the skin on her arm, she knows it. It still looks sensuous, feminine, and inviting. She holds up her forearm and lets Victor smell it. He seems to enjoy the fragrance and the closeness. In spite of herself, she giggles, and before she knows it, she is flirting. With Victor, of all men…

The perfume does smell wonderful. Exotic, sensual, and strangely familiar. She's heard people say that nothing evokes memories better than fragrance, and this one reminds her of someone.

"Thank you," she says to the saleswoman. "You ready to go, Victor?"

Her voice, too brisk and too impatient, dispels the magic cloud of fragrance and flirtation. She only has an hour for lunch. No time for foolishness.

Since she's in a rush, Victor suggests the bar of a luxury hotel nearby. She's passed by it a million times. She always wanted go in. It's the kind of place that's too expensive for her, and she always secretly wanted to go there. Just as she wanted to go to so many other places she could never afford.

Outside it's cold, grey, and the air smells like an imminent snowfall. The typical cruelty of spring in New York. Inside, it's warm, and the room is just as lovely as Maria imagined. They sit in leather armchairs, at a safe distance from each other. A large window offers a view of passers-by huddled in coats, navigating the frosty afternoon. Although she only has an hour, Maria feels relaxed. The fragrance envelops her in its delicious magic. It blends with the scent of leather and the warmth in the room, making her feel spoiled and sexy. And although she cannot remember where she encountered this lovely scent before, she knows that it will be forever in her mind associated with the memory of sitting here with Victor on a snowy day.

"It smells amazing on you," Victor says. "Maybe I should buy it for you."

She smiles. In her relaxed and cozy state, the thought is rather appealing. But why would he buy her a gift?

Then it suddenly comes to her, her recent memory of this exact same fragrance.

"You know, is same perfume our daughter has."

She laughs, thinking it would be silly to wear the same scent as L.

"Is that so? Well, she does look quite like you, our daughter, don't you think? If it suits you so well, it must suit her."

Maria smiles.

"You really think she looks like me?"

"Yes. She's amazingly beautiful."

She loves hearing him say so. How vain of her, she knows it. How nonsensical to cherish a compliment while at the same time trying to suppress all sparks of attraction. How silly, to enjoy that look in his eyes, and to imagine that he still finds her beautiful. She tries to chase the thought away, to concentrate on the mental image of L, hoping her daughter's youthful face will bring her back to safer ground. And she remembers just how badly she wanted to call Victor the other night, after confessing to her daughter.

"She came by Monday," she says. She feels uneasy, opening the subject, but he is, after all, the only one she can share this with. "I talked to her… I hope it will help. I talked to her about this Greg, and about marriage. And I spoke to her about, you know…" In spite of their last conversation, she's still uncomfortable mentioning her betrayal. It's almost impossible to say it, and it's definitely impossible to meet his eyes while doing so.

"Scranton," she finally says, staring at the cloth napkin on her lap.

The weight of the word hangs in the air, as heavy as the guilt pressing down on her shoulders.

"Yes, Scranton," he says. There's something rusty in his voice. But he smiles, and she's relieved to see it. "Your big wild adventure.

You know, we are in a hotel, and I'm pretty sure they serve bagels, since that seems to be your idea of a crazy good time."

"Fuck you!" she says, laughing.

They end up ordering the bagels, gourmet bagels, with cream cheese, lox, and scallions, a far cry from the bland pieces of dough she had in Scranton. They drink champagne, and she feels slightly tipsy. It's snowing outside, big flakes dancing around, falling peacefully onto the dirty New York sidewalk.

They talk about L. She feels better after telling him how quiet their daughter was the night of her confession. How she seemed so withdrawn. She shares her fear that L will this time really and truly cut her off.

"She might just need some time to process it," he says. "It was brave of you to tell her."

"But you still think I shouldn't have."

"I guess we'll have to wait and see. L is smart, underneath all her immaturity. She might be taken aback now, but I think she'll come to appreciate your honesty."

They drink more champagne and watch the snowflakes dance. Soon she'll have to leave the magic of champagne flutes, bubbles, and fragrance. She'll have to step out into the winter afternoon, and go back to work. She'd almost risk being late, to prolong sitting here, with Victor, watching the snow.

"You know, I meant it about that perfume. You should let me buy it for you. When was the last time I bought you a present?"

"Other than my apartment?" she asks, blushing.

"I did not buy you your apartment, Maria. You bought it yourself. I might have helped you get it sooner. But we both know you would have saved the money and gotten it anyway. I just wanted you to have it now rather than later. Life's short, and you've already missed out on a lot of good years."

She ponders the thought, taking a sip of champagne.

"And you should be proud of yourself," he says. "As far as I'm concerned, you did it on your own, and it's no small feat, buying your own place in Manhattan. Remember when we came here and you didn't speak English, you couldn't get a job, and you were terrified to even go to the store by yourself? You've come a long way. And you did it in spite of being proud and stubborn, and sending everybody straight to hell, whom you didn't like. Including me."

She laughs.

"But you helped."

"Not really, and not as much as I should have. And that's because you wouldn't let me. But I was hoping that now, that you hate me less… You do hate me a little less these days, don't you?"

She laughs again.

"I never really hated you. I mean really hate, you know. And yes, I do hate you a little less."

"Well, I just thought that maybe you'd reconsider the money situation."

"I don't want your money, Victor. I feel bad enough taking it for the down payment."

"It's your money too. We're married, remember? Legally, you're entitled to half of what I have."

She takes another sip of champagne. She doesn't feel entitled to anything. She was a bad wife. And why should wives be entitled to money anyway?

"Marriage is such weird institution," she says, wrinkling her nose. "I don't think I'm entitled to anything, Victor. You worked for your money. Not me. You should use it however you want."

"And suppose I actually want to spend some of it on you?"

"Why?"

She didn't meant for it to come out as defensive as it did.

"I'm not expecting anything in return, Maria. You don't have to be my friend. And you certainly don't have to sleep with me ever again if you don't want to. I just think you deserve to enjoy life for a change. I'd love for you to let me help you."

She blushes at the mention of sex, and is embarrassed further by his generosity. His kindness is so undeserved. And it allows for the painful hope that he still cares for her a little bit.

"And yes," he says, "you were right when you said I wanted to use my money to…" He fiddles with his champagne flute. His discomfort is palpable. It freezes her in place. "…to make amends. I never took care of you the way I should have. In fact, I always thought it was unfair that we split up just when things started going better for me."

She swallows. She doesn't want to point out that it was her who asked him to leave.

"You didn't have to take care of me, Victor. I was a grown woman, not a child! In fact, I think it's quite an antiquated notion that a husband has to provide for his wife! I don't feel like you ever had the responsibility to take care of me!"

He laughs.

"I'm not trying to bring back the 1950s, Maria!" He takes a sip of his drink, and appears to be pondering his words. "I respect that you're independent. But would it be acceptable for me to say, I would have liked to be able to take care of you?"

"I would have rather liked being able to take care of myself," she says. "I hated that you had to support me for all those years, when I didn't have a job and was living off you."

He looks at her long and hard.

"Is that how you really felt? Did I really make you feel that way?"

She sighs and hides behind her eyelashes.

"I know I wasn't pulling my own weight," she says.

"You took care of our children, you cooked, you cleaned, you shopped, and you denied yourself everything until you couldn't stand it anymore. I'd say that's more than pulling your own weight."

She has to laugh. Whatever happened to him? She never thought she'd hear him talk this way.

"You sound like Josephine," she says. "Our neighbor, the one I babysat for."

"I remember Josephine. You know, I always could tell she didn't like me, and now finally I know why. She knew I treated my wife like a servant, and made her feel bad about it, to add insult to injury."

It isn't funny, but she laughs all the same. She could never tell him what Josephine really thought about their relationship.

"So you think you should finally pay me for being your maid? Is this what this money thing is all about?"

He frowns.

"That's harsh. But I guess I deserve it."

His eyes look darker, sadder. But he laughs.

"No, ma'am. Your services are priceless."

She can't help but giggle at that. Is he trying to flirt in the middle of such an unpleasant conversation?

"Is that so?" she asks.

"I'd never try to put a price tag on you raising our children," he says, "or on many other things you did. It's just symbolic, Maria. I know it's too little, too late, but I'd wish you'd agree to share our money. I know it wouldn't make things right. But it would make me feel better if you'd accept it."

She shakes her head, smiling.

"You don't have to do this, Victor."

"Think about it at least. You don't have to decide right now. Life is short. You should enjoy it while you can."

She drinks the last sip of champagne. It's sad, but she does have to go.

"Fine," she says. "I'll think about it. I don't think I'll ever be comfortable with you giving me money, or buying me stuff. But I'll consider it. And I appreciate the offer."

He shakes his head.

"Stubborn woman."

"What else is new?"

"Can I at least buy lunch?" he asks.

"Anytime you want."

Why did she say that? It's too flirtatious, too inviting.

"As a friend, I mean," she quickly corrects herself.

"If that's what you want."

Her tries to hold her gaze, but she looks away, looks at the napkin on her lap, starts folding it, placing it on the table.

"Yes, that is what I want."

It hurts to say it. But it is what it is. And she needs to go back to work.

He helps her into her coat. They walk together into the cold afternoon. Snowflakes fall on her face. She enjoys the crisp scent of snow. Traffic and city grime yield to the freshness of the winter air. Steam blows out of subway shafts, the breath of the city, from its lungs and from its gutters, warm, stale and dirty, yet slightly sweet, as unmistakable a smell of New York as honey roasted almonds.

"So you really did quit smoking," she says.

"You noticed."

{29}

A Busy Day

It's been two weeks since I helped *Mami* pack. Two weeks since her bizarre late-night confession. Two weeks of restlessness and thinking. And finally, today, after more soul-searching than a gal can stand, I take the day off work. I have three important appointments, two of which are decidedly unpleasant. The third one I'm mildly excited about.

I spend the morning getting ready. I want to look my best, and I need extra pampering to soothe my frazzled nerves. I had trouble falling asleep last night, anticipating the horrors ahead. In the light of day I feel bold, almost rebellious. I make myself a cup of instant coffee. I recently discovered this is a cheap alternative to contributing money towards Rachelle's gourmet coffee fund. I pour skim milk liberally into my cup. It's organic and comes in a colorful carton with pictures of cheerful little cows. *Văcuțe*. Because there are a few things a girl should never scrounge on, and milk is one of them. Even *Mami* buys organic. Or rather, I should say, especially *Mami* buys organic. She's so compulsive about food, after all.

I eat two boiled eggs (also organic), and some whole grain toast (the regular stuff, because I can't afford the really wholesome kind). I set the peeled eggs on a plate, cut them in half, squeeze some lemon juice on them, and surround them with pitted kalamata olives, one of my favorite treats. I spread a thin layer of butter on my toast, and pour some honey on it. A good breakfast is vital, especially on a day like today. Although I made lunch reservations at a nice restaurant, under the circumstances, I'll probably just sit there, picking at my salad, too nervous to eat.

I take a long shower, then slip into a pair of cheap jeans from the Gap, and put on a simple black T-shirt underneath a simple black turtleneck. I don't want to be dressed up today, and I'm certainly not out to impress anyone. I just want to be comfortable, and look relatively decent. The only thing remotely fancy that I wear is my cream leather bag, by now a little beat up, but still luxurious to me. In it I'm carrying over a thousand dollars in cash. It's money I've been saving from Rachelle's French lessons, as well as from my weekly budget. I've stolen some money tricks from Rachelle. I've learned the only way to budget is by giving myself a weekly allowance. I end up with three lean days each week, but that is way better than two lean weeks at the end of each month. I also go through my wallet every now and then, and put each five dollar bill I find into a savings jar. It adds up, you know?

I wonder what Rachelle would think of me blowing the entire French lesson fund. She was so sassy in warning me to save it. I guess she can go fuck herself. It's my money, not hers. I needn't give anybody explanations for what I do with my own stack of cash. 'Today, I am a woman,' I tell myself. I check out my reflection in a storefront window. A touch of elegance, the leather bag, but other than that, just an ordinary girl, a little drab, and a little scared. 'Today, I am a woman,' I tell myself again. But I'm not sure.

The restaurant I chose is a French Bistro. I've been here with *Tati* and Momo. It's not casual, yet not quite elegant. It's a nice place for lunch, although my guests are used to fancier fare. At least it's nice enough for me. Cozy, and European. And the food is delicious. Too bad I'll be too nervous to enjoy it. A wooden board on the wall announces that oysters are in season. Oysters. *Huitres. Stridii* (?) I love oysters. It's *Tati* who taught me to like them. I haven't had any this year. But in my state of agitation, whatever I order will be wasted. And throwing away oysters, good, juicy, salty oysters, would be a sin.

Sitting alone at the table, I wonder if they'll even show up. Then, finally, here they are. I force myself to smile. I watch the hostess direct them to my table, admire Joan's silhouette in a well tailored suit, notice that Gretchen has changed her hair color.

Greeting each other is awkward. Joan remains cold. I mirror her demeanor. I force myself to continue smiling. I won't bend over backwards to be nice. But I'll be polite. Politeness is important.

Gretchen only acknowledges me with a subtle nod. She sits down, taps her manicured nails on the table. The red hair doesn't really suit her.

We order drinks. Joan asks for iced tea. Looking at her Cartier watch, she says pointedly that she'll have to return to work soon. Gretchen orders a mixed drink she discusses in great detail with the waiter, asking for simple syrup made with Splenda. I order a glass of champagne. Joan shoots me a hostile look. I smile. I guess I feel like celebrating, just a bit.

After all these months, facing Joan and Gretchen is not as nerve racking as I imagined. I decide to order the oysters.

Conversation is sparse and frosty.

I wait until I'm halfway through my oysters, before addressing the money issue.

"So, I finally am in the position to settle my debt to you, Gretchen."

Gretchen raises her eyebrows. Joan removes a leather-bound notebook from her purse, and pages through it.

"My records indicate that you owe my sister three thousand dollars," she says. "Rent for the months of June, July, and August, of last year."

Her eyes meet mine. I smile.

"Actually, I owe her one thousand dollars. Rent for August. I am finally prepared to give it to her now."

"No. You lived there four months. My sister kindly has waved the rent for the first month. But you must pay for the other three. I cannot believe that after all this time, you asked us here in order to offer to pay only a third of what you owe."

I eat another oyster, enjoy its salty sliminess, take a delicious moment to savor the aftertaste.

"I understand where you're coming from, Joan. I did live there for four months. Still, Gretchen is only entitled to one month's rent." I look at my former friend, who is stirring the ice in her now empty glass with her straw. "Here's how things work, Gretchen. You cannot invite someone to live with you and then, a few months into it, start making demands you neglected to make at the beginning. You never mentioned rent to me when I moved in. You invited me to stay with you. For free. Three months later you changed your mind. You can't do that. You can't give something away, then demand to be paid for it later. I will pay you for August, because that is the month that I chose to stay after you decided to charge me."

The corners of Gretchen's mouth twitch.

"I will take you to court," she says.

"I guess you could. But no judge is going to rule in your favor. You can't charge someone rent after you invited them to live in your house for free. It's like having guests over for dinner, and then presenting them with a bill."

"You were not a guest! You were my roommate!"

"No, Gretchen. I was a guest. A roommate signs a lease, and gets a key. I had a key for the month of August. I will pay for the month of August."

I reach inside my purse and pull out the manila envelope full of cash. Fives and tens spill out on the table. I love the sight of my heap of bills in small denominations. I know it's a negligible sum for Joan and Gretchen. But I bet they've never been confronted with a table full of fives and tens before.

"Here is the thousand dollars I owe you. I took the liberty of adding ten percent interest. And there's an extra hundred to cover this lunch."

I finish my champagne, suck up the last oyster, then stand up to leave.

"Goodbye, Gretchen. I hope you figure things out in your life. It was nice knowing you, Joan."

Outside, in the chill of early spring, I feel strong and empowered. I take out the folded newspaper from my purse, and look up the address again. In spite of the cold, I will walk.

I fish inside my pockets, and put on my gloves. Good leather gloves. A present from *Mami*. Of course, they are not the expensive kind she sells for a living. But they are good quality leather gloves, snatched up at a sale somewhere. I remember appraising them at about twenty bucks, and being irritated with *Mami* for buying me a cheap present. Yet this is the second winter I'm wearing them, and each time I put them on I feel elegant and special.

I reach the headquarters of the organization. To my surprise, it's a beautiful brownstone. I kind of imagined a not for profit in a building crumbling with decay, where roaches roam freely, and everything smells like mold, weed, burned coffee, and stale cookies. In spite of the nice building and clean modern lobby, I cannot suppress my doubts. Of course, helping people, 'volunteering,' sounds good in theory, but in practice, I harbor a secret distaste for the martyr nature of people who make such things a priority. A bunch of tree-hugging, self-righteous hippies, who wear ragged clothes, don't wash their hair, and probably smoke too much pot.

I press the buzzer. I tell myself I'll have to shed my prejudices. After all, I decided to give this a try, at least for a little while, if they'll have me. It's my lame attempt to counter the bad karma inherent in the horrible thing I'm about to do.

To my surprise, the young woman sitting behind the receptionist's desk is not dressed like a hippie, and her hair looks clean. She's wearing slim cut jeans, and a white T-shirt with "Speak Free", the name of the organization, printed in bold black letters on the front. I wonder if they'll give me a T-shirt too.

"Hi, are you L?" she asks. "I am Andrea. I will be interviewing you." She motions for me to sit down on a black loveseat across from her desk. "Sorry, we don't have much space. And we are rather informal around here."

I sit down. Andrea pulls over an ottoman, and gets a notebook. She looks over my resume, nodding and smiling a few times. "Wow, so you speak four romance languages! And a bit of German. That's amazing! And you have a B.A. in English, that works well for the teaching position. Now, why are you interested in working here?"

I adjust my purse on my lap. I'm surprised to find that I'm actually nervous.

"I… I just think it's a great thing to do, teaching people English, you know?" I sound like an idiot, I know it. And for some reason, I want to make a good impression. "I'd like to do something that helps people, you know."

"So do most of us," Andrea says. "But there are many ways of doing something meaningful. Why this particular one? What exactly about this position attracts you?"

I shift from playing with my purse to playing with my hair.

"Well, I've always been fascinated with language."

"I can see that," Andrea says.

I try to will myself to say something intelligent.

"I've been teaching my roommate French, and it has really been a very rewarding experience so far."

"I'm sure. But working with first-generation immigrants who sometimes don't have the faintest notion of English is very different, and very challenging. You'll be able to communicate with the Hispanics, of course, but a large percentage of the people we serve are Asian. They will not speak anything remotely similar to the languages you know."

"That does sound challenging," I admit. "But… I guess the reason I want to do this is because I can really relate to what these people are going through. I'm a first generation immigrant myself. Of course, I came here as a child, and my parents took care of me, and I adjusted, as kids do. But I know how for grownups it's so hard. I really admire these people for being able to leave behind their lives and take a leap. And I do know how hard it is for them. I might not have gone through that myself, but when we came here my mom spoke no English at all. It took her years to learn, and she was miserable, practically a captive. I wish there was a place like this for her to go to, but we didn't know of anything, and we didn't have any money. Which is why I think it's so nice that you guys do this for free. I mean… Sorry, I guess I'm rambling."

"No, no. This is actually very interesting. You seem to have a strong personal reason to do this. And we are looking for people who are giving and passionate."

I feel myself blushing. Giving and passionate. It sounds a bit corny, but I like it.

"Well, I'd say you pass," Andrea says. "But of course, we'll have to try you out first, put you into an actual classroom, and have one of our more experienced teachers observe you, before we can officially hire you."

"Hire? I thought this was a volunteer thing…I mean position."

Andrea laughs.

"Oh, no. We pay our teachers. And our other employees too. And we give full time staff a full benefits package."

"Oh." I'm confused. "I thought it was a non-profit organization."

"Yes, it is. Our students do not pay for their classes. But we have an endowment to pay our teaching, recruiting, and fund raising staff. Of course, our salaries are nothing like what you'd get in the corporate world. But it is a fabulous place to work."

She stands up, walks to her desk, and hands me a pile of colorful brochures.

"I've put together some materials on our organization. And I will give you a brief tour of our state-of-the art classrooms. Then I'll introduce you to some of the recruiters. They are the ones who help our students actually get to us. Without them, our classrooms would be empty."

"Do they ever go to women's shelters, you know, like, for battered women?"

Andrea thinks about it for a second.

"You know, I'm not sure. But that would be a great idea. You can ask them yourself. Let me show you the classrooms first, and then we'll call one of our teachers and schedule for her to observe your teaching demonstration."

The third appointment of the day is the hardest. I can feel my stomach contracting, and my knees trembling, as I stand on Greg's doorstep. In my purse, in a small velvet box, is the engagement ring he gave me.

{30}

Easter

In my mind, Easter will always be associated with the scent of the vinegar *Mami* mixes in her egg dye. There's nothing pastel about Romanian Easter. Eggs come in bright colors, red being by far the most popular, and *Mami*'s favorite. Every few years, she sends me to one of the Romanian grocery stores in Queens to buy red dye. This red powder, combined with vinegar, could paint the whole world bright. I love to see the eggs soak in Mami's viegar-dye concoction until the color deepens to a shade that's not pink, not orange, but unapologetically, and unmistakably red.

Mami positions the eggs in their cartons to dry. Once they cool down, we grease them with bacon to make them shiny. I doubt anyone in modern day Romania still does this, but I enjoy the ritual.

As *Mami* likes to point out, Easter is the most important holiday of the year. Celebrating it is a big production. First, people fast for forty days (at least theoretically). And even those who don't, like me, observe a strict vegan diet on Good Friday. *Vinerea mare*. After the fast comes a feast, the highlight of which is lamb.

But first there's midnight mass. Everybody congregates in front of the church, and at midnight they light candles and sing a song about Jesus rising from the dead. *Tati* told Alex and me how, in Romania, where churches are built in traditional cross-shaped Orthodox fashion, and do not have to share a block with a Korean laundry and other businesses, the entire congregation, with their candles aflame, would circle the church three times.

Mami never goes to mass with us. It's no secret that her dislike for the community outweighs her desire to go to church. Even on Easter. It's *Tati* who takes Alex and me to midnight mass. *Mami* waits at home with an elaborate Easter meal, dyed eggs, gourmet sardines, stuffed grape leaves, olives, *taramosalata* from the Greek store, different types of feta, and then of course, roast lamb, crunchy, salty, yet so tender it falls off the bone, a crisp fresh spring salad, spinach pie, and sweet cheese pie with raisins.

This year will be the same, yet different. *Mami* won't be making the meal. We will, instead, after church, gather at *Tati*'s, to eat the lamb he made. *Mami* and I will dye the eggs at her new place, then *Tati* will pick us up, and take us to his house. Alex is home from school and sleeping at *Tati*'s, because, there's no home for him to go back to. *Tati* will take Alex and me to church, as usual, and *Mami,* I guess, will wait until we return, watching the lamb (as if the roast lamb could run away, or get bored without an entertaining companion). After church, we will eat our feast at *Tati*'s. Then he will drive *Mami* and me back to *Mami*'s, where I will spend the night. Only my crazy Romanian parents could come up with such a complicated arrangement.

Once I finally get to see *Mami*'s new place, I understand why everything is different this year: There's no room for a family dinner here. There is no table, and there are no chairs.

My mother occupies one sparsely furnished room. It's beautiful and very Zen, but far from practical. There's nothing here, except hardwood floors, bookshelves, and a big white bed. 'Very comfortable,' *Mami* says, and after sitting on it, I agree. A long white curtain can separate the room into bedroom and kitchen areas, and there is a similar curtain by the only window. The kitchen consists of a white cupboard built into the wall, a sink, stove, and fridge too close together, and then, across from these appliances, a chrome workstation topped with a wooden carving board. That's it.

Mami has classical music on. Vanilla scented candles are burning on the windowsill. She has already opened a bottle of red. She seems content, relaxed. But it's more than that. There are some surprising changes about her: *Mami*'s had her hair cut, dyed, and styled. It's still shoulder-length, and still wavy, but there are textured layers in front. Her color is the same rich chestnut, but the white strands are gone. Instead, her stylist added subtle (read: expensive) highlights and low-lights. It looks completely natural, hardly noticeable to the untrained eye. She glows. I'm shocked. *Mami* sports the hair of a Park Avenue princess, the pricey, well groomed, yet understated style of the upper crust of the Upper East Side. It's not surprising that she wanted it, nor that it suits her. But never in a million years did I imagine she would splurge on such a thing.

She's wearing a simple white T-shirt. Of course, only *Mami* could pull off dying Easter eggs and then tending to the lamb (whatever that entails) in an immaculate white T-shirt!

But the real shocker are her designer jeans. I have to look twice, and cannot help asking. She laughs. She blushes. "I treat myself," she says. "You like?"

What's gotten into *Mami*? Designer jeans, a salon style, a new apartment, and then some. I could pick out that scent out of a thousand. *Mami* is unmistakably wearing my *parfum secret*. In her hot jeans, and her alluring scent, she is walking around her overheated apartment barefoot, displaying ten beautiful toes with nails all perfectly groomed and painted red, bright red, like the Easter eggs, but even shinier.

They look good, but they just don't fit. There's something sensual about bright red varnish, but doesn't she know it's all wrong? Doesn't she know that upper class ladies on the Upper East Side, ladies with subtle highlights and even subtler lowlights, would rather go for natural and understated? Doesn't she know how many shades of pale pink there are in this city? Could she not have noticed? She sees these women every day. She talks to them, smiles at them, and sells them gloves for their perfectly manicured hands. She must know their look inside out. Maybe she doesn't care. Maybe she's simply having fun. I guess it's about time she did. But what gave, I wonder.

Yet it's my own fingers, unadorned, with slightly bitten nails, that steal the show this evening. *Mami* grabs my hand before even offering me a glass of wine.

"Where's ring, my sweetie?"

"The ring is gone, *Mami.* I gave it back to Greg."

"So wedding is off?" she asks. She jumps with joy, hugs me, and hurries to pour wine to celebrate.

I'm not sure her display of excitement is appropriate. I feel relieved at having broken the engagement. A weight has been lifted. Still, I feel guilty, sad, and more than a little ashamed.

"*Tati* doesn't know yet," I say. The thought of telling him gives me nightmares. What will he think of me? "I think I have to tell him…tonight. Will you help me tell him, *Mami*?"

Mami raises her eyebrows, then goes on pouring our wine.

"Help you? No. I don't help you. You are grown woman. You tell your *Tati* yourself. Now, let's drink toast to freedom!"

I clink glasses with her, but take no pleasure in the wine. I feel betrayed.

"Don't worry," *Mami* says. "He won't be upset. You think he want you to get married? No. He wouldn't say anything, but I know he hope you wouldn't get married."

Her words are little consolation. I can't imagine *Tati* being pleased. Even if he didn't want me to marry Greg, he'll disapprove of the way I acted. And he'll be right. He usually is.

"Don't pout, L," *Mami* says. "You are grown woman, remember? You old enough to live on your own, old enough to get engaged, old enough to realize it's not good to get married, old enough to break engagement. You are an adult. You owe nobody an explanation. Why be afraid to tell your father? Now, telling that boy, that must have been difficult. That took guts."

She raises her glass, and once again we toast. I smile a vague smile. I know *Tati* will not feel the same.

*

The greased eggs are waiting on the counter. L is sulking into her wine. Victor and Alex arrive. Maria shows Alex around. He seems indifferent as ever. She shouldn't have expected anything else, but still, it hurts.

Victor, on the other hand, is full of compliments on her apartment, on her appearance, on the wine. He brought her flowers. Tulips. Her favorite. They break her heart. As she arranges them in a vase, she almost wants to weep. Of course, she knows, she's being too dramatic. She's a little too touchy today, too sensitive to even the slightest possibility of pain. It's the excitement of it all: her children seeing her new place for the first time, her seeing Victor, which even now that they are friends, still unnerves her. Not to mention the prospect of going back to his place, where she spent her crazy night of passion with him. And she'll have to act normal, like nothing ever happened. She couldn't sleep all night thinking of it. To make matters worse, this morning she got her period.

Now she's completely miserable, a wreck of nerves and sadness. Not even wearing her new jeans makes her feel better, not even her outrageously expensive hairstyle. Everything hurts, the slightest inconvenience annoys her, and the futility of Victor's desire makes her want to weep. There is desire in his eyes tonight. He still looks at her like that, after all these years, now that it's too late for the two of them. It's too sad for words. She has to remind herself that she didn't get her hair done for him, but rather as a treat to herself, and that she hasn't bought those crazily priced jeans for him either, but rather so she can feel young and fun again, and take some pleasure in her own appearance. She's not trying to attract him at all. They're friends now, and it's wonderful. Any spark of desire is nothing but an accident. And that's ok. Yet tonight she feels vulnerable and sad. Tonight she'd love to let him put his arms around her, to feel protected, safe, and maybe loved. But she knows that's the dream of a foolish girl who doesn't want to acknowledge, after all this time, who Victor really is, a girl who built him up into a romantic hero. She's no longer that girl.

She's a grown woman and she's had enough experience to recognize people for who they are. Victor is a good man. Kind, generous, and wonderful in many ways. But not a man whose shoulder one could cry on. He'll make a dependable friend. But he'll never be emotionally available as a lover. And in his heart of hearts he'll never forgive her betrayal. After all, can she blame him?

She sighs, and rinses the last of the wine glasses. They're all waiting for her. Thinking probably that she's obsessive compulsive for not just leaving the dishes in the sink. But they have no idea how badly she needs a few minutes away from them, how she craves a little aloneness, the comfort of warm water on her hands. The wine glasses look pretty. She loves good crystal. She smiles. Soon enough she'll be a crazy old lady who thinks of objects as her friends. In a few years she'll probably be talking to her wine glasses!

With Alex carrying the dyed eggs in a wicker basket, and appropriately rolling his eyes at this unwelcome chore, they finally head for Victor's apartment. She relishes in the thought that she'll be left alone there, that they will go to church and leave her by herself. She wishes they'd just hand her the keys and go. But no, they have to come upstairs, they have to bring the eggs, they have to keep chatting like they always do, and in the midst of it all she has to deal with the anxiety of being back at Victor's, has to pretend nothing is going on, that she's not thinking of their night together, months ago. She has to act like the tornado of emotions blowing through her is not there. Now how does one do that?

She's only been here once before, on Thanksgiving, for her guilt-ridden night of passion with her husband. She doesn't even remember the place. She was all too consumed that night, first with Victor, then with disappearing as quietly as possible.

His apartment, to her, is foreign. The other woman's territory, not her own, the silent witness to Monica's years of intimacy with Victor. Maria is a trespasser, a stray prowler who fled before dawn. To the other woman, the décor of Victor's life must be as familiar and comforting as her own. The apartment surely holds vestiges of her role in Victor's life. Her lingering scent on the couch, some personal effects in the bathroom, an accent or decoration she might have picked, a plant, maybe, she used to water.

As Victor turns the key in the lock, Maria thanks God that the lobby is dark, so her husband and children can't see her blush. She sticks her hands in her pockets so nobody can see them trembling. She feels weak. And it's not just her period, though the cramps and the dizziness don't help. Of all possible days, why did her fucking period have to come today? Isn't it bad enough that she has to visit her estranged husband, and pretend, in front of her children, not to have had wild passionate sex with him all over his apartment?

As she enters Victor's place, she wonders if she should pretend never to have been here before. Would it be tactful, or would it be ridiculous? Would Victor be relieved, offended, or amused? After all, she doesn't recognize the place. She doesn't have a general sense of it, doesn't feel like she's really visited. And yet he once took her home and fucked her up against the wall, and on the couch, and again and again in the bedroom. Desire courses through her, like a jolt of electricity, and she hates herself for it, hates Victor, hates this damn apartment, hates the images she can't help recalling. She's revolted at thinking in such vulgar terms. But then again, wasn't it vulgar, her experience here? Wasn't it primitive in some sense, raw? And didn't she like it that way?

Victor helps her out of her coat.

"You already know the place, but I can show you around if you like." She blushes. So he isn't going to pretend that it never happened.

"Actually…I…don't really remember where anything is," she says, thankful that he's busy hanging up her coat and not really looking at her. She realizes that she's doing nothing but embarrassing herself by admitting to her sex-induced amnesia. But Victor seems unfazed. Is he trying to be a gentleman, or has he really forgotten the nature of her previous visit? She bites her lip so hard it hurts.

"I'll show you around." His voice is warm, but she can't detect the note of tenderness she longs for. "Would you like a glass of wine? Kids, wine?"

Her heart sinks. He's treating them all the same. He's just being friendly.

She sits on the couch, next to Lili. Her eyes wander around the apartment, and despite herself she looks for traces of the other woman. It's a painful exercise, and rather fruitless. The objects in the room offer no clues. They seem as impenetrable as Victor. Poker faces all around. He could have bought all these things himself. They are tasteful enough. And they fit well together.

"I can't tell him," Lili whispers, as soon as Victor disappears into the kitchen. She looks at Lili, and sees the sadness and worry on her little girl's face. How selfish of her to sit here, obsessing about Victor's love life, when next to her, L is in such obvious distress.

"Of course you can," she whispers back, and reaches over to smooth the hair out of her daughter's face. Lili keeps fidgeting, rearranging her position on the couch. "Just try to sit still, take a few deep breaths, then just say it."

"What are you two whispering about?" Victor asks, handing each a glass of wine.

"I'm not marrying Greg anymore."

L's face is lobster red. Her eyes glaze over. Maria hopes she's not going to cry.

"You're not?" Victor's voice betrays no emotion.

"What did he do?" Alex sounds ready to pounce on poor Greg.

Lili looks down. She's blinking fast. The corners of her mouth are twitching.

"He… He didn't do anything, Alex. I just…" Her voice falters, and she looks to her mother for support. "I don't love him. So I can't marry him."

"Did you tell him that?" Victor asks.

L nods, unable to speak.

"She did," Maria says.

Why are they all so gloomy? It's good news, after all. Victor didn't want her to marry that boy, and Alex couldn't possibly have grown too fond of him the one time they met. Why does she feel like she's the only one who can truly appreciate this happy news?

"Let's drink to that!" She raises her glass, and her son gives her a nasty look.

"Let's drink to L being free!" she insists.

Reluctantly, the other glasses rise to meet hers. Poor L seems completely crestfallen. Victor has a stern look on his face.

Maria is desperate for a drink. Her family truly is getting on her nerves. She can't wait for all of them to leave. She'll find some sort of comfort once she's alone. She'll curl up on the couch in front of the TV, and enjoy some more wine by herself. Maybe she'll even give in to her impulse to cry. After all, there's plenty of time to freshen up before they all come back.

Of course, now that L has brought up her engagement, they're bound to sit around and talk about it.

"Are you angry with me, *Tati*?" L looks at her father with big pleading eyes. Maria hopes he'll be kind enough to reassure her.

"No, Lili. I'm not angry. But I do hope in the future you'll think twice about making a commitment like this. An engagement is a serious thing. You can't just get excited and say yes, then change your mind later. But certainly, I'm glad you changed your mind. For many reasons."

Maria hopes that he'll go on to say something nice, something to make their daughter feel better. She knows Victor wouldn't say anything he doesn't mean. Still, she tries to urge him with her eyes to say something, anything reassuring. They exchange a brief look. Does he understand how important this is, how badly she wants him to be kind and supportive?

"Well, at least I won't have to pay for the wedding," he says.

Is that the best he can do? She can see the first traces of tears forming in the corners of L's eyes, and it breaks her heart.

"Actually," she intervenes, "I think you should have party for her anyway."

Victor laughs, shaking his head.

"But she's not getting married. And, happy as I am that she won't ruin her life, I don't think, as a father, that getting engaged to some guy she didn't have strong feelings for, then dumping him, is the kind of behavior I should reward."

He does have a point. But Maria resents him nevertheless. Victor, the educator! Once more, he's the adult, and she's the unfit parent.

"Yes, getting engaged was stupid. But you know, Victor, to realize is bad for her, and to break engagement, that took guts. And that should be applauded."

"So you want a party to celebrate the fact that your daughter is not getting married!"

Maria nods.

"Yes! I think we should celebrate Lili not doing stupid thing!"

"But Lili, did do a stupid thing. She just didn't go through with it. So while I'm happy she realized her mistake, I really think this wine is celebration enough."

She sighs. He's like a wall sometimes.

"Explain this to me, Victor, because I really don't understand. If your daughter go ahead with this foolishness, and marry a man she don't love, a man she don't even know well, then you honor her bad choice, which you don't approve, by throwing her nice wedding. Now that she finally make wise decision for herself, like grown woman with solid backbone, you won't throw a lousy party to celebrate that. Why you would be happy to throw wedding so she can fuck up her life, but not have party for her now that she's not?"

Victor smiles.

"I would not have been happy to throw the wedding, and you know it. But I would have, because that's what a good father does. And you would have been there for her that day too, right? In spite of all your reservations. I even think you were gonna get her something..."

"Shoes."

"Shoes. Well, happy or not, I guess you and I both would have respected her choice, and we would have had a wedding, because that's what people do. But now that she's called it off, well, I'm happy and relieved that she's come to her senses. But I'm not gonna go as far as to throw a party to celebrate that my very immature daughter has finally realized marriage is not just about a ring and a fairy tale wedding. I don't think her behavior in this matter deserves a reward."

Maria inhales sharply.

"Well, I do," she says. "And too bad I'm not in position to throw party for her. Because I really think my daughter being young and free and not having lost her head and marry the wrong guy, deserves bigger celebration than a fucking wedding, no matter what people do. Actually, what people do, is all fucked up. Weddings glamorize marriage to point where young women like L start dream about it. I think having party to celebrate not getting married is really so much healthier..."

Alex lets out a little laugh, but she ignores him. She turns to L, who's being sad and quiet, like a little mouse. She reaches over and pats her daughter's knee. L's bones feel sharp through the denim. The girl should really eat more.

"I guess you don't have party, my sweetie, but for what is worth, I think you deserve it. And I, for one, still buy you shoes. And guess what, young lady? You just been upgraded from fucking Daffy's to Manolo Blahnik."

Victor laughs and shakes his head.

"So you are bent on rewarding this kind of behavior?"

She straightens her back, assuming what she hopes is a dignified pose.

"Well, I am proud of my daughter. And, in spite of what you saying, I want her to be very proud of herself."

L reaches for her hand and squeezes it.

"You don't have to buy me Manolos, *Mami*." Her voice sounds like a scolded child's.

"But I want to, and I will."

Alex exhales puffs like an angry horse.

"How can you even afford, Manolos, mom?" he asks. "Do you even know what Manolos cost? I thought you were Miss Thriftiness."

Maria smiles.

"I got credit card now."

Alex rolls his eyes.

"You have to pay for what you charge, mom. With interest."

"Actually," Maria says. "I not have to pay anything."

Alex looks at her like she's a dumb cow. That's probably how he thinks of her. He's probably formed his opinion of her back when she was lingering around, useless, a burden to her family, a woman too lost and confused to function properly.

But she can't let it get to her. She smiles as if she didn't even see the look he gave her.

"I have no money to pay credit card, Alex." And here she pauses for effect. "But your father does. And guess what? I'm his wife. So I decide I will spend his money. See, Alex, I if I get credit card and get in debt, my debt is your daddy's debt as well. Apparently we are legally one financial entity."

She wonders if Victor still remembers his own phrase.

Alex shakes his head and looks at his father, as if to say 'I can't believe what she's done this time!' Her self-confidence falters. If Victor returns Alex' sentiment, if they sit there, looking at her like she's some juvenile delinquent, she won't be able to stand it. She'll probably hurl her wine glass at Victor, to hell with acting dignified! And to hell with their so-called friendship! She'll never forgive him, if after all that talk of making amends, he'll dare betray her now.

"If you don't like that, Victor, then you should have divorce me years ago."

Victor smiles.

"You know I'll be honored to pay your bills."

"Not all my bills. Just credit card."

But she's touched by his generosity, just like she was that day when he took her to lunch and tried to convince her she's entitled to his money. She's still not sure about that, after all she's done. But it was too much to resist.

"Buy whatever you want, Maria. In fact, I think you should buy yourself a pair of Manolos too."

"Thank you," she says. "I think about it. But what I really want is not designer shoe. What I want is party for my daughter."

He laughs. She tries to hold his gaze. Silly, to think that he would offer her so many things, but be so stubborn about the stupid party.

"You want that party that much?"

She smiles. Would he really give in? For her? Because she asked? Then again, she doesn't want the party for her sake. She wants him reassuring L, telling her he is proud of her no matter what.

"Why we don't talk about it? When is just you and me? Now, of course, if I am real bitch, I charge whole non-wedding party, and then you have to pay for it in the end. But I wouldn't do that, since you don't approve. Manolos, though. That's different story. I don't even care how you feel about it, I buy our daughter those shoes. Good quality shoes are important, you know?"

She looks at L again, poor child! Her mood didn't seem to improve even with the promise of the most fabulous shoes known to womankind.

"You know, L, I spend years in bad shoes, shoes that don't fit. I torture myself with them. And trust me, is not worth it."

L's eyes light up, as if she's just put together a puzzle.

"Those shoes, *Mami*, the small ones, the ones you gave away, they didn't fit you either?"

Maria still can't believe her daughter's fascination with her old sandals.

"They fit, when I was younger. Until I get pregnant with Alex and my feet grow whole size. You know, pregnancy is just the weirdest thing, like your body is taken over by aliens. All these weird things happen. So my feet, they just grow, and then, well, I cannot find shoes I like to buy during communism, and after we came here, we just couldn't afford any."

Her son puffs like an angry horse again.

"Oh, come on, mom! Why you always such a drama queen? We were never that poor. We could always afford shoes!"

She looks down, embarrassed. She doesn't want to discuss their poverty in front of Victor. She shouldn't have mentioned it in the first place. After all, what's the point of bringing up the past now, when he's clearly trying to offer her some sort of compensation?

But it's Victor who speaks.

"Actually, Alex, we really couldn't. For the longest time, we couldn't buy your mother a decent pair of shoes."

Hearing him say this, she feels sad for him, just as she did when they had lunch and he said that he would have liked to have been able to take care of her. It must have hurt him to not be able to provide for them, to have his wife rely on other people's charity. She didn't realize it back then. She was too busy resenting him for their poverty. Looking back now, she knows that for him too, it was hard. And she wants to stand up for him in front of his children, in front of himself.

"Of course, it was my own fault," she says, "because I was so picky. I should have got something very cheap, but I was so spoiled and clueless and vain..."

Victor interrupts her.

"You were not spoiled and vain. You put up with a lot of shit, and you did so very gracefully. I mean, look at this, our kids don't even know how poor we really were. Really," he turns to Alex and Lili. "Do you guys remember ever going to bed hungry?"

They shake their heads. They look so uncomfortable, she feels sorry for them.

"Well," Victor goes on, "I certainly worried many times about what the hell we were gonna feed you, and whether we were all gonna starve to death just because I was crazy enough to bring my family to America in pursuit of some fantasy. But your mother always managed to whip something up. Every breakfast, lunch, and dinner, there was food on the table."

"It was good, too," Alex admits. "We never had a bad meal that I can remember."

It's probably the nicest thing he's said to her in a long time.

"How about macaroni and cheese with side of banana?" she asks, laughing.

"Are you kidding, mom? I loved mac and cheese and bananas! I thought you only made it so rarely because it was bad for us, or something."

"Well, is not the most healthy thing. And your father hate it."

"It really wasn't bad," Lili says. "And we never had to eat anything gross. I know people who grew up on spam."

"Or baloney," Alex adds.

"Or canned ravioli," L makes a face.

"Well, at least I can say I never feed my children that." Maria says. She knows that avoiding nitrates, preservatives, corn syrup and food coloring still doesn't make her a good mother, but she decides against saying it out loud. Instead, she says to Victor. "I never thought we would starve, not even for second." She meant to make eye contact, and to say more. She meant to say that after all, he's always been there for all of them, that he provided for them, one way or another, that it was she who bailed out. But the words just stuck in her throat.

"But those shoes, *Mami…*" L says. "They really were small. I can't believe you had to wear those."

"I did. And that's why I want you to have the Manolos. I want you having most fabulous shoes, and when you looking down at them I want you be proud of who you are, and to appreciate that you are free and have your life ahead of you. When I was your age, I was barefoot and pregnant. Literally. I just didn't want this to happen to you, L, to be so young and unprepared for life like me, and have kids. Because is so hard. You have to be older, and you have to be sure what you really want. I was too young, and had no idea what I was in for. I'm not sure I even want kids back then." She didn't mean to say that. And of course, there's no way to take it back now. "I mean, I did, but…" At a loss for words, she looks at her watch. "Is late. Why you not go to church?"

"Oh, no, this is very interesting!" Alex says. "Go on, mom… So having kids basically sucks…"

She shakes her head.

"I don't mean like that. All I mean is, is better to be older and be prepared. Is just so complicated."

She takes another sip of the wine, and looks fondly at her son and daughter. She cannot imagine her life without them.

"For what is worth, I like you guys very much. And I'm very glad I have you. My point is just..." But she feels dizzy from the wine, and she can't remember her point.

"Don't get married, and don't have children?" Alex asks. "Don't worry, mom, growing up with you was enough to put me off marriage forever."

It feels like he slapped her. The silence in the room is ringing in her ears. Her hand trembles as she raises the glass to her lips. Why don't they go to church already, and leave her alone?

"Alex, that is an awful way to talk to your mother!" Victor says. "I don't care how old you are, I don't ever want to hear you talking to her that way!"

She tries uselessly to blink back tears. Victor reaches out to her, his hand touches her knee, but she moves away. She takes the napkin from underneath her wine glass, and wipes the corners of her eyes.

Alex is looking down, avoiding her, and especially avoiding his father. She knows that Victor is waiting for him to apologize. And she knows Alex won't. He's too proud. He's her son after all.

"You shouldn't be so hard on him, Victor. He was just a child, and he grew up with us fighting all the time, and he hated it. And then you left, and he missed you, and he blamed it on me."

Alex looks at her and shakes his head.

"Mom, I was being an asshole just now. Why are you defending me?"

She smiles.

"Because I'm your mother, and that's my job?"

"Even when I'm an asshole?"

She laughs.

"Especially then."

"That don't make sense, mom."

"It make sense, Alex."

"Well, I take it back," he says. "I'm sorry. It was a crappy thing to say. I didn't even mean it."

"Is okay, honey. I know you didn't mean. And I'm sorry, too, Alex. I'm sorry you had to hear us fight so many times. I'm sorry I made your father leave. I didn't mean to, but I made a mess of our lives."

"We both did," Victor says. "You can't keep blaming your mother, Alex. It's completely unfair."

Their son looks down. He's fiddling with his wine glass, searching for words.

"I know," he says. "You know, I always wondered. Were you two ever happy together?"

She swallows hard.

He's so young, Alex, too young to remember the days when they still loved each other, she and Victor. To him, it's like those times never existed.

"Your mother and I were very happy, Alex."

Victor's voice is firm.

"We loved each other, and we had a wonderful marriage, and two wonderful kids. We were perfect for each other, and we were extremely happy together until we came here. We never even fought back then."

"Maybe we should have," she says. "Is unnatural not to fight at all."

But she can't imagine it. She remembers herself in her youth, the way she would hang on to his every word, the way she'd analyze his every gesture. What did he need? What did he want? Was she saying the right thing? Was she acting the right way? Did he love her? She wanted nothing but to please him back then.

"You're right," he says. "But you were too young and too sweet to fight with me back then. And you were so in love with me. You would have followed me to the end of the world."

"I did follow you to the end of the world."

"I was a lucky bastard. I was crazy about you, you know that!"

She smiles, but she has a bitter taste in her mouth.

"Yes, you were crazy about me same way people are crazy about luxury car. You see something beautiful and you want to take it home, display it, and have the whole world know is yours! Well, it sucks to be the trophy wife! Is like you're an exotic pet kept in golden cage, and then eventually you realize you're nothing but a live-in servant!"

Victor laughs. But he looks hurt.

"You really felt that way. You weren't joking the last time you said it."

She looks down. She didn't mean to hurt him, now, or the other day, in the restaurant. But where will they get if she sugarcoats all her bitterness?

"A little. Towards the end I felt like I was there just to cook, and clean, and look after the children." She wants to add sex, but she wouldn't say that in front of Alex and Lili. "We talk about this before, Victor. And I don't mean to keep bringing it up. Is all in the past."

His dark eyes still look sad.

"I know. I just hate it that you felt that way."

He means it, by now she knows that, and she feels for him. She wants to reach out to him, to comfort him. But she's too shy, and too unsure.

"Is late, Victor. Why you don't take the kids to church?"

"Why don't you come with us?"

"Me?"

She leans back on the couch. She hasn't been to church with them for more than ten years now.

"Yes, you. The lovely girl I married to keep in a golden cage. Come with us."

She laughs and shakes her head.

"I don't know, Victor. Those people hate me."

"You mean you hate them."

"Well, whatever. I… I'm not going to change who I am."

"Nobody's asking you to change, woman. I'm just asking you to come to Easter mass with your children."

She'd never admit it, but she's tempted. She'd hate to go, of course. But it would be worth it, just to see everybody's faces. Just to feel their eyes watching her, wondering why she's there, standing next to her husband. She'd lean a little closer to him, just to give them something to talk about. But no, it would be silly. She's not going to freeze her ass off standing in front of some church in Queens just so a bunch of insufferable old farts can gossip about her.

"And who be watching lamb, then?"

Victor laughs.

"The lamb is dead. It isn't gonna run away!"

"But if it burn?"

"Well, actually, the lamb is already cooked."

"Oh, no, Victor, you shouldn't cook it ahead of time! It be cold and dry when you get back!"

She knew she shouldn't have let him prepare Easter dinner, as sweet as it was of him to offer. She enjoyed the luxury of not having to do anything. But why on earth did she trust him with the most important dish?

He smiles, confident and content. He probably thinks his dried out lamb will be delicious.

"Come here. Lemme show you something."

He takes her hand, pulls her towards the kitchen. A heavy-duty pot is resting on the stove. It's one of those expensive French ones she's always wanted. Victor lifts the lid and she takes in the savory scent of lamb and spinach. Unable to resist, she decides to break her fast early. With two fingers she grabs a piece of lamb. It tastes divine. Juicy and flavorful, with just the slightest hint of mutton. She reaches for a spoon to take another bite. The spinach, crisp and tart, lingers on her taste buds. The mustard greens add just the right amount of spice. It all blends perfectly with plum tomatoes and a dash of curry. It's the kind of daringly different Easter meal she would have loved to cook herself, if only she thought that her children would accept it.

"You make this or you buy?"

If there's a restaurant that sells this, she needs to know where it is.

He laughs.

She takes another spoonful.

"Seriously, you make?"

"Yes, ma'am."

"Is amazing! How you learn to cook like this?"

She replaces the lid. But even after covering up the pot she still stands there, spoon in hand, tempted by the idea of yet another bite. She feels ravenous and weak. Her period, the wine, the nerves, it's all wearing her down, making her hungry. Victor hands her a plate and helps her to a steaming pile of stew. She eats it standing. It's the best meal she's ever had.

She notices him watching her, looking her up and down as if assessing her figure in the new jeans.

"So, you finally decided to take advantage of some of our new found wealth," he says.

"Your wealth, not mine," she corrects, placing the empty plate in the sink, and running water over it. "And just so we're clear. You're not supporting me. I'm paying my mortgage and everything I need. You're just buying me expensive gifts every now and then."

He leans closer, his dark eyes intense upon hers.

"I don't want to put you in a golden cage."

"I won't let you."

He's still looking at her, his body dangerously close. He reaches for her, but she shakes her head.

"I thought you said no strings attached. No… expectations."

He holds up his hands.

"None whatsoever."

He takes a step back. They are now at a safe distance.

"So what did you buy yourself nice?"

She smiles.

"Let's see. So far, you buy me this hair do, jeans, and perfume you liked."

He nods.

"Apparently I have quite good taste."

"Flawless," she says. "And a good heart too. You make generous donation to women's shelter, fund for starving children in Africa, humane society, and hummingbird society."

"Is that so?" He laughs. "Hummingbird society?"

"Yes. Helps environment. Good karma."

"Well, thanks for watching out for my immortal soul. I guess that's what a good wife does."

It feels good to be relaxed enough to joke around. Maybe in time, it'll be enough. Maybe in time she'll stop feeling sorry that that's all there's left.

"But..." she adds, "You do pay off full balance, right?"

"Yes, ma'am. Don't worry, we won't go into debt because of the hummingbird society."

"So..." she looks down, suddenly, not knowing how to phrase this. "So you can pay full balance, how much can I spend?"

She feels like a child asking for an allowance. She has to remind herself that she's an independent woman, making ends meet by herself, and that she only accepted his money because he insisted, that she only allowed herself to take him up on his offer because after all, life is short and it'd be stupid to deny herself pleasure out of pride. But will he think of her as greedy?

"Don't worry about it," he says. "Just spend what you like. When you feel more comfortable with the whole money issue, I'll take you to the bank and we'll go over the accounts together. But for now, if you'd just use that card of yours and spend on whatever you please, I'll be a happy man."

"How you have so much money, Victor?"

She can't help herself. She's always wondered. Yes, the store seems to be doing well, but how well can a business like that do, with the rents in Manhattan, and God knows what other expenses?

He laughs.

"It's not that much money, hon. But it's enough for us to be comfortable. When you feel up to coming to the bank with me, I'll show you. There's the store, there's investments, there's some savings. You'll see."

"Ok," she says. "But I still not come to church."

She starts walking back into the living room.

"You should."

"I... I don't know." She feels herself hesitate. Yes, in a sick way, part of her would like it. Just to show people. Like a victory lap. But that is vain and silly. She hates those people and she shouldn't care what they think. It'd be so much nicer to stay here, curl up on the couch, relax, drink wine, take a little nap maybe.

Her children's eyes are watching her. They both want her to come along, even Alex.

"Come on, mom! What's the big deal? It's just Easter Mass! And we'll probably be late anyway!"

She's flattered. She can't believe her son, of all people, wants her to go. Maybe he still feels guilty for his snarky comment earlier, and now he's forcing himself to be nice.

"I need use restroom," she says.

The bathroom is small. She finds that she enjoys the comfort of this sheltered little room. She takes pleasure in its neatness, tries to find calm and comfort in its symmetry. She surveys the dark tiles, the beige shower curtain, the stack of black, white and beige towels, everything clean and ordered, the way things tend to be in Victor's world. She enjoys washing her hands with the big white bar of soap. It smells fresh yet neutral. Pleasant enough, but not something a woman would pick. She can't imagine 'Momo' choosing that. Or rather, she doesn't want to imagine it, doesn't want to think of Monica in this bathroom, doesn't want to picture her slender body wrapped in one of these towels, standing in front of this very sink, examining her perfect complexion in this very mirror. But she does picture it. In detail. She can see every perfect inch of the other woman's body, can feel the luxuriousness of her smoothing lotion on her shins, her breasts, her shoulders, can almost hear her brushing her teeth and her shiny black hair, smiling at her own beauty in the mirror, getting ready to join Victor in bed. She swallows her pain, forces her mind to silence and refocus. Then she just can't resist. Here it is, right in front of her, a shrine of secrets, the cabinet behind the mirror. She hesitates before opening it, but once her hand slides the glass cover aside, what's done is done, it is what it is, and she knows she'll be ransacking everything like a thief. It must be in here, the other woman's stuff. Her make-up remover and her cotton disks. Her night cream. Her eye serum. Her toothbrush.

She looks at the neatly ordered shelves, cataloguing the objects one by one, reassuring herself that they are all so masculine, all exclusively, unmistakably his. A fancy electric razor. Shaving cream. Aftershave. Men's deodorant. Nicotine patches. So that's what helped him quit.

She reaches for his bottle of aftershave. She lets herself enjoy his scent. She feels naughty snooping around. His fragrance turns her on. It's so silly! There's obviously nothing in here, and she's acting like a teenager with a crush. She hopes she can remove the scent of aftershave from her hands, or they'll all know what she's been up to. She places the bottle back on its shelf, pushing the other things around to make room for it. She can't remember its exact position, and she's not sure just how well soap can remove fragrance. But maybe there's rubbing alcohol in here. She once read in a magazine that it can erase even the strongest perfume.

She reaches for the plastic bottle, and her heart stops. Behind the rubbing alcohol, besides a box of aspirin, there are five orange tubes of prescription pills. She pulls them out one by one, her hand shaking. She doesn't need to read the labels. She knows what these are. But she reads their names anyway, over and over. They advertise this stuff on TV. Blood pressure medicine. Bloody blood pressure medicine. He's been taking that, for God knows how long, and she didn't even know it!

Her heart racing, she sits on the edge of the tub. How sick is Victor? How long has this been going on?

She sometimes forgets that he's a mere mortal, that he can get sick, just like the rest of us, that something bad can happen to him, that he will die one day. Terror courses through every inch of her body. What if it's actually happening, what if it's happening now?

With trembling knees she walks back to the living room.

"Victor, can I speak to you in bedroom please?"

Her children are only too familiar with such scenes. Alex sighs. Lili looks down and bites her lips. She probably thinks they're about to fight because of her cancelled wedding. Poor kids! They'll both be sitting here, waiting for the yelling to start in the other room.

But as Maria pulls Victor into the bedroom, fighting is the last thing on her mind.

Still trembling, she asks.

"What is wrong with you?"

He gives her a puzzled look, and it takes her a moment to realize that she needs to be more specific.

"Your heart?"

Still, she can see, he doesn't understand.

"I found medicine, in bathroom."

She suddenly feels exhausted, and sits down on the bed. Victor sits next to her.

"It's not a big deal," he says. "My blood pressure is just a bit higher than it should be."

She sighs, a cold shiver running through her.

"I don't understand. You never even get angry."

"Apparently that's not that good for the heart."

He laughs.

"Oh, Victor, this is horrible! How long have you had this?"

"Just a few months, and really, it's not that bad. I just have to take the medicine, and I already quit smoking, I avoid salt…"

She gives out a deep sigh. The thought of him being sick, any sickness, is just unbearable.

"Come on, woman. Don't be such a drama queen, like your son says. I'm not dead yet, there's no need to mourn me! And apparently if I do die, I guess I'm all set, given my recent charitable contributions."

"Don't joke about this! Don't you dare joke about this!"

"I'm touched that you care."

"Really, don't joke!" By now she's nearly crying. She looks around, hoping to find some kind of geometrical figure. Something neat and ordered to rest her eyes upon, something to count to distract herself from crying. In the simplicity of the room, she finally settles on the buttons on the front of the flat screen TV, but she's unable to concentrate on them. She imagines Victor in his bed, watching this

TV, and she wonders if he ever gets lonely. When the other woman isn't here, when he's alone, going to sleep in front of this big flat screen, is he content to be alone, or does he feel like he's missing something?

"Seriously. I am touched that you still care this much about me."

He takes her hand and brings it to his lips. She knows then, that she won't be able to hold back her tears.

"Come here." He puts his arms around her. She rests her head on his shoulder. It feels good, his body against hers. She lets herself be hugged, lets herself cry.

"It's ok, honey. It's all going to be ok."

She nods her head softly, but doesn't stop crying. It's such a relief, such a luxury, to just let herself go, to stop pretending that she's so damn strong all the fucking time.

"It's gonna be ok."

She knows he isn't talking just about his health, and she knows she's not crying just over that either. She's needed a good cry for ages. And she especially needed a good cry today. She loses track of how long she cries for, how long he holds her, but when she finally lifts her head, still sniffling, and gives him a weak smile, she feels profoundly satisfied.

He looks at her, and wipes away her tears with the cotton sleeve of his shirt. She laughs. It's such an uncharacteristic gesture for Victor, Victor who likes everything neat and clean. Now there are mascara stains on his crisp white shirt, and he doesn't even seem to care.

She sniffles a few times still, but feels herself relaxing, growing calmer. She even manages a proper smile.

He's looking into her eyes, intent on something.

"Ok, now, what I really want to know is what exactly you were looking for in my medicine cabinet." She feels blood rushing to her cheeks. "Would you also like to look in the closet? Or have you done that already?"

She laughs at her own silliness exposed. She can't well say she needed a tampon, now can she?

"Seriously, Maria. If you want to know something, you can just ask me."

"Are you still seeing her?"

"No, ma'am."

"Since?"

"Since before Christmas, when we broke up."

"Is there anything else?" he asks. She shrugs. "Like maybe, you might want to know if there are others?"

She frowns, chasing away the image.

"I guess that's not a pleasant prospect to you," he says. "Then maybe you should say so. If you don't want me going out with other women, well… then you should say it. In fact, I'd like to hear you say it."

She bites her lips. Whatever happened to them just being friends?

"I don't want you to see other women, Victor."

"I won't. And I'd like you to not see other men."

She smiles. She decides then and there that she'll never tell him he's been the only man in her life.

"I guess I could give up other men," she says, smiling as if she's promising to turn her back on a long list of lovers.

He seems to want to say something, but he hesitates.

"Could you trust me?" He finally asks. It's a heavy question, one she didn't anticipate, and is not prepared to answer.

"I'll try," she says. She wishes she could sound more confident, but she doesn't want to lie. "But… It might take me a while to really be with you again, I mean, really be with you."

She searches his eyes. Will he be willing to wait? There are so many attractive women out there, in this city, who wouldn't hesitate a second before going to bed with him, and here she is, his own silly wife, having so many issues, so many fears and apprehensions.

"That's ok, honey," he says. "I understand that."

They are both quiet for a while.

"I'm sorry I cheated on you. And I'm sorry I acted like I was entitled to it, like you were to blame."

She swallows hard. As angry and hurt as she's been, has she herself not always felt that his straying was her own fault? That it was the natural consequence of her kicking him out of their bed? That it was well deserved punishment for her own betrayal?

"Wasn't I?" She feels tears burning in her eyes again, rolling down her cheeks. "Was it not my own fault for…" She sobs, and her words are stifled, the question suspended in the air.

He reaches for her hand.

"You have to stop thinking that everything bad is your fault, that you deserved it somehow. You are wonderful, Maria. You are strong, and smart, and incredibly beautiful. You can be impossible, but you are truly wonderful, and I love you. I should have told you that every day, especially when you were most inclined to doubt it. When we came here and you couldn't fit in, and you felt guilty about not having a job, and about hating our new life, I should have told you every day that I was happy you were with me, that I was lucky to have you, lucky you came with me, that you stood by me."

It's the nicest thing anyone has ever said to her. It has to be. But she cannot stop crying, cannot stop feeling guilty.

"But I did not stand by you. I left you."

"You have to forgive yourself for that."

"Can *you* forgive me?" It's the question she wanted to ask him years ago, the words she could never bring herself to say. After her return, she'd lie in bed beside him, thinking of whether he'd ever forgive her, whether his quiet anger would ever go away. They rarely made love in those days, but each time they did, each time there was at least a fleeting moment of tenderness, she wondered if she should ask, if she should take advantage of the glimmer of closeness, and ask for his forgiveness. She never dared, and the moment was lost. The more time went by, the more horrible and unmentionable her deed seemed to her, the more afraid she was to bring it up, and still, the more she yearned for his forgiveness. The pain of lying there, next to him, thinking that he could never ever forgive, that she could never ever ask, was so strong it was almost palpable. It kept her awake at night, tossing and turning, wallowing in her guilt. She grew resentful.

She never woke up determined to be nicer, or sweeter to him. She woke up feeling mean and spiteful. As if she had already asked and he had already denied her.

Now, after all these years, the words are out. He's heard them. She cannot take them back. All she can do is hold her breath, and wait for his answer. She feels his hand, still holding hers, and she grows hopeful.

"Can you forgive *me*?" He asks.

"Yes," she says. "But I need you to answer me, Victor. I need to hear you say *you* forgive *me*."

"Of course I forgive you, honey."

"You mean that? You're not saying it just to be kind? You're not saying it just so I stop crying?"

"No, honey. I really mean it." His hand squeezes hers, and she gives him a light squeeze back. But she keeps sobbing.

"I'm sorry. I just can't stop crying." She tries taking a few deep breaths, and wipes her eyes with the sleeve of her shirt. "I just got my period today. I get so emotional the first day. And I'm in horrible pain. And I feel weak and dizzy, and then I drank that wine."

She blushes. She was taught by her mother not to discuss 'female issues' with her husband, and she abided by that through most of her marriage.

"I guess this is too much information," she says.

Victor laughs.

"Absolutely not. You've come a long way, you know? Remember when you were too shy to talk to me about birth control?"

"Yes, and then I got pregnant like an idiot."

"And I sent you to have an abortion, like an asshole."

They are quiet again. They've reached another sore spot. But she doesn't feel anger, looking back. She thinks of how he must have felt, how hard it must have been for him to not be able to support his family, to have to ask his wife to go have an abortion, because there was no way they could feed another baby.

She squeezes his hand.

"I didn't want that baby, Victor. I'm glad I didn't have it."

They sit quietly for a while, still holding hands.

"I had this weird dream, just before Christmas," he says. "I dreamt that you were pregnant."

"You mean, you had a nightmare. Knock on wood." She laughs, and reaches over to knock on the TV stand.

"No, I know it's strange, but it wasn't a bad dream. You were pregnant and we were walking down Fifth Avenue together, shopping for a plastic giraffe for the baby."

She laughs.

"Well, if there was a giraffe, then it must have been a great dream! Giraffes have good symbolism. I don't remember exactly what they stand for, but they're the animals with the biggest hearts… The funny thing is, I did think I was pregnant, after… you know, Thanksgiving. I was in a doctor's office, and they told me I was not pregnant, and…"

"You went to see a doctor? You should have called me!" He seems horrified by the prospect of her going to the doctor, alone. She remembers feeling utterly deserted, thinking he didn't care. It feels good to know she was wrong.

She shakes her head, recalling her near certainty that she was pregnant.

"I'm never having unprotected sex again! I really hope our children don't do that!"

They look at each other and laugh.

"I hope our children are smarter than their parents." Victor says. "I'm sorry you had to go through that. I'm really fucking sorry I acted like such an asshole. I should have called you after that night. I should have driven out to fucking Queens when you didn't pick up your phone. I just… I was angry you left."

So he did call. She had unplugged her phone. But he did call.

"I'm sorry I left. I was afraid you wouldn't want me here in the morning."

"I did. I really wanted you here."

They are silent again.

"Don't laugh at me," she tells him. "But when the doctor told me I wasn't pregnant, I… I was so disappointed. How stupid is that? I really don't want to be pregnant, I really don't want another child! But I just thought of all those things, you know, like in your dream, shopping for a plastic giraffe together, things like that. I kept imagining we'd go for the ultrasound, and it'd be cute."

He smiles and nods, caressing her hand.

"That would be pretty cute… It is odd," he says. "But maybe it's because now our children are grown…"

"I know. And they are what kept us connected to each other. When you asked me for lunch, last summer, I thought you wanted to ask for a divorce."

He shakes his head.

"Maybe the pregnancy thing is just a metaphor for us both still wanting something holding us together."

She smiles. But then she wrinkles her nose. "But not another fucking baby! And not some stupid piece of paper. You know, I don't even believe in marriage anymore. It's all nonsense. I like the idea of nothing really binding us together. Just being together because we want to. Nothing more. Except…"

She looks at him and smiles.

"What? You eyes just lit up. What do you want, aside from that ridiculous party?"

She laughs.

"A dog! Victor, we should get a dog!"

He shakes his head, laughing.

"No way."

They're still holding hands as they walk out of the bedroom.

Their kids already have their coats on.

"I guess we're late for church," Victor says. "But your mother is coming with us."

"Am I?"

"You are."

She opens her mouth to protest.

"And your father is getting a dog," she announces, laughing.

"We can discuss this, as a family, after church," Victor says.

"Really?" for the first time this evening, L looks hopeful. "Like from the pound?"

"Maybe," Victor says. "But probably not. Come on, we've never been this late for church."

Alex helps her into her coat.

"Don't worry, mom. We won't let anybody mess with you."

It must look obvious that she's been crying. She should have washed her face. But in the end, she doesn't really care. Her children have seen tears before, and she couldn't give a rat's ass about those idiots at church.

They barely make the end of mass. They arrive just in time for Maria's favorite part, the lighting of the candles, but being late, they don't have any candles to light. They hover at the outskirts of the crowd. She searches for familiar faces. She leans against Victor. He puts his arm around her.

At the end of mass, people rush and scramble, pushing in front of each other, the way Romanians do. They all want Easter bread, dipped in holy wine. Victor volunteers to fight his way through the crowd to get their share. Maria stays behind with the children. It's chilly out. She and Lili hug each other, trying to keep each other warm.

Then she sees her. A tall brunette, a lonesome figure next to an older couple. Maybe her parents? It's unmistakably Monica, Victor's former lover, clutching her candle, shielding the flame from the wind with her cupped palm. Her gaze is not following Victor into the crowd. At first, Maria thinks the woman is looking at her, then she realizes who she's really staring at. And it kind of makes sense.

She nudges her daughter gently.

"That lady over there. She looking at you. You go say hello."

L seems reluctant.

"Mom!" Alex says. "You don't know who that is! Stay here, L!"

She's touched. She realizes that, in his own way, her son does feel loyal towards her. But she still knows the right thing to do.

"Oh, I know exactly who that is, Alex! Is a lady who, over the years, has been very kind to your sister. L, sweetie, if you want to go, go. Is ok. Is not nice to turn your back on your friends."

L goes along. Maria pulls Alex close. He tries to shake her off. "Aw, mom!" But then he lets himself be hugged, and puts his arm around her, replacing his sister as a source of warmth.

They watch people scramble for the holy bread, talking, joking, and arguing. They watch L and Monica laugh together, like old friends. The other woman looks towards Maria and gives her an appreciative bow of the head.

"That was big of you, mom." Alex says. "I thought you would ask me to kick her ass for you."

She laughs.

"I generally prefer you not kick ass. But I appreciate you would do that for me."

She rocks Alex in her arms, and he grumbles, pretending once more to hate being hugged.

"And if she gets anywhere near my husband I will kick her ass myself, I promise."

"So what is going on, with you and your husband?" Alex asks, not missing a beat.

She chuckles. He's not stupid, her son.

"I don't know what you mean."

"Come on mom, it was obvious all night! Are you guys hooking up or something?"

Maria laughs.

"Hooking up? No, that's what you kids do. We not hooking up. And that is not how young men should talk to their mothers!"

Alex rolls his eyes.

"Give me a break, mom!"

"Well, if you are really interested, your father and I are working through our differences."

It sounds very formal, but at least she said it correctly.

Alex laughs and raises his hand in the air. It takes her a few seconds for her to realize he wants to give her a high five.

Their hands touch in the air. A suspended handshake. A truce, maybe?

She pulls him close and squeezes him tight, ignoring his obvious protest. She's his mother, and she's not going to settle for a fucking peace treaty, suspended air-borne American handshake notwithstanding.

{31}

Not a Wedding Party

Alex can't believe his parents are actually having a party to celebrate L's broken engagement. But then again, there are worse reasons for a party, and this one is destined to be a small affair. L's guest list is short, and who on earth could his parents invite? Mom only has one friend, and happens to hate most of Dad's acquaintances. He himself is doing his share by bringing a date.

The party is held at his father's furniture store. Here they are, a bunch of people thrown together haphazardly. There's his sister, of course, wearing her new Manolos. There's a pretty girl he's never seen before, whom L introduced as her new friend from work, just before she announced that she changed jobs and is now working for a non-profit, teaching English to immigrants. There's L's roommate, who brought her kid. Then there's *Tanti* Madalina, Mom's friend who disapproves of him, with her boyfriend. His father invited two couples, an elderly Romanian couple who've always been fond of L, and his old buddy Amir, with his wife. They're friends from way back when Dad still drove a cab, and Amir is still is a taxi driver to this day. He's always been nice to Alex and L, and Alex is quite happy to see him tonight. And then, last but not least, as if dogs were the most common occurrence at parties, there's his father's newly acquired pet, Shirley, a shy dog with a long muzzle and the sad eyes. Alex takes to her immediately, and decides to feed her small pieces of smoked salmon each time his date goes to the restroom to reapply her makeup, which is so often, that he seriously fears for Shirley's waistline.

He notices his mother, who looks stunning and glamorous in a red dress, making a conscious effort to stay away from the elderly Romanian couple, yet trying to be polite when she speaks to them, alternating each fake smile with a sip of champagne. She looks so phony trying to be friendly to those people. But then again, these days he's trying not to judge her. He notices his father stepping towards her, saying something to break up the conversation, steering her away, his arm around her waist. Dad whispers something into Mom's ear, and she laughs while bringing the champagne flute to her red lips. She looks amazing. Happiness becomes her. As his father goes in search of the bottle to refill her glass, Alex is left wondering how these two managed to find a way back to each other. He wonders if eventually he'll be comfortable enough with Mom to ask. She seems prone to confessions these days.

He slips one more piece of salmon to Shirley, then goes looking for his sister.

"Congratulations on not getting married, sis!"

She raises her champagne flute, laughing.

"Interesting non-engagement party. Remember to invite me each time you choose not to get married."

"Don't be fooled," she says. "This is just an early birthday party."

Her birthday is indeed coming up. She'll be twenty-four. That's freakin' ancient, but L looks like she's aging well.

"I don't know, sis'. I think Mom has found a way to persuade Dad to give you a non-wedding party. She seems to have him eating out of the palm of her hand these days."

His sister looks around as if to make sure nobody is watching them. Then she leans in and whispers:

"Alex, *Mami* and *Tati* are… back together, sort of."

Alex laughs.

"So you finally got the memo?"

"You mean you knew?"

"Well, sort of."

L straightens her back and assumes an air of importance.

"Well I know for sure." She leans in closer and continues whispering. "I went shoe shopping with *Mami* last week, and she just wouldn't shut up about it. It's like, they both realized that they made mistakes, and they both really love each other, and they've forgiven each other for lots of really horrible things they've done in the past, which apparently is extremely liberating, and she's just so happy, she's practically floating on air! She didn't even buy herself shoes because she said she doesn't need anything these days, she's happy just the way she is."

She pauses for emphasis, but Alex is unimpressed. He's heard a similar discourse from Mom.

L seems miffed by his blasé attitude.

"But they are not living together," she points out.

"I was wondering about that." Alex is staying with his father. And other than Shirley, which Dad told him, was Mom's idea, he could detect no signs of his mother's presence in the apartment. He talks to her on the phone quite frequently these days, and she did tell him they are back together and that she's happy, but he cannot bring himself to ask if they moved in together yet. Mom never volunteered the information.

"Well, apparently they have no intention of moving in together either!" L says. "She told me so. Apparently she loves living by herself in her apartment, and just 'dating' *Tati*."

Alex looks at his parents. Mom and Dad are talking to Amir and his wife. He notices his father introducing them, and realizes that these are friends dating back from a time when his parents were still living together, but had no social life in common. It's strange and sad to think that Mom has never before met Amir and his wife, two of *Tati*'s closest friends.

Next to him, L is rolling up a slice of prosciutto, and feeding it to Shirley. She looks happy, and he's glad. It's her non-wedding party after all. She should be enjoying it.

"You look good, sis. I guess breaking up with that guy was good for you."

L blushes. Alex wonders if she still feels bad about it. It was, after all, shitty, what she did, and poor Greg didn't seem to deserve it. But leaving him after marriage would have probably been worse.

"I'm sure that must have been hard," Alex says. "Break-ups are tough, and getting over them takes time."

She nods, but she looks close to tears. He puts his arm around her. She's so skinny, her bones almost hurt him. Why on earth do all girls starve themselves to death?

"You'll be ok, sis. You're curiously strong for a skinny girl, remember?" L laughs at this allusion to their childhood fights, which were often quite violent.

"I am actually pretty happy these days," she says. "I think I'm more relaxed about stuff now, you know? I used to worry all the time. I used to feel like I was going nowhere, like my life had no purpose and I had to find one. It was scary. I always imagined I'll not be able to support myself, that I'll become a bag lady someday. And I think now I've stopped."

"What changed?"

"Nothing. I just started thinking about things differently. I just take it day by day and think that a good day is a day when nothing bad happens, no drama, no crisis, and I eat all my vegetables."

She laughs and looks at him, as if to tell if he's listening.

"Oddly, now that I've stopped worrying about my future, I've kind of started coming up with a plan for not becoming a bag lady after all. I… I think I'm gonna go to grad school after all, the way *Tati* wants me to. Not because it's what he wants, though. I mean, I want to. I think I'll get a Ph.D. in foreign languages and then maybe I'll teach."

Alex nods. That sounds sophisticated and very much up L's alley.

"I always thought you should do something like that, sis. So, have you told Dad yet?" The moment he says it, he realizes it's a stupid question. "I mean, you're not doing it for him, of course, but I know it will make him happy."

"It does. I told him about it as soon as I realized that I wanted to do this, and he was just besides himself. He offered to pay for it, but… if I get an assistantship, it would all be free. Can you imagine? And I could continue working where I do, and I really want to, so… But anyway, I won't start applying before the Fall, but I spoke to my professor from CUNY who said I could probably get into the program at NYU. Isn't that awesome?"

She's talking very fast, and her eyes light up. She's so funny sometimes.

"Anyway, *Tati*'s very happy. With me. I think that's why he even agreed to this party."

Alex nods.

"So our mother is celebrating that you're not getting married, and our father is celebrating that you finally decided to go to grad school."

L smiles and takes another sip of champagne.

"Yes. Though I think I'm still on probation. You know, they came up with some sort of punishment for me. It's quite ridiculous."

Alex raises his eyebrows.

"Do tell."

L chuckles.

"Well, I guess it's not so bad. But once a week I have to go pick up *Mami* at the store after work. We go to the supermarket and buy groceries according to a budget and to what's in season. Then we go to her place and she shows me how to cook a meal out of it. And then we drink wine and talk and I have to sleep over."

"Sounds like Mom's idea of the perfect mother and daughter experience."

L laughs. Alex gives her a long look.

"Come on, I know you secretly enjoy it! There's nothing wrong with that either!"

L blushes. In the heyday of his immaturity and their sibling rivalry, he used to call her a spineless sucker for being completely ga-ga over Mom. Now he almost feels her.

"I'll tell you a secret, sis. Mom's plan to infiltrate our lives is elaborate and far-reaching. You know she started calling me after

Easter and leaving all these messages: 'I'm your damn mother. (Yep. She said 'damn'). You call me or I come to upstate and kick your ass like you never imagine!' I swear, I have no clue where all the profanity comes from, and she never used that tone of voice with me before, it was always 'my sweetie, please call *Mami*, *Mami* love you so much, why you not call back?'" He rolls his eyes and tries to imitate Mom's voice. He must be doing a good job because L can't stop giggling. "So guess what, sis, I finally picked up the phone and called 'my damn mother', for like the first time since going to college, and then once I set the precedent it was kind of hard to stop, so now she makes me call her at least once a week. And we've moved from talking for five minutes to actually chatting for half an hour. And seriously, I think I might just have to grow up and admit it, there's nothing wrong with talking to your damn mother once a week, and there's nothing wrong with actually enjoying it."

"Well, at least she doesn't make you chop vegetables!"

"Mom and her vegetables! I usually know it's time to get off the phone when she asks me to list the vegetables I had that day, or to read the list of ingredients on the frozen meals in my freezer. 'No, my sweetie. That stuff so unhealthy. Look at salt content. So bad for you. I want you stop eating corn syrup. Corn syrup like poison. Causes diabetes'."

L laughs.

"No way! That's crazy! But then again, that's *Mami*!"

"Yeah, it's almost cute. I picture her sitting there with reading glasses and a dictionary, trying to figure out if my food is slowly but surely giving me cancer."

They laugh. They drink more champagne. They feed Shirley until she's ready to burst. His date returns, her nose powdered to perfection. L's friend summons her over, the one with the baby. She's carrying a giant bag and seems to have that little guy all ready to go. Alex shakes her hand goodbye, and L follows her through the crowd of people.

*

Maria steps outside to see Rachelle off. It's clearly and irrevocably summer. The air feels hot and sticky, almost stifling. Her eyes follow the noisy avenue into the horizon. She sees lights, and cars, and people bustling about, a charged and energetic sort of harmony, the lifeblood of this crazy, dirty city. The summer air clings to her skin. She welcomes it. She's happy. And so the question comes to mind that she's been asking herself these days. Now that everything is well in her world, is she still sorry she came to America, or does she finally concede that Victor's choice has been a good one? She'll never know what could have been, and tonight, tipsy on champagne, and floating on happiness, she finally sees things clearly. It doesn't matter in the end. In truth, she knows, there is no way to deem Victor's choice good or bad. We have only one life, and there's no way to know how other lives could have turned out. Speculation is useless, as happiness is unpredictable. She'll never know what could have been. Their alternate lives might have been better, worse, or maybe just the same. All she can know is that now, in this very moment, things are good. The twists and turns, the choices and chances that led here might have been wrong or right. What use wondering about it all? We only live once, and our pasts are as impossible to qualify as they are to undo. The key is to let go and to enjoy the moment. After all, it is what it is.

Made in the USA
Middletown, DE
27 January 2024